I0736541

In Love with an Alien

Liv Joanka

In Love with an Alien by Liv Joanka

On the distant plant Alloca, the presidential Council's rigid policies and regimental control was unchallenged. Through forced interracial marriages, they would create a single race of people. Now in less than one month Carrie would be shipped to New World city to marry a total stranger. Resisting the council's plan would mean war.

Carrie was convinced she did not have a choice, until she was kidnapped then rescued by an alien.

Copyright Information

Peltrovijan Publishing
P.O. Box 9473
Silver Spring MD 20916
peltrovijan@yahoo.com
https://peltrovijan.com/

The author does not guarantee and assumes no responsibility on the accuracy of any websites, links or other contacts contained in this book.

In Love with an Alien
All rights reserved.
Peltrovijan Publishing/ published by arrangement with the author

PRINTING HISTORY
February 2023

ISBN: 978-1-937143-67-1
Copyright © 2023 by Liv Joanka

This book is licensed for your personal enjoyment only. This book may not be re-sold or given away to other people. If you would like to share this book with another person, please purchase an additional copy for each recipient. If you're reading this book and did not purchase it, or it was not purchased for your use only, then please return to your favorite book retailer and purchase your own copy. Thank you for respecting the hard work of this author.

No part of this book may be used or reproduced by any means, graphic, electronic, or mechanical, including scanning, photocopying, recording, taping or by any information storage retrieval system without the written permission of the publisher except in the case of brief quotations embodied in critical articles and reviews. Please do not encourage piracy or plagiarization of copyrighted material in violation of the author's rights. Purchase only authorized editions.

For purchase information contact:
Peltrovijan Publishing: peltrovijan@yahoo.com

ACKNOWLEDGMENT

Thanks for the support from my family and friends

Table of Contents

****

Prologue: Segaan

The *Jirga* Kaiser watched with narrowed, yellow eyes as *Zha* Obeel cautiously approached him. Rule had been thrust upon the *Jirga* suddenly, with the unexpected accidental deaths of his first brother and his father. Having eliminated just about every disease known, an Azar was virtually an immortal and could technically live forever, barring accidents. A crushing injury to the torso or depriving the brain of oxygen — as in a drowning — were some of the few unavoidable causes of death among the Azars, which was why the death of two royals in a transporting accident 400 cycles ago had stunned the nation. The current *Jirga* had assumed rule in the midst of the present crisis, and unfortunately, the deference due a *Jirga* was seriously undermined because he was viewed as a young, brash second son with a ferocious temper. He now waited in silence, impatient with *Zha* Obeel's slow approach.

Beside *Zha* Obeel walked, *Loya* Favood, the most powerful psychic of Segaan. At the required twenty paces, *Zha* Obeel stopped and prostrated himself on the floor. *Loya* Favood stood silently next to him. The psychic's eyes were open but his gaze unfocused in concentration. His robe and hood covered his form from head to toe leaving only the pale blue of his face and hands visible. As a tenth-degree psychic, and leader of the psychics, he only could remain upright in the presence of the *Jirga*.

"Eighty full cycles ago Loya Favood made contact with the aliens. He has disabled their outside communication system and the controls of their flying machine. They were forced to land on Segaan and cannot leave." Zha Obeel voice was monotonous as he raised his head.

His mental words reached all, including the *Jirga*, who grunted in assent.

Zha Obeel resumed his mental report. *"We have captured some of the aliens and Loya Favood been studying them carefully."*

Slowly the *Jirga* extended his hands from his robe to touch the pads of all four fingers with each other. Within the last 100 cycles his skin had taken on a translucent hue. Although a reversible process, it was a sure sign of stress among the Azars. And the *Jirga* was under a great deal of stress. As imperial ruler his responsibilities would have been enormous. With the turmoil of the past forty alifees, the *Jirga*, and indeed the entire nation, were now at risk. Unfortunately, the stress had not only caused his translucent skin, but it had also drastically worsened his notoriously short temper.

Nevertheless, the *Jirga* Kaiser was determined to find a solution to save his people–hence this new experiment. He now waited in silence, impatient with *Zha* Obeel's slow approach.

Although he had requested this meeting, he was unsure how it would develop. Normally, his central receiving chamber would be bustling with advisors. This cycle, however, the hall had been cleared. Even the guards had been banished to the other side of the closed doors. The *Jirga* had allowed only four of his most senior advisors to be present. They were standing silently behind him and would remain silent unless he requested otherwise.

Zha Obeel head was bowed as was customary. *Zha* Obeel was neither a minister nor an advisor within the imperial government. He worked as a Blocker for the Psychics. The Azar's system of government had two branches: the *Jirga* and the Psychics. And although the *Jirga* was the ultimate ruler of all Segaan, in the history of the Azars, none had ever dared to ignore the powers of the Psychics. Within the Psychic chambers *Zha* Obeel's position was undoubtedly revered. The imperial rule, however, consistently refused to grant Blockers the almost mystical privileges reserved for the Psychics. Here in the *Jirga's* chambers *Zha* Obeel was regarded as an ordinary citizen.

Zha Obeel continued mentally. *"We have captured some of the aliens and Loya Favood has been studying them carefully."*

"My advisors say that you have brought twenty-one of the females and one male into the sector. What have you learned so far?" The mental question was addressed to the psychic standing silently in front of him. But again, it was *Zha* Obeel who answered. A psychic could communicate only through his blocker and even then, communication was mental. Without a blocker, communication with others was often difficult, many times impossible. There were recorded incidents in history of psychics dying from mental jamming in attempts to communicate directly. The psychic needed the blocker as a shield to filter the mental static of others, especially a high- level psychic such as *Loya* Favood.

"Contact is dangerous, but Loya Favood believes we are compatible."

"Believes?"

"Loya Favood wishes more time, Jirgaar."

"We have no more time," the Jirga roared. "So inform Loya Favood. Have him send an image of these beings."

Loya Favood remained impassive as he communicated with his Blocker.

"Loya Favood wishes to study the beings more before...."

But the *Jirga* interrupted harshly. *"An image!"*

"It is as you wish, Jirgaar."

The same fuzzy image began to form in the minds of all present. It slowly took shape, showing three aliens. They were naked and unconscious, lying on a smooth surfaced, table-like structure, in a sterile-looking chamber. All were female.

"These are the first females we captured and the ones we are studying. The others are in a conscious state and kept in separate chambers."

Initially, the *Jirga's* face remained expressionless, as he stared at the females. Unlike the Azars, the skin color of these beings was pinkish — a skin color unknown to the Azars. Stranger yet was what looked very similar to hair, concentrated on their heads and groin area. The Azars did not grow hair. Two of the beings had thick, shoulder-length, yellow-brown head hair. The third had flowing black head hair that almost reached her waist. Lower animal life forms were the only living things on Segaan to have such hair.

"Are these intelligent beings?" Now the *Jirga* did not disguise his disgust.

"Loya Favood is convinced they are intelligent. Their flying machine is superior to our travel technology."

The *Jirga* did not like that comparison. *"We have the ability to develop flying machines. We choose not to do so. It would be suicidal for us to travel in the sky!"*

"As you say, Jirgaar." Zha Obeel tone was carefully respectful.

"What of the males?" the *Jirga* was now frowning deeply.

"We have only captured one male. The others were accidentally killed on the Upside. He is being kept in a separate chamber."

"Is he like the females?" the *Jirga* demanded.

With the *Jirga's* repugnance obvious, Zha Obeel was now blinking nervously although Loya Favood remained impassive. Two of the advisors shifted in disquiet.

Despite the general unease, nothing prepared them for the next image. He was undoubtedly male, and he too was naked. But he seemed totally unconcerned about his nudity as he stood shouting at someone unseen. Despite the fact that he was caged, his angry expression and the enraged shaking of the bars on his cage caused advisors to gasp.

The *Jirga* gave the mental equivalent of a growl. *"They look nothing like us."* Now his voice reverberated in anger. *"The Loya Favood said these beings were as we are."*

Certainly, the male was even stranger than the females. Although tall, he was still not nearly as tall as the average Azar, and his skin color was a dark honey brown with eyes that were either dark brown or black. Like the females, he had hair that was noticeably thicker on his head and in his groin area. Unlike the females, his head hair was tightly curled, sitting like a cap on his head but he also has short, yet clearly visible hair covered his entire body.

The *Jirga* was furious and seemed actually repulsed. Azar's eye colors were all varying shades of yellow making the black color of this being's eyes seem even more shocking. And none in Segaan had ever seen anyone without the blue skin of their own people. Add these differences to the body and head hair—phenomena unknown to the Azars—and the result was total abhorrence mixed with fear. They had also noted the absolute fury on the face of the male.

"Outside appearances will not matter if we are compatible," Zha Obeel rushed to explain. *"Loya Favood thinks they have the appearance of our early ancestors. Loya Favood is still investigating their biology. It is most difficult. He cannot see their insides clearly."*

Unfortunately, the *Jirga's* disgust had hardened. *"Already the Loya Favood has spent eighty cycles examining them. Our early ancestors were primitive being and lacked intelligence. If these beings are in a primitive stage of their development, they are useless to us. What more time does he need?"*

"Perhaps twenty or more cycles. Loya Favood needs to confirm...."

"We do not have twenty cycles to waste. It was the plan of the Loya Favood that we use genetic material from the female aliens. Surely, he has already tried this. We need to know the results of his experiments!"

The *Loya* Favood was finally indicating possible emotion, not in his features, but his stance widened slightly.

"Loya Favood begs more time Jirgaar. It is critical...."

"Enough! The Loya Favood can continue his examination of the beings already captured. We need not bring any more Downside. How many more are there?"

"Loya Favood has touched 153 females and 215 males, Jirgaar."

"Tell the Loya Favood to send a pulse to destroy them all."

"A pulse is not possible Jirgaar. Touching the alien mind is proving extremely dangerous. This first-cycle the mental contact killed one psychic."

"Very well. We will send a small party Upside. We can wait no longer."

There was a brief pause. The *Loya* Favood remained expressionless and *Zha* Obeel, still prostrate on the floor, lowered his head in obeisance. *"Loya Favood submits to your wishes Jirgaar. However, let it be known that only one psychic will accompany the Upside party. Segaan cannot afford to lose another psychic."*

The *Jirga* grunted. As the *Jirga* Kaiser, he was determined to find a way to save the Azar race. After over eight thousand alifees of civilization, the Azars would not all die—not while he was *Jirga* Kaiser. He would do whatever it took to save his people, which was why he had reluctantly agreed with his council when *Loya* Favood first made his proposal.

However, now that he had seen the strange beings, he did not think this plan would work. The aliens looked repugnant. He did not wish children from these beings populating his world. To change course, he would need to eliminate *Loya* Favood. That would be difficult if not impossible. There was no other psychic powerful enough to challenge the *Loya* Favood—assuming he could even find a psychic willing to oppose their own leadership. A better alternative would be to pretend to go along with *Loya* Favood's plan. Perhaps he would spare the females for a while and let *Loya* Favood continue with his experiments. The male, he would have killed immediately. That too would be difficult to arrange, but it was feasible.

It was certainly not necessary to have any live alien males on the planet. Besides, even the *Loya* Favood admitted that they were a danger. He did not want even a remote chance that any would survive. And without males the aliens would not be able to reproduce.

With an abrupt mental command, he dismissed *Loya* Favood and his Blocker, *"Go! I will allow you more cycles to study the aliens you have captured. But the ones on the Upside will be destroyed. Also, we must have an alternative option. This I will think more on. Our survival is in the will of Tooaal."*

****

300 Years Later

Arapmo

Chapter 1

Arapmo was the only outpost of the colonists and the town's existence was due solely to the sheer determination of twenty men. It was nine years ago that Dennis Classet, together with nineteen other mavericks, decided to petition for an expedition to venture into the interior. Of course, they each had their own agenda. The Council's rigid policies and regimental control was unchallenged in the close environment of New World City, but would the Council be able to maintain control of its citizens if the population were more dispersed? The expedition plans did not sit well with the Presidential Council.

The Council was unaware of the secret alliances of the men, but even so, their fear of possible dissidents would not have been their sole objection. No expedition could be undertaken lightly. Because their initial population was so small, one of the guiding rules of the Presidential Council was the preservation and creation of life. Through a policy of careful planning, the population of the planet Alloca was steadily increasing and no one — not even the dissatisfied minority — wanted to put the population at risk. For the Presidential Council, however, pragmatism won. After 300 years the colonist had mostly exhausted the supplies of the First Valley. They needed to venture out.

With the Council's approval, the expedition was set. Most of the population of New World City predicted disaster. Even now, 300 years later, stories of the attacks by the revos were still chilling. The revo was not the only wild predator on Alloca, but they were the least understood and the most feared. These huge animals were said to be over nine feet tall, hairy and vicious. Yet, there was no accurate description. No one had ever seen a revo up close and lived to tell about it. The early colonist had no defense against the hairy monsters. The weirdest thing about the attacks was that the revos always took away the female bodies of their victims yet left behind the males — dead yet strangely unscarred. The early colonists were never able to figure out the cause of death. It was believed that the revos ate their victims and preferred female flesh. Only one male body was unaccounted for and suspected eaten by a revo. The colonist lost almost a quarter of their population before the attacks stopped as suddenly as they had begun. In the last 300 years no one had ever seen a revo again. The speculation was that the early colonist might have passed on some disease to the revo that had wiped them out. Now, the sole monument commemorating the attacks was the names of all forty-four victims inscribed in a memorial in the First Colonist Museum.

In the first expedition attempt, the group headed north. But they found temperatures even more extremely hot then that of New World City. Since no one wanted to deal with temperatures averaging over 120 degrees every cycle, the second expedition headed south. To the south of New World City, the terrain was hilly, and the elevation got higher and higher. Yet this time around, to the chagrin of the doomsayers, the expedition was a roaring success. The explorers traveled for over a month and again, they encountered unexpectedly harsh weather. But at least, because of the higher elevation, the temperature dipped in the other direction. Arapmo in fact, was discovered purely by accident as the explorers tried to avoid the extreme freezing weather. It was a beautifully sheltered valley. Arapmo escaped most of the harsher dips in temperature experienced by the surrounding countryside. Which was why, even though the town did not have all the conveniences of the city, the people of Arapmo loved their little town. And with the discovery of the precious metal—moonglitter—the town's future was secure. It was expanding rapidly, too rapidly some older members of Arapmo were saying. They were afraid that the town was attracting opportunist and thrill seekers.

But right now, Arapmo was a safe outpost—this despite the simmering tension among its citizens. There were no recorded murders in Arapmo's short history. And even petty crimes were almost nonexistent. The main problem was that the twenty colonists to finally win approval for the venture had one thing— and only one thing—in common; they all wanted freedom from the Council's laws. Unfortunately, it was only after founding Arapmo that they discovered the hidden agendas within the groups. Still, they had achieved one goal. And with an unsteady alliance still holding, seven of the original mavericks formed the Arapmo Town Council—the ruling body of the town. They all recognized that even greater than the threat of open warfare among the citizens of

Arapmo, was the danger posed by the Presidential Council.

It was the united goal of the two factions living within Arapmo to keep the Presidential Council out of their town. Now with rumblings from the Presidential Council, some in Arapmo were fearful of a showdown. Yet, the majority of Arapmo still favored independence from the Presidential Council.

Carrie Classet stood by her window and watched the dawn of first-light. She was so worried. What if the Council sent the Presidential Guards to enforce their order? What then? War?

She knew some in Arapmo favored moving even further inland to escape the Council's reach. Already the town's population was starting to take sides. Those willing to fight to keep Arapmo independent of the Presidential Council, even if it meant fleeing, and those willing to give in to avoid a confrontation.

She had nothing planned for this cycle. She hated that her issue could lead to war. And it was getting harder and harder to wait patiently. In less than one month, word should reach them from the Presidential Council. She was waiting on a ruling on her petition to refuse her marriage agreement, and the waiting was killing her. What if they received a negative ruling? It was a distinct possibility. Carrie knew her father would never accept the Council's authority.

What would happen then was anyone's guess. She knew where her father stood. He had founded Arapmo and he planned to fight, if a fight was needed, to keep the Council out of his town. Carrie did not want to leave Arapmo. She loved Arapmo and had lived here most of her life. The very thought of having to live in New World

City with a stranger for a husband was scary. But neither did she want to be the cause of a rift between Arapmo and New World City. And a war! Her father kept insisting that the Presidential Council was too protective of lives to go to war. Carrie was not so sure. And Arapmo was too small to take on the Presidential Guards! When she thought of the effort her father had put into building this town, she felt like crying.

Carrie stirred. She could not stand here forever. She would go to the fluar's watering hole. No one in Arapmo had ever tamed a fluar. No one on the entire planet had ever tamed a fluar! The animals travelled in pairs and were incredibly shy. Catching a fluar was not the problem. The problem was that the animal usually died almost immediately upon capture. The longest one had lived in captivity was two cycles. She had watched this particular fluar every first-light for the past three weeks, and already it seemed tame. One light, it even came within two feet of Carrie. Perhaps, she though morbidly, this would be her parting gift to Arapmo — taming a fluar.

She dressed quickly, pulling on a thick jacket and ankle boots. The jacket came only to her hips, but that was okay because she wore a thick divided skirt, which reached to her boots. At this time of the year, first-light in Arapmo could see temperatures in the fifties. Carrie opened her door quietly and padded down the hall. No one was up. The house was so large and spacious that it took Carrie a few minutes to negotiate the downstairs rooms. Her father had amassed a vast outpost and he had specifically built their home to mirror a typical New World City mansion.

Originally, her father bred zigs, but he also owned one of the largest moonglitter mines in Arapmo. Carrie quietly left the house. She was headed first to the barns, which were just a short distance behind the house. Within minutes she was sneaking in through the small supply door at the back. Carrie moved silently down the stalls to her zig. She knew the animal would not welcome her at this hour.

Zigs were notoriously lazy at just about all times. Although great at pulling heavy loads, they were not as intelligent as the fluar. The zig and the fluar were the only large animals that the colonist viewed has having any potential as safe domesticated beast of burdens. The zig was easily trainable and reminded the early colonists of an old-world animal called a mule. However, it was twice the size of a mule plus much slower and lumbering. It was called zig because of its tendency to wander in mindless zigzag patterns when feeding in the wild. The fluar however, was still a mystery. Faster, taller and sleeker than the zig, it looked to be an incredibly smooth ride if one could ever tame it.

"I tell you we can easily increase the loads. These zigs can take twice what they are carrying now. Plus, now we have the cabin to use for storage."

Carrie instinctively ducked below one of the stalls. She did not recognize the voice and she knew every worker on her father's outpost.

"It takes almost two full lights to reach the cabin. That's too far for even a zig to carry such a heavy load."

That was Tim's voice, Carrie thought. Tim had started working for her father only five cycles ago. He should be at the mine camp, not here at the outpost.

"I'm giving both of you a fair cut. It is enough for now. We will keep the load the same."

Carrie did not recognize that voice either. Who were these men? Her heart began pounding. Whatever they were planning did not sound good. She had to get back to the main house! Carrie began inching back toward the door. As she passed a stall, one of the zigs grunted. Carrie froze!

"What was that?" Tim asked.

"Quit sweating. A zig probably groaned." The first man was contemptuous of his friend's fear.

"Chris, go and check," one of the strange voices ordered.

"It was just...."

"Check!"

There was no way the man, Chris, would not see her if he came in her direction. Abandoning caution, Carrie turned to flee.

"What the bolt!"

Carrie rushed toward the door in terror. She almost made it. Less than two paces from the door, the man slammed into her. They both fell to the ground.

"Who the fire bolt is it?" Tim asked. He and the other man had also rushed forward.

Carrie was too stunned to move even when the man rose off her. She groaned as rough hands flipped her onto her back.

"Carrie!" Tim stared at her in amazement. "What are you doing here at this hour?"

"I was going to ride out early." Carrie was unable to keep the fear out of her voice, "to look at the fluars."

Tim turned to the stranger. "She is Mr. Classet's daughter. We can't.... That is...." his voice trailed off miserably in the face of a sharply raised eyebrow and an incredulous look from one of the strangers.

"I'm sure she heard us," the stranger stroked his clean shaved chin as he gave Carrie a contemplative look. "So, this is the pretty thing that has the entire town in an uproar."

Carrie's heart was hammering. She had never seen anyone with such cold eyes—as green as the Allocan skies—they terrified her.

"I... I..."

"Don't bother denying it." He interrupted her with a dismissive wave of his hand before turning to the two men. "She may come in useful in the future. Tim, saddle one of the zigs. Chris will have to take her to the cabin."

This man was clearly the boss. He moved decisively toward her.

"No!" Carrie screamed as she tried scrambling away. "Tim! Please!" she turned terrified eyes to Tim, but the young man turned beet-red and refused to make eye contact. Chris grabbed her firmly and clamped a hand over her mouth. As Carrie wriggled and kicked wildly, the stranger pulled a small injector from his pocket. She was able to get only one solid kick to the stranger's shin before he slammed the injector into her thigh.

With a moan Carrie collapsed forward.

****

Caleel- 9 Alifees Ago

Chapter 2

"Perhaps we should have taken more boys?"

"No. Only fifteen boys were born from the experiment. Taking more than five would be too risky."

"The Soosan would never know."

"The current *Jirga* does not track the boys, but the previous one did. If this one lives..."

Zooric couldn't pinpoint exactly when he began making sense of the sounds he was hearing. There were two men in the room and they were discussing him. He struggled to open his eyes but the lids felt unbelievable heavy. Drugged again! He did not even have the energy to summon his past rage. He wanted to give up. Could he will himself to death? Even as the thought surfaced, he realized—I am thinking! In his past drugged state, he had been unable to put two thoughts together.

"He's coming awake."

That voice! Zooric became absolutely still but he knew he would never be able to fool them. He could already hear his frantic heartbeat— in his head.

"Zooric!" One of the men tapped him lightly on the face.

He tried to turn his head but his muscles seemed disconnected from his brain; he was not sure how much movement he actually achieved and not even to save his life could he open his eyes. An involuntary groan escaped, startling him. Was he in pain?

"What do you think?" It was the same voice.

Suddenly, Zooric felt a burning pain in his upper chest. Again, he groaned and helplessly tried shifting his head, but fortunately, he truly was unable to move his upper body. What were they doing to him?

"He is not really responding." This was the other man. Zooric feared them both but this man, Deeknor, was a monster.

"Dees! I thought you were going to kill him."

"With a knife? Deeknor laughed. "That would be too messy. And how would we explain his death from a knife wound? Apply some pressure. I do not want his blood dripping on the floor."

"His brain is probably fried."

"He definitely cannot move," Deeknor sounded satisfied. "No one could remain still while being stabbed."

"So, what do we do now?"

"We will keep him here for a few more cycles. He is waking up. The other boy never regained consciousness although he lingered for four cycles. If this boy wakes, even if his brain is gone, we will use him until he reaches puberty."

Zooric's breathing was labored as the pain slowly faded. Only vaguely was he aware of a pressure on his chest. They did not want him bleeding to death. They would still use him. He did not care anymore. He slipped back into unconsciousness even as despair filled him.

It was dark when he woke again. He knew because he shocked himself by actually opening his eyes. He tried to lift his head but the effort was beyond him. As he relaxed on the bed, he was jubilant as he realized that he was aware — his brain was working again — he could think. He was naked, lying under a thin sheet covering; he could turn his head but he couldn't lift his arms and he was not sure his legs were actually attached to his body. If this was the effect of a drug it was something new. He searched his mind — tying to recall anything of his past — and a fierce joy filled him as his memory came in bits and pieces. It wasn't much but he could now remember his family. This definitely meant he was no longer under the influence of the mind-numbing drugs. With a sigh of relief, he closed his eyes and drifted off.

****

When he woke again there was light, and the sounds of a quarrel.

"*Onke* Deeknor sent you to change him."

"I changed him last cycle. It is your turn."

"It is not my turn. And you did not change him. You always get Raekon to do your dirty work. I brought him his food. Onke Deeknor said we were to take turns..."

Restric and Shron were two of the boys living in the house. Both were Zooric's age, not harmless, but not an immediate threat, so he ignored them as he again took stock. Since he was feeling stronger, he cautiously tried moving his arms and legs. Yes, he was definitely recovering. Now that he had some control over his muscles, he would have to hide that fact from them. How long had he been unconscious? It had to be at least one cycle for certain, but perhaps two. Each cycle was 25 *eens* but a cycle was broken into first- light, which was five *eens*, followed by three *eens* of first-dark. The cycle continued with second-light, which generally lasted eight *eens*, and then nine *eens* of second-dark. It was light now but he was not sure if were first or second light.

Since the boys were still busy arguing, he carefully turned his head to look around the room. This was not the room he normally shared with the other boys. Was he even in the same house? In his regular room there were no windows and he and the other boys slept on pallets on the floor. This room had a large window and, in addition to the bed, a closet completely covered one wall. From this vantage point, he could not recognize any landmarks. In fact, he could see only the green Segaan sky. It was also impossible to tell how secure the window was. However, if he was in the same house, he could be in one of the rooms that he had never been allowed to enter. Before he was drugged Restric had told him about those rooms, and he knew that they had unsecured windows. He was afraid to hope, but now that he could think rationally, he had to plan. This could be his only chance to escape.

He was brought back to the present by the slamming of the door. Restric had walked out. He was never changed but at least Shron fed him, and later that cycle the boy Restric came back with another liquid meal.

"You stink," Restric sounded pleased.

Whose fault was that? Zooric thought surly. However, he deliberately gave no indication that he understood. He now knew it was second-light. And he was in the same house. He hadn't dared leave the bed, but he had been able to raise himself enough to take a peek out the window. He recognized some of the landmarks. Also, throughout the cycle he had been regularly exercising his muscles, carefully hiding his actions whenever anyone entered the room. His bed was wet with urine because no one had come to assist him from it and he was not about to let them know that he could speak or move. A wet bed he considered minor. He had learned that he could live with discomfort, besides, after an entire cycle he could no longer smell himself. He now waited in silence for what he knew would be minimal help at best, torture at worse. It was Restric's specialty.

Shron had propped him up with pillows to feed him the thin liquid with a spoon. Fortunately, he was still in the same propped up position as Restric brought a full bowl to his mouth.

"Here! Eat! Do not expect me to feed you."

Zooric kept his expression blank. He dared not move. Predictably, since he was unable to swallow fast enough, most of the liquid poured down his chin and onto the sheet. It was steaming hot and Zooric was unable to stop a hiss of pain. As he gasped, even more of the hot liquid poured over him. Zooric's breathing was hard, his eyes wide and staring as he struggled to blank his mind — to control the pain. His biggest struggle was controlling the urge to move or push the bowl away.

Restric began giggling. "Poor Zooric. It is a pity you cannot understand."

The bowel emptied. Zooric slowly unclenched fists that were fortunately hidden by the covers.

Restric grinned at him. "If you are lucky Shron will clean you." Restric continued grinning as he pulled away the covers, exposing Zooric's naked body to the cool air. "You need air to dry and perhaps get rid of the smell." He was turning to go when the door opened.

Deeknor entered.

"How is he?"

"I tried feeding him but he does not swallow. Look at the mess he made." It was said with exactly the right amount of indignant concern.

Deeknor came over to the bed. "Why was he not changed?" he demanded.

"You were not here Onke Deeknor, when I begged Shron for help and he refused. I tried but could not turn him by myself. I was just now about to replace the sheet he soiled as I tried to feed him."

"Shron refused to help?" Deeknor's eyes narrowed.

Restric tentatively reached out to touch Deeknor's arm "I even threatened him. I told him I would tell you of his refusal but he said he would accuse me of lying."

Deeknor patted Restric's hand reassuringly. "I will take care of Shron. Go find him. Tell him to go to my room immediately. I will be there shortly."

Zooric did not have time to feel pity for Shron. As Restric left the room Deeknor bent over the bed.

"This is probably for the best."

He forced himself to stare blankly as Deeknor removed a knife from his belt. Zooric eyes tracked the knife as Deeknor absently tapped the blade against his open palm. This is it, he thought. Yet his heart was not even racing. He was in fact feeling unnaturally calm.

The other man entered. "I have been checking on him throughout the cycle. He is fully awake but he still does not move."

"Are you sure?"

"Positive! I checked him with my knife."

He had done no such thing but Zooric was not about to argue the point. The boys had been his only visitors this past cycle.

Deeknor straighten. "It is senseless to keep him alive if he cannot even feed himself."

"We will be left with only three boys," the man was clearly nervous.

"That means you will have to be very careful. We cannot afford to lose another boy." Somehow his words seemed to carry a threat, perhaps to the other man, yet Zooric gave an involuntary shiver. Fortunately, the men were no longer focused on him.

"I have heard that the sizzle can have a numbing effect on muscles. It has been only two cycles. Perhaps we should wait at least one more."

"Perhaps, but I never intended him to live much longer. We could not keep him drugged forever. Besides, now that the boys from the experiment are approaching puberty, the Soosan Protectors may begin making enquires. We could give them a dead boy but there is no way to explain how a boy could get sizzled."

The other man was nodding. "You are right. How..."

"A blow to the head. That worked before."

Zooric's eyes flickered. He could not believe he was listening to a discussion of his own death. And such an emotionless discussion! Deeknor could have been discussing the weather.

"I have to travel outside of Caleel within a cycle." The monster continued. "I will take him then."

"We told the parents of the other boy that their son ran away. What will we say for this one?"

"He did not like the strict disciplined training that a Soosan must follow. He fell out of the window when trying to run away. They are poor. It is unlikely that they will question us if we pay them well. Also, like before, I will give them the body."

They continued talking as they left the room. Zooric was now shaking so badly his teeth were chattering. It was not only from the cool air. His emotional numbness of a few minutes ago had evaporated. He was now terrified! If he wanted to live, he had perhaps one cycle to plan his escape. As the door closed, he resumed the careful exercises he had started earlier. Hopefully someone would come soon, both to change him and to cover him up. It was risky exercising his limbs when he was so exposed, but he had to be ready and the exercise would warm him. He was freezing!

****

Present Day

Chapter 3

Cautiously, silently, Zooric eased the window open. It was pitch dark outside, but this was good. It was less likely that anyone was about, giving him a better chance of escaping undetected. The window squeaked as he raised it. He froze in place with his leg lifted in preparation to climb out. He was struggling not to panic as he strained his ears, even closing his eyes for a second, to better concentrate—but nothing. There was no movement outside his room and hopefully the entire house was asleep. Quickly this time, he adjusted his bundle— it did not hold much, just a few items he had gathered from the room, things he felt he would need to survive—and scrambled out. Zooric was not sure how long it would take him to walk home. However long it took, he would make it; there was no turning back. He would die rather than return to this house.

Caleel during the dark was eerie, with the dome shaped houses and buildings looking like miniature stepping-stones in a giant's pond. After leaving the house, Zooric deliberately kept to the shadows, his bare feet made no sounds on the rough pavement. As a pre-pubescent, he had no special senses to help him. But even that fact would work in his favor, because if he remained motionless around others, there were no electro-signals for even a Soosan to detect.

Silently, yet as swiftly as possible, he walked away from the house. He knew running would attract too much attention so he resisted that urge, besides he felt too weak to run. However, with an almost paranoiac fear of discovery, he found himself looking back every few seconds. But there was no hue or cry—no alarm was raised. Again, he made a silent vow. He would never go back. And he had no plans of stopping until he was well clear of Caleel.

His first act after leaving the town was to wash. It was a small body of water but with an almost frantic obsession to be clean, he did not care. He went in, clothes and all. For him it was almost a ritual. In cleaning himself, washing, he was effectively washing away the past—putting it all behind him. He was dripping wet when he finally walked out of the water, but he made no effort to dry himself. In his mind, the act of natural drying completed his mental cleansing ritual.

He continued walking until first-light approached. The lightening skies found Zooric searching for a hiding place. Deeknor would be searching for him. This he did not doubt.

Like the town itself, this area was a fertile and lush region. Centuries ago, much of the forest had been cleared, allowing roads to crisscross the region. Through the ages, poor upkeep of the roadways had allowed the proliferation of sates, a naturally occurring purple ground cover that grew to ankle high. Sates seemed to naturally repel the dense woodlands and many farmers outside Caleel proper, after clearing the land, used the plant to keep the forest at bay.

Zooric finally found the ideal spot in one of the scattered remnants of the area's wooded past. It was in the middle of the ylieen tree. With branches as wide as an adult's torso, and leaves just as broad, the ylieen tree would provide an effective cover and would hide him completely from any casual observer, even one standing directly below the tree. However, getting into the center of the tree was tricky. The ylieen tree, when in bloom as this one was, often produced numerous multicolored buds. They were beautiful but caused painful ylieen burns on the skin. Within a few cycles of contact, the skin would become irritated and swollen, forming unsightly white blotches that could take up to ten cycles to clear. Since Zooric was hoping he would not meet anyone, an unsightly even painful skin condition was the least of his worries. He climbed a good distance off the ground to find a comfortable branch then hitched his bundle to the branch above. As he settled down to rest during the light, he examined his arms and legs. His skin was smooth, brown, virtually hairless, and as yet showed no signs of ylieen burns. But he wore a sleeveless tunic. It was the only clothing he could find in the room, and although the adult size of the tunic covered him completely, actually reaching to just above his knees, that still left all of his arms and most of his legs uncovered. He just hoped the ylieen burns he knew he would have to endure would be worth this effort to escape.

He closed his eyes with a sigh. But, as his body relaxed, images began crowding his mind. *Saac ga!* Not now! He did not want to deal with the emotional trauma of his immediate past. Unfortunately, his brain had other ideas. Even with his eyes squeezed tightly shut he was unable to banish the scenes of horror. The worst was the fuzzy nature of his memory. He would recall the end of a scene but not the beginning, or the middle but not the end.

With a grimace he sat up. Pulling his knees to his chest, he wrapped his arms around them and stared aimlessly through the branches. He was exhausted, but unable to sleep.

Just how he had escaped with his mind intact would remain a mystery. Yet he was thankful. The incident had allowed his escape.

As far as he was concerned, the past was the past and he wanted it to stay that way. But with his brain playing tricks on him and intent on reliving hazy scenes that he had no wish to recall, he knew there would be no sleep for him this light.

The rest of the light was spent planning the best route home and designing a protective cover for his feet. He cautiously left his perch to retrieve flexible leaves and branches from other shrubs. There was no hurry and he wanted a sturdy foot cover. He knew the path from his father's farm to Caleel was well traveled and much of the territory was familiar because he had made the trip numerous times with his father. The problem was he would have to avoid the well-traveled paths. And travelling in the woods without foot protection would be painful if not impossible. However, now that his brain was finally free of the mind-numbing drugs that they had been giving him, he knew he had a good chance of surviving. True he would have to avoid the open, but if he stayed to the edge of the forest, he would not get lost. And much of the vegetation on Segaan was water rich. There were also numerous edible fruits. Besides, even without the water-filled plant life, he would not die of thirst. There were enough rivers and streams between here and his home.

His biggest worry was really an attack from any of the various wild animals. The deadliest was the feera.

They were particularly vicious scavengers, but as nocturnal animals they hunted during the darkening. By traveling in the darkening, Zooric was hoping to avoid contact with others, but a plus would be that his constant motion should reduce his risk of attack. He could sleep in trees during the light. The one wild animal capable of climbing trees was the wolar. But it was too big and lumbering to launch a silent attack. The wolar depended on its size to subdue and kill its prey. He was sure he would awake long before a wolar could plan an attack. Zooric was confident that he would survive—if only he could forget the past.

****

At second-dark, he climbed down from the tree and continued his journey. Because he had carried no food, he stopped periodically to scrounge around for wild nuts and fruits along the way. Initially, he planned to go directly to his parent's farm, but by the third cycle he felt the first simmering of awareness. *Saac ga*! It was happening!

Zooric stopped. As he stood absolutely still, a tingling of electricity ran throughout his body. He closed his eyes and breathed deeply. Why now? He wrapped his arms about his body as a powerful surge gripped him. It was the beginning of his electro senses! Now he would need a medic! During the first ten cycles of onset, his electro senses could fluctuate wildly. Only a medic could stabilize the electrical surges. He had heard that some boys went crazy without a medic. To get a medic he would have to return to the Caleel. Zooric took deep breaths as another wave of awareness gripped him. It was followed almost immediately by that tingling of electricity. Even as he hugged himself protectively, he was mentally rebelling. No! No! No! No way was he going back.

Zooric opened his eyes during another powerful surge. It was pitch-dark, but he could now 'see.' Despite the urgency of his need, he looked around in wonder. It was unbelievable! Already his special electro-senses were displayed. Now, by sending small electro- pulses out into his surroundings and monitoring the return signals, he had a picture of the area around him. He could 'see' across the open land to the next group of trees. He could 'see' the animal life that had been invisible to him in the dark. It was even possible to 'see' where the land dipped and disappeared into the horizon. A bitter expression pulled at his features. Was this the reason he had survived that last incident? Although the fog of numerous drugging had slowly faded, his memory was still hazy. Yet, he knew he should have been dead or badly sizzled; instead, he had been stunned. Perhaps puberty started in the brain long before the electro skills showed. It was the only explanation he could think of.

Now he could no longer go home. If he went home, by law his father would have to take him to a Soosan medic for first-link testing and for treatment. All Owoon boys must undergo first-link, a test of their electro skills. And as a child of a Soosan, most likely he would test sensitive—and become a Soosan. He had already been initiated into the life of a Soosan by Deekec. He wanted no part of it.

Slowly, reluctantly, Zooric changed course and began heading into the underdeveloped area to the South of Caleel. Yet, mixed with his reluctance was a curious relief. True, he wanted to see his family. Of course, he missed his parents, his sister and his brother. By leaving home, he had already accepted that he would never see them again. Returning now would mean he would have had to tell why he could not stay in Caleel. It was also possible that the men would demand his return—perhaps even force his father to give him up.

Zooric stopped, lifted his head and stared at the twinkling sky. The silence of the universe looked down at him. He was alone yet.... Zooric took a deep breath and, for the first time since his ordeal began, he cried. They were not silent tears, and they were endless. The emotional onslaught left him huddled on the ground; his arms wrapped tightly around his body. When the tears finally stopped, he slowly rose, sniffing and wiping his face on his shoulder. Now he could admit a truth that had been nudging at the edge of his consciousness ever since he started this journey. He wanted to be alone. Here, there was no one to ask uncomfortable questions, and no one to force him to recall what he preferred to forget. He would not live in the wilds forever, but he would stay for as long as he could. Yes! He would at least learn to control his special senses. He even preferred the risk of going crazy. Perhaps with time he would learn how to hide the fact that he was a sensitive, was perhaps Soosan!

Over the next few cycles, Zooric slowly learned to manage and control his new skills. With constant practice, he was able to stretch himself to the limits of his abilities. He had always been told by both adults and others his age that the initial surges were uncontrollable. This was definitely so, but they did not drive him crazy. They were an annoyance, yes, but functioning was not beyond one's capabilities. It was like a background noise that was irritating, but with determination could be ignored. The great positive was that, with his new skills came food. It took him two full cycles of practice before he learned how to generate a pulse just strong enough to kill his prey without burning the animal to a blackened crisp. The fact that he needed to practice control was positive proof that he was a high sensitive and could be a Soosan. For an ordinary Owoon, normally the difficulty was in generating a pulse strong enough to kill. But he also debunked another myth when he found that generating a pulse, even to kill a prey, did not reduce the violently swinging surges. Yet there were other advantages. Now that he could scan the surrounding area for movement, he no longer feared attacks by wild animals. He found that he could scan vast distances of level land, but mountain ranges or even large trees blocked his senses. There was one curious fact: he could detect the electro signals from even the smallest animal! Zooric never knew that there existed Soosans with that particular skill, but since he had never lived among real Soosans he was not concerned. After all, no Owoon really knew everything about the Soosans.

Zooric had been traveling for more than 100 cycles, in a southerly direction when his senses picked up some low-grade electrical impulses coming from a mountain range. The signals were so faint that had he not been actively scanning the area; he would have missed them. This far from Caleel, the land was uninhabited, but it had been explored by his people. Although he was now traveling during the light, in all that time, he had only seen two animal trappers. Trappers tended to travel with a pack of hunting rocleers and were notoriously protective of their territory. Like wild animals, some trappers would fight to keep others out of a given area. With his electro detection skills, Zooric was able to locate any trappers long before they were even aware of him; he was therefore careful in giving them a wide berth.

It was possible this was another trapper. Zooric stopped to get a better feel of the signals. The vegetation here was much the same as around Caleel, although there were less of the purple sate ground cover, and more dense areas of forest. This type of terrain was not ideal for long-range signals. Yet, the signals seemed to be coming from a distance. Curious, he slowly and cautiously tried to locate the source. Yes, they were coming from the looming mountain range. The question was, where? It could not be trappers—they did not travel in packs—maybe another settlement? He had never heard of another large settlement of Owoons. As he got closer, the signals did not become stronger. Puzzled, because somehow the signals did not seem normal, he tried again to pinpoint the source. It was then that he realized why the signals felt so strange. They were mechanically induced and not from a living being! Dense sates covered the pathway that led directly up to the mountain. There, on a narrow ledge about his height, were six large stones—each about the size of his head. Zooric stared. The stones were emitting the signals! They were large and oval and even as he gazed at them, understanding dawned. He had found an ancient Azar sector!

Frowning, Zooric tried to remember from past lessons whether an Azar entrance opened out or in, up or down. Hopefully it opened in, or down, because the door would never be able to open out with over 300 alifees of sediments collected behind it. Next, he tried figuring out how to open the entrance. From history lessons, he knew that the stones were the key. By pulsing the stones in a specific combination, the door would open. However, there were six stones. Ancient Azar poems that he had studied gave combination keys only for four stones. This meant that, unless he got lucky, it could literally take a lifetime to figure out this combination! Yet he intended to try. Taking a deep breath, he concentrated—focusing his electro-pulse on first one stone then another. Nothing happened. After a period of trial and error, he realized that four of the stones had a slightly different signal. Perhaps those four stones were the key? Throughout the course of the cycle, he repeated his efforts, concentrating on the four stones, trying out different combinations learned from history lessons.

Five cycles later, after again pulsing the series of four stones, Zooric though he heard a sound. Frowning, he tried again. This time he both heard then felt something. The door was opening! Slowly, noisily it opened downwards. Zooric scrambled out of the way as it fell with a thud. A blast of debris cascaded around him. Coughing and gasping, Zooric fled further away. When the dust finally settled, he moved forward, cautiously climbing over large and small rocks, as he made his way inside. What a find! His heart was humming with excitement. Soon he would have to report this to the Soosans —but not yet. This would be his one and only chance to explore.

****

Two alifees later Zooric was still exploring. It was not that he had changed his mind about reporting his find. Rather it was because of his fear—he was terrified he would be returned to the house in Caleel. Fortunately, he had not spent the time alone. About thirty cycles after his find, he found a young rocleer. The animal had a terrible injury to his back, likely the result of a fight, and was on the verge of dying. More than likely a trapper had abandoned the animal. It was so sick it gave just a token growl as Zooric bent to examine the injury but did not otherwise protest when Zooric carefully picked it up. It was another twenty cycles before the rocleer, now named Soor, fully recovered. By then he was Zooric's faithful friend and companion. Rocleers were the domesticated cousins of the wild feera and Zooric suspected that his rocleer was half feera; it had grown so tall—reaching almost to his waist. The feeras in the wild were taller, although, like his pet, they too had small bodies in comparison to their massive heads and long skinny legs. Like the wild feeras, Soor also had short but thick black hair covering his entire body.

In truth, with Soor for companionship, and the comfort of the sector to live in, Zooric did not miss civilization. The sector had huge reading rooms that were still intact and he spent many cycles using his electro-skills to read the embedded electrical disc that was the Azar's primary recording method. As he explored deeper into the sector he was, however, assailed by guilt. The Azars had even more advanced technologies then his people. He really needed to report this find. It was his guilt that finally prodded him to travel north to Caleel. While living in the sector he had tamed two female pageens. The pageen was a smart four-legged mammal strong enough to carry an adult male on its back. They travelled in herds, typically lead by a male, ranging from a minimum of 2 to a maximum of 8. They needed at least a pair to survive. The best way to tame one was to separate a pair from the herd.

The smooth easy ride of the pageens could have easily reduced his journey to Caleel by half, but Zooric lingered. With Soor as a guard during the darkening, he no longer had to literally sleep with one eye open in fear of attack by any of the numerous wild animals, especially the feera.

Instinctively, he continued to avoid others. Using his electro detection abilities, he found that he was able to sense others long before they were even aware of him. But as he approached the town, his senses were swamped with more and more electro-sensory information. He was literally picking up the electro signals of hundreds of citizens. At first, the static was overwhelming. Zooric dismounted. He allowed his pageens to walk slowly. Breathing deeply, he caressed the animals, while striving for control. Finally, he stopped. He was on a wooded rise just above the center of town. He knew he could not go on —not because of the electro-sensory overload. True blocking was one skill that he was weak at —he had never had to practice. But he had easily learned how to block much of the incoming electro-sensory signals and as he drew on them, his skills improved. No. His problem was his deep-seated fear of capture. As he got closer to the town, long forgotten nightmares began plaguing him again. Zooric stood and gazed in silence. He could see the lights of the town at this distance. Soor, sensing his unease pressed closer.

"I know Soor," he murmured. "There is nothing to fear. It is unlikely that they will even remember me."

Yet he could not move! His mind was already screaming in blind panic. Also, with his block fully in place, he had lost one of his senses. It was like going deaf. He felt exposed, plus like a phobia, no amount of rational reasoning could convince him that the people of the town would not immediately pounce on him—or take him back to the house. Zooric turned away. He would have to find some other way to tell the Soosans about his find. Decision made; he began a rapid retreat. He was a full cycle away from the town before his heartbeat settled back to normal. But Zooric did not pause in his flight. He pushed his mounts, determined to reach home in record time. With two mounts he was able to rest one while riding the other. It took less than fifty cycles to get back to his home in the Azar sector.

****

It was almost another four alifees later that Zooric next ventured out for Caleel. He had explored the entire sector and as he read his way through the vast selection of discs in the sector's massive reading rooms, he was amazed and astounded. Was he the only one with this knowledge? As more discoveries unfolded, he realized that he truly could not keep this find to himself. There were ancient maps… writings and artifacts. The people of Caleel needed to know. The Soosans had to be informed. The problem was getting the information to them.

On this attempt to reach Caleel, Zooric carried animal skins that he had collected. And this time luck was with him on his journey back. He met and aided an injured trapper. This was his first contact with another person since his escape and Zooric was surprised and pleased to discover that he could easily block the trapper's single electro signal while still maintaining his ability to detect other signals nearby. That was reassuring and helped to ease his fears as they approached the town. However, as he got nearer, he was again forced to put up a total block. Zooric fought his feelings of helplessness. Fortunately, the trapper was exceedingly grateful. Assuming that Zooric was new to the animal trade, he gave Zooric valuable information on selling animal skin and hair; he also offered Zooric a place to stay when he learned that Zooric's family did not live in Caleel.

Five cycles later, with cash on hand and a completely new outfit, Zooric again left Caleel–this time for his parent's farm. His stay in Caleel had relieved some of his fears of capture but instinctively he continued to travel in the woods, avoiding all contact with others. Now, for this last part of his journey, he would have to use the path.

"Come Soor," he said to the rocleer at his side. "It is time to go back."

The rocleer wagged his stubby tail and pressed its massive head against Zooric's leg. Zooric rubbed the animal's head then reluctantly straightened. Leading his pageens, he made his way down the lightly wooded slope and onto the main path leading to the farm. Soon a cart, pulled by two caceens pulled up. The caceens was also a four-legged mammal capable of caring an adult. However, the animal was viewed as less intelligent, when compared to the pageen, and was often used to pull wagon or carts. One big difference between the two animals was the huge head of the caaceen. Knocking on the caaceen's head produced a hollow sound similar to knocking on a hollow log.

"Do you need a ride, *Zha*?" the driver asked while keeping a close eye on the rocleer.

Zooric nodded his thanks. He was finding speech, or just communicating with others, difficult. For the last six alifees, just about all his conversations had been between him and his rocleer.

"Uh... I can't take the rocleer," the Owoon said.

"No problem. Soor can follow." He swiftly tied his pageens to the back of the cart.

"Are you from this area?"

Zooric cleared his throat a couple of times before speaking. "I am Zooric. I left here about eight alifees ago." It was a risk giving his name, but he could think of no way to avoid it, especially since he intended to visit with his family.

"Zooric!" the driver stared. "*Saac ga*! Zooric! I cannot believe this. I am Bmees."

At the driver's expectant looks, Zooric stared. Bmees was his younger brother. The last time he saw him he was a ragged youth of eight alifees. This was amazing!

Bmees was grinning widely. "You are Zooric aren't you?" He did not wait for an answer. "Yes. I recognize you now. You are so different. It was difficult at first, but I did immediately think you looked familiar. That was why I stopped." Without pausing he continued. "But where have you been? The man who took you, *Zha* Deeknor, he and a friend came looking for you after you ran away. When you did not return here, we all suspected you had died trying to return home."

Even now, eight alifees later, just the mention of Deeknor's name was enough to cause Zooric to flinch. "I have lived as an animal trapper," he said, after what he knew was a noticeable pause. "I knew that I would get in trouble for running away. I was afraid to come home." He was very thankful that, when he had escaped Deeknor's house, he had changed course and headed south.

Bmees nodded understandingly. "*Eeng. Zha* Deeknor was very angry when he came looking for you. *Zha* Deeknor gave father a lot of money for the honor of training you as a Soosan. When he realized you were not here, he wanted his money back and at first threatened to have father arrested for breach of contract. But father retaliated by accusing *Zha* Deeknor of ill-treating you and causing you to run away." Bmees grinned. "Of course, *Zha* Deeknor backed down. He knew he was at fault for causing you to run away. But it is indeed fortunate that you were not here or he would have been sure to take you back. But why did you leave? What did he do?"

Bmees was naturally curious but Zooric was not up to satisfying his curiosity. This was just what he had been afraid of. Questions! "I did not like living with Deeknor," he said flatly. That must have been the biggest understatement of his life! Yet he knew that if he began any explanations it would lead to more questions. He had no wish to answer questions.

"Did they not treat you well?" Bmees was puzzled and possibly confused by Zooric's use of Deeknor's name without a title. Politeness and respect were very important to the Owoon people. They routinely used titles to show respect, indicate relationships or delineate status. In fact, titles were omitted only among close friends or family. Therefore, for Zooric to omit the title of a non-relative was an extreme insult. "Were they not able to give you the life of a Soosan?"

Zooric tensed. He could not do this. Even after all this time, he still was not able to deal with his past. "I... I did not like it there," he repeated.

Unsatisfied, Bmees stared. "But why? After *Zha* Deeknor approached father, father went to the Soosans. He had promised *Zha* Deeknor he would not, but he did not want trouble with the Soosans in the future. He only wanted to let them know that you were missing or possibly dead. But the Soosans were very interested in father's story. They paid us handsomely for information on *Zha* Deeknor. We heard later that *Zha* Deeknor had three other boys living at his house. And soon after, they took all the boys away from *Zha* Deeknor. The boys were taken to the Soosan sector but *Zha* Deeknor and his friends disappeared. No one knows what became of him after the boys were taken away." Bmees shrugged. "You know the Soosans. They tell us nothing of Soosan's business. We suspect the boys must have eventually become Soosans because we have not heard from them again. There was a rumor that the Soosans were upset that *Zha* Deeknor had collected the boys and had punished him. No one knows for sure. Did he not give you the life of a Soosan as he promised?"

Zooric hunched his shoulders. "He did. I just did not like it."

"The Soosans also collected all the other boys of Soosan fathers."

"What did they do with them?" Zooric cautiously asked his first question.

"They lived with Soosan Protectors until first-link." Bmees paused then added thoughtfully. "We all thought that all children of Soosan fathers would automatically become Soosans but there were a few boys that the Soosans did not take at first-link. These were boys who never lived with *Zha* Deeknor. Can you imagine how very disappointed they were not to become Soosan?" He paused again, this time in mortification. "I am sorry Zooric. I did not mean..." For the first time since their meeting, Bmees was at a loss for words.

With relief, Zooric realized that Bmees thought that he too had proven non-Soosan at first-link. He hastened to reinforce Bmees belief. "I have had time to accept," he said. "And I really do not mind that I am not Soosan."

Bmees stared in astonishment. "You do not wish to be Soosan?"

"*Zte*," Zooric said firmly. "I like my life as it is. I have lived as an animal trapper outside Caleel for some time, and I like it." He did not add that after living in Deeknor's house, he had no wish to repeat the experience as a Soosan.

"How are mother and father?"

Fortunately for him, Bmees went along with the change of subject and was happy to bring him up to date with news of their parents. By the time they arrived at the front entrance of the farm he had learned that his sister had bonded. She lived on the farm with her mate and three children.

No one rushed out to meet them as Bmees pulled the cart up beside the dome- shaped animal house. But that was not usual. At this hour, the family was likely preparing for the end cycle meal. The place looked prosperous and almost unrecognizable. Because his parents had been poor, Zooric was surprised at the condition of the farm. Remembering Bmees mention of a reward from the Soosan, he imagined that his father had used the money to expand.

"Hurry," Bmees urged him.

Bmees had already watered and fed his caceens but Zooric was taking his time, fussing over his pageens. However, finally acknowledging that he was delaying the inevitable, he gave the animals' one last pet before following Bmees to the family's living quarters. It was located just a short distance from the animal house. Zooric breathed slowly as he tried to control his fear. He could only block one strong signal while maintaining a partial block and already he was sensing strong electro signals–

indicating the presence of others. Again, Zooric found the sensory overload enormous. He knew he would be able to function only by blocking the entire electro signals—using full block. Now, as much as he longed to see his parents, he wondered if he could just leave his information with Bmees then leave. But already they were at the door! Very reluctantly, he followed Bmees into the house.

"Look who I found!" Bmees announced as he walked in the main room.

The words made him the focus of all eyes. There were four adult Owoons in the room. Zooric recognized his parents easily. And the children he placed as children of his sister, which made the other female Owoon his sister, and the male, her mate.

Bmees began chuckling at their blank stares. "This is Zooric!" he stated triumphantly.

"Zooric!" his mother cried. "Zooric! I cannot believe this." She began crying as she hurried toward him with outstretched arms. "Zooric!"

Zooric was enfolded in her arms. "Mother!" Despite his effort to block, he was swamped with her emotions. Zooric tried to pull away as he realized the contact was inhibiting his blocking skills—but his mother refused to release him. She was squeezing him and crying at the same time. As his father also approached, Zooric tensed, expecting another flood of emotions, but to his surprise he was able to block his father. Yet he could not relax, not with his mother's intense emotions on the verge of overwhelming him. It literally felt as if she was projecting her emotions into his head. Yet, there was no time to analyze this strange effect. He could not remember the last time he had thought of his parents. Mentally he had chosen to survive, and for the longest time surviving for him meant forgetting the past. Unfortunately, forgetting the past—although the less traumatic alternative—had included forgetting his family. Now, unable to block his mother's feelings, the memories and emotions were almost unbearable. Sniffing and blinking he tried hard to hold back from the emotional onslaught, but tears were trickling down his cheeks as he returned their hugs.

"We thought you were dead." His father voiced the thoughts of them all.

"I am fine," Zooric said as he gently pulled out of his mother's hold. As loving and caring as her emotions were, they were too much, and there was a limit to how much he could take. Even when he finally stepped away, Zooric found that he was still struggling to block her. "I have spent my time away as an animal trapper."

"But why did you not return sooner?" The question came from his sister.

"I was afraid. I knew... I knew Deeknor would come looking for me. I was not sure how... when he would stop looking."

"We cannot understand why you ran away," his mother was still upset. "Did he ill- treat you?"

Their questions were endless, yet Zooric's answers got briefer and briefer.

"I did not wish to stay." It was all he would say. And his answer was just as unsatisfying to his family as it had been to Bmees. Like Bmees, they all tried to pry more information from him. Like Bmees they soon found that the happy, cheerful boy, who had left home, could in no way be compared with this guarded and wary adult.

Unlike the average person who would be spurred into speech, just to break an uncomfortable silence, Zooric clearly felt no such compulsion. And as the questions continued, his preferred method of dealing with those he did not wish to answer became silence. Without embarrassment, fuss or noticeable discomfort, he just refused to answer questions not to his liking.

After the third such uncomfortable gap in the conversation, his family gave up. Fortunately for them all, Bmees was Zooric's opposite, in that he seemed driven by compulsion to fill any significant pause in the conversation. He took Zooric to his room to change and clean up for the end-cycle meal, then later began eagerly feeding Zooric news of the farm, their neighbors, even the most trivial of current events.

Zooric could see where others would find Bmees chatter exhausting. He didn't—at least not initially. It was strangely comforting to realize that holding up his end of the conversation only required him to nod, shake his head or otherwise give some indication that he was listening. However, by the time Zooric and Bmees returned to the main room to eat, even grunting 'yes' or 'no' was a strain. He was convinced that he had heard Bmees' entire life story, and then some. Now he was actually beginning to worry about surviving the meal. But he lucked out. It seemed food placed a temporary halt to Bmees chatter. During the meal his brother's speech was strictly limited to requests for more food. Thankfully, Zooric settled down to eat as he listened to the flow of conversation without joining in.

Traditionally, the entire family gathered after the meal. It was an informal gathering where they would often play games or just socialize. As they sat, Zooric began removing a total of five objects from his pocket.

Then initiating the conversation for the first time, he revealed his staggering find.

"I have discovered an ancient Azar sector. It was a small one, perhaps home to about 5,000 Azars. It was called Nergeet and is will take about fifty cycles to reach it if traveling by pageen. It is south of Caleel.

"What!" His father jerked up right.

"*Saac ga!*"

The astonishment was universal. They gathered around in amazement, eying the unusual artifacts. Included was a very old map, yet it was made of a parchment very similar to what the Owoons now used for writing.

Zooric pointed to the map. "I believe that many alifees ago Owoons had to have lived in the sector. There are other finds but I brought this map as proof because the Azars did not store information on parchment."

"No one has ever discovered an Azar sector," Bmees commented as he fingered the finds.

"This is unbelievable!" his father commented. Carefully he opened the map. "This map shows various Azar sectors. Look!" he pointed out the closest sector to the North. "Here is another one that is close to us — named Yotse. And it looks much larger than Nergeet. We must tell the Soosan."

"Will they reward us, do you think?" his sister's mate asked.

"It is very possible. This is really an astonishing find. But with the Soosan as it is, a reward is uncertain."

"Uncertain?" Zooric queried.

His father nodded. "There has been much grumbling about many of the recent judgments of the Soosan. Many do not like the direction the new *Jirga* has taken and the policies that have been adopted." Here his father shrugged—a reflection of the general acceptance of the Soosan's rule. "But nothing can be done."

They all nodded in agreement. In fact, no Owoon would even dream of overthrowing the Soosan, forcing a change, or even questioning the edicts of the Soosan. Soosans were the rulers and that was an accepted fact.

"Soosan policy has changed for the worse," Bmees said. "They are not as fair as they were in the past. Many do not like the current *Jirga*. If only he was close to the end of his life-cycle."

"Unfortunately, this is not so," his father said as he picked up a curious instrument. "The old *Jirga* died suddenly and the current *Jirga* is very young, only about twenty-two alifees. We have never had so young a *Jirga*. Perhaps that is the reason for the erratic leadership."

Zooric was not interested in the age or leadership abilities of the Soosan. He was not interested in the Soosan, period!

At his lack of response, his father continued, after only a slight pause. "Regardless of who the *Jirga* is, we must take this information to the Soosan. Zooric, would you be able to find your way back to the sector?"

Zooric nodded. "I have prepared a map with instructions on how to find the entrance."

This, he brought out and placed it on the table.

"We can take this to the Soosan the next cycle." Bmees said excitedly.

Their father agreed. "*Eeng*. This should definitely be taken to them immediately."

Bmees nodded. "It would indeed be serious if we did not inform them of this at once."

At that comment, Zooric wisely refrained from telling them that he had discovered the sector a good six alifees ago.

They planned into the darkening. Bmees and his sister's mate would go to the Soosan sector with the information. Zooric would stay at the farm for a few cycles before leaving.

"But why leave?" his mother asked.

"I wish to remain an animal trapper," he said. "I will not disappear forever. I will return often."

Again, his family did not understand, and again Zooric refused to explain. He could not tell them of his discomfort around others. To prevent the swamp of emotion, he had to block out all incoming electro sensory information and with his blocking skills so poor, that effort took most of his concentration. It also left him sensory deprived, and he was definitely not accustomed to the sensation. Perhaps his skills would improve with use, but he had another major problem—what if the Soosan suspected him to be a sensitive? Even informing the Soosan of his find was a risk. However, since some of the boys of Soosan fathers had tested normal, he was hoping that they would assume him to be a normal Owoon who had just accidentally stumbled on the correct combination to open the Azar sector.

Nevertheless, he would have to take care, even with his family. How could he admit that he had never had first-link? More than likely he was the first Owoon male to miss first- link and he was sure there was a penalty—he just did not know what it was. There could also be a punishment for hiding his sensitive nature. Again, he did not know. For certain, if the Soosan discovered him, they would take him to the Soosan sector.

****

Early the next cycle, the Owoons left for Caleel. But like many plans, this one did not work out as expected. Less than four cycles later, a large contingent of Soosan Protectors arrived at the farm. The Soosan was holding both Bmees and the mate of Zooric's sister. The men would be released only if Zooric returned to the Soosan sector. No explanations were given. The Protectors were all Owoons except for the officer. He was *Gaare* Retran, a Soosan and the head of the Soosan Protectors.

Zooric did not attempt to escape. They did not say why they wanted him, but Zooric recognized that such a high-level delegation meant business. Besides, he could not in all good conscious leave his brother in the custody of the Soosan. So he went with the guards to the Soosan sector, a place he had vowed never to enter. It was another horrendous cycle later, after a short but violent fight with the leader of the Soosan before he was free again. In the confusion after the fight, they had willingly allowed him to go. Zooric was still not sure why he was released, but he did not stop to question his good fortune. He had even secured the release of his brother and the mate of his sister. Still, Zooric hated his time there. Not only were his memories still too painful, but there were also Soosans now who provided a constant reminder of his past. The only good that came from his time in the sector was that it proved that Deeknor had distorted the lifestyle of Soosans for his own sick and corrupt propose.

However, with his release he was not about to chance the Soosan changing course and perhaps again demanding his return. He would have to leave. True he would miss his parents, his brother and his sister. He had enjoyed playing with the children of his sisters and had even begun learning to live with the flood of his mother's emotions. While he was reluctant to leave them, his fear of recapture was too strong. He knew he could not stay. This time he decided to head north. During his time in the sector to the south of Caleel he had read extensively. And from the writings of an Azar psychic named *Loya* Favood, he had discovered the secret the Soosans were hiding from the Owoons people. He would find this alien race of people, the Tifoosas.

****

Caleel

Chapter 4

Zooric watched as the male Tifoosa began climbing the narrow path into the mountains. The female he carried was still slumped over on his caceen. Although they both wore thick outer coverings, he was almost sure the rider was male and the one slumped over the caceen he assumed to be female because her head was covered with long curling black strands of hair that had become loose. The hair on the male's head was shorter and was a light brown in color, but different hair colors also corresponded to the Writings of *Loya* Favood and did not surprise him. According to *Loya* Favood, the Tifoosas came with hair and skin colors ranging from dark brown to a pinkish white. These two definitely fit the descriptions given by *Loya* Favood. They even had different skin colors, with the male a golden yellow color and the female pale brown. Even so, her skin was not as dark a brown as Zooric's.

Zooric exhaled excitedly. He could not believe.... When he began his journey, he never imagined he would actually see any of the Tifoosas, especially so close to Caleel. Traveling steadily, it had taken him almost 200 cycles to reach this valley. His first shock was the discovery of the Tifoosa settlement within the valley. The Azar's settlement of Yotse was not a shock—this he had expected to find, and he did. But the Writing of *Loya*

Favood told only of a Tifoosa settlement further north. He was now glad he had chosen to leave Caleel. If not for the event in the Soosan sector, it is unlikely that he would have ventured so far from home. But once again, he had learned valuable information for the Soosan. The Tifoosas were a much larger group than he or they had imagined — and they were spreading! Later he would decide how to leave the Soosan this new information. Right now, he was not sure he was willing to take the chance of going back.

The cycle before, just before first-light, he had discovered the entrance to Yotse. Getting in was not a difficulty, but by then he was too keyed up to remain there or to probe deeper into the sector. He left Soor guarding one of his pageens, while he explored the surroundings. It was then that he spotted the Tifoosas shortly after they left one of the large resting areas of their settlement. The Tifoosa's settlement was not as large as Caleel, but even so, he had bypassed it, fearing to show himself to such a large population. Now, here were two Tifoosas close at hand. He was itching to make contact. His greatest wish was to make contact. This may well be his best chance. These two were alone. Ever since discovering the existence of the Tifoosas, Zooric had been excited at the very idea of meeting them. The problem was deciding how to go about first contact. He knew of the Tifoosas — but the reverse? Would they attack him or run? The good thing was that at least he would be able to communicate somewhat with them. During his time in Nergeet, he had carefully studied both the written and verbal form of their language. He did not know it fully, but hopefully he knew enough to get by.

Undecided, Zooric continued following them on his pageen. Zooric found it strange that the Tifoosas preferred to ride the lumbering caceen and not the faster pageen. But then, he was finding much of their behavior strange. He wondered what was wrong with the female. Zooric did not think the female was dead. The male was being too careful with his burden.

He paused now, as they vanished around a steep bend. There was only the one path. He held back, giving them time to move ahead. Zooric did not fear detection, he was sure he could easily follow from a safe distance where he would not be seen or heard. He had soon confirmed that the Tifoosas did not possess the special senses of the Soosans, or even the Owoons. In this again *Loya* Favood was correct.

To the left was the steep face of the Orongeen Mountains. On the right, the path fell off sharply—a ragged and dangerous drop that could be fatal. Although the lush pink and purple vegetation hugged the mountain, the path itself was mostly free of vegetation—more than likely it was created eons ago, perhaps by the agile gos-gos, a small herbivore. However, it had been noticeably widened and the male Tifoosa traveled with the confidence of someone who clearly knew where he was going.

The Tifoosas traveled throughout the first-light of the cycle. As the bright, shining sun was slowly covered by one of the moons, first- dark approached. The male had excellent timing, another indication that he had traveled this way before. They were perhaps close to the summit now and the path was widening to form a small clearing. The male approached a small resting place made from the wood of the Aceed tree. A mounting block stood in the clearing. After the male dismounted, he pulled the female from the caceen and carried her into the resting place. In less than a minute, he returned to care for the caceen, leaving the animal securely tied in a crude animal house.

Frowning, Zooric dismounted and led his pageen to the back of the resting place toward a small tree close to the edge of the clearing. It seemed this was the end of their journey. He could detect no others inside. His senses also told him that the female was coming awake. He was picking up something else besides the male's signal. Zooric's frown deepened because these signals were different —noticeably stronger. But that was not all. He was unable to pinpoint the exact difference. This is weird! The signals were definitely coming from the female and although still inconsistent they were getting steadier. There was no way Zooric could leave without finding out what was going on. It would be dangerous for him to stay on the outside during the darkening, without any shelter, but he had no choice. The cabin was the only shelter in the clearing. Now he would have to stay awake in order to stay alive!

He circled the resting place, examining it for another opening besides beside where the male had entered. There were none, but the place was not well built. The wood of the Aceed was not fitted to seal all the gaps. Zooric peered through a small opening.

The male Tifoosa was bent over the female. He slapped her face, forcefully, and Zooric realized he was trying to bring her to full awareness.

From his hiding spot, just outside the cabin, Zooric continued his intent watchfulness. The female was sitting up. She held her head and was obviously in pain. At this distance, not only could Zooric see her clearly, but he could also even hear her moan. Her eyes looked to be a shade darker than his, but he could not make out the actual color. His gaze shifted to the male. This Tifoosa's eyes looked blue. That color was nonexistent as an eye color among his people. Yet, with his flared nostrils and thick lips, the alien's features were not much different from those of his people. Apart from height, it seemed to him that the other differences between his people and the Tifoosas were the skin, eye and hair color.

Suddenly, the female doubled over and brought up the contents of her stomach. Zooric quickly looked away. His breathing was jerky. It was happening again. It must be that she was sending out electro sensory signals! But how was that possible? With the signals from the male so weak, Zooric had not needed to put up a block, but the female's signals were stronger and almost overwhelming. He took slow, deep breaths and tried to focus on his pageen. Through the ages, there were legends of how Owoons had helped stranded pageens and vice versa. Some even said that the crazy electro effects of puberty could be eased by linking with a pageen. Zooric had tried this technique when he first escaped to the woods rather than making first-link. At the time, he had been determined to survive without first-link or any outside help, and he was willing to try anything to get through the stress caused by the surging electrical activity at puberty. Focusing now on his pageen did not block the disturbing signals he was receiving from the female. It was like being offered a sip of water in the face of undying thirst. But as in the past, it did help somewhat, and gradually he was able to calm both himself and the pageen.

When he looked back at the Tifoosas, the male was holding the female. She struggled weakly. Zooric frowned as he tried to understand what was happening. To him it looked as if the male was attempting to remove the outer clothing of the female. She would surely freeze in the darkening temperature.

Then she began struggling in earnest— crying out as she did so.

Zooric jerked. He almost groaned aloud. She was in pain and afraid. Her emotions had reached him! Mentally! As a clear buzz! But that should not be possible. She was a Tifoosa! Zooric rocked back on his heels as he struggled to separate her emotions from his. As he did so, he realized she was terrified— terrified of the man holding her. Again, she cried out, but although he had studied the language of the Tifoosas, he could not understand her. Her accent made the words strange and incomprehensible to him. But he really did not have to understand the language to realize the female was calling for help.

The male shouted back at the female then slapped her face again. This time with enough force to rock her head back.

Zooric flinched. Again, he felt the sting of her emotions. Although he could have easily blocked, that was not his choice. He rose from his stooped position and walked around to the opening of the resting place.

Teen laree! Teen laree! Leave her!

The male looked up, then his eyes widened in shock. The female took the opportunity to scramble out of the man's loosened hold, but she too was terrified. Without thinking Zooric made mental contact.

"Oo ee t'regaan — I will not harm you."

It didn't seem possible, but her eyes widened further. Clearly, she had heard him even if she did not quite understand.

She was still staring in shock, when suddenly she lifted one hand to her mouth to stifle a cry.

Zooric had been focused on the female. Out of the corner of his eye he saw the male move. The male was lifting a curious shaped object to point it at Zooric.

The female shouted a warning before lunging at the male. But Zooric was already on the move. The object was unknown, but he assumed that it was a weapon of some sort. The man's arm jerked, then a loud report filled the air. Something whooshed within inches of Zooric's head. Fortunately, the male was distracted by the female — which was enough to upset his aim. But Zooric had unwittingly moved almost directly in the new path of the missile spurting from the weapon!

"Oh, you killed it!" Carrie cried.

****

Chapter 5

Chris was breathing rapidly in nervous excitement. The alien had dropped to the floor, but the being was now slowly shaking his head as if dazed. Chris began moving cautiously toward the alien. "Don't go near it," he muttered although Carrie, if anything, had inched even further away. "It's still alive."

Carrie looked up at him and realized that her captor was going to shoot the being again. "No! Don't! No!" She cried.

But Chris did not get a chance to shoot again. He suddenly grabbed his head with both hands. The gun dropped to the ground with a clatter.

"Aggh!" he was screaming in agony, literally pulling tufts of hair from his head. Within seconds he had collapsed to the ground screeching and twisting in pain.

Carrie stared in horror, as Chris' face got darker and darker, his eyes bulging. Then a slow trickle of blood began coming first from Chris' mouth, then nose and ears. Carrie whimpered as he finally fell silent, his arms slack, but his body still twitching spasmodically. She brought her hands to her mouth in an effort to hold off her rising nausea. Then the awful smell of feces and urine permeated the cabin.

She lost the battle to hold down the last of the contents of her stomach.

When she stopped retching, her gaze swiveled back to the being on the ground. To her shocked surprise, the alien was having just as much trouble holding onto his stomach contents. He had rushed for the door, but unfortunately didn't make it.

The stench in the cabin was now unbearable.

Carrie continued watching as the alien backed further away from Chris. He was now supporting himself, one hand on the door, as he stood bent over. Dry heaves continued to rack his body. Slowly he raised his head. From the distance across the cabin, it was easy for Carrie to see that he was shaking.

Carrie bit her lips with uncertainty as she watched him. He seemed deeply affected by the death of her kidnapper, so although still afraid, Carrie could not help but feel sorry for him. Was Chris' death an accident? Perhaps? Still, he had a strange weapon that was amazingly effective. She wanted him gone. But even as she watched, his intent gaze turned back to her. He wiped his eyes and mouth with the sleeves of his robe. Carrie began scrambling away.

"Please...." she whispered; then blinked. He was speaking and as before she was hearing him in her head. She did not understand him, but somehow his words were curiously soothing. Carrie shook her head and continued to back away slowly.

"Get away from me. Get out of my head!" she cried. Her heart began pounding, her palms sweaty as she backed into the far wall of the cabin. She could go no further. They stared at each other for endless minutes.

He was almost a foot taller than her and dressed in a thick flowing purple robe that stopped just above his ankles. The color was a perfect match of the mountain's vegetation. Heavy boots showed below the robe and since he also wore black gloves only his face was bare. It was a curiously still face, smooth and free of any evidence of a beard. That lack of facial hair made him seem ridiculously young, yet she suspected that he was older. His skin was the color of the old-world coffee, and with his slightly flared nostrils and full lips, he looked human. Rather like pictures in her history books of some of the early colonists. Even his eyes looked normal. They were a light brown-hazel.

He pushed back a cape-like covering from his head, revealing tightly curled black hair that was very unevenly cut. Slowly he pointed to himself, "Zooric." This time he spoke aloud.

Carrie swallowed. "Oh my god! Oh my god!" She clasped her hands to her heart. The beat was still abnormally loud and erratic.

At her movement, he cocked his head to one side. His intent gaze followed her hands and Carrie sensed he was puzzled, not that his intent facial expression had changed. It was more a feeling she had. He continued staring without making any effort to come closer. She however, inched further away along the wall then stopped, wetting her lips nervously. He was blocking the door. There was no way she could get out without passing him.

"Please...."

Again, he pointed to himself, "Zooric."

Carrie swallowed. Think! Think! She chided herself. But she just couldn't. The only thought in her mind was to run. He moved. "No!" she screamed, close to becoming hysterical. Arms extended to ward him off, she pressed into the walls behind her.

The alien stopped. At last, he was showing some facial expression. Not that it was reassuring. He was glaring at her and repeating the same foreign sounding words.

Confused and terrified by the events of the past few hours, Carrie sank to the ground and started to cry. She had been kidnapped, almost raped and now... and now. This was impossible. They were the only inhabitants on the planet. How could another species of intelligent life be here now? But he looked human. Was he a descendant of a deserter from the original Colonist population or had another spaceship crashed without their knowing? It didn't seem possible. Through her tears she saw the being move again. Again, she scrambled along the wall in terror. "Get away from me! Get away!"

"I... will... not... hurt... you."

He was really looking furious now, she thought. Yet, because he was now drawing out each word in anger, it suddenly dawned on her that he was speaking English. His strange accent made it difficult for her to understand him, but his words were definitely English. And he was madder at her actions than at her. Her fear was making him angry! The blind terror abruptly left her. She was still fearful, but somehow, she did not think he meant to harm her. He had been too deeply upset by Chris' death. Carrie sank back down, bent her head in her hands and bawled. She did not even raise her head when she heard him moving about the cabin. Fortunately, he did not touch her or close the distance between them.

When her burst of hysteria finally ended, she looked up to find him still exploring the cabin. He was moving the few utensils on the table about and peering into the pots. He had also opened four bags that were stacked against the wall. They were filled with moonglitter! But although the alien seemed interested in the precious metal, and spent a few minutes examining the rough stones, he soon moved on. Not that there was much more. It was only the one room. A crude table was pushed against the wall near the door. Next to where she sat, were the makings of a bed–just a moss-like plant- piled on lengths of raised wood. A small fireplace, beside the bed, was empty. Chris had made no attempt to light it. Carrie looked around, but there was no sign of her former captor—or the gun. And although the doors were open, the smell of death and vomit was still there. A closer inspection revealed the bloodstains and marks on the ground, indicating that the alien had dragged the body out of the cabin and into the clearing. So those were the sounds that she had heard!

Seeing her watching, he stopped his exploration and squatted within a few feet of her. Again, he pointed to himself, "Zooric," he said aloud.

Carrie sniffed and wiped the back of her hand across her nose. It was indelicate, yes, but what did she care.

That intent look was back on his face. Although his face remained expressionless, Carrie got the impression he was amused.

Her face heated at the thought of him laughing at her.

How dare he laugh? She turned her back on him in a huff then realized how ridiculous her actions were. She looked over her shoulder. He was actually grinning. It gave his face such a boyish look that Carrie stared. Could he really be as young as he seemed? He looked about mid-teens. What was a teenager doing here by himself? Her fears melted as she convinced herself that despite the strange power that he had used on Chris, he was only human. He had to be a descendant of a deserter. He's going to think I'm an idiot, Carrie though in dismay.

Straightening her spine and sitting up, she firmly pointed to herself

"My name is Carrie. Carrie!"

His eyes brightened as he repeated. "Caree." He then pointed to himself again, "Zooric."

Carrie nodded. "Zoo...zooreek."

He nodded; satisfied that she got his name right.

"I am sorry about your friend. I... It.... I did not mean that he die."

This time he was speaking slowly enough for Carrie to understand. She nodded.

After giving her an uncertain look, he stood. "Wait here. I must bury the body."

Again, Carrie nodded. She watched as he went back outside; then stood shakily, fixing her clothing as she rose. He had covered Chris' body with blankets and was now covering the blanket and body with stones large and small.

Finally finished, he approached her again.

"We cannot stay here," he said. He pointed to the zig standing patiently in the clearing outside the cabin. "We go."

Go where? Carrie suddenly realized she had no idea where she was. The last thing she remembered was being grabbed in the barn and injected with the slumber drug. How was she going to get back home?

"Leave?"

Zooric nodded; then he repeated. "We cannot stay here."

He turned to the zig and led the animal to the large mounting block. Carrie followed hesitantly. Yes. She knew that she couldn't stay here. But where was he taking her?

He kicked a small stone out of his way. "Vees," he said pointing to the stone.

"Vees," she repeated. This word was easy. He was trying to teach her his language, she thought in amazement.

But Zooric shook his head. He pointed to himself again, "Zooric," Then he pointed to her, "Carrie." Next, he pointed at the stone, "Vees." Now he looked at her expectantly.

Oh! Carrie now understood. As least she understood what he wanted. He wanted to learn her language! But she thought he already knew it! "Stone," she supplied.

"Soon."

"No, stone"

Seeing his difficulty with the word, Carrie repeated it a couple of times.

"Sone."

He was still unable to get the "T" sound after the "S" But Carrie guessed that would have to do. She used the mounting block to scramble onto the zig, wondering why he made no effort to help her. By the time she was up, Zooric had also learned what the animal was called. Zeeg he called it.

Once she was mounted, he gave the equivalent of a whistle. Almost immediately there was a rustling sound and a large fluar appeared from behind the cabin. The contraption around its face and mouth was clearly a bridle of some sort, but there was no saddle on its back, rather there was a thick folded blanket. Carrie stared in amazement as Zooric vaulted onto the back of the animal.

"Oh my god! You tamed a fluar."

That curious intent stare of his focused on her once more. Then they went through the language circle again with him pointing to the fluar. She finally understood. From his words, Carrie soon discovered that her difficulty in understanding him was mainly a pronunciation problem. His accent gave even the words that he knew a strange sound.

But she still could not get over him riding a fluar. The colonists had been trying to tame one for ages. The fluar took the lead and they started—to where Carrie had no idea. The only certainty was that they were going down the mountain path. Carrie had no knowledge of how she came to where she was, but she assumed she was in the mountains above Arapmo, therefore going down seemed like the best idea. Traveling was extremely slow. She was terrified of falling down the sheer sides of the mountain, but Zooric seemed to know where he was going. It was almost fully dark before they reached a smaller clearing. Here, the sides of the mountain were ragged, and the overhang formed a small cave.

He dismounted as agilely as he had mounted and looked around the small clearing.

Carrie watched him for a few minutes before realizing that he was looking for a stone for her to use to dismount. She turned sideways and slid clumsily down the side of the zig.

Zooric gave her a nod of approval. "*Daat...*"

Carrie ignored him. She was puzzled over why he had made no move to help her off the zig.

Zooric removed some supplies from a pouch strapped to the side of his fluar then indicated that she should go into the cave. Carrie hesitated then nervously went in. She really did not have a choice since there was no question of her continuing down the mountain in the darkening. She would have to trust him. She had no idea what she would do if he attacked her. Her only reassuring thought was that he clearly did not want to touch her. But where would they sleep? And what about wild paws? They were nocturnal creatures, with a body similar to that of the old-world coyotes but with a head twice as large. They also had very long legs. The paws were extremely vicious, but generally preferred to attack defenseless animals or people. They were known to be attracted to blood or even sleeping campers. Plus, because they usually traveled in packs of four or more, fighting off an attack was next to impossible.

The cave was small, and the space became even smaller after Zooric dragged both animals in. He then lit a fire at the entrance before unpacking food. He shared everything with her, telling her the names as they ate. The food was not familiar to Carrie, but much of it was delicious. She especially liked a corn-like vegetable he called norson and wondered how easy it was to grow. They spent the meal trying to communicate or rather; he spent it learning how to pronounce as many words in her language as possible. But throughout their meal, he carefully avoided touching her, even when passing her food. In fact, at one point he actually scrambled out of her reach when she accidentally came too close. Carrie was hard pressed to hide her smile. He was afraid to touch her! Perhaps there was something in his culture that said males couldn't touch females. The idea was extremely comforting. At least she did not have to worry about him hurting her– especially now that she realized how close their sleeping quarters were. And he was definitely older than a teenager!

Carrie wanted to rest after eating, but Zooric merely continued more language lessons. Not only did he seem determined to master the pronunciation of her language, but he was also bent on teaching her his language! They spoke well into first-dark. Despite the light from the fire, they could hardly see each other, yet Zooric was relentless. Carrie finally began yawning to get her message across. When that didn't work, she decided on a more direct method. She rubbed her eyes and squeezed them shut with a big yawn. "Zooric, I'm sleepy."

That got her nowhere. Zooric only stared, his face impassive, yet she was sure he understood. She was equally sure that if she did not resist, he would continue lessons throughout first-dark. He was very intelligent and curious, and unfortunately showed no sign of sleepiness.

"Sleep," Carrie mimicked lying down to sleep, "I'm sleepy," she repeated.

Finally, reluctantly, he agreed. For a bed, Zooric made a rough padding with the leaves of the Weeping plant, so called because the main trunk of the tree often grew to about nine feet yet remained completely bare. At the very top, the plant produced leaves that were long black strands that drooped in all directions. The strands were often close to the length of the plant itself hanging like a waterfall around the trunk. She learned that his people called the same plant an Aceed tree.

Zooric indicated where she should lie down and even provided her with a thick wool-like blanket. Carrie thankfully wrapped herself in the rough bedding. The winter temperature in Arapmo was lower than that of New World City. In New World City both darkening temperatures sometimes dipped down to the 50's in the winter. But in the summer first-light temperature sometimes soared to over 100 degrees and even second-light could see high temperatures in the mid 90's. The colonist had already surmised that the higher elevation of Arapmo affected the region's temperature. The temperatures in Arapmo ran ten to twenty degrees lower than New World City, but only because Arapmo was protected by a ring of mountains. Outside the valley, the temperatures dipped even lower. But at least so far, they did not have to deal with firestorms. In New World City, whenever the temperature hit the upper nineties, there was always a possibility of firestorm. The tiny particles fell from the sky and could cause severe burns on the skin. In extreme firestorms, large fire bolts fell from the sky, some as big as a fist and only someone bent on suicide would venture out.

Carrie snuggled deeper into her blanket. She was sleeping outside for the first time in her life. She was with an alien, and she had absolutely no idea where she was or how she would get back home, yet somehow his presence was reassuring. She fell instantly asleep.

At second-light Zooric got up to take the animals from the clearing.

"Stay," he told her.

Carrie stood immediately, "Where are you going?"

"Stay. I come back."

She had no idea what he meant. Carrie stood biting her lips as she watched him leave the cave. Then realized this was an excellent opportunity to perform her morning ablution. Finished, she briefly considered leaving. But where would she go? There was no way she would make it down the mountain without transport. Carrie restlessly paced the cave. She was jittery and unable to relax as she worried about finding her way down the mountain. What if Zooric did not come back? Finally, she heard him coming. She breathed a sigh of relief. She was no longer alone.

During the next few minutes, she busily followed Zooric's directives as they packed and prepared to leave. She had wondered how he was going to get her back on the zig if he refused to touch her. But Zooric found a large . stone for her to use as a mounting block.

Since she was still heading toward her home, Carrie was happy, and, as the path widened, she tried to ride side by side with Zooric. He would have none of that. Each time she attempted to come up beside him he would frown, tell her to go back and then forcefully gesture for her to do so. Yet he offered no explanations. Although annoyed, Carrie finally gave up. Much as she wanted to find out more about him, he clearly had some hang-ups about women!

"No you don't," she laughed, as she playfully rapped her zig lightly on the head. She named her zig, West. West was a lumbering beast that constantly tried to nip at her legs. He was so slow at turning, that each time he tried, Carrie easily read his intent. "Give it up West."

Zooric turned on hearing her laughing amusement, directing his intent stare at her then the zig. He said something in English, but again Carrie had no idea what he was saying. Seeing her puzzled look, he rapped on his head and repeated slowly. "Head, *soosag*. Head empty."

"Soosaag," Carrie repeated. "That means, 'head' right? "Head." She rapped at her own head.

Zooric nodded. He pointed to the zig. "*Soosag zareed*, head empty," he repeated.

Carrie laughed and took a guess at what he meant. "Are you saying his head is hollow?"

Knocking on the zig's head did produce a hollow sound—almost similar to knocking on a hollow log—because the zig's large head was filled with air spaces. Most mature zigs grew to over 15 feet tall and this zig was already close to 10 feet. But the fluars could be even taller. The one Zooric was riding was much taller that Carrie's zig. As she watched him in envy, she decided that his ride definitely looked smoother than hers. She wondered if she could convince him to let her have a go on the fluar. With that thought in mind, she tried to explain her wish to Zooric.

"Can we switch? Can I get to ride the fluar?" Carrie tried pantomiming gestures to get her point across. After all this would not involve him touching her, just switching mounts. He understood all right. She could tell when he did, but, as with her request to ride beside him, this desire also got her nowhere. Zooric just shook his head. When she persisted, she got a firm 'no', which he repeated in his language for emphasis.

"*Zte.*"

That was definitely a 'no'. What Carrie didn't understand, was why? But Zooric refused to even try explaining. Carrie gave him an annoyed glare, which he totally ignored.

As they neared the foot of the mountain, Zooric veered off the broken path and onto a ragged trail. There were times they both had to bend low over their mounts to avoid contact with the vegetation. The path had also narrowed again. Carrie looked around in confusion. Was this the way home? The dense woods left just a narrow path, probably made by a wild animal. But shouldn't she still be headed downhill? For a while she followed Zooric's lead, until she became convinced that she was going across rather than down the mountain.

Carrie no longer feared him but as second-dark, and one complete cycle approached, she did began fearing that he was taking her to his people and not hers! Why didn't she think of this possibility before! Her family was likely frantic by now. Abruptly, she stopped. Zooric immediately halted.

"I need to go home," she tried explaining to Zooric. She wanted to go home before the end of this cycle! When the first colonist landed on Alloca, they had speculated that an Allocan year was about one Earth year. They later found that comparison meaningless, since one Earth day was not the equivalent of one cycle on Alloca. Before long they decided to work with a light and dark system of cycles because unlike on the old world, here on Alloca a complete 'day' consisted of approximately 25 Allocan hours broken into five hours of first light followed by three hours of first dark, then eight hours of second light and nine hours of second dark.

Using this system, the colonist worked out one complete Allocan year was approximately 400 cycles. But because initially there had always been the hope of eventually returning to the mother Earth, the colonists decided to stick with their old-world system of calculations, therefore maintaining a link to Earth. Their compromise was to equate 10 days or 10 cycles to one week, although they kept one Allocan year as an approximation of one Earth year.

Zooric now shook his head at her. "Come! *Spior!*" he said, urging her forward.

Carrie refused to budge. "I need to go home," she told him. She tried everything—she mimicked, she even pantomimed. Zooric just watched her with narrowed eyes. At the end of her performance, he repeated the one word, 'come!'

"I won't come," Carrie insisted. And just in case he missed her determined look and mulish expression, she repeated it in his language. "*Zte spior*. You must take me home. I want to go home."

"*Zte!*"

This was said sharply. Zooric was now getting annoyed. Well good. She was annoyed as well, plus she missed her family.

"Yes! I'm not going any further. I want to go home! Home!" She pointed in the general direction of her home. She was sure her home was further down in the valley.

The main town was in the middle of the valley and her father's outpost was on a high ridge on the outskirts of the town. The first colonists to Arapmo tried growing the staples pani and lapin in the valley. Later some attempted to breed zigs. Since finding the moonglitter her father mostly concentrated on mining. He still bred zigs and had made numerous attempts to capture and breed the fluars. But her father, as one of the original explorers, owned vast areas of Arapmo where moonglitter was mined. The fact that moonglitter was the only precious metal discovered so far on the planet had only enhanced its value. And with the wealth from his mines, her father really did not need to worry about other sources of income.

"No," Zooric said, still shaking his head at her.

"But I have to get back home," Carrie insisted. She was so comfortable with him she could not believe he was not going to take her home. Then she realized she was being silly. Even though he was human, he knew nothing about her people. Most likely, he wanted to show her off to his people. What was wrong with her? That drug must still be in her system. It was the only explanation she could find for her irrational behavior. She abruptly decided it made no sense pleading with him when he didn't want to understand. There was nothing stopping her from riding off. True his fluar was faster than her zig, but how would he stop her? It seemed he couldn't or wouldn't touch her. Plus, she was riding behind him. All she had to do was to turn around and ride off! Simple!

"No! *Zte! Spior ee narkee* Come back!" Zooric shouted.

Carrie ignored him. Suddenly, she felt a blinding pain in her head. "Aaagh!" she gasped. Releasing the reigns of the zig, Carrie clutched at the animal's long hairy mane. She closed her eyes and tried taking deep calming breaths. But the pain... it was nearly unbearable. She felt as if her head was splitting in half.

It was a few minutes before she was able to open her eyes. The pain had eased somewhat. She looked down to find Zooric in front of her zig holding its reins. His face was no longer expressionless, worried eyes were anxiously scanning her face. "I am sorry! Caree I am sorry! I did not mean for you to hurt."

Although the pain had eased, Carrie closed her eyes again. "Caree," Zooric called again.

She didn't want to look at him. Carrie was fighting back tears. Now she knew. She had thought of him as her rescuer, but she was just as much a prisoner with this alien as she was with Chris. The tears won. She was unable to stop the tears from trickling down. How could she have forgotten that he had killed Chris? She dashed a furious hand across her face. She hated for him to see her crying. What was going to happen to her? Suddenly, hysterical, Carrie began screaming and storming at him.

He gasped, and as he backed away from her, Carrie felt what could only be described as a spark of electricity in her head. Although she screamed, this surge of electricity was not painful as the previous one.

In a fit of sheer terror and fury, she reached down to push him away. "I want to go home. I'm not going to go and be a museum piece to your people. I want to go home. Do you hear me.?"

As she touched Zooric, he doubled with a moan and again Carrie felt that surge of current. This time running through her body! Abruptly Zooric stood, released the reigns of the zig, and hauled her from the zig and directly into his arms. He gasped again; then began muttering in his language. "Caree! *Oo galee*. Caree."

"Zooric!" Carrie was too terrified to rant at him. Again, it was like a charge passing through her, but then she was flooded with his feelings. He wanted her! She stared up at him in dread.

But his eyes were closed; his face screwed in concentration as his arms tightened around her. Then his eyes flew open; their eyes locked as his mouth sought hers. "Caree, Caree. *Oo...Oo...*"

He was shivering! Shudders were actually racking his body.

"No! Zooric! No!" Carrie cried again. She was terrified, both for herself and for him, as another charge, this on even more powerful than before, ran through her body.

****

Chapter 6

Zooric had been afraid to touch the female. Unlike in the time of *Loya* Favood, the mind sizzle with the male Tifoosa had not rebounded to kill him or make him sick. However, the female was different. He was aware of her. Her presence, her emotions were like a constant background noise in his mind that he was finding harder and harder to block. He had never felt anything like this before, and the feeling was beginning to scare him. It had to be that she was giving off constant electro- signals. And he was afraid they were taking over his mind. What power was it that this Tifoosa had? When he left her in the cave earlier that cycle, he had felt tense and jittery because, almost like a rope, her electro-signals had been tugging him back to her. Zooric had been terrified to touch her, afraid that any touching could enhance the electrosensory signals!

But then she started screaming in fury. Her words were like missiles piercing his brain. He couldn't take it! Zooric tried sending her a gentle buzz. He needed her to stop! As she reached out to push him away, the pain in his head increased. Zooric again tried to buzz her but to his shock, the low signal went through them both. It had formed a circuit! Zooric's mind went into shock! It was a linking! True it was a low-level linking, but Zooric inhaled deeply. *Saac ga!*

"Caree! *Oo galee*. Caree."

He had never experienced a link. His entire body tightened in need as he sensed that she would be able to take his electro sensory discharge. Zooric felt a flood of emotions... confusion... fear...then surprised pleasure. These were her emotions! He was only half-aware that he was sending her the same feelings. He tightened his hold as he sent her another low surge of current. Then, for the first time in his life, Zooric released the rigid control he had always kept on his electro- abilities.

"Caree, Caree. Oo...Oo..." Zooric tried, he truly tried to calm her, but he literally could not speak. He had no control! His lips sought hers as his body craved a deeper contact— a deeper link. He poured into her—a surge of current that he had always thought was involuntary and would only occur at sexual completion. The erotic result was instantaneous. He was already rock hard! He had to have her. Here! Now! Without releasing her, he brought them both to the ground. His one thought was to bury himself in her—to the hilt.

But she was getting frantic. Linked as they were, he was not just feeling her fear he was living it. It was impossible for him to ignore how it was swamping her pleasure. She could not cope with his emotions! She was still too terrified of him.

"No! Please No!" She was struggling as well as crying. Zooric groaned as he tried to pull back. He was going too fast, too soon! He did not want her to be afraid. But did he have the strength to stop? Sweat poured off him as he fought for control. He had linked! He could not believe it! Fortunately, the linking had ended. He had discharged mentally, even if not physically. He wrenched his mouth away and buried his face in her neck. However, he was totally unable to let go completely. He held her tightly as intermittent shivers racked his body. At least her panic had subsided somewhat. Almost involuntarily, he again sent a low buzz. To his surprise, he found that the return signal provided a degree of calm, even if it in no way satisfied his sexual hunger. But from the emotional response he was getting from her, he also realized that the low current flow was calming her also. Zooric breathed deeply as he puzzled over these new feelings. It didn't seem possible, but it actually felt like a form of linking. Confused, he lifted his head.

"*Oo galee. Tipaat ee.*" He forgot that she could not speak his language.

But Carrie nodded—she was able to decipher his meaning. "I'm okay."

Zooric's mind went blank. He stared at her. He understood! Despite his knowledge of her spoken and written language, he had been having a lot of difficulty understanding the reality of her speech with its distinctive accent. Now he understood her as clearly as if she were speaking in Gavaa, the language of the Owoon.

"I can understand you now," he said aloud marveling at his sudden ability; to not only understand her, but to communicate clearly.

Carrie was puzzled. "What do you mean, you understand?" she asked in her language.

Zooric released her and rolled away. He did not understand what was happening, first the low-level linking and now this. No! What about the high-level linking—and without sexual intercourse. He had never believed that such was possible!

"Zooric, what is it?" Carrie asked worriedly.

Zooric turned to glare at her in confusion. He was angry because what was happening was beginning to scare him. Then another thought occurred to him. He asked abruptly "*Ee ou rimeem?*"

Carrie stared. "What?" She was clearly puzzled.

Zooric however, was relieved. At least the reverse was not also true. He had asked her if she understood him. But Carrie did not understand his language; she would still need to learn it. Perhaps the linking could only enhance abilities already present. He finally responded to the worried looks Carrie was giving him.

"I find that I now understand your language much better than before. I do not fully understand why this is so."

Carrie's eyes widen in shock. "I can understand you better. Was it because of what just happened?"

"*Eeng!*"

"Oh God!" But Carrie was still puzzled. "What happened? I don't understand?"

"I do not either!" Zooric said grimly. Yet he knew it was the linking. He abruptly sat up. *Saac ga!* He had linked! And she was unhurt and alive! This was truly remarkable and definitely not normal for his people. And there was the enhanced language skill—and the low level linking throughout. Something strange was occurring between them.

As excited as he was over the fact of his first linking, Zooric moved further away, trying to put mental as well as a physical distance between him and the girl. He had taken her with him because he was not sure what to do with her. He had immediately grasped that he had a major problem on his hands. First, he did not want to return her to her people—at least not yet. He needed to understand her language and her people, and she needed to understand him. Besides, he could just imagine the massive uproar if he took her back and she told all her people about him and his people. And if they had so large a settlement here then their first settlement would be even larger, which meant that the Tifoosas outnumbered the Owoons. He was fearful the Tifoosas would try to hunt down to kill or capture every Owoons! He also had another problem. He had no home, so he could not take her to the Owoons.

Zooric mounted his pageen automatically. What should he do now? This linking had been spectacular. He wanted to repeat it—with him deep inside her! He knew of the sexually enhanced pleasure of a linking, but this too was something that he had never experienced. Yet she was dangerous. Her emotions had been mentally painful, and he could not block her. Would all her people have the same effect on other Owoons? If so, the Tifoosas had a deadly weapon against his people. He turned around to look at Caree. She was now standing beside her zig with her arms wrapped protectively about her body.

Zooric dashed a hand warily across his face and indicated that she should mount her zig.

"I want to go home," Carrie insisted.

"I cannot let you go. You will tell your people of mine."

"What if I promise not to?

As he stared at her in silence, his control slipped. A flood of fear reached him. *Saac ga!* They were her emotions! And they were much stronger than before!

Zooric quickly raised his block. He needed more time. He hated puzzles and mysteries and the strange connection between them was something that both intrigued yet spooked him. "We cannot make it to your home this cycle. We will go to my camp this dark."

Carrie stared at him, her eyes wide with fright. "What of your people?"

"I am here alone."

"Will we go to your camp only for this darkening?"

"We will rest there this darkening, yes."

Now it was Carrie's turn to stare. Zooric met her gaze unflinchingly. He realized then that he would have to take care because he could easily send her his emotions. He just hoped she did not have the ability to force them.

"Okay," Carrie finally agreed, apparently reassured by his deliberate calm.

Zooric gave a brief nod before going over to give her a boost up. As soon as he touched her it happened again. He immediately lost his ability to block! Zooric released her arm as if stung. This was impossible!]

"Zooric?" Carrie sounded scared at his abrupt withdrawal.

Ignoring the question, he turned to find a large stone. Somehow, she would have to mount herself. He was not touching her again. His control had barely held for the first link. It definitely would not hold for a second. And he did not think she was ready for the contact he craved. Zooric rolled the stone into position. "I cannot touch you. Use this to mount," he told her.

Carrie complied reluctantly. She opened her mouth twice to speak but each time shut it again, intimidated by his scowling expression.

Zooric remounted easily. "Follow me," he instructed.

The second-dark was generally darker than the first and before long they were forced to dismount and walk their mounts to avoid injury from overhanging branches. But Zooric was determined to reach camp that cycle. His number one reason being that it was just too dangerous to stop. There was no covering, and short of staying up during the dark, he would not be able to protect himself, the animals, plus the female. This was why, despite his exhaustion, he pushed on. And his exhaustion was both physical and mental. The female was constantly sending him her emotions and blocking them was proving mentally draining. Zooric sensed both her weariness and determination to prove to him that she could keep up. He needed that determination. Hopefully, if he ignored her pleas to slow or stop, her determination would be enough to keep her going. She was silent now—resolutely following him. Good! Stopping was not an option and slowing would only prolong the agony.

****

Carrie did not think they would make it to Zooric's camp that cycle.

Zooric had not spoken to her since deciding to take her to his camp. Carrie couldn't see what he was so angry about. She was so confused over what had occurred. She was even more confused because instinctively she wanted to trust Zooric. How could she trust an alien that she had just met? She had reversed her former opinion and was now convinced he was an alien. No human had such weird abilities. Yet as ridiculous as the idea of trust between them was, there seemed to be a disconnect between the reality of what she should be feeling and what she actually felt. She needed answers!

"Why don't we just camp here," Carrie asked.]

Zooric did not respond. Not that she blamed him. It was a silly question. They could not sleep in the opening without some protection. Paws would eat them. The paw never attacked a moving object. But since it was attracted by the smell of blood or heat of any life form, a sleeping human could literally be eaten alive. Now she scowled at his back. "Fine, be a baby and sulk!"

He continued to ignore her. They walked in silence for the next few hours. She was now exhausted but determined not to call him again. Even if it killed her, she would keep up. She began muttering under her breath. "I know you are doing this just to get back at me. Just you wait. Carrie stumbled. She cried out; her arms outstretched to break her fall. Fortunately, she fell into her zig

"Keep moving! Come!" Zooric urged without stopping.

"Beast!" Carrie muttered as she leaned wearily on her zig. "What are you anyway? A machine?" She took a deep breath, straightened, and then started walking again. Just one foot in front of the other, she thought, left foot, right foot, left foot, right foot. She stumbled again. "Oh God,

Carrie raised her head; she could just make out the outline of Zooric ahead. He did not stop. Would he leave her if she fell? This time her body wavered before finally settling in the standing position. Carrie blinked. Left foot.... Right foot. She wasn't sure she was going to make it. Her zig abruptly bumped into Zooric's fluar causing Carrie to crash into it. The animal gave a trumpet of disapproval Carrie blinked, her uncertainly. Had they stopped? She stood swaying unsteadily. Her brain had ceased functioning some miles back.

"*Caree,*" Zooric's voice sounded different. Then Carrie realized that the words sounded in her mind. He began mentally urging her on. Carrie was too exhausted to protest this new invasion.

"We are at my camp. Come! I will prepare a bed for you. You can sleep immediately. Come Caree. You must move. I cannot touch you."

Carrie moved. Like a zombie she followed his instructions. The beds were where he indicated. Carrie sank wearily to her knee then literally passed out the instant her head touched the bunched-up creation that she assumed was the pillow.

****

Chapter 7

Hours later, Carrie was jerked from a deep dreamless sleep by a sharp agonizing pain in her left leg. "Aaah," she cried out, reaching protectively for her leg. Then, as suddenly as it began, the pain disappeared. Her eyes snapped open. Carrie sat up groggily and viewed her surroundings for the first time. She was in a.... A what? The surrounding ceilings were high—about 12 feet and made of what looked like rock. It could be a cave—a large cave. The room itself was over 20 feet square and scattered with strange looking furniture—someone's house? Had Zooric brought her to his people even after his promise not to?

Carrie pushed shakily at her tangled mass of hair. The sun's light was streaming into the structure from an open doorway. Sunlight! That meant it was well into the first-light! She must have slept for hours! She pushed away her blanket and got up hesitantly. She had been lying on the floor, on a bed made of grass-like vegetation, and on it was another thick blanket. Curious, Carrie slid off and made her way toward the sunlight. Two fluars and her zig were camped directly outside the structure. Two fluars? Carrie stared uncertainly at the large animals. They were wide-awake and stared unblinkingly back. The zig on the other hand was still asleep. Lazy animal, she thought in amusement. One of the fluars suddenly gave a loud bellow. Carrie became startled.

"I guess you want food, uh," she asked. "Don't worry I'm hungry too." She was in fact starving. But where was Zooric? And more importantly, where was she? A low stone fence surrounded the structure, which Carrie now assumed was a house. It was just high enough to stop the animals from wandering off. Ignoring the animals for the moment, Carrie walked toward the sunlight. She stared down at the wide passageway paved with the same stone material of the fence. This is a street! A huge wall blocked one end, but the other end led to what she assumed was the exit—that was where all the light was coming from. The building she was in was the only structure in sight. On the opposite side of the 'street' was a steep rock wall. She looked up but the wall curved to form the ceiling. Was this a large cave? But what was a house doing in a cave? And it was such a large house. She was actually in the front yard of the house!

Carrie was just beginning to panic at the thought of meeting other aliens, when a large paw jumped the fence and bounded toward her.

Carrie screamed. "Aaah!" She scrambled back, and then began backing slowly toward the house she had just exited. "Zooric! Zooric!" She looked wildly around for help. Even another alien would be welcome now. But no one appeared.

I have to keep moving, she thought frantically as she inched along the walls of the house trying to find the entrance without turning around. She was afraid to leave her back exposed to the paw. But the paw did not come any closer. In fact, it was acting downright weird. It stood by the fence and gave a loud howling bark. Then it jumped the fence again, momentarily disappearing from sight. The animal immediately returned, only to repeat its actions. Carrie stared. What was it doing? Was it tame? Did it belong to Zooric? But where was Zooric? The third time, the animal howled at her before running out. Finally, Carrie got the message.

"Oh my god! It wants me to follow it." Where was Zooric when she needed him? This animal had to be a pet, but Carrie was still afraid. Then she remembered the pain that woke her. "My leg," she looked down. Her leg felt fine. She pulled up her divided skirt. Her leg was smooth and free of blemish. There was no wound, no cut, and no bruise.

"Zooric! Zooric must be hurt!" At her words the paw gave another loud howling bark. Ignoring her fear, Carrie ran towards the fence, and scrambled over. As soon as the paw saw her coming, it bounded away.

"Not so fast," Carrie cried as she hurried to keep up. The paw ran down the wide passageway that Carrie assumed was the street. From there they exited suddenly onto the sloping pathway of the forest. Carrie paused to stare but the paw was not tolerating any such stops. It howled at her again.

"Okay, okay, I'm coming."

It ran off and soon disappeared into the shrubbery. Carrie started forward then stopped. She had no idea which direction to go. The animal reappeared. It was smart enough to return when it realized she was not following.

"Good boy or girl or whatever you are," Carrie praised as she started running again. This time the paw made sure she was always in sight. It stopped and waited for her, sometimes even returning to her side if she didn't immediately catch up.

Carrie heard the water before she came to it. She emerged from the woods then gasped. The water was beautiful. Natural water in the rivers and oceans of Alloca was always a deep blue green, a reflection of the skies. This water was flowing in a layered waterfall, and with the sun reflecting the varying colors, it truly was spectacular. It flowed from a height of about twenty feet to create a small pond at the base. The pool was shallow but wide, with large stones protruding from the water. Carrie could see where getting to the other side without getting wet would be tricky. It would involve using the rough stones as steps. This was what Zooric could have been attempting. He was lying in the middle of the pond, his left leg projecting from his body at an unnatural angle; and the water flowing away from him was bright red!

"Zooric!" she shouted.

"Oh no! Oh no!" Praying he was not dead, she hurried into the water. In her one attempt to use the stones, she almost slipped and fell. Yes, that definitely must have been what happened to Zooric. The stones were extremely slippery. It was much safer wading in the water. The paw scrambled after her sending huge splashes in its wake.

"Ouch," Carrie cried as a particularly large splash hit her face. She was soon soaked. She wiped impatiently at the flood of water streaming down her face and scrambled the rest of the way across. Then, with her heart pounding, she bent over Zooric. He was unconscious but his chest was moving, proving that he was not dead. Carrie sank back on her heels in relief.

Now she had another problem. How was she going to get him back to the camp? She stared at the paw that was now panting, with its face within inches of Zooric's. The animal didn't look tame enough to pet, but clearly, he or she was devoted to its master.

I'll bet you are a male, she thought. She carefully turned Zooric onto his back. His head was resting on a rock with his face just clear of the water. The rock may have bashed his head in, but she was also sure it had saved him from drowning—by keeping his head out of the water. There was a deep cut on his head, just above his right temple, and it was still oozing blood. She would need something to stop the bleeding, but she had left the camp with nothing. Carrie thought of the blanket.

She could cut that up. Another idea came, but first his head. She would deal with the leg once she got him to the camp.

Carrie tore strips off the shirt-like garment he wore under his robe. Using a number of strips, she was able to make a pad, which she tied tightly around his head with another strip. She checked his leg. It was broken, but although the skin was badly bruised, no bone was protruding. Satisfied that at least he was no longer bleeding, she stood up. Next task would be getting him out. She would deal with his leg later. She grabbed him, one hand under each armpit and started dragging him out of the water. Was he heavy! Carrie was panting after moving him just a few feet. The paw soon got the idea that she needed help and sank his teeth into Zooric's clothing, near his shoulder. Together they both heaved—another few feet. Carrie stopped and straightened. Her back was already killing her.

It took three more pulling efforts to get him out of the water. Carrie was ready to collapse. She rested her hands on her knees and bent over. After a few minutes of heavy breathing, she stood. She would need to go back to the camp for the blanket. As Carrie started toward the woods, the paw, after watching her intently without moving, gave a low growl.

Carrie stopped. "What now? I'm not abandoning him, but I need something to help get him up." Carrie spoke soothingly to the animal, hoping it would understand. The animal only growled again.

She backed away, afraid of an attack. What if he thinks I'm leaving? She thought.

"I'll be back. I promise," she said. Then she realized how idiotic she sounded, talking to a paw. Worse, she was speaking in a language it probably didn't understand. She decided to try out her few words in Gavaa.

"*Tvox, oo spior narlee.* Stay, I will come back." At least she hoped that was what she said. Fortunately, it seemed to work. This time the animal only whinnied when she turned to walk away.

Good!

Carrie ran all the way back to the cave. At least the running warmed her up! Breathlessly, she ran up the passageway. The animals were still in front of the house. Carrie rushed in. Panting, she stared around, noticing for the first time two large bags in a corner of the main room. Riffling through them she found a knife and a rope. Then she rushed over to her makeshift bed and grabbed the thick blanket she had discarded only a few minutes before.

"This will have to do," she muttered. She turned to go but stopped at the sleeping zig. It just might work since there was no way she would be able get Zooric onto the fluar. Carrie woke the reluctant animal, saddled it, and dragged it with her into the forest.

Back at the pond, she placed the blanket on the ground and carefully rolled Zooric onto it. That done, she wrapped the blanket around him, and tied it tightly. Carrie tied another length of rope around the blanket and scrambled back to the zig. She tied the other end of the rope to the pommel of the zig's saddle, then caught the leading reins of the zig and urged the animal forward.

"Come West! Come!" The zig slowly lumbered forward. After a few feet, Carrie stopped the animal and went back to the edge of the pond to check on Zooric. He was still tied in the blanket. The plan was working. Good! She was going to have to pull him all the way to the camp. Carrie urged the zig forward again. The paw followed, keeping up with its master's progress. She had to go very slowly, so it took forever before she finally reached the cave.

"You did it West! You did it!" Carrie praised the animal; then ran to Zooric. It had taken hours not only because she had to go so slow, but she also had to stop repeatedly to adjust the blanket and rotate the part at the bottom as it became frayed. The first-dark was approaching when Carrie finally inched Zooric into the cave. Despite her exertion, she was shivering. She carefully dragged him all the way to the house.

He was still unconscious, and that fact was beginning to worry her. Surely, the wound on his head was not that bad. She ran a finger along his jaw. No wonder he looked so young. This close she could see that his face was covered in a fine, short, and almost invisible hair. No shaving was necessary.

Carrie carefully unwrapped him from the now ragged blanket, and then bent to check his injuries. First his leg; the break was just above the top of his boot. Carrie frowned. A year ago, her brother had broken his leg. Now she tried to remember all that was done at the time. She needed to get the boots off and set the bones. Carrie considered the rest of his clothing. She hesitated then decided to get everything ready first. She would need something to keep the bones in place- and water. She remembered seeing a container full of water. But first, she needed to change.

After borrowing some of Zooric's clothing, she got a fire going, grateful that she had watched Zooric carefully the last darkening; then she set some water to boil. The animals began complaining. Carrie realized that they had not been fed at all this light—neither had she for that matter. But she was too keyed up to eat right now. She rushed back outside to collect brush for the animals and also some long twigs to use as splints. After feeding the animals, she settled down. Enough delays; now to remove his clothing.

Under his tunic, he wore baggy pants-like clothing. That would have to go; besides it was torn and wet. He also wore what looked to be loose under shorts. Carrie was relieved. As she removed his pants and cut away his boots, she stared at his long legs in envy. They were legs a female would die for. They were smooth, the same brown as his face, yet it was not his skin color that inspired envy, but fine hair that covered his entire body!

Finally, taking a deep breath, she felt around for the broken ends of the bone and firmly pulled the lower end.

"Aarh!" Zooric jerked, then moaned.

Carrie screamed. An unbelievable pain was concentrated in her leg; then a low throb started in her head. Carrie released Zooric's leg and doubled over, pulling her leg protectively to her chest. Tears started in her eyes. Zooric was slowly regaining consciousness. Oh god! He was sending her his pain. Carrie bit her lip until the metallic taste of blood filled her mouth. She was beyond understanding how this was possible. She could only gasp again as another wave of pain hit her leg.

"Zooric please! Zooric!" Carrie was aware the instant Zooric regained complete consciousness. He immediately started trying to control the pain he was sending. Carrie looked up. His eyes were still closed, but his breaths were deep and harsh. Sweat was pouring off his body. The pain in her leg subsided to a dull ache. The same was true of her head. Dare she try again?

"I have to set the bone," she told him. There was no response. "Zooric?"

Would he live if she did not set the bones? Because she was unsure, Carrie very hesitantly clutched his leg again. The pain was not as sharp—perhaps because she was prepared this time, or maybe Zooric was still exerting a measure of control. Carrie pulled, jerking the bones into place. She felt another flash of pain, then nothing. Zooric had passed out. She gasped. But at least she was now pain free. Shakily, she used finger pressure to check the break site. Finally, she straightened both of his legs and compared their length. Although she was not a medic, they looked even, and she was confident that she had done the best she could. Now she had to put the splint in place before he woke up again.

As she reached for him, again she marveled at the difference in their skin color. He was much darker than she was, and she was perhaps one of the darkest settlers in Arapmo. She knew that a few of the original colonist were dark skinned, but the marriage program devised by the Presidential Council was deliberately geared to guarantee one race. The idea was that, with so few people, they could not afford to have racial strife or discord. The deliberate policy of forced intermarriages between the different races was fast producing a single race of similar looking people, but it was one of the biggest sources of discord between the Presidential Council and the citizens. Many, if not all of the people of Arapmo, disagreed with that particular policy. The problem was there were two opposing factions now living in Arapmo. There were those who wanted no intermingling of the races. They wanted to preserve each distinct race by banning interracial marriage. Then there were those in her father's camp. They just wanted freedom of choice — to marry the person of their choice regardless of race.

She was working on tying the last knot on the strips, keeping the splint in place, when Zooric woke. She knew he was waking when she felt the now familiar flash of pain. She looked up, but his eyes were still closed. As he became more fully awake, the pain slowly subsided.

"Zooric?"

His eyes flickered open. They were dull with pain. She reached to check the wound on his head. He flinched. Carrie felt unexpectedly hurt at the rejection. She started to withdraw her hand.

"*Zte*," the command was mental. Carrie stiffened at the mental invasion. "*I do not have the strength for verbal speech.*"

Because he seemed to be reading her thoughts, Carrie was reluctant as she again reached toward his head wound. He had closed his eyes, and now he turned his face towards her hand, almost like a baby rooting. Tentatively she reached out, only the tips of her fingers touched him, yet again there was that flicker of electricity. Carrie tensed, expecting pain but this time there was none.

She slowly relaxed trying to ignore the electrical flickers. As she did, Carrie began sensing his emotions. He was feeling content and sleepy and became even more so as the electrical flickers continued. However, even as he relaxed, she began feeling a slowly building pool of pleasure.

"Do you have any medicine?" She hurriedly withdrew her hand. The question was more a distraction than a plea for information.

"*My bags*," he murmured. Again, she heard the words in her head, and somehow his words increased her vague erotic feelings. "*Zte, do not stop yet.*"

Zooric's eyes were still closed. But his heavy breathing was slowing. Carrie, however, was tense. She did not like the way her body was reacting, and she did not want to get his emotions. She bit her lips.

"*Are you still feeling my pain,*" he asked.

"Just a dull ache. Nothing like what you must be feeling." Reluctantly, she touched him again, resigned to the tingling of electricity her touch produced. "Is this a normal ability among your people?" Carrie was getting both uncomfortable and embarrassed. She needed to concentrate on something else!

"*Nothing between us is normal. And I can control the pain better when you are touching me,*" he murmured. Even his mental words sounded weak.

"You feel less pain?" Carrie asked in surprise. She had thought he felt terrible pain when she touched him. "Why were you afraid to touch me in the past?"

"*I have only just realized it.*" His eyes flickered open to stare at her. He gave a faint smile. "*If you would relax and enjoy the sensations of our touching, you would feel better too.*"

Carrie snatched her hands away, as she felt her face heating up. Did he know what she was feeling? If he could send her his pain, was it possible to send and receive thoughts as well?

"Go get the medicine." Now there was a wealth of amusement in his voice.

Carrie fled to rummage through his bags. Zooric turned to watch and gave instructions. She finally located what she sought. "What is it?"

"Oeeln, from the oeeln plant. It stops infections"

"We desperately need antibiotics. Most of what we have is grown in labs, and the supplies are running low. Our scientists have begun experimenting with different plants, but so far, they haven't found any that have antibiotic properties."

"This plant grows in the lowlands."

"What are these others?" There were six different packets of medicine in his bag

"Pain killers, antidote, for the poisonous wicee sting and drink for strength, for fevers..."

"Wicee?"

Zooric explained but Carrie did not know of any snake-like animals. It was possible the wicee was native only to Zooric's home area. "Do you want the pain killer?"

"Zte."

"You may need it later." Carrie said, warning him that his pain could get worse later.

"You will still be here later, besides, with the painkiller I will have less control," he pointed out.

Again, Carrie was embarrassed as she realized what he was implying. But she did not dispute his assumption. More than likely, she would be here later. She seriously doubted she would be able to find her way down the mountain on her own.

She brought over the antibiotic and gave it to him with a small container of water. Stooping beside him she lifted his head to help him drink, again the tingling. This time it was not as sharp and they both ignored it—Carrie, because she was concentrating on carefully placing the container to his mouth, Zooric perhaps because he was too sick.

He drank deeply then asked mentally. *"Did you feed Soor?"*

"The paw?"

"Paw?" Carrie explained.

"Soor is not a feera—they are wild." Zooric said as soon as he recognized the animal she was describing. *"He is a rocleer."*

"We have never seen them."

"They live with Owoons as pets. Distant cousin to the feera."

"He looks like a paw or feera— whatever you call them. I thought he was going to attack me." Carrie related what happened.

"There is no need to fear Soor. He would never attack unless at my command. How did you get me here?"

She told him, and then asked. "Where are we?"

"In the travel hall of an ancient Azar sector."

The words were meaningless to Carrie, but she did not want to get distracted. She decided to stick to her main concern. "Are we the only ones here?"

"Eeng."

That was a relief. Carrie was bursting with questions but could see and feel that Zooric just was not up to answering them. Already his head was getting heavy on her hand. She carefully helped him to lie down as she realized his strength was fading. "How are you feeling now?"

"*Better*," he said from his supine position. "*Have you eaten?*"

"No. What is there to eat?"

Zooric instructed her on how to prepare their meal, but halfway into the preparation, he either lost consciousness or dozed off. Carrie decided to let him sleep.

He didn't wake up until the middle of first-dark. Again, she was first aware he was wakening by the throbbing pain in her leg.

Carrie hobbled over to him. "Zooric!" She cried. The pain became muted, but it was still there.

"Zooric please, you have to stop sending me your pain."

He turned to her. "*Touch me,*" he muttered.

She hesitated slightly, and then placed both hands on his chest.

He closed his eyes, as he took deep breaths. Carrie was also breathing deeply as a low surge of current went through her, and a deep pleasurable throbbing began to build, concentrating in her groin. At least the pain in her leg was easing. Did she dare enjoy this pleasure? As her pleasure built, Carrie shifted restlessly. She wasn't sure what she wanted. Zooric's eyes were closed. She could feel him slowly relaxing. Uncertain what to do and how to react, Carrie felt her restless tension grow. Finally, unable to take it anymore, she withdrew her hands. The pain in her leg was gone, so she assumed that he was feeling better. Carrie pushed herself upright and stood rubbing her hands on her thighs as she looked down at him in frustration. She did not like these feelings. Her entire body was tingling, but Zooric did not seem similarly affected. From the emotions she was receiving, she was aware that the electrical tingling relaxed him. Again, he had fallen asleep! With a distracted sigh, she left his side to get some food in the form of a thin gruel.

"Zooric! I have some soup." Carrie called a few minutes later.

Carrie stooped beside him, but Zooric's eyes remained closed. She knew he was awake however, because of the low throbbing in her leg. "Zooric! You have to eat." Carrie spooned a mouthful and carried it to his mouth.

He turned his head away. *"No. I'm not hungry."*

"You have to eat," Carrie repeated. "Come on Zooric. Just a little."

Carrie was able to coax him into taking only half the bowl. Even the effort to eat seemed to exhaust him. His brow was covered in sweat again, his breathing once again harsh and irregular. Carrie placed the bowl on the ground and left him to get a rag. She carefully measured out a small quantity of water. The big jug was all the water they had, and she had no intention of going to the stream now that darkening was approaching. She would need more water for food and for the animals, but she would worry about that in the next cycle. Going back to Zooric, she began wiping his brow. His eyes flickered, more in response to the immediate tingling that accompanied her touching him than to her effort, however he did not open his eyes. Carrie continued stroking him until his breathing evened out. He was asleep again.

She rocked back on her heels and stared worriedly at him. He did not look good. His skin was now almost gray and was becoming ashy, despite his bouts of sweating. Carrie got some more of the medicine for his leg but this time he absolutely refused to swallow it, allowing most of the liquid to spill to the ground. Carrie grounded her teeth in frustration. She carefully opened the bandage around his leg. The site of the break felt warm but didn't look severely infected. But why was he so pale and lethargic? What would she do if he died? She was at least one cycle, perhaps more, from home. Carrie chewed on her lips as she considered her situation. She was in an alien town, but it was clear that the town was abandoned. That left her alone with an alien who could be a danger to her people if he could kill others so easily. Yet she did not want him to die. If she left him, he would surely die. But if he died, would she be able to find her way back home? She was not sure. If she stayed, at least there was a chance they would both survive.

Carrie slept fitfully throughout the short hours of first-dark. Not only did her leg ache, but she also had a splitting headache. His thoughts had even invaded her dreams. They were a confused jumble of emotions. Sometime during the darkening, exhausted from lack of sleep, she rolled closer to hold him, hoping to calm him enough so that at least she could sleep. She thought wistfully of her bed at home. They were both sleeping on a bed made of the grass-like plants found in this region. It definitely needed more padding! Finally, he either fell deeply asleep, or lost consciousness; either way her pains stopped.

****

When Zooric next woke a new cycle had arrived. He was more alert but still had no appetite. However, since he offered no objection, Carrie literally forced as much food in him as quickly as possible. Finally, he feebly pushed her hands away, again spilling much of the gruel. She sighed. It was pointless getting mad with him when he was so sick. At least he had consumed more than half the bowl. But she was still worried. From the returning pain in her leg, she knew his control was fragile. She knelt over him, rubbing his brow and determinedly ignoring the pleasure it brought her, until he fell asleep again.

Zooric dozed on and off for the rest of the cycle. At one particular lucent point, he told her to go with Soor to the stream for more water. Just before the darkening, Carrie got him to eat a little more and take some of the medicine. He was not eating enough to sustain a baby much less a man of his size. But no amount of coaxing on her part could get him to take more. She finally left him to sleep.

The next cycle, Zooric was definitely better. He finished his meal then announced that he had to get up.

"That is just crazy!"

He only gave her a look before slowly turning in an effort to drag himself forward.

"Zooric!" Carrie cried.

"I have to go," he growled.

"Oh!" Carrie dipped her head to hide her embarrassment as she realized that he needed to use a bathroom. "Let me help you."

"*Zte!* Leave me!"

She refused to leave him, however. She had already explored the house and knew what room he was heading for. Six smaller rooms led off the central room that they occupied. He finally gave up fighting her and allowed her to help him crawl through to another room. There she left him to do his business.

"Call me when you are finished," she shouted as she left. She was slightly reassured by the fact that he was speaking aloud. Hopefully, that meant he was getting well and could manage.

Of course, he didn't call. She first realized he was in trouble when she felt the now familiar stabbing pain in her leg. Carrie rushed to the room. Zooric was attempting to crawl out.

He stopped when he saw her. He was panting heavily and had somehow managed to open the cut on his face. Blood was pouring down his right side.

Showing extreme restraint, Carrie managed to avoid shouting at him. She silently wrapped her arm about him preparing to support his upper body.

"Both hands," he muttered, resting his head on the ground and returning to mental-speak.

"What?"

"It is a link — like creating a circuit. It will be better if there are two points of contact."

"Oh." Carrie placed her other hand on his chest. The zing of electricity was immediate and a lot more intense than on the last few occasions. Carrie gasped. Zooric instantly tried to pull back.

"No. No. It's okay." She took a deep breath and felt the control Zooric was trying to exert. If he could maintain control so too, could she. Her challenge in controlling her emotions actually involved trying to keep still. She found herself fighting an almost unbelievable urge to run her hands up and down his chest—to explore his body! As before the linking helped him. He was still weak but together they managed to get him back into the main room. He was listless and shaky by the time she had him covered in his makeshift bed.

He was still gray and ashy a few hours later. Determinedly she removed all his upper clothing to give him a sponge bath, hoping to hydrate his skin. She was too worried to be embarrassed and he was too weak to forestall her. He mutely suffered her ministration.

He was so still when she was finished that she started worrying again. "Zooric are you sure you are alright. Should I touch you again?"

"Go ahead."

Carrie stretched out beside him and rested both arms on his chest. His rapid breathing slowed as he relaxed. But Carrie waited until the dull ache in her leg was totally gone before releasing him. Again, he slept.

He slept deeply throughout the first half of the cycle, but when he got restless and the pain started in her leg again, Carrie prepared to stretch out beside him. He was burning with fever. He stirred restlessly. Carrie began receiving his emotions.

Although his emotions were no clearer than before, she panicked calling, "Zooric. Zooric."

"W...what? ..."

Carrie was totally confused as she tried to separate her emotions from Zooric. "Zooric please. I can't handle this."

Zooric muttered indistinctly. His head was shifting restlessly on the bedding.

"Zooric!" Carrie called again. She reached for him, using both hands to hold his head steady, and gasped. Instinctively, Carrie tried to pull away from the pain of the powerful surge of electricity. But this time she couldn't. She was taking not just his pain, but also his thoughts. This was too much all at once. "Zooric!" she screamed.

Zooric's eyes flew open, as he jerked fully awake. He stared blankly at her for a few seconds before he put a lid on both his emotions and his thoughts. Then within a few seconds, the pain in her leg was muted. Carrie's body went limp with relief.

Throughout the next cycle Zooric rested. He was still weak and seemed to be running a low fever. The good thing was he started eating more and no longer had a pale sickly look. Carrie was vastly relieved. He was recovering. This strange connection between them was beginning to have a profound effect on her. She still slept beside him however, instinctively holding him during the darkening when the pain in his leg got too much for him to bear. She was also adapting. Sometime during the last two cycles, she had stopped regarding him as an alien. It was impossible to hate or fear someone who spent a lot of time worrying about her safety. From his emotions and sometimes chaotic thoughts, she knew he wanted her; but she was also aware that he was worried about her. He hated the fact that he was not able to help and for some reason seemed to believe that she was putting her life in danger every time she left him to go outside. Men! She found that just as Zooric had advised; if she relaxed, she did enjoy the linking more. It was definitely pleasurable!

At the end of the second-dark of the third cycle, Carrie yawned after another low level linking. She snuggled closer seeking something, she wasn't sure what. She was lying with her upper body draped over his. Resting her head on his shoulder, she collapsed with a sigh.

"Caree you should not..."

Carrie did not hear whatever else Zooric was trying to say. She was too exhausted. All this past light she had been busy caring for the animals plus Zooric. She had made two trips for water and right now didn't have the strength to raise her head. The last thing she remembered thinking before she went off to sleep was that Zooric's body was feeling much cooler. His fever had finally broken.

****

Chapter 8

Zooric woke to find the girl draped across his chest. She was using him as a pillow. He lifted one hand to cautiously touch her hair. She had braided it. Curiously, he examined the thick braid resting on her back. Her hair was as black as his, but her curls were larger, looser — giving her hair a wavy appearance. A slight smile touched his lips as he fingered the thick braid, careful to avoid disturbing her sleep. His other hand drifted to lightly stroke her cheek. She was not beautiful in the same sense as the women of his people. But neither was she much different. Her lips were not as full as his, her nostrils not as flared, yet he suspected among her own people she would be considered beautiful. The perfect symmetry of her face was pleasing, regardless of her race.

Soor came over to investigate what his master was doing. Zooric stopped stroking the girl and petted his rocleer. The animal flopped down in delight.

"Thank you Soor. I guess you saved my life, again... Do you think you could get us some food?"

The rocleer got up eagerly and gave a low rumble. Zooric gave him one last pat. "Food!" he said in Gavaa and watched as the rocleer loped out of the room, then he looked around. Through the open doorway he could see that both pageens were up, but the caceen was still sleeping. When he first arrived at the Azar's sector, he had meant to go deeper into the sector but changed his mind, instead choosing to explore the outside and the Tifoosas. They were actually camped out in a traveler's receiving chamber. They should go inside. It was most likely safer, and the accommodations would be great.

Again, he focused on the girl in his arms, lightly stroking her back. He suspected that she would have a problem dealing with living in the sector. Perhaps he would just stay here, at least until he recovered. She had saved his life, and not just once; he did not want to upset her. She stirred. Zooric paused in his stroking, but she did not wake. Relaxing, he released the breath he did not even realize he was holding, to continue his gentle stroking along her back. This mental link between them was almost too strange to believe, he thought. That linking was undoubtedly helping him heal. He no longer fought the feelings she generated in him although a part of him still resented that he had little control when they touched. He had also realized an important fact. Caree wasn't sending him any signals. It was all coming from him. He was so sensitive that he was involuntarily picking up every signal coming from her and responding by initiating a link.

But what did she feel for him? From her emotions, he knew she was no longer afraid of him. But he had known about the Tifoosas. For her it must have been a shock to find out that her people were not the only race on this planet. What he needed now was a plan. He wanted her, but even more he wanted her to want him, and he did not want to share her, not even with his own people. He certainly did not want her to go back to hers. But what would he do if she insisted? Zooric's hand tightened, instinctively, possessively on her back. She belonged to him!

He felt her coming awake. Because they were in contact, he was unable to block her emotions. Not that he was trying. With his mind open he was aware of her surprise at finding herself draped over him. Her instinctive panic was immediately replaced by embarrassment. She looked up. Zooric gave a brief smile of amusement. Carrie looked down in embarrassment as he lifted a finger and gently touched her face. Her brown skin was actually getting red.

"This does not happen to me."

His question distracted her, momentarily staying her disconcertion. "What are you talking about?"

"Does your face always get red when you are embarrassed?"

"Oh!" Her confusion cleared. Carrie planted both palms on his chest to push away from him.

Zooric did not tighten his hold, but neither did he release her.

She glared at him. "Perhaps your embarrassment does not show because of your complexion. Now let me up!"

"I can read your emotions," Zooric stated calmly.

Her eyes widened.

"I can give you mine," he added.

"What?" she squeaked.

He suited action to words and immediately flooded her with his feelings. "See, I am just as confused as you are."

As suddenly as it began, the flood stopped.

Carrie sat up in cautious surprise. This time he allowed the action but did not completely release her. "Can you still get my emotions?"

"*Eeng.*"

"I don't want to send them.

"Perhaps with practice you will be able to stop." Zooric was not particularly interested in having her learn.

Actually, he liked getting her emotions. In fact, he found her emotions extremely soothing.

"How?"

"I am not sure. You just not send it." He shrugged his disinterest. Recently he had begun keeping his senses wide open, literally wallowing in her emotions. The freedom to do this, after a lifetime of imposing a rigid control over his senses, was exhilarating. Ever since his escape, he had struggled to put his past behind him. With his immense control, he had managed to force his conscious mind into submission. Trying to sleep, however, was another matter. It was during the dark that his unconscious mind took over. In the past, his only means of getting sleep was to exhaust himself during the light, and even then, sleep often eluded him, interrupted by nightmarish childhood memories. Not anymore, and he was sure that feeding on Caree's emotions was the cause. He shifted slightly and released her; aware that she was again conscious of where she was still lying.

She darted at him a nervous glance before moving to sit beside him. "Until I can stop sending you my thoughts, I want you to block them. It's not fair that I can't get yours and you can get mine."

"I get your emotions not your thoughts. I can't read your mind to know what you are thinking." He said seriously. "If you are sad or happy, I will know, but not the reason why."

"Thoughts, emotions... I don't care. Just block them."

"Always blocking is impossible." That was true. It was also true that he could only block when not touching her.

Carrie stared.

He stared back. Recognizing her uncertainty, he tried to reassure her. "I can give you my emotions," he offered.

She gasped as he flooded her mind with his feeling. "No!" Carrie clearly did not want to deal with his emotional needs. She switched the subject. "What is this electricity charge between us?"

"It is a linking. We will eat first then I will explain."

****

Glad that at last he was hungry, Carrie jumped up to prepare their mid-light meal. In just a few hours it would be first-dark. Next, she fed the animals; then gave Zooric his medicine. He grimaced when she said she had to examine his leg, but for once she felt no pain as she unwrapped the bandage from his leg, examined it, then rewrapped it with clean bandages. His leg looked free of infection and the bruising was healing nicely.

"It's only been three cycles and it already looks healed," she exclaimed.

"We heal faster than you do."

"How do you know?"

"I know of your people." She looked up. "But how?"

Before Zooric could answer, the rocleer returned with a baby gos-gos in its mouth.

"Let's take care of this first," Zooric said.

"It's a baby," she wailed.

"It's food," Zooric disagreed. "The gos-gos is very agile. They live in tunnels in the ground so I am not surprised that Soor could only capture a baby." He told her how to skin the gos-gos and cook it on the small fire. By the time she was finished feeding the rocleer, and feeding the other animals, half the light was gone. Next, she had to go to the stream for her daily wash and get more water. When she got back, she found that Zooric had used her time away to wash up and change his clothing.

Carrie was aghast. She insisted that he lie down so she could examine his leg again, "You are lucky you didn't open your wounds again," she told him grumpily as she checked. Fortunately, the splint and bandages were still in place.

Finally, she flopped down beside him. "I hope you realize that you owe me big-time."

He stretched out on his back, placing his hand behind his head. "I will not forget," he reassured her.

"Good. Now eons ago, you promised to tell me about this extra knowledge you have of my people and about linking."

"Yes. Linking." Zooric chose to answer her second question then paused to gather his thoughts. "After puberty all Owoons have the ability to link."

"But what is the linking?"

He shrugged. "It is an electrosensory ability. We have the ability to send pulses of electricity into the environment. The return pulse gives us information. I find that each person has a distinct electro frequency in the brain. If I pulse a person—send an electric signal out to someone—from the return pulses I can identify who it is—if I have met that person in the past, or I can get an unknown signal— meaning it is someone I have never met. The same principle works in the dark. I can use my electro sense to find my way—to 'see' objects and to differentiate between animate and inanimate objects. I can also send a mental pulse—mental-speak—to others, or send a buzz, which means I can send a small amount of electrical current to the brain. A buzz can cause pain. It depends on the intensity."

Carrie stared. "So, the linking is electricity energy?"

"Linking is a discharge of electricity," he hesitated. "Linking is unlike a buzz in that the buzz sends the electricity directly to the brain while linking sends electricity throughout the body not just concentrated in the head."

"That is exactly what I felt. Like an electric current passing through me."

He nodded. "Ordinarily, Owoons do not have this low-link. But when I touch you, I always have to control this urge to link with you."

"Are you saying I force you to link?" Carrie was indignant.

He gave her a hooded look.

"I am not forcing it," she deduced. "You sometimes have no control, and you don't like it."

Zooric inhaled and exhaled sharply. "In any linking you lose a measure of control. There is an exchange of emotions. In this low- linking that we share, the extent of the exchange depends on how much control I retain. It is true that you do not force me to link, but it is also true that when I am weak, I have little control, and when we touch, I also have little control. But something else happens when we link." He hesitated, reluctant to tell her more.

"What?"

Zooric looked away. "The linking that we have is not a very high energy linking. Never have I heard of such a low level linking. And you are capable of taking some of my pain, my hurt. I think that in the process of taking it, I heal faster. Last time... if I totally lose control, you get all — my emotions, my thoughts, and my electro energy, especially if the linking moves to a higher level. That would not be good. As yet, you cannot handle it all. That is what happened at our first linking. But if I control and sent you just a little, I feel better." His intent gaze was directed at her once again. "None of this happens when Owoons engage in normal linking — it is always a deep involuntary link. And once the linking starts, they have no control over the depth of the linking."

"Are all Owoon like you?"

"Like me how?"

Carrie looked down and absently pleated the folds of her shirt. She wanted to ask him more about this strange linking, but she was afraid. She settled on a neutral topic. "The same color hair, eyes skin."

Zooric shrugged. "Our skin color varies a lot. Many have my color; some are lighter, some darker. The shades vary. We also have different hair and eye colors. But most Owoons have brown or black hair and varying shades of brown eyes."

"Yours are hazel," Carrie pointed out.

Again, Zooric shrugged, this time with a grin. "Hazel, I do not know. My eye color is light brown. It is very common among my people."

"No, it's hazel." Carrie insisted then gathered her courage and returned to a more probing question. "How did you kill Chris?"

"Chris?"

"The man who kidnapped me." Zooric was momentarily distracted.

"Kidnap? Did he take you by force?" When Carrie agreed he seemed relieved. She was puzzled until he explained that before he had assumed that Chris was her friend.

"Oh no! Chris is … was a bad guy. He took me from my home although I didn't want to go." She did not think the time was right to tell Zooric exactly how she was kidnapped. But Zooric had other ideas.

"Why did he take you away?"

"You were supposed to tell me how you were able to kill him," she protested.

But Zooric folded his arms across his chest. "First you will explain why he kidnapped you," he insisted.

Her glare had no effect. With a final scowl, she accepted the futility of trying to out-stare him and told him what had happened to her. "So, you see I need to warn my family. These men are stealing from my father."

"When I am well, I will take you back to your family," he promised.

She wanted to believe him, but she was still fearful. Yet at this point, there was not much she could do but believe him. Although perhaps she could have killed him while he was ill or maybe just not helped him. He would surely have died had she not brought him back to these caves and cared for him. But there is no way she could have lived with herself if she had aided his death. Her best bet now was to stick to getting information. She went back to her original inquiry. "So how did you do it?"

He had no problem following her thought process. After a moment of hesitation, he reluctantly admitted. "I… It was an accident. I did not mean to. I only wanted to stop him, but he startled me. I generated a burst of electricity and projected it into his mind. It's an electro- buzz. The step-up is an electro-sizzle. The intensity of the electro-buzz or sizzle can be varied. I did not realize... I did not think the intensity I generated would kill."

"Can every Owoon do that?"

"*Zte.*"

Carrie stared at him. Now she was even more afraid. He was an alien. And he had extraordinary powers. My god, he could kill!

Zooric was definitely feeling her fear. "Caree. I would never hurt you. I did not mean to kill him. I only wanted to stop him from hurting you or me."

"But what about the rest of my people? You can read minds. And your people could easily kill all of mine."

"I cannot read your mind, and neither can my people," he corrected.

She shrugged that off with a wave of her hands. "You know what I mean," she cried. "Why are you here? You could kill us all," she whispered. "Your people sent you here to spy on us, didn't they?"

But although he looked startled by her accusations, he was silent, seemingly unsure of what to say.

"When are you going to admit it?"

Instead of denying her assumptions, he asked curiously. "Are you sensing my emotions?"

"I don't know. I just know you aren't telling me everything."

Zooric stared off into space. He started slowly. "All Owoon have some form of electro-sensory ability, some more so than others. At puberty all males are tested in a process called first-link to determine their level of electro-sensory skills."

"Is your ability more than others?"

"*Eeng,*" Zooric admitted. "I am a sensitive." He said nothing further.

As she stared at him, Carrie was abruptly aware that she was getting some of his feelings. They were indistinct, but clearly her questions pained him in some why. Still, she needed to get answers!

After a few minutes, during which Zooric made no effort to break the silence, she tried again.

"What is a sensitive?"

He stirred, flicked a glance at her then finally decided to answer. "We who have more electro-sensory ability."

"How much more?" she insisted.

"Others cannot electro-sizzle," he bunched up the bed to prop himself up against the wall then bent his head back, staring at the ceiling. "A sensitive can. Others can only electro-buzz, we can electro-speak—send mental messages to others, or private messages to one person at a time. It is very dangerous for sensitives to link with someone who is not a sensitive. Unless the sensitive maintains total control, the weaker person will be killed by the electricity generated at the linking, or they will receive a sizzle—just enough to fry the person's memory but not enough to kill. That is worse than death because then the person becomes like a shadow."

"Why are you suddenly being so open with me?" Carrie asked, and then added suspiciously, "Are you going to renege on your promise to take me back?"

"*Zte*, I will take you back," he stated flatly, giving no indication of his true feelings.

Then, clearly unwilling to continue with the topic, he moved on. "Now tell me of your people."

"One more question. How did you know of my people?"

"Your people were brought to this planet by the Azars. They were the original inhabitants of this planet, of Segaan. They had incredible strong electro sensors. The flying ship your people traveled in was orbiting near our solar system when it attracted the attention of one of their strongest electro sensors. He was able to bring it here. They disabled the controls so your people could not leave or contact outside help." Zooric was a lot freer in giving this information.

Carrie jerked upright. "Yes. Oh my God! Yes! The first colonists could not understand why their controls wouldn't work. They were unable to call for help. They did not even plan on landing on any planet. They were on a long-term exploratory mission into deep space. They had traveled for over fifty years and were actually on the return journey to Earth, which is our mother planet, when they found their spaceship drawn into this planet's orbit. According to our history they had to make a landing or crash."

"*Eeng.* Centuries ago, the Azars lived on the surface of the planet. They experimented first with animals such as the pageen, and soon discovered how to manipulate the genes of their people. They developed electro-sensor abilities, but in the process their skin became extremely sensitive to any rays from the sun. They could no longer live on the surface of the planet. Even a few minutes of exposure to direct sunlight was enough to cause terrible skin burns or even kill them. They became underground dwellers. They lived in many different underground towns and cities called sectors. We are now in the entrance of one of their sectors.

"That is why we have never found traces of them," Carrie said softly. "Our scientist only found evidence of an ancient civilization; over 10,000 years old. They speculated that a calamity wiped out the entire race."

"The ancient people of Segaan were the Azars."

"Did they look like us?"

"*Zte*. They were very tall, many close to ten-feet tall. They also had big heads and were very thin. I have never seen any images of an overweight Azar. Their feet and hands were much narrower than ours. They also had no body hair —not even on their heads. And their skin color was blue."

"Blue?"

"*Eeng*. They had blue skin. When under stress their skin would take on a translucent hue."

"That must have been weird looking. What color eyes."

"Most were yellow, some were light green."

"But what happened to the Azars? And where did your people, the Owoons come from?"

"The Azars reproduced artificially. The male sperms and the female eggs were kept in special reproduction banks. When the citizens were ready to have babies, they would place orders for a specific type of baby. They could even determine the baby's personality. Their babies grew outside of the female in special breeding houses. Unfortunately, a defective electro-genetic link was introduced in the female eggs at the main reproduction bank. It was not discovered at first because it was a very subtle brain defect.

The Azars believed it was deliberately manipulated by a deranged or vengeful scientist. Although they were successful in isolating the defected gene, they had no normal replacement genetic material. Also, since the Azars harvested the female eggs at birth, the defect eventually spread throughout the entire nation. Over time, the defects began producing children with severe life-threatening abnormities, most did not survive. And unfortunately, all Azars carried the defective gene. And with each generation, the severity of the abnormality increased. Finally, the Azars were forced to stop all births. The few live births were both physically and mentally defective and were unable to reproduce. This is why they brought your ship down. The plan was to use genetic material from the eggs of your females to replace Azars' defective eggs.

"So, they used the revo to capture our women and kill our men."

"Revo?"

"When the first colonist arrived, they were attacked by a hairy animal we called a revo." She described the attacks.

"Those were not animals. They were Azar people."

"So, they dressed as animals and kidnapped our women."

"They did not dress as animals. Their skin was sensitive to the sunlight. They had to wear very thick animal skin-covering to protect their skin from the sun, and even so, they could remain on the surface of the planet for only a few hours."

"Whatever," Carrie muttered enraged with Zooric's apparent defense of Azars.

Zooric gave her a hard stare. She refused to back down and glared angrily back at him. Sighing, Zooric turned away. "Perhaps what they did was not right but try to understand. They were trying to save their people."

"How can you even try to excuse what they did?"

"Very well, I will not," he snapped in unexpected anger.

"Okay, okay. Just tell me what happened next." Zooric had lost his impassivity, which really surprised Carrie. She watched uneasily as he struggled to contain his unexpected irritation. It was a while before he continued.

"Unfortunately, the breeding program did not work as they hoped. According to the Writing of *Loya* Favood, their great psychic, they were able to get a viable intelligent life form only when they reversed the process, when they introduced traces of the Azar genes into the human genome. It therefore followed that the children of their breeding program looked nothing like them. These offspring had less than one hundredth of one percent of the Azars genes and did not have even a tenth of their abilities."

"Your people," Carrie guessed.

"*Eeng*. My people."

"Even before they realized that the plan would not work, the ruler at the time wanted to destroy your people. The *Loya* Favood was able to prevent him. The *Loya* Favood also survived numerous attempts by the ruler to have him eliminated. However, the *Loya* Favood knew that once the Azar ruler realized that the plan was not working, nothing would stop the destruction of your people."

"If they couldn't live then no one would. What a race!"

"Something like that," Zooric admitted reluctantly.

"So, what happened?"

"The *Loya* Favood was able to keep his experiment going. He managed to convince the Azars that his plan needed a few generations before proving itself. He kept your people alive and did not inform the ruler. He was also able to move many Owoon children to a safe sector. In the time of *Loya* Favood, already forty alifees had passed without the birth of a single Azar baby. The population was not reproducing, so the Azars would eventually all die. I think the *Loya* Favood sped up the process and helped in the destruction of his own people rather than let them destroy your people and ours.

He must have introduced a slow acting poison or something. There were many reported deaths from unknow causes and at that time the Azars were virtually immortal. These deaths were unusual. In his writings he blamed the defective gene in the population for the deaths.

I have been into another of the Azar's sector. It is to the south of my home. They are fabulous places. These people had technology far in advance of ours. I think the sector I visited was the last fully inhabited sector of the Azars and was perhaps the safe sector that Owoon children were taken to."

"Wow!" Carrie was silent for a minute. "In a way I guess I feel sorry for them."

Zooric nodded. "It is a sad history."

She turned fully to him. "But do you realize what this means?"

"What does it mean?"

"You are human."

"Meaning I am no longer a monstrous alien," he said teasingly.

"You promised not to read my mind."

"I cannot read your mind and I did not even have to read your emotions. It was clear what you were thinking."

"Humm." Carrie said as she started to rise.

"Wait. It is time for you to tell me about your people." Zooric invited.

Carrie sank down again. "Did your people never try to contact us?"

"I am not sure how much they know. Many alifees ago I discovered an old Azar sector and I found the electro writings of the great psychic, *Loya* Favood. But I do not think this information was known to my people. Before I left my home, I gave the rulers all the information that I discovered. So, it is possible my people will try to contact yours."

With a nod of understanding Carrie started her tale. "Well, there really is not much that I can tell you. New World City was the first settlement. There, the Presidential Council dictates everything. Those bunch of stooges control every aspect of life in the New World City. After girls reach puberty, seeing a boy alone, or even after a marriage contract is signed, is strictly forbidden. All women are required to contract and marry by age eighteen — men by age twenty-five. The Council must approve the marriage contract and the marriage has to take place no later than four years after the contract. And there is worse. Once married, the Council determines when you can have a child and how many children you can have.

"Why is your Council so rigid?" Zooric focused on the most puzzling aspect of her words.

She sighed. "Because there were so few of us in the beginning, they wanted to ensure there was always the correct male to female ratio. Also, all the people on planet Earth did not look alike. There were many races and often the races did not get along. The Presidential Council wanted to create one race of people here on Alloca. They did not want race wars over minor differences in skin color, hair color, features or anything. No one is allowed to violate the rule. I don't think anyone has ever violated a rule of the Presidential Council."

"Is the punishment very severe?"

"Yes! Minor punishment could involve several years of forced labor, or if they find that you disagree with a policy, they will force you to marry someone closest to someone you most dislike. You dare not refuse, and it is like living with a spy in your household for the rest of your life. Everything you say or do is recorded. We know of two men who are living this punishment. One tried to commit suicide after only 700 cycles of marriage. The suicide attempt failed so now he is in permanent forced labor. But he was also forced to give sperm transfers to his wife so now she has three children. Permanent forced labor is usually used as a major punishment, but they could also take your children away and give then to another couple or give them into servitude. In the New World City my seventeen-year-old cousin, is only one year younger than I am and is already contracted to marry."

"Are you contracted to marry?"

"Yes," she gave him a haunted look. "My father founded Arapmo. We all thought that Arapmo was far enough away from the city to escape the dictates of the Presidential Council. And at first, they left us alone, but for the last few years they have suddenly decided to get involved with us. Perhaps because we have begun to draw so many people from New World City. I am the third person to get a marriage contract. The other two—a boy and a girl—both went back to New World City to marry."

Zooric straightened. "When?" he asked abruptly. "When do you have to go?"

"I don't want to go. I want to marry someone here in Arapmo and my father doesn't want me to go either." Carrie drew up her knees to her chest and wrapped her hands around them. She looked down. "The Arapmo Council agreed with him. We petitioned the Presidential Council to cancel the marriage contract. Now we have to wait for their answer." She turned to him. "Oh Zooric. I am so afraid there will be a war. And Arapmo is too small to win. I'm just afraid. My family may be forced to move back to New World City as a punishment."

****

Chapter 9

Zooric reached for her. There was absolutely no way he was going to let her go to a strange Tifoosa. Caree was his. He wanted her. True, she was affecting him in ways that left him frustrated and uncertain. The last time he had felt such widely swinging emotions, he had been a pre-adolescent. Since meeting Caree, he had lost much of his emotional control. Yet he knew that his irritation was mostly directed at himself. She was upset by his attitude, and he was annoyed because her distress was affecting him. Striving for calm, he continued to hold her. He also needed her. But now was perhaps not the time to bring up his needs.

Immediately the now familiar zing of a linking started. He slid back to the ground taking Carrie with him. For once in his life, he wanted to deliberately lose himself in a linking. Slow even breaths he cautioned. But he was only just maintaining a measure of control. His nostrils flared as he forced his breathing to slow. He held her tightly as he stared at the ceiling.

"Zooric?"

He could sense her discomfort at the feelings generated by the link.

"Shhh," he murmured soothingly. "I will not do anything more than a low-link."

For a few minutes Carrie was still. But then she began shifting nervously and Zooric realized that she could not relax and enjoy the pleasure she was undoubtedly receiving. Reluctantly, he released her. She was not yet comfortable with him. Still, he was not worried. Time was on his side. He would be patient and gentle— giving her space and time to become accustomed to him and to trust him. But he meant to have her in the end!

Over the course of the next 20 cycles, Zooric slowly healed. He tried to strengthen the original support Caree had made for his legs; however, it still did not permit walking so he was unable to help Caree gather wood for their fire. With a makeshift crutch, he was able to stand for short periods, and he did get the well working, which saved Caree the need to get water from the stream. Like most of the Azar's machinery the well operated by electricity. Fortunately, Zooric was able to bypass the electrical operation and install a pulley system, which allowed them to suspend a bucket into the well each time they needed to collect water. The cooking units were another problem. Despite his best efforts—and he tried repeatedly—he was unable to get any to work. Perhaps some other mechanical part was broken.

"I don't mind getting wood for the fire," Carrie tried to reassure him.

"I mind," Zooric shot back. "I do not like that you have to leave here and go out alone." He also hated it when she when outside his sensory range. It was something that he had not mentioned to her.

"There is no one in these woods. And I go in the light so there is no chance of a paw attack."

"There are other wild animals."

Clearly, she did not believe him. "I do not know of any animal that would attack a large moving target in the light."

He scowled because he knew she felt he was trying to scare her "Perhaps not, but all animals are predators.

They will attack if they are hungry enough, so you must still be careful. Always take Soor with you."

It was with mild frustration that Carrie accepted Zooric's suggestions. He realized it was given more to placate him rather than her belief in any apparent danger. Their disagreement over the perceived danger led to their first big quarrel and some startling revelations. It began simple enough.

****

One cycle, in her search for firewood, Carrie heard Zooric's mental call.

"Caree you are going too far."

"How do you know how far I am going?" Carrie demanded then realized that he could not hear her. While she could hear his mental-speak across distances, she could not speak back. Carrie slowed, even stopping to look around. She was following a small animal's trail and had just passed the river and waterfall where Zooric had fallen. But she was growing to love the sounds of the woods. The birds of Alloca were a colorful lot—and so numerous. Even in the light, the sounds of their calls and cries were like music. Eventually, she planned to sit and study all the birds and their sounds. Humming softly to the tune of one of the birds, Carrie decided to continue. However, less than a minute later, she stopped. She was getting goose pimples on her arms, and plus she was beginning to feel uneasy. Was Zooric okay? Then she heard him again, mentally.

"Caree! Why are you going so far?"

Rubbing her arms, she looked around. Soor was happily investigating the shrubs. There was nothing wrong! Yet she felt uneasy. Was Zooric the cause? She suspected that Zooric could somehow sense where she was, and it irked her that he refused to admit it.

"Come back!" He now demanded. Carrie was about to turn when she felt it—a sharp pain in her head. He had buzzed her! She was outraged, although it was not even half as bad as the first time he had done so. Blinded by a rising fury, Carrie began running back in the direction of their camp. How dare he try to control her? How dare he buzz her?

She was still furious when she burst into the camp. Zooric was sitting. To her surprise he was holding his head, almost as if in pain. Carrie paused momentarily, but as he lowered his arms her fury returned. Standing breathlessly in front of him she began shouting.

"Don't ever do that to me again! Do you hear me?"

"Caree, I am sorry."

She continued screaming at him in fury and was angrier still when he remained silent, his face tautly expressionless as he stared at her.

When she finally paused for breath Zooric again apologized.

"Oo galee." Zooric had switched to mental speak, but at first Carrie was still too angry to notice. However, it suddenly dawned on her that he was acting strangely. He was too still, too silent plus, he was speaking mentally and he only did so when too weak to communicate otherwise.

Her fury fled. "Zooric are you alright?"

His response was to close his eyes. Then he released a ragged breath and slowly lowered himself to theground. Lying supine, he brought both hands up to support his head.

"Zooric?" Carrie was suddenly frantic.

"Caree, please no more," he begged without opening his eyes.

"What? What are you talking about?" Carrie bent over him. "Zooric?" She started getting panicky when there was no response.

At that Zooric opened his eyes to stare straight at her. She was close enough to realize that his eyes were clouded in pain.

"Your leg?" She asked, turning to look down.

"No," he muttered. *"Your emotions."*

"What?"

He groaned. *"Your anger. It hits me here."* He pointed to his head.

Carrie was still puzzled. "What do you mean?"

"I cannot block your emotions easily when you are so angry. You send them like missiles in my head. It hurts."

She rocked back to stare at him in amazement.

"My anger makes your head ache?" she questioned skeptically.

"More than a hurt. Pain. It is pain like someone digging a hole through my brain."

"I see." She didn't, not really, and although Zooric must have sensed her puzzlement, he abruptly began withdrawing.

"It does not matter. I am sorry I buzzed you." He was struggling to rise, and as he spoke, he averted his face.

Carrie watched with a frown. "So why did you?"

When he turned to look at her, his face was once again impassive. "I will not do so again."

It was not an explanation and Carrie was getting angry again. She had noticed that it was a bad habit that Zooric had. He resorted to silence and refused to answer or discuss certain topics. It was an annoyingly bad habit, she was thinking.

"Zooric, don't you think we should discuss this?"

"What is there to discuss?"

"How did you know I was going too far?" she demanded.

Instead of answering, Zooric turned away. "I will get the water."

That did it! White-hot rage hit her. But Carrie didn't get a chance to act out her rage. Zooric gasped, staggered, lost one of his crutches and then his balance.

"Zooric!" she cried out, reaching for him. As she touched him, she felt the zinging of the linking. It had been twenty cycles since they had last experienced this. Carrie had scrupulously avoided touching Zooric because she did not like the feelings generated by the linking. Why he had avoided her had been anyone's guess. Now as she tried to stabilize him and prevent him from falling, she knew!

****

"*Saac ga!*" He cried as he released the other crutch and his arms tightened around her. Then he bent his head sealing her mouth with his. The muted flow of emotions became a flood. Zooric groaned, pulling her tighter against his body.

"Zooric you will fall!" Carrie cried. She was afraid. She had never felt so overwhelmed before. Then she remembered. This was like the first time — in the woods — and as before she was flooded with Zooric's thoughts, with his emotion. Now she knew. He was afraid of the power he felt she had over him—afraid that she would hurt him. Carrie thought it ludicrous that he felt she had too much control over him. She had always thought she

137

was the one in danger —she was the one with the least power. But for Zooric, this linking that they shared was not as equals. He could only access her emotions, but unless he maintained rigid control, she could get his thoughts, his every feeling. And pressed tightly against him as she was, Carrie was suddenly fearful of his present feelings. She was not totally innocent. She was well aware of Zooric's arousal. But she was not sure she wanted this— not now, not with him. Pulling her lips away, she buried her face in his chest. He was shaking—shivering really.

"Zooric!"

With another groan, Zooric tried pulling away both mentally and physically. They both staggered.

"Sit down!" Carrie was also beginning to feel a throbbing pain in her leg, which she knew was from Zooric. "You need to sit. Zooric!"

He allowed her to guide him to the floor.

"Leave me now," Zooric muttered.

But Carrie had no intension of even releasing him. Although she was sure he would never admit it out loud, she now knew that he had very strong possessive feelings for her, and these feelings were not solely based on need. But Zooric was still too secretive by far. Nevertheless, the insight she had just gained into his character had calmed her own fears. She was secretly thrilled by the discovery of her powers. So, the colonists were not totally defenseless after all! Finally free of fear, she relaxed. She was now willing to do whatever she could to help. As she held him, she could still feel his mental struggles to stop sending her his emotions and thoughts. But he was doing an extremely poor job. Somehow, she had weakened his control over his electro-sensory skills.

Her leg was still throbbing with an intensity that was beginning to worry her. But then she realized that Zooric's biggest struggle appeared to be his effort to control his passion. He wanted her but wanted her to be willing. Given choices—and here he had to choose between controlling his thoughts, his emotions or his passion—he had chosen to first control his passion. He did not want to scare her or force her sexually. Then, as much as he hated exposing his deepest thoughts to her, his next priority had been to control the pain he was sending her—his emotions. The total unselfishness of what he was doing moved Carrie deeply.

Kneeling beside him, she began gently stroking his face. "Does this help or make it worse," she asked.

Zooric's eyes were closed. "A low-link will help." Tiny shivers were now racking his body yet he was sweating, his breathing ragged.

"You should have told me."

Instead of responding, he initiated a link and Carrie felt the low tingling of electricity— a low-link.

"Instead of ordering me to stay close, all you had to do was explain that you could sense when I went too far out and explain that it worried you."

Again, no response, but she could tell he was listening.

"I also get panicky when I go too far from you, but I did not understand that you were the cause. Just now in the woods I came out in goose-pimples, but I just assumed that I was scared of being left alone."

Although he still did not respond, Zooric was now staring at her. And she was also aware of his curiosity.

Carrie nodded. "I now understand the reason. I am picking up your signals to me, so I can sort of sense when you are near. How do you think I feel to have an alien invade my mind and read my thoughts?"

"Your emotions. I can only read your emotions. You can read my thoughts."

"Only when you lose control."

"As I just did," Zooric growled.

Carrie smiled. He had regained control. She was no longer getting his thoughts— unfortunately. She traced his lips with her fingertips.

Zooric's eyes narrowed. "Do not play with me Caree," he warned.

She flushed, abruptly withdrawing her fingers. "I did not mean..."

Her voice trailed off as Zooric unexpectedly caused a linking by bringing the palm of her hands to his lips. He watched her as her flush deepened. "You do not know what you want."

She didn't. But it was an exhilarating feeling, knowing she had so much control over him.

"Does my anger really cause you much pain?"

He nodded, his eyes darkening. "I can always pick up your signals—just general signals announcing your presence. Then you unconsciously send your emotions, which I can normally tolerate or block if they become too disturbing. But when they are intense, as in anger, I find it hard to block them, and if we touch, I definitely am forced to take them. It is like the linking. They are so intense that I suspect you may be able to control the sending of them."

"I will try," Carrie was doubtful. She had not even realized that she was sending anything.

"Perhaps with time..." he allowed his voice to trail off as he again brought her palm to his lips.

Carrie's mouth opened on a gasp as a bolt of pure pleasure coursed through her with the linking.

"You said...." she was trembling slightly as she attempted to remove her hand.

"I know what I said, but I have changed my mind. As long as I am not weakened or hampered by your anger, we can both enjoy the pleasure of a low linking. There is no harm in it."

"There isn't?" Carrie was uncertain as she pulled away.

But Zooric's normally expressionless face broke into a slight smile. "There is not." He was emphatic.

****

Chapter 10

The next 10 cycles were totally different from the previous twenty. The biggest difference being the repeated low-level linking that Zooric encouraged. He was constantly touching her, kissing her hands or fingers, prompting her to link with him. Yet it was never enough for him to lose control. Carrie did not get his thoughts, although his emotions were clear enough. Besides, even though he never brought her in close contact with his body, his arousal was obvious, and soon the linkings were leaving her weak with longing and wanting more.

They had established a routine by now. Carrie usually left at first-light to collect firewood, while Zooric, still unable to walk fully upright, was forced to drag himself about the rooms. He was getting increasingly frustrated at his inability to help. Most cycles, apart from tinkering with the machinery, he could do little else but help with the cooking. Meanwhile, Carrie had to care for the animals, drag buckets of water about, plus help him.

After a frustrating morning of again trying to fix the cooking machine of the Azar, Zooric decided to try walking. After all it was now thirty cycles since his injury. Using his makeshift crutch and holding to a piece of furniture, he dragged himself upright. His leg throbbed in warning. He gritted his teeth and held on; then taking a deep breath he tried to take a step.

"Aaah," he gasped. The throbbing in his leg had increased and he knew he would not be able to make it.

Carrie suddenly rushed in. "Zooric!" Her voice was high in panic. "What happened?"

Zooric turned abruptly, but the sudden movement caused him to lose his balance. He only just managed to twist so that he landed on his good side. Even so the sudden pain was nearly unbearable.

As he laid panting and striving to control the pain shooting up his leg, Carrie bent over him.

"What did you do to yourself? Oh, Zooric. I told you not to try walking. What if you broke your leg again? Oh, Zooric!"

Her panic reached him, but Zooric couldn't answer immediately. He needed all his concentration to prevent the pain from overwhelming them both. And he knew he was having only moderate success.

She reached for him. "Let me link with you."

"*Zte.*" Zooric tried to push her away but did not have the strength. It was one of those times when a low-level linking could easily spiral out of control. After the initial first few cycles, when he had been too sick to care, he found these low-level linking as pleasurable as she did. But after these past cycles of repeated linkings he was finding it increasingly difficult to maintain control over his reactions. At any other time, he would have been able to handle the linking but not now, not when he was barely in control.

Now, as she held him after his one feeble attempt to push her away, Zooric gave up. He breathed deeply as the linking flowed through them both. He needed this!

"*T'veetox!*" Zooric sucked in a gasp of air as his control slipped. Carrie shifted in his arms again, despite his urging her not to move. "Caree!" Caree did not seem to realize the power she had over him. There was no way he could control this linking.

"It's okay Zooric. It's okay."

He gave a guttural laugh. It was far from okay. He would not be able to stop! With a groan, he gave up the losing battle, treaded his fingers into her hair and brought her mouth to his. The result was even better than their first attempt in the woods. The surge of pleasure almost blew his mind. Zooric rolled over tucking her under him. A stab of pain reminded him to take care of his leg.

"Your leg," Carrie had felt the pain too.

"Hush. Hush," he murmured, feverishly running his hand over her clothing, in his need to find an opening.

"Wait!" Carrie unexpectedly came to his aid.... perhaps not so unexpectedly. He knew she was feeling as much pleasure as he was. On contact he had lost the battle to block her emotions or even stop feeding her, his.

Carrie brought her hands up and quickly released the looping ties of her blouse.

Zooric fumbled impatiently with the ties on her outer clothing. He had never done this before, but his knowledge was not only instinctive. He had made it his business to learn as much as he could about Tifoosas, both males and females. And the Writing of *Loya* Favood contained detailed observations of their mating rituals. However, the dry clinical knowledge he had obtained in no way prepared him for the reality of the intense emotional onslaught. Besides, at this point, he was too desperate to show much finesse. "Caree... I need.... Caree..." He could not wait! He bunched up her loose skirt seeking an entrance. He was in!

"Aaahh," Carrie cried out and Zooric flinched at her pain. He drew a ragged breath. He had realized too late that this was Caree's first time. He should have prepared her more. But at least now that he was where he wanted to be, he was no longer so frantic.

As she whimpered and pushed ineffectively at his chest, trying to pull away from him and ease her pain, he understood. Linked as they were, Zooric felt both her fear and her needs. She wanted him—but she was not ready. He knew he would have to take care of her fears and meet her needs before continuing.

He murmured, stroking her intimately —calming her, both mentally and physically— forcing himself to slow down and ease her fears because no way was he going to withdraw.

Carrie finally gave up her feeble protest. As she relaxed, Zooric's urgency returned. He began to move inside her. Carrie's breath was coming in gasps as waves upon waves of pleasure swamped her. She wrapped her legs around his thighs, pulling him deeper. Zooric suddenly groaned aloud, lifting slightly for one last plunge. With an explosive shout, he poured a liquid heat into her body. It was accompanied by a surge of electricity that tingled every nerve ending.

Zooric breathed in her disbelief, her amazement. Her scream was one of pure mind shattering pleasure. He was barely aware of collapsing on her. He knew she was in a semi- conscious daze. In fact, for the next few minutes, neither of them was aware of anything.

****

It was the pulsating pain in Carrie's leg that finally forced her to awareness.

"Zooric," she murmured. If she was in such pain, she couldn't imagine what Zooric was feeling.

Zooric reluctantly shifted his position to ease the pain in his leg. He gently lifted Carrie's chin to meet her eyes. Carrie flushed. She still could not believe what she had just experienced.

"Are you okay?" he asked.

She nodded shyly. She had never done this before. But from their intimate linking she also knew that neither had he. What she wondered was why? As far as she knew, within her family circle, only her younger brother had never had a woman. Often Carrie had secretly listened to her older brother and Derrick as they discussed their relationships. And Zooric was only a year younger than Derrick. Derrick! She had not thought about him since meeting Zooric. It was not long ago that she had hoped to marry him. Carrie shifted guilty, causing Zooric to shift again.

"Your leg," she cautioned.

Zooric grimaced. He was making no effort to hide his emotions—Carrie was getting both his pain and his pleasure. He literally did not have the energy to stop the open electro- sensory flow. After resting a few more minutes, his hands began gently caressing her again. He was also removing her clothing. Carrie willingly brought her mouth up to his. This time the kiss was a gently giving. A delicious throbbing began spreading throughout her body. Carrie could not believe the intensity of her feelings. She shifted restlessly, moaning her needs. Zooric's mouth moved to her breast, then back to her lips, as he began moving inside her again. At the intense mounting pleasure, Carrie locked her hand around his neck, as Zooric surged into her again on another powerful discharge. An unbelievable euphoria high filled her. It was spectacular! Minutes after her tumultuous release, intense shivers still racked her body. Zooric had collapsed on her again. Carrie soothed her hands over his sweat slicked back. She was replete. She was also drowsy but the pain in her leg was keeping her awake.

"Zooric," she murmured. He was a dead weight.

"*I cannot move,*" he muttered.

Carrie giggled.

However, the stabbing pain soon got him moving. He rolled over again taking her with him. They were still linked, both mentally and physically, but this time Carrie was on top.

Carrie lifted her head only to bury it in his neck. As they both relaxed, other feelings and emotions took over. The low electro link had not ceased. It was weird. At first Carrie was confused as she began receiving the tortuous scenes. They were indistinct— never lingering long enough for her to figure out what was happening. Then it clicked. She was getting Zooric's thoughts, snippets of his past! As her horror mounted, she raised her head.

"Zooric?" Carrie was appalled.

He said nothing; he did not have to. The level and length of the linking had weakened his control. Once started, it seemed the flood of thoughts could not stop. Carrie was getting it all—the abuse, the beating, and the torture—both physical and mental. Even worse, the abuse was often ghastly superimposed on the special privileges his parents had lavished on him…. Then there was his desperate craving to be normal….

Abruptly, Zooric tried to dislodge her.

Carrie held on firmly. She was now aware of Zooric's frantic and largely futile attempts at control. She knew he wanted a privacy that he had no hope of achieving with her close contact. And she did not want him putting his control back into place. Not now! Not when she was so close to understanding him.

"I do not want your pity," he cried.

"You know I don't pity you," she protested.

"You feel sorry for me. You...." Again, he tried to move her.

But Carrie stubbornly held on. "I don't pity you Zooric. Whatever happened should never have happened. I am sorry you suffered so, but that isn't the same as pity," she insisted. "How can you blame yourself when someone does something bad to you?"

"Leave me," he said harshly.

"No! Zooric, listen to me. You were a child. The adults were wrong, not you. I don't pity you."

Zooric made a sound—much like an animal in pain. Carrie tightened her hold on him. He broke down. Carrie was surprised yet pleased as he buried his head in her chest. His shoulders shook as he cried—silently. She was sure he would never have revealed so much of himself to her if he did not trust her. As she stroked his back, Carrie was fiercely glad that the intimacy they had just shared had given him the confidence to trust her. He needed this release!

Knowing it would sooth him Carrie wished she could initiate a link. "Link with me," she urged.

Still, he hesitated. Carrie continued holding him until he relented. As she had suspected, the linking soothed him. With a deeper contact, such as during the sex act, the linking was incredibly erotic. By itself, Carrie surmised the linking was a mild pleasurable feeling, both calming and healing.

Carrie began abstractedly smoothing the healing scar on his temple. It was not that obvious even though it was a bit jagged because the wound was never stitched. Zooric did not move. His face was still buried in her chest and although his breathing was now normal, she was still getting his chaotic emotions.

She ran her fingers through his hair. She had cut it just twenty cycles ago at Zooric's request, and was quite pleased with her effort, especially considering that it was the first time she had ever given a haircut. And her hair cutting was a marked improvement over the jagged mess that was Zooric's best attempt. She gently pulled at the tight curls. As she pulled a single strand loose, she marveled at its length. She released the strand and watched as it settled contentedly among its fellows. Very reluctantly she looked up. She hated disturbing this calm, but she had only received disconnected snippets of his past. She needed to understand; she wanted to understand and Zooric needed to talk!

"Why?" she asked when he remained silent.

Zooric slowly raised his head. His eyes met hers briefly. They were suspiciously red and cloudy, but he quickly closed them in a deliberate effort to shut her out. Carrie persisted. "Your past is like a wound. It will fester if not exposed and cleaned."

He refused to make eye contact.

"Zooric?" she pleaded. He shifted, lifted his head and pulled her up. For a minute, Carrie was fearful that he would push her away, then to her relief he abruptly tucked her head into his shoulder and began to talk.

"The Soosans are the rulers of the Owoon people." His voice was low, hesitant... Carrie could literally feel his reluctance. There was a substantial pause before he continued. "A Soosan does not develop his unique sensitive ability until first-link at full puberty. But only males develop these skills, so all Soosans are males and there is no reproduction. They live in an all-male society in the Soosan sector and can fill their ranks only by depending on the sporadic birth of a Soosan in the general population."

"You told me you were a sensitive," Carrie raised her head. "Is that the same as being a Soosan?"

"Perhaps... most likely. All Soosans are sensitive but I was never tested."

He did not explain further and although Carrie had more questions, she relaxed on his shoulder, deciding to wait and let him tell his story at his own pace.

"At puberty all boys are tested. If they test sensitive, they become Soosan, and they leave their family, friends—everyone—and move into the Soosan sector. There they stay, learning the tenets of the Soosan, sometimes for the rest of their lives. No Soosan under forty alifees is allowed to leave the Soosan sector, mainly because they believe that over that age a Soosan would have more control of his talents and would be less likely to accidentally kill an ordinary Owoon."

Although Zooric did not immediately continue, Carrie did not prompt him. She kept her head on his shoulder and began drawing mindless patterns on his body with her fingers. She was determined to wait him out, and her patience was rewarded when he took a deep heaving breath.

"Because no Soosan had ever given birth to a child, not many boys were becoming Soosans. Many cycles ago, a Soosan leader, *Jirga* Restric, decided that the gene that gave rise to a Soosan was becoming diluted in the general population. The Soosans were able to convince about thirty women to volunteer to have babies with a Soosan father. The women were brought into the Soosan sector, then artificially given a sperm transfer."

"Artificially?"

"Soosans do not have any form of sexual contact with women. Because of the linking, any sexual intercourse with a woman will either kill the woman or leave her permanently maimed."

"But we..."

"You are different. I do not know why. Perhaps all the women among your people are like you." He paused thoughtfully, "Or perhaps the Soosan never thought to test our females." He was now absently caressing her as he continued. "Twenty-two children were born from the experiment. Fifteen were boys."

"You?"

"*Eeng*. Everyone thought all fifteen of us boys would grow to be sensitives, to be a Soosan. We were all told we would soon be Soosan, so we did not need to learn or do any of the normal chores of ordinary boys."

He gave her a brief background history of his family. "My family lived on a farm outside Caleel. They were very poor when they decided to take part in the Soosan's experiment. The parents of any Soosan child are usually greatly compensated, but the compensation would not occur until the child reached puberty. However, money alone was not the only reason my parents participated. It was considered a great honor to have a Soosan child. Very soon however, my parents became apologetic because they could not give me the idle life of the other boys of Soosan fathers. They tried so hard to give me extra privileges, to do things that I knew they could not really afford. They refused to listen when I told them I did not need anything extra. I did not mind the work—this was all I knew. I really enjoyed helping my father on the farm. He also tracked animals and sold animal skin so I would spend many cycles living and sleeping in the woods with him, checking, emptying and resetting the traps. Then everything changed when I reached fourteen alifees."

This pause was so long that Carrie decided on a prompt, "What happened when you were fourteen years old?"

Zooric's body was tense again, yet when he finally started talking, he did not really answer the question. He seemed to be backtracking. "There were three areas that these boys of Soosans fathers were. Five were on the outside, far from the town, six lived in Caleel—in the town, and the rest were near the Soosan sector. The lucky ones were the four raised near the sector. They were under the direct eye of the Soosans; no one bothered them." He stopped. "Caree...." His voice trailed off.

Carrie said nothing. He was a smart man. She was sure he would eventually accept that she was not going to move until he told her the entire story.

His hands tightened in her hair as he reluctantly continued. "A man named Deeknor came to our farm. He told my parents he had raised a Soosan before and knew how a Soosan should live. He would give me all the privileges of a Soosan lifestyle now. I would live a life of luxury until my first-link. He brought with him the son of his sister. This boy was named Restric. Restric too told us how much the brother of his mother would help me. He told me how much better life would be for me if I lived with others like me. He showed me images of a large house in the town where I would live. I did not want to go, but my parents were convinced it would be better for me, and although I did eventually believe him, I just did not want to leave my family. But they had always felt guilty about not providing what they felt was best for me. This they thought would be good. Besides, they and I both thought that I would test Soosan at first-link. I would have to leave them anyway. To make the deal even better, Deeknor offered to pay my parents enough so that my father would be able to hire help for two alifees. He said it would be an honor to be able to teach a Soosan."

"So, you went to live with Restric and the other boys?" she asked when he again stopped.

He was silent.

This time Carrie did not attempt a prompt, and when Zooric finally started speaking, he was again using delaying tactics, giving other related details.

"There was another man. I now believe that the men felt that if they could control us as children, they would be able to control us later. They wished for control of the Soosan. For the first time in history, they thought they knew who would be a Soosan." He took a deep, ragged breath. "Hold me," he muttered.

Carrie wrapped her arms around him, understanding his plea to link.

He breathed into the link. It calmed him somewhat, but his breathing was still uneven and his voice even lower when at last he resumed. "In all Deeknor collected five boys. Most, like I, came from the outside. Their parents too, sought to give them a better life. We were all brought to the house he had shown us in the picture. But Restric was the only one who could come and go. Restric and another boy were named after the *Jirga* Restric who first planned the experiment. But because he was leader, the boy Restric was the only one allowed to use the name."

"Was Restric the oldest?"

"We were all born around the same time. He was the second oldest. But he was the biggest and strongest — mentally — even then."

"They shaved our heads and kept us naked." A rough sigh followed. "I was told that this behavior was normal for the Soosan. We were told we needed to prepare for life in the Soosan sector. Only a male can become a Soosan. This I knew to be true. They also insisted that we live the lifestyle of the Soosans."

"What lifestyle was that?"

No answer.

"If we were good, we got extra privileges."

Carrie was afraid to ask what 'good' was. Lying on him as she was, she could feel his racing heart and was unable to avoid what were clearly his painful emotions however, he had regained enough control to block his thoughts.

Again, a long pause.... Carrie thought he was not going to continue, and when he finally found his speech, it was halting and low. Although she was lying on him, she could hardly hear him.

"The men... the men were... they were sexually abusing the boys — abusing us. We... we had to... we were... expected to practice... to practice on each other."

"Is that the life style of the Soosan?"

"Soosans do not abuse children," Zooric said violently, "Besides they are adults. None are forced into unwanted relationships, and anything can be normal with consenting adult."

Again, he tried to push her away from him, but once again Carrie refused to budge. Zooric finally dragged them both until he was sitting upright, leaning against the wall.

He sounded angry with himself as he continued. "We all wanted to live as Soosans — as good Soosans. They were able to convince us that we had to do this. I wanted so much to fit in that I pretended I liked what they were doing to me. But for us boys, the aim was to achieve an erection and to climax. This was the way to show that we enjoyed what we were doing. It was drummed into us that we had to enjoy this. If you could not enjoy yourself, we were told we would never be good." Zooric drew a ragged breath. "So, we had to pretend we liked what they were doing to us and what we were doing to each other." He stared up at the roof. "I can't believe I am telling you this," he muttered.

"Well, you needed to tell someone." Carrie said fiercely. Her heart tightened when she thought of his years of both mental and physical abuse.

He sighed but did not look down. "I hated it! *Saac ga!*"

Carrie lifted her head to stare at him. "It was a form of brain washing. What they did to you was cold blooded abuse."

Carrie gave him a squeeze as he grunted, refusing to answer. Then she again tucked her face into his shoulder. "Go on."

"I had never heard of sexual abuse of children within the Owoon society. I had never even believed that such was possible. Normal linking for the Owoon is an involuntary act at sexual completion, and if a man did such with a child, the child is maimed for life by a sizzle. A mentally damaged child would draw the notice of the Soosan Protectors. These men got around that by always withdrawing before completion." Zooric gave a rough laugh. "The only boy who really loved it was Restric."

"The leader?"

"Hmm." Zooric grimaced. "I think Restric truly loved Deeknor. Would you believe, while we all tolerated the abuse because we felt this was something we had to like, Restric saw the abuse as a treat. He was jealous, and we all suffered whenever he was not the one chosen by Deeknor."

"Maybe he was just too badly brainwashed and abused," Carrie suggested tentatively."

"*Zte*! That I do not believe! Restric was evil! Not only did he enjoy the abuse, but he also enjoyed inflecting pain one anyone who dared to oppose him." Again, he paused. "One light, about 200 cycles after I arrived at the house, I decided I could take it no longer. I was done with pretending. Besides, I was finding it harder and harder to pretend — to perform. Sometimes I was unable to, which was twice as bad as.... I was mocked... The other boys...." he did not continue, instead he abruptly moved on. "I wanted to leave, especially when the men accidentally sizzled and killed one of the boys. I do not know how they were able to hide his death from the Soosan. I asked them to take me home, but first I was told that my parents had already spent the money and could not repay the men for the time that they had trained me. Then they refused to let me write to my parents or contact them in any way. They insisted that as a Soosan I would not be able to see my family again, so I should get used to it. This was true, but still I became angry. Finally, I just refused to cooperate and refuse to do as they asked."

He slid down onto his back, pulling Carrie with him. His hands restlessly massaged her scalp, running down her back only to move back up again. This time he did not continue.

Carrie looked up. His eyes were closed. He could not block his emotions, but he was actively blocking his thoughts. She could feel him withdrawing. "Zooric?"

"It was almost 50 cycles later before I escaped." His voice was soft, and he had switched to mental-speak. Even without getting his swirling emotions and feelings from the tension gripping his body, Carrie knew that whatever had happened in that time, Zooric could not yet speak of it.

Carrie began stroking him gently.

Zooric continued flatly. *"Eventually I went back to my family."*

"What happened to the men who kidnapped you?"

Some of the stiffness left his body. "After I escaped, they came to my father's farm to find me. Fortunately, I was not there. I lived in the woods south of Caleel for 6 alifees, mainly because I was afraid the men would capture me again. When the men left my father's farm, my father reported Deeknor to the Soosan. I recently learned that when the Soosan found out what Deeknor had done they arrested him. Deeknor and his friend were brought before the Soosan Grand Assembly, evaluated and sizzled." Zooric's voice was devoid of expression.

She stared up at him. "You mean..."

He nodded. "After a sizzle you become a shadow of your former self. The Soosan can give very precise electro-sizzles. Because the sizzle is concentrated in the frontal lobe of the brain, it can be just enough that the person will no longer be able to retain a memory of any future event. They will have a memory of their past—of everything up to the point of the sizzle —but after that nothing stays in their minds. They will meet you now then meet you just one hour later and not remember the first meeting."

"That is awful."

"It is a living death," he agreed without apology. "Those who have been sizzled are called subeets. Perhaps I should not wish it on anyone, but these men deserved it. They now live under the protection of the Soosans — they work either for the Soosan or are hired by the hour by anyone wishing menial labor."

Carrie shivered. "What other crimes do they electro-sizzle for."

"Murder. I know of only two other subeets in all of Caleel."

"It is a very final type of justice."

"So is murder."

Again, his voice was without expression, yet Carrie was still getting his raw emotions. She wanted to ask more questions but knew that Zooric needed her right now. He was still holding so much in! She looked up. His expression was stark — his eyes almost black with remembered pain. "Oh Zooric." She pulled herself higher pressing her mouth to his, and immediately they linked.

Zooric inhaled sharply. "Caree..." A throbbing need gripped Carrie as Zooric took control of the kiss. He brought his hands up to caress her breast before moving to replace his fingers with his lips. Next, he moved his hands further down, intimately caressing her. Carrie felt boneless as she shattered in an explosion of pleasure. Zooric still held her tightly, although this time she noticed that he was in full control. She no longer had access to his thoughts. He shifted slightly to the side but not to dislodge her. He was merely reaching for the blanket. He pulled it over them.

"Perhaps I can help your people." Zooric murmured in her hair.

Carrie looked up startled. "Your people would help us."

"I cannot speak for my people. But I will definitely help."

"Oh Zooric!" Carrie's mind raced as she considered the possibilities. Even with only Zooric's help, the people of Arapmo had a better chance. She snuggled closer, and they easily fell asleep.

****

Chapter 11

Five cycles later, Zooric decided to tell Carrie about the Azar sector. His leg was much better now and with his crude crutch, he was able to walk for short periods of time. Most of that time was spent exploring the area they were in. Six separate rooms entered directly into the main hall. Some of those rooms then lead into other chambers. Two were large public bathrooms but there were also private bathrooms attached to some of the other rooms. Zooric was unable to get the plumbing in any of the private bathroom working so they had stopped using them since the result was to smell up their living area.

A passage off the main hall also led to separate living areas. There were distinct bedrooms and cooking areas. The problem was there was no light, so Carrie could not explore. Zooric could, because, whenever he went, he used his electro skills to light the area.

They had moved their belongings to a room off the large main entrance. Now, with Soor providing regular meat and water that was available, their only need was firewood.

"Come here Caree," he called out soon after they finished the first cycle meal. As she followed him outside, he pointed to the blocked walls. "Watch the walls," he directed.

"What walls?"

"We are at the entrance of the Azar sector. This was their traveler's receiving center. Every large sector had one. And according to the Writings of *Loya* Favood, this was a very large sector. The population, during the time

Loya Favood lived, was about 20,000. See those stones?" He pointed to some rather large yet almost totally spherical rocklike balls that rested on a rock shelf that was about ten feet high.

Carrie nodded.

"The Azar were master electrosensors. Most of their world operated using some form of electricity either generated by themselves or by water."

"Sort of how you are able to light those other rooms and I cannot."

"*Eeng*. I found out about this sector while living in Nergeet. Nergeet is the sector south of Caleel. This sector is constructed similar to Nergeet, except that Nergeet does not have this receiving entrance. Entering all sectors involves sending a series of electrical current into the various stones. Somewhat like opening a locked door using a combination of numbers. I found the combination instructions for this sector at Nergeet. Watch!"

Zooric focused on four of the large stones in succession. Staring intently at each for about five seconds. Suddenly, there was a grinding sound. Carrie jumped and tried to back away but Zooric grabbed her, pulling her firmly to his side. She stood and watched as the wall slid into itself. Almost like a sliding door. Revealing a long, wide passageway. Light from the cave's entrance could not penetrate this far. The dark passage sloped gently downward. But even before Carrie had a chance to appreciate this usual sight, a musty smell reached her. She wrinkled her nostrils.

Zooric stepped back, taking her with him. "It is best that we wait for the odors to dispense before venturing in. Perhaps by the next cycle we can explore."

"My god! I don't believe this," Carrie exclaimed. She stared at the shadowy structures lining the wide passageway. "This is the main road, isn't it?"

"*Eeng*. When the Azars lived, these entrances were kept closed. Travelers would be processed from this building we are in. Then, according to *Loya* Favood, if they had the correct travel documents and could pay the travel fees, the officials would then activate the cave-wall opening. It needs a strong burst of electricity to activate the opening. Now, only a sensitive can do so."

"But why is it so musty in there. Didn't they have any ventilation?"

"*Eeng*. But it is possible that some of the ventilation shafts are blocked after so many alifees. On the next cycle we can explore."

However, the next cycle, they did not get very far. Zooric could not negotiate the slope without pain. And he did not want her to go alone. Carrie did not care to go alone either, so they decided that the exploration would have to wait.

The next ten cycles went by slowly. The most important chore was still the collection of firewood from the forest. Unfortunately, this chore was still Carrie's. Using his crutches, Zooric could hobble around only for a few hours before the pain in his leg forced him down. With increasing mobility, however, he was able to tinker with even more of the ancient tools and equipment in the house. Not that he could get many working. But he even found two rusty zooreels, a form of electric car, that the Azar's used for transportation. It could be made to hold two or four people at a time. The two they found were both four-seaters. Zooric explained that his people used a similar means of transport in the town.

In Love with an Alien

****

Early one first-light, 45 cycles after breaking his leg, Zooric was sitting in the front of the house, tinkering as usual, when he felt the first flutter. His head jerked up. Someone was approaching! And Carrie was out collecting firewood! Zooric grabbed for his makeshift crutch but in his panicked struggle to get up quickly, he slipped and fell.

"Aaah," he gasped. Caree! He had to warn Caree! Zooric began sending her urgent mental messages. *"Caree! Hide!"* Then he dragged himself toward the main entrance. With the cave blocking electric signals on three sides, he was unable to accurately assess the danger. Was it his people or hers? *"Hide Caree! Someone is approaching!"* Zooric could not tell if he had reached her in time. Hopefully, Soor would protect her. He was still hobbling toward the entrance when he sensed her terror. He was too late! They had found her! Then came the pain. He gasped in shock, his mind reeling.

The pain faded slowly, but Zooric was trembling. He could no longer sense Carrie. She was either unconscious or dead! At the cave's entrance, he concentrated fiercely. Owoons! There were seven of them; three were Soosans. He focused on the oldest Soosan, sending a compelling mental question.

"What have you done to her?"

"Zooric! Where are you?" Came the immediate reply.

Zooric ignored the question. *"What did you do to the female Tifoosa?"* He demanded.

"How did you know of the Tifoosa? How did you meet her?"

Zooric sent a blast of pure fury at the Soosan. He knew that it translated as a little more than a buzz when the man gasped.

"What did you do to Caree?" He demanded again.

"Dees Sous Zooric! That hurt! Sous Raekon merely stunned her."

"Her system is different. She was in a lot of pain. It was much more than a buzz."

"We are unable to check her, a rocleer is standing guard. How did you know what she felt? And where the dees are you?"

Soor! Zooric thought quickly, and then sent the equivalent of a mental whistle to Soor. He was now glad that he had spent the time training Soor to respond to his mental call.

"Tooaal! Sous Zooric the rocleer is actually leaving. Gaad Sorgan will check the Tifoosa now."

Zooric gave them less than a minute before demanding. *"Is she alive?"*

"Eeng. She is alive. Who is she? How did you meet her?"

Again, Zooric ignored the questions.

"Bring her to me. I am in the Azar sector."

"Are there other Tifoosas around?"

"Zte."

There were more questions but Zooric refused to answer. *"I will answer your questions when you get here with her,"* was all he would say.

He knew there was a strong possibility that he would be placed under arrest. But right now, he did not care. He just wanted to make sure Caree was well. As he started back toward the traveler's center, Soor bounded in. The animal was so clearly agitated that Zooric had to spend a moment calming him down. "It's okay Soor. She will be all right. Those Owoons will be bringing her here in a few minutes." He hugged the rocleer, trying to reassure them both.

Within a few minutes the seven Owoons appeared. Zooric stood, propped up by the wall, and watched them as they approached. He knew one of the Soosan, Raekon, very well and wished it were otherwise. The other two Soosans, *Loyas* Modnar and Meestric, he knew from his brief visit to the Soosan sector. They were members of the Soosan hierarchy. *Loya* Meestric was also second under the *Gaare* Retran, the head of the Soosan Protectors. Of the four non-sensitives, he knew one. All were members of the Soosan Protectors. *Gaad* Keefav, the Protector he knew, carried Carrie. Soor began a low howling bark.

Zooric reached down to calm the rocleer with a pat. "Put her here." He indicated blankets on the floor.

The Owoons could not contain their amazement. They were actually in an Azar sector. Only *Gaad* Keefav, and the *Loyas* Modnar and Meestric entered. Raekon and the other Soosan Protectors remained outside, looking around and exclaiming at the new wonders.

"Dees! You opened it. And this must have been a very large Azar sector," Raekon briefly entered the room. He was brimming with excitement. Like all Soosans, he communicated mentally, directing his comments to all.

Zooric ignored them all. Right now, he could focus only on Caree. He sank to the ground, lifting her head gently to his lap. What if she had been sizzled? His thoughts skittered away from such a horror. Soor, sensing his distress, kept trying to push his large head in Zooric's face, offering comfort in the only way he knew.

"Caree!" He gently stroked her temple, automatically speaking aloud as that was his preferred method of communicating.

"Wake up!"

"How badly is your hurt?" *Loya* Meestric, like Raekon was directing his mental- speak to everyone. He pointed to Zooric's leg.

"Sous Zooric?" He queried Zooric privately when Zooric did not respond.

Zooric looked up. Much as he would like to, he could not ignore them forever. Again, he spoke aloud, this time in Gavaa. "It was broken but it is healing well." Actually, he wasn't sure how it was doing especially after re-injuring it earlier when he fell. There was still a dull throb. He rested his back against the wall of the room and gave them his full attention. He needed to concentrate on blocking their electro signals. He could do nothing for Caree except pray to Tooaal she had not been sizzled. Now he needed to find out why the Soosan had tracked him down. Was he to be punished after all? With his partially healed leg, escaping with Caree would be difficult if not impossible.

"He also opened the true entrance!" one of the Protectors called out. They were still outside looking around.

"What!" *Loya* Meestric, who had been about to sit, instead stood. He exchanged a look with *Loya* Modnar then gave Zooric an astonished look, to which Zooric did not respond. *"I must see this,"* he said as he left the room. The excitement of the others was clearly contagious.

Loya Modnar and *Gaad* Keefav remained. *"Gaads Sorgan and Egell are medics,"* *Loya* Modnar said. *"Perhaps they could take a look at your leg."*

Gaads Sorgan and Egell were outside looking around. "Perhaps," Zooric agreed. His leg was the least of his concerns at the moment, but he kept his tone neutral. It would not do to argue with someone so high in the Soosan hierarchy, besides of all of them present, Zooric respected *Loya* Modnar the most—trusted him the most also. "Why was she buzzed?"

"She screamed when she saw Sous Raekon. He was afraid she would alert others and wished only to silence her."

It was a reasonable explanation, but Zooric's lips tightened. He wanted them gone. "Are you not interested in examining the sector?"

Loya Modnar gave him a gently smile. *"Later."*

Zooric gave him a considering look; then looked toward *Gaad* Keefav. "Is he guarding me or you?"

Loya Modnar looked surprised. *"You have misunderstood Sous Zooric. You are not under arrest."*

Zooric raised his eyebrows in disbelief. "Then why are you here?"

But *Loya* Modnar would not be rushed. *"I would first like to know how you are doing, and why the female Tifoosa is here."* At Zooric's clear expression of impatience, *Loya* Modnar continued calmly. *"But see to her."*

Annoyed, Zooric turned to Carrie. As long as Caree recovered, he did not care what they choose to do with him, but he needed to plan. He did not want her to be hurt. Perhaps they would allow her to go freely if he cooperated. First, however, he wanted her to wake up. Once again, he bent over her, then paused as he heard the others returning.

"We will need light," Raekon was saying as they re-entered the room. They were all brimming with

excitement. *"Will you give permission for us to explore Loya. I have never been in an Azar sector before."*

"Have you forgotten that the sector where we live is an ancient Azar sector?" Loya Meestric asked, smiling indulgently.

Raekon discounted that with a wave. *"You know what I mean,"* he said grinning at both *Loya* Modnar and Meestric in turn. *"This is new. Never been explored before."*

Zooric watched and listened to the by-play.

"Have you been in?" Loya Meestric left Raekon discussing the plans to explore and came to sit by Zooric, *Loya* Modnar and *Gaad* Keefav.

"Zte." Zooric pointed to his leg.

Loya Meestric nodded.

"How did you track me to this sector?" Zooric asked. The question was directed at *Loya* Modnar.

"Your interest in the ancients — your interest in the Tifoosas. We studied the maps that you got from Nergeet and suspected you would either head back to Nergeet or come here. We tried Nergeet first, as it was closer, then headed here." The elder Owoon shrugged. *"We have been searching for over 400 cycles. The current Jirga insisted we find you."*

Zooric nodded. "Are you arresting me?" he asked again. They must have been truly determined to find him to have traveled so far. He was actually surprised. "Did Restric not recover?" He knew he had injured Restric when he escaped the Soosan but he did not think that it was a serious injury. A short search he had expected, but not such an extensive one. And certainly not one aided by three Soosans.

Loya Meestric frowned. *"Zte! You misunderstood. Restric has recovered but he is the one under arrest. This to prevent him from again controlling the sector."*

That speech made no sense to Zooric. Before meeting Carrie, he would have clammed up. Now he frowned in query. "How did he control the sector?"

"Restric had enormous power. Because he was such a high sensitive, he was able to control the Soosan sector. Not many realized this. The current Jirga is extremely grateful that you were able to stop Restric. That is why we allowed you and your relatives to leave."

When *Loya* Meestric paused *Loya* Modnar continued. *"It was only later that the Jirga determined that the extra skills that you and Restric have need to be studied. We cannot trust Restric so we had to find you."*

The implications were clear. But this was news to Zooric. And he did not like it. He wanted to be normal. It was bad enough when he had imagined himself a sensitive. Was he even more different? He could not believe that his electro-sensory skills were more than normal—he did not want to believe. He stared uncertainly at them both. "What extra skills?"

"You were able to open the Azar sector at Nergeet."Loya Modnar explained. *"Only Restric has been able to open closed sector doors in Caleel. It truly would be irresponsible for the Soosan to ignore such skills."*

Zooric could only stare. He refused to be drawn into a commitment. Had he recognized that his skills were different, he would never have made them known. "Did you know about the sector south of Caleel?"

Loya Modnar nodded *"We did, but we were unable to open the entrance door. We tried for many countless alifees, but although we knew the combination, no one in the Soosan was ever able to generate the power necessary to open the entrance."*

At that Zooric frowned. "Did you not detect the various energy pulses coming from the stones at Nergeet?"

Again, the elder *Loyas* exchanged looks.

What now? Zooric was annoyed at being excluded from the exchange. "You have wasted your time. I cannot..."

Loya Modnar held up a hand for silence. *"We will not discuss this now,"* he added *"We of the Soosan sector are prepared to meet your needs Sous Zooric..."*

"You know nothing of my needs," Zooric said abruptly.

"Restric..." *Loya* Meestric began.

This was too much too soon. Zooric felt nauseous. "Do not speak to me of Restric."

Loya Meestric fell silent.

Loya Modnar stared at Zooric's taut expression for a few seconds before beginning again. "A promise was made many alifees ago — a promise to your true father, the great *Jirga* Restric. We of the Soosan have failed, in the past, in protecting his son. We wish to correct the errors of the past."

"My true father?" Zooric was incredulous. He had always known that one of the men of the Soosan sector was his true father. But to learn that his father was the great *Jirga* Restric! He stared at them. "Is this the truth?"

"Eeng," Loya Modnar said. *"Your true father was one of the greatest sensitives ever. Had the Soosan sector continued under the guidance of your father, it is doubtful that many of the errors of his experiment would have occurred. And it is unfortunate that he did not live to see you as an adult."*

Zooric dipped his head to hide his emotions. His true father! Saac ga! As a child he had read stories about the many deeds of the great *Jirga* Restric. "When did he die?" he muttered.

"He lived a very active life. At ninety-eight alifees he succumbed to old age. You were just past your fourth alifee at his death."

Zooric lifted his head. "Did he know me? Personally?"

Loya Modnar nodded. *"At that time the policy of the Soosan was to closely monitor all the children of Soosan fathers. It was after your father's death that the policy was unfortunately changed."*

Again, Zooric looked down. He really wanted to discuss this further, but Raekon was approaching. He did not know how much Raekon, as a junior Soosan knew. He knew nothing of the Soosan. He was only now discovering that there were different levels to a sensitive's power. But he did not know where Raekon placed.

"Have you been in yet? Have you explored yet?" Raekon asked, looking expectantly at Zooric.

Silently, Zooric pointed to his leg.

Loya Meestric stood; he gave Raekon a smile to which Raekon responded.

"Now I understand when you speak of Sous Zooric's powers. Is he really is as strong a sensitive as Restric?" Raekon paused for a response, looking inquiringly at all of them.

Remembering Zooric's outburst, neither *Loyas* Modnar nor Meestric felt comfortable answering the question. They too looked to Zooric for guidance; however, the totally blank expression on Zooric's face left them clueless. After a significant pause, *Loya* Modnar cleared his throat, but he was spared the need to answer.

Carrie was coming awake. Ignoring both Raekon and his questions, Zooric began murmuring to her.

"Just relax Caree."

Raekon blundered on. *"Is she..."* he began just as Carrie groaned.

"Get lost Raekon." Zooric spoke without turning around. He did not want them alarming Caree. "You had better hope she recovers or I may just sizzle you."

Raekon backed up sharply, shooting a panicked look at *Loyas* Modnar and Meestric.

Loya Modnar gave Zooric a warning look. *"Do not lightly use such words."* He turned to Raekon. *"Come. He is upset. We will spend some time exploring and leave him with the Tifoosa."*

They all left, thankfully leaving Zooric alone with Carrie.

****

Chapter 12

Carrie had been picking up wood chips when Soor began growling. At first, she ignored the rocleer, thinking he was just upset at a passing animal, but when the growling persisted, she got worried and stopped to look around.

"What is it Soor? I don't see anything." Then three things struck her almost simultaneously. First, she got Zooric's pain. That was followed, almost immediately, by his mental warning. She did not get a chance to react to either. She saw them! Carrie screamed. That was the last thing she remembered before a blinding pain struck her.

Now she moaned as remnants of the pain returned.

"Caree," Zooric anxious voice reached her. "Are you okay?"

"Zooric?" She tried to sit up but he was holding her too tightly. She relaxed in his arms. "What happened? My head..."

"A buzz. Not by me. Link with me and give me your pain."

Carrie turned to bury her face in his chest. She breathed deeply at the linking. Zooric continued to stroke her gently. Carrie recognized that he was trying to put her to sleep and with the pain slowly fading, she did feel pleasurably drowsy. She was drifting off when an alien voice intruded.

"*Daat ebil teen?*"

"She is fine," Zooric responded in Gavaa.

Carrie blinked awake as her panic returned.

"Easy." Zooric's voice was soothing as he smoothly switched to English. "Do not worry. No one will harm you."

"Zooric?" Carrie clutched at him. At her words, Zooric turned worried eyes on her.

Although Carrie was reassured by his lack of alarm at the alien's voice, she struggled to sit up. This time he allowed her to. Carrie looked around. An Owoon had just entered and was standing not far away, his clean shaved head clearly outlined. Two others were standing by the door. At least these two had hair on their heads, hair that looked very much like Zooric's—still —she gasped in fright.

"They will not hurt you," Zooric reassured. Nevertheless, Carrie swallowed nervously. She could not help staring. They all were similarly dark-skinned, yet they were giants. They had worked out that Zooric was over six feet tall, but some of these aliens were taller. The tallest, the man by the door, looked close to seven feet tall! Now she knew why these rooms had such high ceilings. The Azars must have been taller still!

Even as she watched, another Owoon entered. His eyes were dark, almost black. He said something in his language.

"*Zte*," Zooric replied. He grabbed his crutch and struggled to his feet, "Can you stand?" he asked Carrie in English.

At her nod, he continued speaking to the Owoon in Gavaa. He spoke slowly so that she could understand "The buzz gave her head an ache."

Carrie frowned. At Zooric's urging, she stood shakily. She could understand Zooric but had no idea what the other Owoons were saying. "What did he say," she asked.

"He just wanted to make sure you were fine. They are very sorry about what happened." This was added with a scowling look at another Owoon who had just entered.

"Why are they here?" she asked.

"They were trying to find me. They wish that I come back with them to Caleel" Zooric did not explain further. "Let me introduce you," he said turning completely around to face his people.

Yet another Owoon entered as he spoke. This one had the lightest eye color of them all—a pale yellow that was almost golden. He removed his cape, as he stepped closer, revealing a clean shaved head.

"This is *Loya* Meestric," Zooric said. "He is second in command of the Soosan Protectors— similar to your Presidential Guards. Next to him is *Loya* Modnar, an elder in our society."

Both Soosans stepped forward. The *Loya* Modnar smiled at her then turned to Zooric. Zooric nodded then *Sous* Raekon and the others came forward. Zooric introduced them all. The tallest was *Gaad* Trateen, but the others all ran close seconds.

Carrie nervously stood and gave what Zooric had told her was the standard Owoon greeting, a bow from the waist.

Loya Meestric cleared his throat a few times but did not say anything—or rather Carrie didn't think he had said anything until Zooric turned to her.

"*Loya* Meestric is again apologizing for hurting you," Zooric explain.

Carrie looked startled. "He did?"

A brief fleeting grin touched Zooric's lips. "He just told us all—unfortunately he was unable to 'send mentally' to you," he apologized.

Carrie frowned as she realized that she was the only one not 'hearing.' "I can see where mental speaking is a great advantage." Her frown deepened as Zooric turned to *Loya* Meestric, obviously listening to another question or comment.

Whatever he said came as a surprise to Zooric. Zooric fired off a few rapid questions in Gavaa that Carrie had no hope of understanding. Carrie took the time to more closely examine the Owoons. As Zooric had explained earlier, it would be too simplistic to say they were all dark- skinned. They truly did come in various shades of brown. *Sous* Raekon's complexion was just a shade darker than hers. The common thread was their hair color, height and build, at least among the Owoons. The Soosans were all completely bald. But they were all tall and slender. Even the shortest, the one Zooric introduced as *Gaad* Sorgan, was only an inch or two shorter than Zooric.

Finally, Zooric turned to her and explained using their private mental pathway. *"They can understand you. All Soosans and Soosan Protectors are required to learn your language. It is a part of their training. He wants to know why you are frowning."* He continued aloud in Gavaa. "She is fine *Loya* Meestric. She is no longer upset. She has accepted your apology."

Carrie queried with raised eyebrows. Her acceptance of the apology was news to her.

"Smile and look sorry." Zooric directed her privately.

His directions caused Carrie to bite her lips—so much for translators. She tried for a contrite expression so as not to prove Zooric a liar.

"You are speaking aloud. Why can't they?"

"The preferred method of communicating within the Soosan sector is mental-speak," he said in English then added in a private mental aside to her only, *"Believe it or not, it is possible to lose the ability to use your vocal cord to speak aloud. There are some within the sector who have been there for over sixty alifees and can no longer speak aloud. I do not believe Loya Modnar or Meestric can speak aloud even if they wished."*

"What about the others?"

"Raekon?" Again the question was directed only to her.

She nodded.

"He can speak aloud." Zooric did not add to that comment. And as Carrie looked inquiringly up at him, he ignored her in order to return to another query by *Loya* Modnar. "As you can see, I cannot travel until my leg is healed. This should give you ample time to explore the Azar's sector."

They were all eager to comply. *Loya* Meestric soon had them organized. Carrie found much of the Owoon's technology totally foreign. She watched in amazement as they unpacked their supplies. None of the Owoons approached her although she got numerous curious glances. But their overwhelming interest was centered on the Azar sector. It was something they couldn't resist. They all wanted to explore.

As Zooric hadn't been in, he could offer no advice on where to go. But he had explored Nergeet. He could tell them what to expect. And for once he lost his reticence and became actively engaged in the conversation. Within less than an hour they were ready to go, leaving Carrie with a clearly bored Zooric. He too wanted to go exploring! His next preference was sex but when Carrie refused, he became so grumpy that she quickly decided it was in her best interest leave him to his own devices. Since Zooric did not want her to leave the sector again, she resolved to spend the time cooking. With seven more mouths to feed, she would need a lot of food. Besides, her main reason for leaving was to gather sticks and branches for the fire. There were now enough able-bodied men, so gathering sticks would definitely no longer be a problem.

****

First-dark was approaching when the men returned.

Loya Meestric led the way in. *"Is the Tifoosa well?"* He asked.

"She is fine," Zooric responded; then cautiously asked, "What did you find?"

"Many interesting things. But we will need you to open some more doors. They are locked to Modnar, Raekon and me," he paused. *"Now do you understand why we need you in Caleel?"*

Zooric chose not to respond as he absorbed these new ramifications. "When my leg is better, I can easily open any doors in the sector for you to explore," he pointed out.

But both *Loya* Modnar and Meestric were shaking their heads.

"You have yet to understand." *Loya* Modnar commented. *"You are needed in Caleel. The sector needs you."*

Zooric stared, his lips tightly compressed. "Explain."

But the others were restless and hungry. *"We will, but later,"* *Loya* Modnar promised. He indicated that the others should pass and enter.

"Did the Tifoosa prepare this," Raekon asked looking around at the food.

"Eeng." Zooric's response was short.

Raekon smiled at Carrie. She started a smiling response, which faltered and died as she noted Zooric's scowl. Zooric in turn ignored Carrie's searching look. His people were a complication he did not need. Fortunately for all, Raekon made no further overtures to her. The Owoons sat down at the low table to attack the food.

The conversation was focused on their discoveries in the Azar's sector. Zooric listened avidly.

"Perhaps at the next light we could carry you down Sous Zooric," *Loya* Meestric suggested.

Zooric agreed. He was definitely interested in exploring the sector even if he did not like the company. As it got dark, torches were lit. Zooric shot a grinning look in Carrie's direction. She grinned back because she now understood why it was only recently that Zooric, at her urging, had reluctantly decided to spend first-dark resting. Unlike the Tifoosas, the Owoon did not sleep or even rest during first-dark - they continued as normal. This first- dark was spent chatting and preparing for the trip at second-light.

After the meal *Gaads* Sorgan and Egell, who both had medic training, offered to examine his leg. At first Zooric was hesitant. He was blocking all incoming signals to himself at the moment, but he was not sure if blocking would work when he was in contact with the individual. It certainly didn't work when he was in contact with

Carrie. He was, therefore, tense as *Gaad* Sorgan bent to examine him.

"It is healing nicely," *Gaad* Sorgan said after an initial examination. He looked at Zooric's taut expression. "Do you need something for the pain?

"*Zte*," Zooric refused with a glance at Carrie, relieved that his block had held. She came closer, but he shook his head explaining quickly and privately what was happening, then continuing in English to the medic. "I will be okay. I am controlling it now."

"But why fight for control of pain when painkillers are available," *Gaad* Egell asked.

Raekon looked up with a giggle. *"Did he not tell you? Sous Zooric does not like any medication. He will take it under duress only. Is that not true Sous Zooric?"*

Zooric ignored the question and the resultant scowl from Raekon. Turning to *Gaad* Sorgan he asked. "Will I be able to walk properly once it is healed?"

"You should. The main bone in the leg is now in place, although the other smaller bone is not. But you should be fine. The smaller bone in the leg does not support the body anyway. But if you wish, it can be corrected once we get you back to Caleel. For now, we will make you a sturdier splint."

Zooric nodded his thanks.

"He also needs a haircut," Raekon inserted. He seemed determined not to be overlooked.

Since Zooric did not respond, *Gaad* Sorgan repeated the comment as a question. "Would you like a haircut, *Sous* Zooric?"

"Caree has already cut my hair," Zooric said.

"As Soosan you should not have any hair on your head," Raekon pointed out. His comment drew the others'

attention to Zooric's head. Raekon was right. The heads of all the Soosans were cleanly shaved.

Instead of responding, Zooric turned to *Gaad* Keefav. "How soon will you be able to fix me a better crutch?"

There was a short uncomfortable silence before *Gaad* Keefav said quickly, "Within a few eens."

Raekon was furious. He turned to *Loya* Meestric. *"He is Soosan. He should cut his hair. This is...."*

"Enough Sous Raekon." Loya Modnar interrupted. *"Sous Zooric is only now learning the customs of the Soosan. Give him time."*

Raekon was clearly unhappy. But *Loya* Meestric pulled him aside, allowing the tension to settle. Then, true to his word, *Gaad* Keefav, with the help of *Gaad* Trateen, spent the rest of the darkening making Zooric a perfect pair of crutches.

****

With his new splint and crutches Zooric could stand more easily and even walk without pain. He was delighted. Now his only problem was getting used to the absence of his 'detection' sense. With the presence of the Owoons and Soosans, he had to maintain a near constant block. It was not a feeling he welcomed, and he began experimenting in trying to achieve a partial block—to reduce all incoming signals to a bearable level. Fortunately, he only had to worry about blocking when he was in the same room with the Soosans because the walls of the Azar sector stopped all signals. The Soosans could communicate mentally in the sector only when they were within sighting distance of each other.

Despite the fact that he would have to maintain a constant block if he traveled with them, Zooric was not about to be left behind in this planned exploration of the sector. As soon as second-light broke they were ready. Zooric, supported by *Gaads* Sorgan and Keefav after bluntly refusing Raekon's aid, stopped to speak to Carrie.

Carrie could not understand exactly what was happening. While Raekon was constantly trying to draw Zooric's attention, Zooric either ignored him or was deliberately rude. Even the other Owoons were beginning to get uncomfortable. Carrie decided not to go with them. She was already uncomfortable with Zooric's blatant rudeness and an entire cycle of it would be too much.

"Why will you not come?" Zooric demanded.

"Because I want to wash. I need some privacy, and once they come back, I will not get any," Carrie explained.

Carrie really didn't expect him to be satisfied with her explanation and he wasn't. "That is not all."

"No," Carrie agreed; then looked pointedly at the men waiting for him.

"I wish you to come."

Carrie began backing away. "I do not wish to go." It would take too long to go into an explanation now. "I'll tell you more when you get back."

Zooric wanted to argue further but thankfully for Carrie, the Owoons were impatient. Most were already outside urging the others to hurry. They were also looking puzzled, probably at Zooric's persistence in trying to convince her to come.

"They're getting impatient," Carrie pointed out, since Zooric seemed to be totally focused on her. He did not even seem to be aware of the looks the Owoons were sending his way. "You can't hold up the entire party. Besides, I should be safe here. Soor will stay with me."

"He was with you when they found you in the woods. He did not prevent your buzz." Zooric's scowl deepened. "Besides, I want you with me."

"You did warn me, and so did he. I just did not listen," Carrie objected. "And don't be silly. I'm safe here. I'll see you later." She turned and with a smile walked away before he could protest further. In fact, Carrie knew exactly why Zooric wanted her to come. He hated not having her in mental range. When firewood hunting, Carrie was now always careful to keep within 'sensing' distance of Zooric. But if she were to go back to her home, they would have to learn to survive without each other. They would have to adapt. Yet, as Zooric disappeared down the hill and into the sector proper, Carrie almost changed her mind. She forced herself not to; she would eventually leave. This was good preparation.

Nevertheless, throughout the first part of the light, her thoughts kept skittering around. She felt goose pimples on her arms at odd moments and almost had a panic attack at the thought of something happening to him. This would not do. Carrie decided it was in her best interest to stop thinking of Zooric. She focused on doing what she said she was going to do. She washed her hair, took a leisurely bath and spent the rest of the light preparing a big meal. The activities did not fully stop her odd unease, but at least they got her through the cycle.

Second-dark was approaching when Carrie 'heard' from Zooric. They were on their way back. She was pleased that she had timed it right. The meal was just about ready. Ignoring her sudden increase in heartbeat, she met them at the door.

"Tell them that we have no more meat," Carrie told Zooric. She was trying to hide her relief that he was okay and striving for a light tone. Zooric however, came to stand immediately in front of her even ignoring Soor who had bounded out to greet him. He was crowding her and Carrie backed up—uncertain. Standing not quite touching—there was about two inch separating them—he simply stared.

"Zooric?" Carrie looked nervously around him at the other Owoons. All eyes were on them. Had she not had so curious an audience, she would have linked with him. She wanted to—she was acutely in tune with him emotionally, and the separation of the past few hours had clearly increased their mutual need. Indeed, Zooric was sending wave after wave of an unbelievable demanding pulse. However, instead of linking she took another step back. She was actually fearful of totally embarrassing herself with her need.

Zooric blinked. Carrie was sure he was picking up both her embarrassment and her need as he made an obvious effort to control his desire and converse normally, even to the point of responding to her original comment. "They will have to hunt if they want to eat." He bent to pat Soor who went ecstatic.

Loya Meestric stepped forward. He said something to Zooric while staring intently at Carrie.

Zooric focused on him before turning to Carrie. "*Loya* Meestric wanted to know if we are out of food. He also says not to worry; they will hunt the next light."

Carrie started to reach for him but this time it was Zooric who moved—so suddenly that he almost fell.

Gaad Sorgan rushed forward to support him and the others pressed even closer as they worried over Zooric's sudden weakness.

"I am fine. My leg is the problem," Zooric muttered, as he responded to the numerous questions. *Gaads* Trateen and Keefav supported him and helped lower him to the ground.

Carrie bit her lips nervously as she again moved forward making no effort to hide her concern. Her heart was thudding. Zooric had pushed himself too much. She had felt a slight throb in her leg indicating the pain that Zooric was now feeling. "Zooric?"

"Do not touch me Caree," his mental words were strained and his eyes were half closed as he struggled for control. *"We would link and I wish for more than a low linking now,"* he continued privately.

Carrie abruptly stepped back and hugged herself—a poor substitution for the comfort she craved. Then her face flooded with heat as she realized all the Owoons were staring. Backing away she said to Zooric. "Tell them the meal is ready. I will start serving as soon as they wish."

Zooric passed the message along. "They are ready now."

****

The Owoons dug in with gusto. Zooric ate slowly; he was concentrating on containing his emotions. Just now he had made another discovery. If he focused exclusively on Carrie, he could block out the others yet still receive her signals. Of course, that meant that he was bombarded with her emotions, but that was fine with him.

This time the Owoons tried communicating directly with Carrie. Now that their exploration had allayed most of the thrill of the newly discovered sector, all attention was focused on her. They all spoke and understood English with varying degrees of proficiency. Raekon's English was the worse.

"The food was delicious," *Gaad* Keefav thanked her for them all.

"Did *Sous* Zooric show you how to prepare an Owoon's meal?" *Gaad* Trateen asked.

"Some I showed her but others are the food of her people." Zooric answered for her.

"How did you meet her?" This question was from *Gaad* Sorgan, and he too was speaking English although he switched to Gavaa as he continued. "Can you imagine our shock? The Soosans did warn us of the Tifoosas before we started, but we certainly did not expect to meet any this far from their main landing."

Zooric briefly explained, including the fact that he had accidentally sizzled another Tifoosa. "They can absorb very little of our pulses," he added.

"This I cannot understand. According to the Writing of Loya Favood, this should not be possible." Loya Modnar was thoughtful as he chewed.

"Nothing makes full sense." Loya Meestric agreed. *"We were all concerned when Raekon buzzed her earlier. He did it instinctively when she cried out. But we were concerned that the buzz would reflect."*

"But I did not get a rebound," Raekon said. He sounded as if it were a proud achievement.

A pity, Zooric thought, especially as he considered that Caree had only survived because she was different. He was sure that the other Tifoosa, the one he had accidentally killed, would have been seriously hurt or even killed by the buzz Raekon had used.

"I know," Loya Meestric frowned in response to Raekon's comments, not Zooric's thoughts, which

fortunately he could not detect. *"They are different from what we expected. All is not as stated in the Writings of Loya Favood. And this is most disturbing."*

"Something I do not understand." Loya Modnar asked. *"How is it possible that you knew when she was hurt?"*

Loya Meestric looked up startled. *"Sous Zooric?"* Clearly, he had only just thought of this.

Zooric was wondering how soon they would figure out that something was different between him and Caree. "I do not know," he admitted laconically. "As you said, all is not as the *Loya* Favood writes. We are Owoons not Azars. This is only one of the many things that I do not understand."

His explanations satisfied no one, but he was tired, his leg was hurting and he was in no mood to explain further. He looked over in Carrie's direction just as she covered a yawn. Caree, he knew, was unable to follow much of the conversation because, although the ordinary Owoons could speak English, they kept switching back to Gavaa, and besides, the Soosans could only engage in mental-speak. Zooric began to rise. Perhaps the next cycle he would explain. Right now, he wanted to link.

"I am tired. Next cycle, I will explain further. Caree and I sleep in that room." He pointed. "You are welcome to explore and take any one of the other rooms."

Raekon gaped *"Do you sleep with her?"*

"What I do with her is none of your business," Zooric snapped.

At his tone, the four non-sensitives began inching away, fearing an argument between Soosans.

Loya Modnar waited until they were gone before intervening. *"It is a reasonable question, Sous Zooric. You could accidentally kill her with a linking. Look what a buzz did to her."*

Zooric was standing as he directed Carrie to the room they were using as a bedroom. Although he had half turned at Raekon's query, he turned fully to respond to *Loya* Modnar.

"We have already linked."

"What!" Loya Meestric stood slowly, staring incredulously at Carrie. *"How is this possible?"*

"It happened accidentally when we first met." Zooric was suddenly still, his eyes cautious, as the strong emotions in the room penetrated his block. He knew Carrie could sense the tension in his body.

"What is it," she whispered nervously, apprehensive at the astonishment in the eyes of all the Owoons.

"I will explain later," he said privately, touching her briefly in reassurance but reluctant to test his control with a longer contact.

"Tooaal! If you can link with her then I could too." Raekon was immensely excited.

Zooric was outraged. *"Zte!"*

"Why not?" Raekon was angry. *"I too would like knowing what linking with a woman is like. Restric once said. ..."*

"I am not interested in the words of Restric." Zooric cut in. His eyes were like flint. "Hear this all of you. Caree is mine. And I do not share." Zooric's gaze touched them one by one. "I will fry sizzle anyone who attempts to link with her. Is that clear?"

"A Soosan does not easily mention so serious a punishment," Loya Meestric rebuked. *"This is not the path a Soosan should take."*

Zooric interrupted him with a sharp cutting motion of his hand. "I am not interested in the path of a Soosan. She is mine."

At his side, Carrie was taut. Although he was picking up her emotional resistance on this point, Zooric did not care if she became angry at his possessiveness. He wanted there to be no misunderstanding among his people.

Raekon was still looking avidly at Carrie. *"He should share."* He appealed to *Loya* Modnar. *"Soosans all believe in sharing."*

Loya Modnar, perhaps realizing from viewing Zooric's expression that there was no way to win this argument, began backing off. *"Sous Raekon, it is enough that we now know that this is possible. Once we get back to the sector, we can explore this further."* He added an extra touch of reassurance to Zooric. *"Do not worry that any will interfere with your woman."*

Raekon clearly did not agree. *"The Soosan will make him share,"* he said angrily.

His words inflamed Zooric. He almost sizzled the Soosan right there. Carrie, who was becoming increasingly agitated at Zooric's rising tension, gripped his arm. However, the fragile hold he had on his emotions resulted in an instantaneous link.

Zooric took a deep breath as the comfort of the linking almost immediately gave way to passion. *"Caree!"* He pleaded.

Sensing his lack of control, Carrie immediately released him.

But all three Soosans were shocked. They had picked up the low-level surge of electricity between the two.

"*What just happened?*" *Loya* Modnar asked staring at them in astonishment.

Zooric did not answer. Calmer from the low level linking, he coolly assessed their puzzled stares.

"*It is not possible for a Soosan to engage in such a low level linking.*" *Loya* Modnar persisted, his puzzlement deepening as he stared at them both. "*It was a low-level linking was it not?*"

"*Eeng.*" Zooric agreed.

Loya Meestric, like Raekon was still staring. "*Is this the kind of linking you engaged in with the Tifoosa?*" His tone expressed both his confusion and his shock.

Zooric would have loved to let them continue to believe that was the extent of the linking he was able to achieve with Carrie. However, he knew that they would soon realize that both he and Carrie could engage in a deeper link.

"I am able to initiate the low level linking with Caree," he now admitted.

"*But it did not get deeper?*" *Loya* Modnar voiced their confusion.

"It can."

"*Voluntary?*" *Loya* Meestric was frowning as he tried to draw information from Zooric's uncommunicative answers.

"*Eeng.*"

At that response, even *Loya* Modnar frowned. "*I can personally promise you that no one in the sector will force you to share the Tifoosa if that is your concern.*"

"You cannot speak for them all," Zooric objected.

"*I have been given the authority to. We of the sector did not undertake this mission lightly*". He gave a resigned smile.

"We were ready to promise you just about everything to get you back."

"What of Raekon?" Zooric directed his question privately only to *Loya* Modnar without looking at the younger Soosan.

"Sous Raekon will respect the decree of the Soosan." *Loya* Modnar was open in his response and as he spoke, he directed a warning gaze at Raekon. *"When you indicated that you linked with the Tifoosa, were you speaking of the low level linking you just engaged in?"*

This time Zooric flicked an expressionless glance at Raekon before answering. "*Zte.* We can have a deeper link."

"Loya Modnar..." Raekon began, his tone groveling.

"We will leave them Sous Raekon" *Loya* Modnar interrupted firmly. He gave Zooric an intent look as he continued, *"Sous Zooric, the next cycle we will discuss this further."* His tone indicated his annoyance with Zooric's evasive answers.

Zooric merely nodded, refusing to give a verbal promise.

But at least his response satisfied *Loyas* Modnar and Meestric—both of whom turned to go. Wisely, *Loya* Meestric tried for diplomacy in response to Raekon's petulance. *"Perhaps the linking is possible with other female Tifoosas."*

Raekon's expression brightened. *"Then we could take some with us."*

At that even *Loya* Meestric stared in shock.

Zooric had had enough. He pulled Carrie into their room and immediately activated both the door closing and the lights.

****

191

Chapter 13

Carrie stared; she had not even realized the door could close. Unlike the door to the sector, it was not a complete seal. There was an opening of about one foot at the top.

"What was happening?" She asked. Her limited Gavaa and inability to receive the Soosans mental-speak did not permit her to follow the rapid conversation between the Owoons.

As he undressed, he tautly explained what had taken place.

"What happens now?"

"What do you mean?" he asked. He moved over to where she was standing and within minutes had her just as naked as he was.

"Will they insist that you take me to your people?" Carrie did not bother to even try stopping him; having learned from past occasions that Zooric basically had a one-track mind.

Instead of an immediate answer, he pulled her down onto the bed. In the next breath she was lying on top of him. "I promised to take you to your people. I will keep my promise." He began gently caressing her – long strokes from her neck to her lower thighs that caused her entire body to tingle.

Despite her arousal, Carrie lifted her head to stare at him. "You would let me go?"

Instead of answering Zooric kissed her.

"Would you leave me?" He asked instead.

Carrie was being sucked into a pleasurable trance by the deep-drugged kisses. She was unable to prevent her body from responding as the low level linking left her gasping. She buried her face in his chest as Zooric's fingers found her. "I don't know what to do, Zooric. How can I just forget about my family?" In truth she did not know what to do. "We could visit your family. Let them know that you are alive."

Carrie could not think rationally. She moaned in pleasure as Zooric continued his exquisite torture. They made love that dark with the same explosive needs as before. This time, however, another emotion had crept in. There was a tinge of desperation.

Afterward, Zooric fitted her spoon fashion against his belly. Carrie stared bleakly at the walls. Although Zooric must have sensed her distress, he did not speak. What could he say? From reading his thoughts she recognized that Zooric was just as uncertain as she was. He did not know if he could let her go; he still did not know what to do. His arm came around to cup her breast possessively. Carrie shivered. She was so afraid. Could she abandon her family? She did not want to, but very soon she knew she would have to choose — her family or him. How could she live with aliens? They needed more time — time for her to explore these people and to get to know them better. True, she trusted Zooric. But she did not trust his people, and she was very much afraid they would not be allowed the time they needed.

It was a long while before she slowly began drifting off.

****

Zooric was so attuned to Carrie's emotions that until her mind settled, he could not sleep. Within the confines of their room, he could cancel his block and allow his senses free reign. Not that he was able to sense anything. Master psychic that the Azars were, they had designed their building with total electrical insulation. He could sense nothing outside the walls of the room, which was good. That meant none of the Soosans would have sensed his linking with Caree. He shifted into a more comfortable position.

"Zooric?" Carrie asked sleepily.

"Nothing." He momentary tightened his arm and caressed her gently. "Go back to sleep," he murmured.

Soon Carrie's deep breathing and lack of emotion indicated that she was fast asleep, but it was a while before Zooric slept. Since meeting Caree, he had been free of the nightmares that had plagued his sleep in the past. Now, the presence of the Soosans was bringing back memories he had long suppressed. He also hated that he had to operate with the absence of one 'sense.' And then there was Raekon. Regardless of what *Loya* Modnar and Meestric said — he knew he would soon have a problem with Raekon. He would have to be extra careful.

As easily as he had turned them on, he turned off the lights.

****

When Zooric woke at first-light, he remained still as he collected his thoughts while striving to banish disturbing remnants of his dream. Carrie's presence was more than likely the stabilizing factor that had prevented an outright nightmare. This cycle he would make some critical decisions. He also needed to speak with *Loya* Modnar; he needed Carrie's future secured.

He got up to dress and was almost ready when Carrie began stirring.

"Zooric?"

"Hmm."

Carrie raked her hands through her hair as she sat up and watched him. It had become horribly tangled, because Zooric often unbraided it during their lovemaking. "What happens this cycle?"

"First, I will get on my pageen and see if riding it is possible, now that *Gaad* Sorgan made so good a support for my leg."

Carrie's eyes brightened. "Really," she asked excitedly. "And if you can ride?"

"We go to your family." The sooner he faced this, the better, Zooric thought. Besides, he needed to get her away from Raekon. He had decided. At this point her staying with her family was safer. He could always retrieve her later.

Carrie scrambled out of bed and began getting dressed. "Will your people allow you to let me go?"

"I will tell them you have promised not to mention us to your people." Zooric leaned against the door to watch her mad rush, smiling slightly. As soon as she was ready, he opened the door. Soor immediately leaped in and demanded his morning petting.

After feeding Soor, Zooric decided to try climbing onto the pageen. However, within minutes he realized that a trip was still impossible. There was no way he would be able to tolerate one complete cycle of riding. *Gaads* Keefav and Trateen offered to take Carrie back home, but Zooric refused their aid.

"I will take her myself when I have recovered," he decided.

After the morning meal the others left on another explore. This time, apart from himself and Carrie, only

Loya Modnar remained. The *Loya* had patiently listened without comment to Zooric's plans for the cycle. Once Zooric decided to take Carrie home in another cycle, the elder Soosan convinced *Loya* Meestric to take the others back into the Azar's sector without him. Zooric was certain of the Soosan's motive even before *Loya* Modnar spoke to him.

"Perhaps now we could have our talk, Sous Zooric." He indicated where Zooric should sit as Carrie began to walk away. *"Let her stay also."*

"Why?" Zooric was immediately suspicious.

"I wish to try a first-link with her. I get no signals from her, yet you tell me she can receive your linking. This should be impossible."

Zooric's expression remained blank, but he was in fact shocked. To him her signals were a constant, and the lack of them now made him extremely nervous, which was why he got so jittery when she went out of range. He had been speculating on possible reasons none of the Soosans had mentioned that fact. Never had he thought that he was the only one capable of sensing them.

He slowly sat, pulling Carrie down beside him. "He wishes that you stay." Soor, who had disappeared after his morning meal returned to flop down at Carrie's other side.

"Can I try?" Loya Modnar again asked. At Zooric's hesitation he added, *"I wish only to get her frequency. She must have one if you are able to link. Perhaps mental-speak with her will be possible if I get her frequency. Have you tried to mental-speak to her?"*

Another shock! Zooric looked down, slightly veiling his eyes. Because he had never lived in the sector, there was still a lot he did not know about his abilities. He had not even realized his abilities were so different from those of ordinary Soosans. It was during his short visit to the Soosan he had discovered the ability to private mental-speak, but he had assumed that, just as he could tell whenever there was a private mental-speak going on in his vicinity, others could also tell when he engaged in private mental-speak. But it seemed that this was not so. *Loya* Modnar had no idea he had spoken privately with Carrie. The question now was—should he tell?

Zooric looked up and met the calm eyes of the elder Soosan. He made his decision. "I can speak to her mentally. I have done it repeatedly this past cycle. I did not know that you could not detect it."

"*I see.*" *Loya* Modnar steeped his fingers. He had crossed his legs and now rested his elbows on his knees as he thoughtfully regarded Zooric.

Zooric kept his expression carefully blank. He too was sitting with his legs crossed, but his arms were loosely hanging over his legs.

Carrie touched him. "Zooric?"

He knew she was uncomfortable with the silence. "*He is thinking. Do not worry.*" He reassured her privately without turning or indicating in any way that he was communicating with her.

However, *Loya* Modnar's glance swung swiftly between both of them before resting his eyes once again on Zooric. "*Just now, were you using mental-speak?*" He asked.

"*Eeng,*" Zooric admitted.

Loya Modnar sighed. "*I cannot detect it. I had assumed that you spoke aloud because she could not engage in mental-speak but if this is not so, why do you speak aloud?*"

"I prefer to." There was no point in reminding the Soosan that all of Caleel believed him to be an ordinary Owoon. Only Soosans routinely spoke mentally because they could do so to more than one person at a time. Ordinary Owoons could give mental-nudges but could not mental-speak. Speaking aloud was the only practical method of verbal communication.

Loya Modnar nodded his understanding. After a short pause he began a reflective yet determined explanation. *"You need to know what you are capable of. And we need to know also. I know you have no wish to speak of Restric, but he is just as powerful a sensitive as you are. He too is able to detect when others engage in private mental-speak around him. He could not tell what was said, but he could tell they were communicating. Ordinarily, Soosans cannot detect the signals of a private mental-speak. This was one of the ways he was able to assume such total control. Of all the boys, only the two of you developed such a high sensitivity. We do not know how or why this occurred, but we ordinary Soosans do not have much of your abilities. If we are ever to repeat the experiment of your true father, we need to know how to protect ourselves. We must learn how to protect the sector from rogue sensitives. We cannot allow another Restric to take over the sector."* Again he paused.

"We need your help, Sous Zooric. You mentioned varying energy pulses coming from the stones at Nergeet. We had explored that region to the South of Caleel because we knew of the ancient sector. Yet none of us have ever been able to detect any signals from those stones. The sector would have remained hidden had you not detected it. The Soosan need you!"

Zooric rocked back on his heel. He focused on the astonishing information he had just received. Then, as much as he despised even thinking about Restric, he had to know.

"How long did Restric control the sector?"

"Since two alifees. We realized at first-link that he was a powerful sensitive, but even he did not realize how great his abilities were until much later. Like you, Restric could sense signals that none other could detect. We really do not fully understand all of his abilities, and Restric deliberately did not explain. But his power was great, and for that reason we tried to accommodate him. What we did not consider was that Restric would crave power. After realizing his abilities, he wanted immediate control. At first, we made the mistake of accommodating his drive for power. This was because he discovered areas of the sector that had been lost to us. But soon his craving for power became outrageous.

As he got older, he got worse. On one occasion when we refused to gratify him, he deliberately sizzled one of the younger Soosans. He also threatened to sizzle Raekon and even the Jirga. Eventually, we were forced to meet his excessive demands. During the crisis, the Jirga died naturally, and Restric insisted that we induct him Jirga. His control was absolute, and we could not stop him. Somehow, he would always know if we were plotting against him. After you buzzed him, he was incapacitated, but you left before we could explain any of this to you."

"Knowing this, why did the Soosans tell Restric about me?" Zooric had to force down the mind-numbing fear and anger as he recalled the reason, he was brought to the sector solely as a new toy for Restric.

"Nothing can be hidden in the Soosan sector. When the people of your blood came with the news that you had discovered an ancient Azar sector, we immediately knew that only a high sensitive could have found the sector. But Restric told us that you were a friend. We could not request your help because we were unsure of your relationship with him — you could truly have been aligned with him."

Evidently the Soosan was picking up some of his emotions. Loda Modnar's discomfort was penetrating Zooric's block. Zooric's jaws clenched. Restric had made his wishes known immediately when Zooric entered the sector. Zooric did not wish to revisit the horror of that knowing. Much as he had wanted to rescue his brother and the mate of his sister, there was no way he could do what Restric wanted. He also knew that as soon as Restric realized he was determined to resist; he would be forced to…. He still could not bring himself to think about his last months as a captive. After years of battling his childhood nightmares, he chose not to torture himself by reflecting on what forceful methods an adult Restric would deem suitable. Fortunately, he had not gone to the sector unprepared. While in Nergeet he had found and fixed an Azar weapon. Although he had never been able to test the weapon before, he was enormously relieved when it worked by blocking Restric's electro attack. Later, he had buzzed Restric instinctively — his action induced by blind panic. Afterward, instead of punishment from the other Soosans, something he had expected, he had been totally ignored. It was during the confusion that he had requested and was given permission to go. In fact, he was encouraged to leave with his relatives.

"Zooric?" Carrie was sensing his disquiet.

"I am fine," he murmured touching her reassuringly before continuing privately. *"I just need time to digest all he is telling me. I will tell you later."* He turned to *Loya* Modnar "Deeknor kidnapped five boys including Restric. Raekon is here, another was killed and I escaped. What happened to the other?"

"He was the young Soosan that Restric attacked. He is not dead. He is now a subeet."

"Who now is *Jirga*?"

"*Not Restric. The rightful Jirga has assumed rulership,*" Loya Modnar reassured. "*But Restric has recovered. We have confined him to a cell where we can carefully monitor his confinement – he will suffer severe consequences if he tries to inflict harm on others. However, none of us have the power to completely neutralize him. Our fear is that he will eventually overcome his restraints.*"

At that Zooric nodded. There were many ways a smart sensitive could escape, but that discussion would have to wait. What he really needed was to move away from Restric as the subject. "You said the great *Jirga* Restric had planned to monitor the children of Soosan fathers. Why was this not done?"

"*Unfortunately, many of the Soosan did not agree with the original policy under your true father. Some felt it would set a precedent to monitor boys before they became Soosans. However, while your true father was alive, he was respected enough to convince all that monitoring the children was best. When he died the policy was changed.*"

Zooric's eyes narrowed as he realized the *Loya* Modnar was deliberately using the term 'father' to pressure him. He did not like being managed. "Did you always know of the Tifoosas?"

"*Always. This was why all Soosans and Soosan Protectors are required to learn the language of the Tifoosas. We did not want to be caught unprepared. But we knew only of their first landing site. We had no idea that they had traveled so far inland.*"

"It was irresponsible of the Soosans to totally ignore the Tifoosas."

"*Perhaps this was so. But now we have recognized the errors of our past and need your help to make much needed corrections.*"

"Are you not afraid that I will also illegally take control of the sector?"

"We have done extensive research on you, Sous Zooric. The Jirga even questioned other members of your blood. We did not undertake this mission lightly, but we of the sector have determined that we do need you. It is true that there are risks, but we must permanently neutralize Restric, or the sector, indeed our entire way of life, will remain at risk. Our options are limited. So, I ask you: Would you seek power in the manner of Restric?"

"I have no wish to control the sector."

"Good. It is as we thought. You are truly your father's son. You are not Restric."

"You would take my word, just like that," he was incredulous.

The *Loya* actually smiled. *"As I said, you are not Restric."*

His comment caused Zooric to hunch over. Carrie, who was watching, gave him a worried frown then scowled at *Loya* Modnar. "What is it Zooric? What is he saying? What is wrong? Do you want to link?" She touched him again, tentatively, to avoid accidentally linking.

Zooric closed his eyes briefly, wishing he could accept her offer of comfort. *"I wish to, but we should not."* he responded privately. He suspected that the low linking was the equivalent of kissing—with a twist. It had certainly been effective in slowly eroding Carrie's resistance to him. But even he knew that public kissing was definitely not socially acceptable. *"Our low-level linking can be felt by even an ordinary Owoon."*

Carrie blushed and looked up at *Loya* Modnar.

Loya Modnar, in turn, watched them impassively but did not interrupt, although he must have been aware of the private conversation.

"Why are you so upset?" Carrie wanted to know.

"He spoke of Restric" he murmured privatley. He was looking blankly at the floor.

"The leader of the boys when you were a child?"

"Eeng." Zooric muttered again.

"Do they know what happened to you as a child?" Since *Loya* Modnar seemed to be ignoring their private discussion, Carrie continued ignoring Modnar's presence. But Zooric did not respond. His eyes were closed. She touched him. "Zooric?" There was a flicker of charge however, and she immediately pulled away.

His fragile control snapped Zooric out of his dejection. He was unaware that he was sending emotions, but he suspected that it would remain a reflexive ability. With Carrie so tuned to his frequency, her response also seemed instinctive and automatic. They were so attuned to each other's needs that he barely controlled a shiver of apprehension as he considered the future. Would he be able to let her go? And more importantly, could they live without each other?

"Eeng. They know somewhat," he continued privately. *"I will explain later."* He straightened and looked up to meet *Loya* Modnar's concerned expression. *Loya* Modnar had likely picked up the flicker of the aborted link.

"So can I conduct a first-link?" *Loya* Modnar asked, totally ignoring the lengthy break.

This time Zooric nodded. He quickly explained to Carrie what *Loya* Modnar was going to attempt and conveyed her agreement to *Loya* Modnar.

Pleased, *Loya* Modnar placed the tips of each finger, one hand on either side of Carrie's face, near her temple. It was the classic first-link position. He bent his head in concentration. Zooric tensed as he sensed the flow of charge. It was a one-way flow however, totally different from a linking.

For a few seconds there was silence as Zooric watched. Finally, *Loya* Modnar lifted his head. He began slowly, in English.

"Her make up is different from our people. She is a strong receiver, yet a weak transmitter. This is an unusual combination and one that I would have thought impossible. Among our people we are both weak transmitters and receivers, which are the average Owoon, or strong transmitters and receivers — a Soosan."

"I can hear him in my head," Carrie said in amazement.

"Can you understand," Zooric asked.

"A little," Carrie frowned. "He accent...."

"What of you *Loya* Modnar?" Switching to Gavaa, Zooric turned to the elder. "Can you understand her?"

"Perhaps if she spoke a little slower..." *Loya* Modnar suggested in the same language.

Loya Modnar and Carrie tried again. Yes, they would eventually be able to understand each other.

"Tell me some more about this strange ability you have to link with each other," *Loya* Modnar's English was slow and laborious, but he seemed determined to keep at it.

"What do you wish to know?" Zooric asked.

"How did you initiate the low link?"

"That occurred by accident," Zooric looked thoughtful. "I thought at first that Caree was sending signals out, but I have since realized that I am the one sending the signals. It is like a low electrical circuit. It can occur only when we touch."

Loya Modnar nodded *"Perhaps it is because you are such a very high sensitive. We believe that, in addition to your ability to transmit and receive electrical signal, you can also detect signals from others. Restric was the only other person capable of this detection. Look at your ability to unlock the Azar's sectors."*

"Perhaps," Zooric conceded the point.

"Yet it is still a strange linking that you both have. So strange that I wonder if it is something that could be repeated or if perhaps circumstances placed both of you with unique abilities together."

"I plan to take her back to her people, so perhaps then I will find out if there are others like her."

"This could be dangerous Sous Zooric. The Soosan is not yet ready to initiate contact with the Tifoosas. I understand your need to do things yourself, but perhaps it would be wise to let one of the Protectors return her to her people."

Again, Zooric declined the offer. "Very well. I will not contact her people, but I only will take her back." There was no way he would allow anyone other than himself to escort Carrie back home. "How did you assess her without linking?"

Loya Modnar smiled, clearly pleased that Zooric was expressing an interest in a Soosan's ability. "I will show you." But as he bent toward Zooric, the younger man instinctively drew back. *"This will not hurt,"* he reassured.

"I know," Zooric muttered. He just had a lot of difficulty squashing the fears of his past. He had never had first-link, but since he had allowed Carrie to be tested, he could hardly refuse the same testing now. He also had another fear. Would touching *Loya* Modnar cancel his blocking abilities?

He hesitated. Then with difficulty, he managed to reign in most of his fears, bending his head to allow *Loya* Modnar to touch him.

The contact was so brief that Zooric was startled. "That is, it? I did not... "

Unsmiling, *Loya* Modnar staring at him *"Tooaal! You are able to get my emotions!"*

"As you said I get signals from everyone. Usually I can block, but I cannot block Caree and now you when there is contact." Also, my mother, Zooric thought, as he suddenly remembered her hug.

"Are you saying that you can get everyone's emotions all the time?" *Loya* Modnar was still serious.

Zooric thought for a bit. "I can only detect the emotions of Soosans. Perhaps since Caree is also a high receiver, I can detect her emotions also. I get only static from the Owoons, and that I easily block. Perhaps I could get more if I probed deeper or if I am in contact, but I have never tried. When *Gaad* Sorgan and Egell touched me, I did not detect their emotions, and I was able to maintain my block of their static signals." Zooric scowled, "With you and with Caree my block is useless. But why are you surprised? Was this not the same with Restric?"

"It must have been so, but Restric did not tell us this, and it was not a skill present at his first-link." He looked grim. *"It was a great puzzle to us how Restric was always able to foil any plans to overthrow or arrest him. Now I understand. It is as I feared. His confinement is even more uncertain. We cannot delay our return."*

Zooric ignored the *Loya's* reflections on Restric. *"Caree is not able to stop the sending of emotions. Can you?"*

"We would have to experiment," Loya Modnar said. *"It is definitely something I would like to explore. Are you blocking my emotions now?"*

Zooric nodded. "My blocking skills are poor because I did not have to use them much in the wild. I did not block the signals from animals because although they were constant and could be irritating, they were so low that with practice I was able to ignore them. During the time I lived in Caleel, I had to learn how to block, but I find it very disturbing to totally block all signals. That is what I have had to do since you all arrived. I am trying to find a way to allow at least a low level of signals while blocking everything else."

Loya Modnar nodded contemplatively, *"Restric would have perfected his blocking abilities because he lived his entire life among others. It is even possible that he had the opposite problem."*

"What would that be?" Zooric demanded.

"His detection skills may have been underdeveloped. I suspect you have higher detection skills simply because you were able to fully develop your skills in the wild."

"Is it not irresponsible of you to be telling me this?" Zooric asked grimly.

"You are not Restric, and I personally do not believe you could ever be as Restric was."

The involuntary motion that Zooric made with his arms was a telling indication of his aversion to the name Restric. *Loya* Modnar nodded. "I will respect your reluctance to discuss him. Let us discuss more of your skills."

****

While Carrie was preparing the mid cycle meal, Zooric sat with *Loya* Modnar to learn some tenets of the

Soosan, things he would have learned had he been initiated into the sector at first-link. Both he and *Loya* Modnar however, were pleasantly surprised to find that his time in the wild had taught him much of the control that he would have learned in the sector. Zooric well remembered his first attempt to kill a prey for food. Only with patience and practice had he discovered how to give a mild pulse to stun or kill rather than burn his food to an inedible crisp.

Now, although he agreed to sit with *Loyas* Modnar and Meestric as often as possible to learn the tenets of the sector, he absolutely refused to shave his head. With his agreement in mind, he did confide a little more in *Loya* Modnar.

"Did you ever get a chance to explore Nergeet, the sector south of Caleel?" he asked.

"Not really. We traveled there first when we sought you, but only Gaad Soorgan and I returned to the sector when we realized you were not there. The others remained at Nergeet. We immediately formed this group and headed north. We left the others from the first group to explore Nergeet."

"The Azar had instruments that could kill or sizzle— they called them kooknors."

Loya Modnar looked puzzled and rightly so. The Owoons had no sophisticated weapons to kill or maim. In fact, even in the Soosan, the primary means of defense or attack is by using electro sensory powers. *"Kooknors?"*

"A mechanical means of generating a sizzle."

Loya Modnar stared. *"Are you saying...? This would be a tremendous discovery for us."*

Zooric nodded. "With such a weapon the sector need never fear a take-over by a powerful sensitive, even an Owoon could use the weapon."

At this *Loya* Modnar was silent as he absorbed the enormous power Zooric had just handed the Soosans. *"Thank you,"* he finally said quietly.

A slight smile touched Zooric's lips. "They are also capable of detecting the electro signals from anything mechanical or living." Again, he gave a slight smile. "It could be used to detect the signals from the stone combination at the Azar sector, so you will not need me. These kooknors will do the job."

At that, *Loya* Modnar frowned. *"Not so fast Sous Zooric. We cannot abandon our mission. Surely you realize that. The information you just handed me is vital, yes. But remember what I said about you not knowing the extent of your ability. How were you able to operate this weapon?"*

"I pulsed it. I was able to restore one completely." Now seemed like a good time to confess that he had discovered the sector many alifees ago, which gave him sufficient time to explore and work with the ancient Azar instruments.

Loya Modnar was not really surprised. *"This we already suspected."* He said and then returned to the subject of the kooknors. *"Do you have any that we can test now,"* he asked.

"I am sure we will find similar weapons here at Yotse."

Modnar nodded. *"We would need to test these instruments thoroughly. What if none in the sector can generate a pulse to operate them? It could well be that you are the only one capable of using them. I have said you do not know what you are capable of and neither do we."*

Zooric stretched out on the generous padding on the floor without responding. For now, he would keep some secrets. He had no intension of revealing that he had a kooknor in his possession. Anything he revealed to *Loya* Modnar would eventually find its way to Raekon, and while he was willing to trust *Loya* Modnar, he was not sure of *Loya* Meestric, and he definitely did not trust Raekon. Until he could neutralize Raekon, he had no intention of telling *Loya* Modnar the true power of the kooknor. The instrument could also be used to block all incoming signal—to stop a sizzle! And he had already tested it on Restric!

However, as he looked over to where Carrie was preparing their meal, he was more than willing to confess another fact. "Caree does give off energy waves." He murmured. "I thought everyone could detect them."

Loya Modnar looked from Zooric to Carrie and back. *"Even now?"*

"Always."

"I see," *Loya* Modnar finally said. *"Was this also the case with the other Tifoosa you met?"*

Zooric hesitated. "The signals from the other Tifoosa were different. Caree's signals are low yet they are much stronger than..." again Zooric hesitated. "Not just stronger. Different."

He shrugged. "The sensing became stronger after we linked." He paused; then asked abruptly, "Can you detect her emotions?"

"Nothing," *Loya* Modnar confirmed. *"But this also may be proof that your Caree is different from the rest of her people."*

Zooric smiled. He liked that term—'your Caree.' "Perhaps." It really made no difference to him if Carrie was different or not. He was more concerned with another fact. "Then Raekon can detect nothing either, which is good."

Loya Modnar nodded absently, his mind clearly elsewhere. *"So far, she is the only one that you can link with. Perhaps it would be best if you did not return Zerah Caree to her people."*

That sounded like an excellent idea to Zooric. There was, however, a major problem. "I promised her. I cannot go back on my word."

Again, *Loya* Modnar nodded, this time in sympathetic understanding. *"You have a problem. A serious problem."*

That was an issue that Zooric had no intension of discussing. He was well aware of the serious nature of his problem.

*** **

Chapter 14

The others returned close to first-dark, full of euphoria and a curious collection of Azar artifacts. They were very similar to discoveries that Zooric had made while exploring Nergeet; he was thus able to explain the uses of many of the findings. In fact, two of the instruments found were kooknors.

Later, with first-dark ending, the breathtaking nature of the discoveries had worn off and the Owoons now began planning a hunt for food. Zooric got a stick, and after a quick check with Carrie's — more to reassure himself rather than her — went outside the chambers to draw a rough map of the area.

As soon as Zooric disappeared outside, Raekon approached Carrie. She was sitting some distance away working on the next meal.

Smiling, he introduced himself. "I am Raekon," he said aloud.

He was speaking very slowly in English and Carrie understood him perfectly. She gave him a polite smile.

Without seeking her permission, he sat down. "*Loya* Meestric tells me you speak our language very well. Is this true?"

"I am sorry. No. I speak only a little of your language."

That did not deter him. "We will better my English and you will better your Gavaa if we speak with each other," he decided with a confident smile. Then as Carrie gave him an uncertain smile he continued. "You are a very beautiful woman."

Carrie went pink. She glanced hesitantly at the entrance where Zooric stood. Zooric, who seemed to take her for granted, had certainly never given her such a compliment!

Raekon easily read her thoughts. "He has never told you that, has he?"

Annoyed that he was reading her so easily, Carrie backed up. "Please leave. Leave me alone. Zooric will be angry if he sees you talking to me."

"And do you always do as *Sous* Zooric says?"

But Carrie remained stubbornly silent.

Raekon was amused. "*Sous* Zooric may not have recognized that you are beautiful. Unfortunately, because of his past, *Sous* Zooric still has many issues that he has yet to work through. He may be just using you."

Carrie stiffened. How dare Raekon try to turn her against Zooric? Since he still did not take the hint, she stood and walked away. Raekon did not try to stop her, but during the next two cycles, whenever Zooric was busy with *Loya* Modnar or Meestric, learning about the sector, Raekon would approach her. He was never as obvious as he was the first time, but Carrie was aware that he took every opportunity to put down Zooric. At first, she tried to get Zooric to confide in her. Why did he dislike Raekon so? In spite of her efforts, Zooric stubbornly refused to say anything. Carrie knew a sure way to find out would be to bring the topic up after linking with him during the dark. However, she could not bring herself to so abuse his trust in her. He already hated being so vulnerable; she did not want him to hate her.

But that being the case, Carrie soon decided that since Zooric refused to give her a reason not to speak to Raekon, there really was no reason she shouldn't. Raekon could be very pleasant to her even if he tended to be annoyingly arrogant toward the other Owoons. Yet, so too was Zooric. However, Zooric clearly did not think himself better than the Owoons. No task was beneath him and he did not discriminate, generally applying his disconcerting haughtiness toward everyone. It was no wonder then that Zooric's arrogance did not spark the resentments that Raekon's did.

Still, Zooric was the only one to actively show his dislike toward Raekon. That was true until Raekon, unfortunately, decided to offer his explanations for why Zooric so disliked him. It happened just as they were finishing a last-cycle meal.

In general, Zooric would study with *Loya* Modnar or with both *Loyas* Modnar and Meestric together. Somehow, he and *Loya* Meestric did not get along, and they had never studied alone. When *Loya* Modnar announced that he wanted to go into the Azar sector the next cycle, leaving only *Loya* Meestric and *Sous* Raekon to tutor Zooric, Zooric immediately refused the tutoring — rudely.

Loya Meestric was annoyed. *"Is there a reason you insist on insulting Raekon constantly?"*

Zooric remained silent but Raekon spoke up. Throughout the last few cycles, he had been speaking aloud even in the presence of the other Soosans. "We were both kidnapped before our first-link and we were both sexually abused. *Sous* Zooric just resents the fact that I know of his abuse."

There was an awful silence.

Zooric was livid. He stood, glared at Raekon then turned to leave the room.

He was not yet at the door when Raekon looked around with an innocent smile that Carrie knew to be fake. "It's the truth. I do not know why he should be upset. I think it is unfortunate that he is so misguided that he has chosen to focus his resentment on me."

By now, Carrie was feeling quite furious for Zooric's sake, but before she could say anything, *Loya* Modnar turned sharply to Raekon. He said nothing aloud that Carrie could hear, but she knew from Raekon's almost sulky expression that the younger Soosan was being chastised. Serves him right, she thought fiercely. She started to stand—she could no longer stomach sitting at the table with Raekon —but she was only halfway out of her seat when suddenly Raekon gave a terrified scream.

Carrie's heart thudded in fear. She recognized that cry! The last time she had heard someone scream in such terror was...

"Help me! He's buzzing me!" Raekon was gripping his head in blind panic.

He jerked upright, clutching his head, causing the chair to topple behind him.

Carrie was appalled. She could not believe that Zooric had buzzed Raekon.

Loya Modnar and Meestric jumped up. "*Sous* Zooric!!" They screamed simultaneously. *Loya* Meestric rushed over to Raekon. The younger Soosan was now slumped over, his eyes tightly closed; he was also still clutching his head.

"Oh my God," Carrie gasped as she turned to look at Zooric. His face was totally expressionless as he watched, and she could detect none of his emotions.

"Are you okay?" Loya Meestric was anxiously bent over Raekon.

"Dees! My head. I think he was trying to sizzle me." Raekon muttered, his voice sounded weak as he leaned heavily on *Loya* Meestric.

How could Zooric have been so childish? Carrie thought. Zooric was still standing by the open doorway. She gave him a furious glare that he refused to acknowledge.

"Why did you buzz him?" she demanded. "That was totally childish and irresponsible!" Without answering, Zooric abruptly left the room. Carrie truly felt he needed a good shake. She too joined the group gathered around Raekon.

"Is he okay?" she asked.

Raekon looked up, giving her a weak smile. "I think so. I just have a splitting pain in my head."

She nodded. "I remember." Carrie raised anxious eyes to *Loyas* Modnar and Meestric. Although still angry at Zooric's childish behavior, she was not about to let the *Loyas* think he was heartless. "Zooric would never have deliberately tried to sizzle him. He probably just does not realize his power." She really did not believe that Zooric would deliberately harm anyone without a justifiable reason.

The four Owoons began leaving.

"No!" Loya Modnar insisted. *"Stay! Finish your meal."*

"More than once he as threatened to sizzle Sous Raekon. Sous Zooric is young and impulsive. I always knew that coming after him was a bad idea. He has never had the proper training in the sector — his training is even less than what Restric had." *Loya* Meestric's implications were obvious.

Knowing how much Zooric disliked Restric, Carrie had to bite her lips to refrain from commenting. "How is your head now," she asked Raekon instead.

Raekon had closed his eyes again, resting his head against *Loya* Meestric's chest. "Dees! It hurts." Through half open lids he peered at her. "Perhaps the low linking that *Sous* Zooric spoke of will help me."

She anxiously regarded him. Should she link with him? Would it ease his pain as it did for Zooric? She did not really want to, but she did feel guilty about Zooric actions.

"The low link can help ease the pain." Tentatively she touched his arm in an effort to encourage a low link. She instantly realized that she had made a big mistake.

Raekon was not Zooric. He could not initiate a low linking. His only means of linking was the deep involuntary link engaged in by all Soosans. Carrie immediately attempted to withdraw the contact because, despite the presence of two Soosan and four Owoons, he had immediately tried to deepen the contact—reaching to grab her, forcibly subduing her, seeking to join his mouth with hers.

Gasping in fright and revulsion, Carrie doubled her fists and pummeled him on his chest. Instead of releasing her, his hands tightened painfully on her upper arm. He yanked her forward, but as he crushed her lips with his she bit him—hard! He jerked away.

*Raekon!"*The Soosans were now intervening. Even in her fright Carrie could not mistake the horror in *Loya* Modnar's voice.

Then another voice entered the mix. *"Caree!"* Zooric's shock and hurt flooded her mind. The commotion had brought him back into the room.

Then, as if propelled by invisible hands, Raekon was suddenly flung across the room. The four Owoons leaped up from the table, backing away in fear. Both *Loyas* gasped. Such was their confused fear that they were publicly broadcasting frantic mental messages to Zooric.

She stood trembling, her hands wiping at her mouth. "Is he dead?"

Raekon had landed in a heap close to the far walls of the chamber. The *Loyas* ran to him.

After an initial assessment Loya Modnar stood. *"No, he is fine."* His voice reflected his shocked surprise. *"Gaad Sorgan! Gaad Egell!"* He called the two medics over.

Raekon was slowly getting to his feet with Loya Meestric's aid. *"I am not fine,"* he shouted. *"I think my arm is broken. I landed on it."* He was furious. And continued ranting as the medics examined him.

"But you are fine mentally..." Loya Meestric finally inserted hesitantly. *"How did he do it?"* He turned to *Loya* Modnar. *"With the power he had to have used to throw him, how did he spare his mind?"*

"I don't know." Loya Modnar was thoughtful.

Carrie knew they were referring to what Zooric had just done. It showed the extent of their shock that they were not speaking privately. She gathered her scattered wits. "I must go to him," she said. But Zooric had again disappeared and she could not sense him.

Carrie turned to *Loya* Modnar. "Can you reach him?" she asked anxiously.

"I'll try," the Soosan said. But after a few minutes he shrugged. *"The walls of the sector block all signals."*

"I need to go to him," Carrie muttered again.

"Why?" Raekon was still furious. *"Sous Zooric does not know what to do with a woman. I was fortunate to get*

counseling for my abuse; Sous Zooric lived in the wild for much of his boy-growth and he is still like a wild animal."

Carrie was still in shock at his blunt language and unsure how to respond when she sensed Zooric's presence. She looked up. He had reentered the room and was now approaching them.

Carrie wanted to reassure him—to tell him why she had tried linking with Raekon, but she remained silent. Raekon and the others would also hear anything she said.

Zooric's face was impassive and she could not read his emotions.

Raekon gave him a hard stare before turning to Carrie and continuing in a conversational tone. "Since he now wishes to lie with a woman, perhaps I should tell you his favorite position when he is servicing...." he stopped abruptly with a gasp of pain, then doubled over in a scream of pure agony.

She turned in panic to Zooric. "Zooric! Stop! What are you doing? You will kill him." She started running toward him but he stopped her with a furious glare.

"Do not come any closer!"

She stopped. She was only vaguely aware of the shouts from the Owoons plus *Loyas* Modnar's and Meestric's urgent pleas. Hands covering her mouth, to hold in her fear and panic, she stared at him. "Zooric?" she pleaded.

Zooric ignored her as he scanned the shocked faces of his people. "So, *Loya* Modnar," he asked boldly, "Do you really still wish that I accompany you to the Soosan." He had folded his arms across his chest, both his words and his stance appeared challenging.

Loya Meestric gave Zooric a furious glare as he went to examine Raekon. His action galvanized the other Owoons who had been paralyzed with fear. *Gaads* Sorgan and Egell again moved to Raekon's side.

Loya Modnar however, was returning Zooric's challenging stare. *"I am disappointed, yes."* He too had his arms folded across his chest. *"You have yet to learn self-control. This just demonstrates why you need to learn the ways of the Soosan."*

At those words *Loya* Meestric turned to *Loya* Modnar, and although Carrie heard nothing, she was sure they were arguing. *Loya* Meestric was gesturing wildly, his face almost puffing in anger. *Loya* Modnar, however, remained calm. Carrie turned back to Zooric. He was watching the *Loyas*, but his expression was one of disinterest. Sensing her look he turned to coolly survey her, before asking privately.

"Do you wish to stay with him or do you wish to go home to your people?"

Carrie stared in disbelief.

"Well?" He demanded. He was still furious and Carrie could again sense his hurt.

"Please let me explain what happened."

"I do not wish your explanations. I will take you to your people in the next cycle if you wish to go, or I will leave you with him."

Carrie could only gasp in horror. She felt bruised by Zooric's hurtful words. Before she could respond, *Loya* Modnar interrupted.

"Sous Zooric, your behavior was inexcusable. You could have killed him. Now do you understand why the sector training is essential. You need to learn control."

"I have control." Zooric said flatly. "Were it not for my control, he would be dead."

There was a moment of stunned silence, and then *Loya* Modnar again assumed command.

He waved away Zooric's rationalization. *"You agreed earlier to abide by the tenets of the sector, and our number one rule is never to sizzle someone. Ever! It is only the province of the Protectors. For this you will be punished."*

Now everyone was gaping at *Loya* Modnar, even Carrie thought him crazy. How exactly are they going to force Zooric to take any form of punishment?

Surprisingly, Zooric's response was a scowl. "I..." he began.

Loya Modnar did not want to hear his explanation. *"No! There is no excuse!"*

Zooric's scowl deepened, but unexpectedly he offered a reason for his actions. "I did not sizzle him. After you chastised him, he privately insulted me, so I gave him only a slight buzz. He was pretending to be in severe pain. As for his attack on Caree, I merely threw him. There was no sizzle involved. The last buzz was nothing. He continues to pretend that his pain is unbearable."

Again, *Loya* Modnar would allow no excuse. "We will not debate this. What you did was still illegal under the tenets," he insisted. "Do you or do you not admit fault?"

Carrie had to admit that *Loya* Modnar was extraordinarily brave, considering Zooric's abilities—and fury. And Zooric was furious. His fists were clenched by his side as he glared first at *Loya* Modnar then encompassed them all with his glower. He seemed to be generating waves of fury. Carrie could feel it, and from the taut expression on even the Owoons faces, she was sure that they could too. Then without a word Zooric turned and left the room.

"Did you feel that?" Loya Meestric demanded. *"He was trying to smother us with his fury. He is too powerful. Surely you would not still insist on bringing him to the Soosan?"* Loya Meestric was giving Loya Modnar a hard and disbelieving stare.

But to the surprise of them all, Loya Modnar's lips wore a small half smile. *"I am sure that if Sous Zooric wished to smother us with fury he would have. He is powerful, yes. But I believe him when he says he has control."* Loya Modnar nodded as he added softly. *"Yes, I would insist."*

Raekon, who was slowly recovering, intruded in the debate. "I made no threats against him. And he lies, he did much more than a buzz; Sous Zooric just went wild. He has attacked me—three times. I demand that he apologize, and under the laws of the sector I can choose his punishment for violating my rights.

There was a dead silence as a new tension filled the chamber.

"Sous Raekon is perfectly within his right Modnar," Loya Meestric was still angry at Zooric's action. *"Sous Zooric has agreed to the tenets. Let him prove his loyalty. He should accept his punishment as just and learn from his mistakes. Regardless of what Raekon did or didn't do, Sous Zooric's actions were wrong under our laws. He cannot be allowed to escape punishment. If he is not punished or if he refuses to accept his punishment, then I fear for our future."*

Loya Modnar hesitated.

"I am not out for revenge Loya," Raekon pleaded, "Only justice. I was illegally attacked. It is only right that I should seek justice. I will not even demand an apology; I only wish for the right to converse with Zerah Caree. And for his attack on my person, *Sous* Zooric should not sleep or link with her for five cycles. Is that too much to ask?"

"It is not. You are being very lenient." *Loya* Meestric agreed immediately, but *Loya* Modnar was more cautions; his considering look was directed to where Zooric had exited.

Finally, the *Loya* turned to them. *"I cannot detect him. I will return."* He left the room only to return within minutes. Sous Zooric has agreed not to sleep with the ... with Zerah Caree." He sighed, and then called to the Owoons. *"We will make preparations to leave the next cycle. Sous Zooric insists he will be returning Zerah Caree to her people"*

"No!" Carrie cried. She would have gone after Zooric, but *Loya* Modnar gently restrained her.

"It is Sous Zooric who is insisting Zerah Caree. He does not wish to see you now. He has gone further in the sector. But do not worry, his anger will pass."

"What of his leg?" She asked. *Gaad* Egell had removed the splint from Zooric's leg earlier during the last cycle but the muscles were still weak, forcing Zooric to occasionally resort to the help of the crutches.

Loya Modnar hesitated then turned to *Gaad* Egell who had reappeared. *"How is his leg?"*

Gaad Egell hesitated. "I would want him to wait for another cycle. Too much strain now could be very bad for the development of the muscles."

However, Zooric refused to wait. He was leaving with Carrie the next cycle with or without them and that was final.

****

They were ready to leave early the next light. Zooric was tense and strained and Carrie was even more

223

so. She had slept alone for the first time in over five weeks — that was over fifty cycles! It had not been a restful experience. And she was no longer receiving signals from Zooric, neither his emotions nor his thoughts. He had regained full control and was firmly keeping her out. Was this how it would be when she left? Carrie was anguished. She knew she had hurt him when she attempted to link with Raekon. But she still felt angry that he refused to listen to her explanations.

The only plus to the journey was that she was finally traveling on a fluar. The ride was unbelievably smooth compared to the jerky gait of the zig, yet Carrie could not fully enjoy herself. Soor, unhappy since the incident the cycle before, was now cheerfully forging by her side. Carrie suspected that Zooric had ordered the rocleer to stay with her. She sighed; then tried to shrug off her sadness. It was hard. The trail was almost non-existent and in this part of the woods the thick trees and vegetation blocked most of the sunlight, although it was almost still first light. It gave the forest a dark gloomy feel that perfectly suited Carrie's mood.

With such a narrow path, they were forced to travel in single file with Zooric riding in the lead and *Loya* Modnar immediately behind him. She was traveling between the four Owoons and *Loya* Meestric with Raekon bringing up the rear. Raekon, she knew, was sulking because she refused to talk to him. He had even tried to enlist *Loya* Modnar's aid to force her to acknowledge him, but *Loya* Modnar declined to get involved.

"You cannot force someone to speak to you Sous Raekon," *Loya* Modnar had bluntly advised.

Carrie had noticed that shortly after the incident, the four Owoons had appointed themselves her protectors and were working in shifts of twos, to tactfully keep Raekon away from her. Although he was in the wrong, Zooric had gained the sympathy of all but *Loya* Meestric. Raekon, tolerated before, was now almost universally disliked. Carrie suspected that only Raekon's status as a Soosan kept him from being ostracized by the Owoons.

They were still hours away from first-dark when Carrie began feeling a faint throbbing in her leg. Zooric! He had strapped his leg high on the fluar but the traveling was still too much, too soon. The pain she was feeling was the first sign that Zooric was unable to completely block his emotions at will. Carrie was relieved.

She called the Soosan. "*Loya* Modnar. Could we please stop? I... I do not think that I can continue for much longer."

Loya Modnar turned briefly, giving her a worried frown. "*It is not safe in so wooded an area.*" He turned back to Zooric. "*Sous Zooric, Zerah Caree is tired. We will have to stop soon.*"

If Zooric responded it was privately to *Loya* Modnar.

After a few more hours, Carrie tried again. A stabbing pain was now shooting up her leg. "*Loya* Modnar, please!" she cried.

"Perhaps we could carry her," *Gaad* Trateen volunteered as *Loya* Modnar looked back.

"No!" Carrie said sharply. That was not want she wanted. "No! Please! Could we just stop?" What in the stars was Zooric trying to do to himself?

"*Zerah Caree, Sous Zooric says there is a clearing up ahead. We should arrive there within minutes,*" *Loya* Modnar relayed. "*Sous Zooric would like to use it as a rest stop.*"

Carrie breathed a sigh of relief as she rode into the clearing. She looked anxiously over at Zooric. He was still sitting on his fluar, his head bent, making no effort to dismount. *Gaad* Keefav came up to her.

"I will help you down," he offered.

"Zooric," she whispered.

Gaad Keefav looked over at Zooric then nodded. He jerked his head at *Gaad* Trateen who, immediately came over. "Help *Sous* Zooric," he muttered as he assisted Carrie down.

Zooric did not refuse the aid. He did refuse to eat, however. On reaching the ground he simply rolled up in his blankets before the fire and ignored them all.

Meanwhile, as the others sat in groups eating, Raekon came over to where Carrie was sitting between *Gaads* Trateen and Keefav. Both Owoons looked up, but Carrie concentrated on eating. She was not about to forgive Raekon anytime soon.

"I am sorry *Sous* Raekon but she does not wish to speak to you," *Gaad* Trateen said before Raekon could open his mouth.

At that the Soosan scowled. "She can speak for herself." He deliberately turned his back on the Owoon and faced Carrie. "*Zerah* Caree, would you like to sit with me for a while?" he pointed at a spot on the other side of the fire. "I wish to speak privately with you."

"No," Carrie said without looking up. How many times would she have to rebuff him before he got the message that she did not want to have anything to do with him.

Raekon did not move. He just stood staring down at her.

Gaad Trateen stood. "Come *Zerah* Caree, *Gaad* Keefav and I will show you a very unusual plant."

Gaad Keefav immediately rose and bent to help Carrie up.

"I am Soosan," Raekon said angrily. "You cannot ignore me this way."

For once *Gaad* Trateen did not back down. "I am merely offering to show her one of the most unusual plants on the planet," he said innocently.

Raekon's scowl deepened. "You have to speak to me," he told Carrie. "It was one of the conditions." He turned his appeal to *Loya* Meestric. "It is so, is it not? She must speak to me."

At that *Loya* Modnar intervened. *"I have already told you Sous Raekon, you cannot force someone to speak to you. Leave her and get some rest. We still will have a long half cycle of travel."*

Instead of leaving, Raekon turned to Zooric with a cruel smile. Whatever he said produced no response from Zooric. However, *Loya* Modnar rose.

"Leave him, Sous Raekon," the *Loya* said firmly.

Turning to the camp at large, Raekon gave a nasty smile. "I was merely asking if *Sous* Zooric wanted me to entertain you with stories about his boyhood. Well *Sous* Zooric?"

Zooric did not budge, and again *Loya* Modnar would have intervened but this time *Loya* Meestric held his arm. They were clearly disagreeing over something, and as they argued privately Raekon continued his war of words.

"Perhaps I should start by telling how we made you service all of us when we were boys."

Suddenly furious, Carrie scooped up a handful of dirt and threw it at Raekon. It caught him smack in the face.

He gasped in startled surprise then turned on her in fury.

Carrie felt only the first tingling of a buzz before Raekon was again tossed—this time across the length of the camp. He landed in the bushes almost four feet away.

"Sous Zooric!" *Loya* Meestric turned on Zooric in fearful fury, but before he could say anything further, Carrie was screaming.

"He would have sizzled me! Raekon tried to buzz me! Zooric had to stop him." She turned to where Zooric was lying. He was propped on one elbow staring intently at Raekon.

"Yes!" *Loya* Modnar was grim. *"I felt it"*

There was silence while *Loya* Meestric went over to help Raekon.

"I do not believe it," the Soosan said as he carefully brushed the dirt from Raekon's clothing. *"Is this true Raekon? Did you try to sizzle the Tifoosa?"*

"She threw dirt on me! On me! A Soosan!"

"Tooaal!" Loya Modnar cried. *"What of the many cycles of training that you have had? She is a stranger to our rules — to our customs."*

"Nevertheless..." Loya Meestric began.

"Enough!" Loya Modnar interrupted. *"There is no question that Sous Raekon tried to buzz Zerah Caree. I felt it, and I am extremely disturbed Sous Raekon, by your breaking of the Tenets." Loya* Modnar turned to them all. *"Because of Sous Raekon's actions the punishment of Sous Zooric is at an end."*

When Raekon would have spoken again, *Loya* Modnar held up his hand. *"It is final. I have reached this judgment using my authority as elder of the sector. We will have no more discussion."*

As an elder, *Loya* Modnar's word was law and although he clearly disagreed, Raekon reluctantly accepted the rule. He left with *Loya* Meestric to their sleeping beds.

Carrie, who had been holding her breath throughout the discussion, breathed a sigh of relief. She looked over at Zooric, but he was again wrapped in his blankets. He did not stir although she knew he must have heard *Loya* Modnar.

So, he had not forgiven her. Carrie was suddenly angry. Was this how he dealt with problems—by sulking, because that was what he was doing? He had made no effort to hear her side of the story. She had been tried, convicted and sentenced without a hearing. This was hardly fair! Well, he could continue his sulking. She was no longer going to be the one to make up! She declined *Gaad* Trateen's exploration suggestion and decided to use the stop to catch up on some sleep.

Surprisingly, Carrie slept soundly throughout the first-dark. When she woke, she looked for Zooric, but he was nowhere in sight. He could not be far however, because somehow, she sensed his presence. She paused— remaining absolutely still as she tried to figure out exactly how she knew Zooric was close. His essence seemed to surround her. After her experience with Raekon, Carrie was beginning to seriously worry about this close connection she had with Zooric. He was going to leave her with her family. Would these feelings fade over time? As she thought of Raekon's revolting emotions, she sighed. It was too early in the morning for profound thoughts. Raekon and the *Loyas* were having a quiet discussion, and only one of the four Owoons was present.

"I am going to the river to wash," she told *Gaad* Keefav, the only Owoon in sight.

"It is safe," he reassured her although she had not asked. "You will have total privacy."

"Where are the others?" She really meant Zooric but was almost afraid to ask.

"*Sous* Zooric went with *Gaads* Egell and Trateen to hunt for food," *Gaad* Keefav volunteered with a smile. "He is well. Do not worry."

Carrie smiled her thanks and set out. She had Soor who, regardless of his master's behavior, was still her shadow. The water was freezing. Using a ragged bit of clothing, Carrie decided on a wash rather than a bath. Afterwards she sat by the bank to think. Carrie was not sure how long she sat just staring at the flowing water trying to sort out what to do. Zooric no longer wanted her with him so going home should have been an easy decision, yet... She didn't want to leave him! Carrie buried her face in her hands and cried. Soor immediately came over and began butting her in obvious distress. Carrie wrapped her hands around the animal, totally unable to stop the flood of tears.

And that was how Zooric found her minutes later. She sensed his approach but was too upset to even lift her head.

Zooric awkwardly sat beside her after dropping his crutches by the bank of the river. Abruptly he pulled her face into his chest. They immediately linked.

"Oh, Zooric. You wouldn't listen! I'm sorry."

"Hush," he murmured. "I know. I too am sorry." Swiftly, he began undressing her.

"Zooric!" Carrie panicked at the thought of undressing in public. She tried to stay his hands. "Someone could come. And it's cold!"

Zooric did not stop. "I will keep you warm. And I can sense if anyone approaches. Besides, I have left *Gaads* Egell and Trateen on guard. They will stop anyone from approaching or warn me if they are unable to stop the person. I will also send Soor to guard. Soor, guard!"

With a happy howl, Soor looped off but Carrie was still reluctant. She pushed ineffectively at his wondering hands. "No! Zooric!"

But Zooric was extremely persistent. True he would not force her; she knew that he wanted her willing. But he was fully prepared to spend however long it took to prepare her so that her desire matched his. In record time they were both naked. Carrie soon gave up fighting him on with a groan of pleasure.

Well aware of her surrender, Zooric encouraged her to link again. He deepened the contact by pressing his mouth to hers. Carrie was soon lost in a tide of rising passion.

Later, sweaty but replete, they rested.

"I thought he was hurting. I only wanted to help."

"Hmm," his voice was noncommittal as he merely pulled her closer.

She sniffed as she remembered the lost feeling of not having him nearby. Fortunately, the link with Zooric had snuffed out the last of her turbulent memory of the incomplete link with Raekon. Carrie breathed in his scent. But there was one thing she needed to clear up.... "I learned something when I started the link with him," she whispered.

Zooric stiffened. "I do not wish…"

As she snuggled, she realized she was getting his emotions again and, although she recognized that he wanted to forget the topic, she felt this was important. "No! Just listen, please."

She took his silence as consent. Tightening her arms around him, so that he could not withdraw, she began. "I… It was awful—not like linking with you."

Zooric was totally still. "I do not wish that you have even a low link with anyone else. I think the low link that we share is the equivalent of a kiss—an intimate kiss. And just as I do not want you to go about kissing strangers, I did not like it that you tried to link with him."

Carrie soothed him. She was more than willing to agree, as long as he also stayed away from linking with others. True there was no one else here for him to link with—but Zooric had mentioned that because the Soosans tested only males. They had no idea how many sensitive females were in Caleel. This meant that Zooric, if he returned to Caleel, could link with other females. "Will you also link only with me?" she asked.

"*Eeng*," Zooric agreed immediately. "I will never wish to link with someone else. We will be bonded. I will tell *Loya* Modnar so. We do not need an audience; it will be a fact. *Loya* Modnar can record it."

"Bonded?"

"You will be my mate," he explained.

Carrie was annoyed. She pulled away and began dressing. "Aren't you supposed to ask me first to see if I agree?"

Puzzled, Zooric reluctantly released her. His eyes were watchful. "We are to link only with each other. This means you will be my mate." He reached for her again.

However, Carrie tried to break away. "Let me go!"

"Why are you angry?"

She was more than angry. She really wanted to scream. He really was totally clueless about how to flatter a woman. "Raekon told me I was beautiful," she said in a dangerously soft voice.

Zooric abruptly released her. "Do not speak to me of Raekon."

"Raekon was very nice to me."

"Do you wish to bond with him?" he asked expressionlessly.

He was totally missing the point! Carrie stared at him in mounting frustration. "I don't even like Raekon," she screamed.

"Then why do you not wish to be my mate? Why do you speak to me of Raekon?"

Carrie was intelligent enough to recognize that comparing him with Raekon would be tantamount to asking for a catastrophic explosion. Sitting up, she decided on another track. "All women like compliments and praise. We also like to know that we are appreciated."

Zooric was staring intently at her. "Tell me what you wish that I tell you."

This was hopeless. She would never be able to teach him how to compliment a woman.

Sighing, Carrie decided to start small. "One, you do not create bonds without asking me," she checked off on her fingers. "Did you ask if I knew what a bonding is? No. Is it a ceremony? I have no idea what a bonding is, yet you immediately decided we should be bonded. Two –

you do not keep secrets. How can I bond with you when you keep secrets from me? Why do you hate Raekon so?" Carrie paused for breath and looked expectantly up at him. "Well?"

For a full minute she thought he would not reply. However, unexpectedly, he reluctantly answered.

"Raekon and *Loya* Meestric are bonded, but now he wants you. And I do not trust him. There is something not normal about him. I can sense his emotions."

"How can he want me if he is bonded with *Loya* Meestric?" Carrie was not really shocked. She would not soon forget Raekon's emotions during the aborted link but was still puzzled on the real meaning of a bonding.

"I have never lived in the Soosan sector. I do not know all their habits. I do know that the bond is permanent."

Carrie nodded. "If the bond between *Loya* Meestric and Raekon is permanent, why do you fear Raekon? What do you mean when you say he is not normal?"

"Raekon is mentally unstable. Besides, some partners who are bonded allow links with others." Zooric frowned. "This is true of ordinary Owoons, so perhaps it is the same within the Soosan. I am not sure how serious they hold the bond. Our bond will be very serious. You will link only with me."

And God help her if she didn't. Carrie sighed. Ruefully, she wondered what she had gotten herself into. She seriously doubted she would ever penetrate his arrogance. And she really did not see him casually giving out compliments.

"Can a Soosan bond with a woman?"

"Soosans have only ever bonded with other Soosans. Remember, Soosans cannot control the intensity of a link. It is always involuntary and only occurs during intercourse. Such a link would kill an ordinary Owoon female. *Loya* Modnar tells me that I am the only sensitive to ever successfully link with a woman, but I do not think the Soosans have ever really checked Owoon females."

He shrugged. "I really did not expect that I would ever be able to link with anyone, male or female." It was clear that while he did not attach any negative connotations to the Soosan's lifestyle, he did not wish it for himself. Especially after his experience as a child, he was still leery of relationships with males in general. "The Owoons have male and female bonds. My mother is bonded to my father and my sister has a bond with her mate and he is males."

Carrie nodded. She understood that bonds could be with male to male or female to male. She was still curious however because her culture did not promote male-to-male relationships.

"Perhaps linking only with males is not the choice for all Soosans..." Again, Zooric shrugged. "I do not believe these *Loyas* are interested in females and I cannot judge the Soosans from the behavior of Raekon. Mentally, Raekon thoughts are.... disturbing."

"*Loya* Meestric sees no fault in Raekon."

"I think Raekon hides his true nature from *Loya* Meestric."

"Why do you hate him?" Since he was talking, she decided to try for some more information. "There is more isn't there. Why do you think he is unstable? Why haven't you told *Loya* Modnar?"

"What could I tell *Loya* Modnar? He already knows that Raekon and I do not like each other. He thinks I hate

Raekon because we were abused as boys, together in Caleel.

"Is that why you hate him?"

"I hate him because..." He deliberately shifted slightly away from her before continuing, trying to put both mental and physical distance between them. "Raekon is allied with Restric. I have suspicions but no proof. And *Loya* Modnar has already told me that Raekon was not aligned with Restric during Restric's rule of the sector. I cannot remember the whole, but I know he and Restric were best of friends when I was a captive. However, since I cannot remember, I cannot accuse."

"What do you mean?"

"As a young boy...." There was a lengthy pause, as Zooric seemed totally focused on examining the patterns in the water. He finally continued. "After I decided not to cooperate, I began fighting them, so I was drugged."

"Drugged?"

"I remember very little and the little I do remember I have tried to forget," he said quietly. "Whenever the drug came close to wearing off, I was always given more. I can recall only jumbled half memories of those cycles. Sitting straighter, he was still staring at the flowing water. "When my memories do come, they are often nightmarish, and Restric and Raekon feature prominently in most of my worst nightmares. They both enjoyed inflicting pain, mental and physical..." Abruptly he struggled to his feet, then, before she could comment, he unexpectedly dove into the water.

"Zooric!" she cried as he surfaced, arched his body out of the water and then dove again.

Zooric came up, laughing. "It is cold and deep, but it feels good. Come in!"

Carrie stared at his laughing face. It was so rare for him to even smile that his laughter tugged at her heart. She grinned reluctantly, only to receive a splash of water for her efforts.

"Zooric!"

"Come in!"

"Are you crazy? It's freezing cold!" Then, "Don't you dare wet me," she cried as she backed away from a grinning Zooric who was once again filling his cupped hands with water. "You know I don't have a change of clothing." Before the other Owoons had arrived, Carrie had often worn Zooric's clothing, but since their arrival she had limited herself to borrowing only his tunic when her clothing needed a wash. For the trip she had changed back entirely into her own clothing.

Zooric hauled himself out to the water and sat on the bank. He was naked, and the early light sun highlighted the glistening drops of water on his smooth back.

"Put some clothing on before someone comes?" Carrie urged.

Instead, he stretched out on his back ignoring the spreading goose pimples on his skin. "Come here," he urged.

"It's getting late. The others could come in this direction." But Carrie reluctantly came over. Zooric however, only wanted to hold her to his chest. Although her outer garment was getting soaked, Carrie did not protest. For the next few minutes, they remained motionless. She could feel and hear the steady beat of his heart. A feeling of relief swept through her, as both his emotions and thoughts came rushing in. He had decided to put the pain and horror of his past aside. The intense hurt was gone. Lifting her head, she smiled up at him. Zooric grinned back.

"How is your leg?"

"Fine. But *Gaad* Egell suggests that we remain here another cycle before continuing our journey."

Carrie suddenly thought of something, "Does *Loya* Modnar know that you can read their emotions?"

"I did tell them," Zooric admitted.

"Can they read yours?"

"No. It is a skill that only I have."

Again silence. If only they could remain like this forever! Carrie ran her fingers along his smooth cheeks. "Do grown Owoon men ever get facial hair?" she queried.

"*Zte*. It is one of the differences between our people and yours. "

"One of the many differences," she agreed. Indeed, the hair covering Zooric's body had, was as fine as that on his face. As Carrie's thoughts wandered, her curiosity stirred. "Do your people have any particular worship?"

"Worship?"

"Umm. You know... what god do you believe in?"

"Ah." His face cleared. With an impish grin he began reciting parrot fashion. "The only God is Tooaal, and Jesus was his son."

"Tha...Tha..." Carrie sat up; her mouth was hanging open.

Zooric laughed outright.

"But how did...how do you know of Jesus. That's our religion."

"Have I not told you that we are the children of those of your people—the ones that were captured?"

"But... I thought that they all died."

"They died, that is true. But from the Writing of *Loya* Favood, I know that many lived to see their children grown, and so taught their children of their beliefs."

"But Gavaa is nothing like English."

Zooric shrugged. "So, they chose to speak the language of their captors."

"Gavaa is the language of the Azar?"

"Very similar. Of course, there were changes."

"I would not adopt the language of my captors." Carrie was indignant.

"It is now a fact and already a part of our past that cannot be changed. Why should I get upset?"

He had a point. Accept the past as an unchangeable fact and move on—or try your best to forget and move on. Perhaps that attitude explained how he had managed to survive his childhood abuse. Carrie again rested her head on his chest. "This is so unbelievable." She was silent as she digested this new information. "That is why Soosans can understand English!"

"Umm."

"Zooric, are you falling asleep? You can't sleep here."

"I am not sleeping." However, he did not stir.

"How did you escape?"

He had no difficulty following her train of thought. "I was accidentally sizzled— perhaps during one of those incidents from my nightmares. I was recovering, but I suspect that they did not believe I would recover fully. They left me unguarded. It is possible that I recovered only because I was such a high sensitive. Anyway, I climbed out a window one dark."

"What about Restric?"

This elicited a reaction. Zooric stiffened.

Carrie began stroking him soothingly. "You always get tense whenever his name is mentioned. You said he became ruler of the Soosans. What happened to him?"

After a long pause he told her. "I almost sizzled him."

"How?"

"Caree..."

"Zooric..." she matched his pleading tone.

He was silent.

"Zooric you cannot say that and not follow up on how and why. How did you end up sizzling Restric?"

"Remember I discovered Nergeet, the Azar sector South of Caleel. I lived there for many cycles because I was afraid of recapture. When I left, I told my family about my find and my brother and others reported it to the Soosan.

However, the Soosans held them prisoners and demanded that I come. I later learned that the demand was from Restric. Restric had been *Jirga* for about two alifees. He was uncontrollable —and very strong. As soon as I arrived, he took me to his private chamber and demanded to link with me. There is no way... I could not... Not even to save my blood brother. Restric, of course, was furious. He tried to sizzle me, but while in Nergeet I discovered a weapon that could repeal the sizzle. I used it on Restric. It sent him a backlash." Zooric closed his eyes on a scene that was clearly still vivid in his mind. "I also buzzed him.

Restric's screams brought just about every Soosan to the chamber. But I was most surprised when no one tried to arrest me. They were all interested in Restric and the fact that he was injured. They told me I could leave. I was most happy to get out and to take the others of my blood. It after that I headed north and found you.

I have only now learned that Restric had been terrorizing the sector. He had already sizzled one Soosan and numerous Owoons, both male and female. They were actually glad that I got rid of their problem. No one had been able to confront him without harm. But somehow Raekon was never regarded as Restric's friend. I think one reason Restric had such absolute control is that Raekon was acting as his spy. However, *Loya* Modnar thinks Restric's absolute rule was because like me, he too had strong detection skills and could sense others' emotions. This is true, but I have only my nightmares as proof that Restric and Raekon were best of friends."

"But what will you do? Raekon cannot be allowed to get away without punishment!"

"He will not." Zooric was utterly calm.

Carrie decided not to ask for details. Raekon was right about one thing. Zooric was only partly civilized. She feared that Lola Modnar would realize too late that Zooric followed or discarded rules according to a private morality that perhaps only he truly understood. She changed the subject slightly. "You have not had any recent nightmares."

"*Zte*. I have not had any since I left my people; since I met you."

She smiled. "So, I keep away your worst nightmares."

But Zooric was serious. "*Eeng*. But I have told *Loya* Modnar that I will return."

"To the sector?"

He nodded, exhaling forcefully, as he explained his extra abilities. Throwing Raekon across the room and opening Azar sectors where things that only he and perhaps Restric could do.

Carrie had suspected this and was glad to have confirmation.

"Will you come back with me?"

Carrie gave him a startled look. "You promised...."

"I will keep my promise, but I need you with me. I will not keep you from your family. You can visit with them, but I wish you to return with me to Caleel. I want you with me— as my mate."

She sighed. He really did have a one-track mind. It seemed futile to go back to the point she had been trying to make. She tried pulling away, but Zooric wrapped his arm around her and held her close. "Zooric, I don't know. I ... I have to see my family—to let them know I'm okay."

"Then, will you come back to me?"

Carrie hugged him. This linking that they shared was special. But she suspected that Zooric would be extremely possessive, and she doubted he would ever change his solitary and arrogant ways. Should she hold out for more from their relationship or risk losing him? Then there was Derrick, her friend in Arapmo. What could she tell him?

"I have to think some more," she finally said hesitantly.

Zooric held her slightly away and for what seemed like a long time he just stared at her. It was impossible to read his thoughts. Carrie shifted nervously under his stare since she was sure he was picking up her uncertain emotions. Finally, he nodded in acceptance. She wilted in relief. Ignoring her reaction, he took her hand and pulled her to her feet.

"Come. We will return to the camp."

****

Chapter 15

At the camp the others were all chatting and eating.

Raekon watched their approach in stony silence.

"Did you enjoy her like you always enjoyed me," he asked Zooric privately.

Zooric did not respond to his mental needling.

"I could easily buzz her."

"Just try and I will not just throw you about, I will sizzle you so badly your brains will be fried." The total lack of expression in the entire speech somehow made it twice as effective. Ignoring Raekon's gasp of shock, and the surprised look from the other Soosans—they had not heard the private conversation—Zooric gently tugged Carrie over to where the Owoons were sitting. He ignored the three Soosans, as he sat to eat.

Loya Modnar frowned as he privately queried Zooric. *"It is not wise to become too close with an ordinary Owoon, Sous Zooric."*

"I will choose my friends."

"The tenets and guidelines of the sector were made for a reason. We are the rulers. We cannot mingle with our subjects."

"You are a ruler. I have no wish to rule. My wish is to be left alone. I will sit where I please." Zooric refused to budge.

"Even if you try to live among the Owoons, you will eventually have to accept that you are different. You are a high sensitive and would have to live under the constant stress of blocking. At least in the sector the rooms are insulated. There

you would have the freedom from signals. Besides, you would not be accepted in the general Owoon society. You would be feared when they realize that your electro skills can kill. Read the wise words of the ancients and consider the reasons for our guidelines."

Although he heard, again Zooric chose not to respond. He even turned slightly away from *Loya* Modnar, so indicating that he wished to end the private mental conversation. Carrie looked inquiringly over at him.

"I was conversing with *Loya* Modnar," he explained.

She looked over to where *Loya* Modnar now seemed to be having another of those heated yet mental discussions with *Loya* Meestric.

Finally, *Loya* Meestric turned to Zooric. *"Sous Zooric, we wish to speak with you,"*the *Loya* directed.

Zooric reluctantly looked up. *Can this not wait?"*

"Zte!" Loya Meestric said.

"Sous Zooric, Loya Meestric and I have already discussed this." Loya Modnar was speaking privately. *"We do need your input."*

Zooric turned to Carrie and the four Owoons. "Caree, stay here. I must see what they want." He stood and walked over to the Soosans.

"How did you toss Sous Raekon?" Loya Meestric asked as soon as Zooric was close. *"Such should not have been possible."* He allowed only the Soosans to hear his words.

"Is this the reason I was called?" Zooric demanded of *Loya* Modnar.

Loya Modnar gave a faint *smile as he responded privately* to Zooric's impatience. *"Have patience young Sous*

Zooric. You would be wise to respect even if you cannot like Loya Meestric. Remember he is of the sector."

"It that a threat?"

Loya Modnar was immediately serious. "Sous Zooric, we both know that you are a threat to us and not the other way around. But the sector does need you. Believe it or not we are actually here to ensure your safe return."

Zooric gave *Loya* Modnar a considering look before turning to *Loya* Meestric. "The sizzle is dangerous only when it is concentrated in the mind. By spreading the charge, it will go through the entire body. A powerful charge can then be given without necessarily harming the mind. The person is thrown by the power of the charge."

"Have you done this before?" Loya Modnar was curious.

"Eeng. I practiced on the animals for many cycles. If the charge is too large, it causes the heart to have an irregular beat and can kill, but only rarely have I caused any harm."

Raekon, who had remained silent until now, was furious at this perceived insult. *"I am not an animal. I am Soosan. You could not have been certain the pulse would not sizzle or kill me."*

"I have already thrown you twice. I am more than willing to again demonstrate that it was no accident you were not sizzled."

"Zte!" Raekon cried out in panic. *Loya* Modnar frowned.

"I was merely responding to his question," was Zooric's bland defense.

"Very well Sous Zooric. This skill we will also experiment further with, when we return to the Soosan." As

Zooric turned to go, *Loya* Modnar again cautioned privately. *"Consider my advice. You would be wise to eat with us."*

*"Zte."*His response was final. And *Loya* Modnar recognized it as such because he did not press further. With a nod he excused Zooric.

****

They stayed at the camp for two full cycles before *Gaads* Egell and Sorgan judged Zooric's leg ready for travel. It was, therefore, three cycles after leaving the ancient Azar sector, as second-dark was approaching, that Carrie climbed down the last path of the mountain to her home.

"I wish to take her further," Zooric said as they stopped.

"We can easily see her resting home from this point. Where is the need to invite danger?" *Loya* Meestric was frowning heavily.

"There is no need for any but me to go further," Zooric pointed out.

"Zte," *Loya* Modnar was adamant. He again tried to convince Zooric not to go further.

When that didn't work, he tried suggesting that one of the other Owoons take his place. Again, Zooric refused. His second refusal sparked a private mini argument between *Loya* Modnar and Meestric. As Carrie watched it dawned on her that these Owoons were actually here solely to protect Zooric! She was not surprised at the final agreement reached.

Gaads Trateen, Egell and Zooric would accompany her down the final path. At the least sign of trouble, Zooric should mentally notify *Loya* Modnar. Once the plan was set, Zooric requested private time with her. Or perhaps it was not quite a request since he did not even wait for an answer before pulling her out of sight of the others.

Carrie's initial protest faded as she saw the taut expression on his face. As Zooric backed her up against a tree, she was swamped with his emotions. This time he wanted her to know his need. She wrapped her arms around his neck and immediately his mouth came down to meet hers. They linked and Zooric instantly deepened the link.

"Caree... Caree...."

"I promise I will come back," she muttered into his chest when he finally lifted his head.

His tension immediately eased. Silently he traced her lips with his finger. "I will hold you to your promise. You will return in five cycles."

Carrie gave a tremulous smile then rested her forehead on his chest. Trust Zooric to immediately impose a rule! Yet she was sure of her decision, although she was still fearful of the profound effects it would have on her future. There was also her family. She was not sure how they would accept her leaving to live with an alien!

Meanwhile Zooric continued to gently caress her. *"I will know if you are well,"* he murmured mentally.

"I wish I could electro-speak to you too."

"If you are hurt, I will know," he seemed to be reassuring himself.

"But what if you get hurt."

Zooric gave a rueful grin. "With three Soosans and four Owoons to protect me, it is not possible." Then as Carrie continued to look doubtful, he continued, "I will be careful. But you too must take care. Remember, the men who arranged for your capture. They could be dangerous."

Carrie tightened her grip around him. She did not want to leave just yet. But she had to. She really missed her family, and she could not let them continue thinking that she was dead.

"I will take care. I will tell my father about Chris as soon as I get back. And don't worry, I will return. Five cycles is a very short separation." Now she was reassuring both herself and him.

"I know." There was no hesitancy in those words. In fact, it sounded remarkably like a vow. As he bent his head, this time to kiss her gently, he continued. "You will go now. It is getting darker. I wish to see you arrive safe before full dark."

Carrie reluctantly let him go, and they silently made their way back to the others. Raekon, who was still sullen, gave a smirk but said nothing. Carrie quickly looked away. She neither liked nor trusted Raekon now, and it embarrassed her to know that he was probably aware of the linking she had just had with Zooric.

Gaads Trateen and Egell followed as Zooric led to the fluar. *Gaad* Trateen was leading the zig that Carrie would ride to her home. At the last stretch of woods above her father's outpost, the group stopped, and Carrie mounted the zig.

"Be careful," Zooric repeated.

"I will." She gave a tentative smile then slowly made her way into the outpost. It did take long. At the main house she hitched her zig to the railing—provided for just such a use —then slid elegantly down. She looked up, but it was impossible to see Zooric in the dark. Yet she was reassured that he would know where she was. She had drawn and left a rough plan of the house at his insistence. It showed the location of all the main rooms plus all the bedrooms, including hers. She had no doubt that if she did not return to him within her five-cycle window; Zooric would come and get her.

Carrie stepped onto the wraparound porch that opened onto all the downstairs front rooms. She walked toward the door—to the main lounge room. It was very late so she did not expect to find anyone about. The wood of the porch floor squeaked.

"Who is it?" a voice called.

Carrie did not get a chance to answer. The door swung open and her oldest brother peered out.

"Dave!" she screamed before launching herself at him.

"Carrie!!"

He staggered under her weight, barely able to hold her. But as soon as he recovered his breath he started screaming at the top of his lungs. "Carrie is here! Everyone! Carrie is here!"

Within an instant the porch was crowded. In fact, Carrie was dragged inside on a wave of bodies. For the next few minutes, no sensible conversation emerged. Carrie was literally passed from relative to relative as each expressed their delight and joy. In addition to Dave, all her family was gathered in the room —her mother, her father, her younger brother and the baby of the family Kelly who was only eight years. There was even Derrick and also Thia, their housekeeper. Derrick's father and her father had been childhood friends. He had lived with them for over two years, ever since the death of his parents.

"We thought you were dead."

"We could not find you anywhere..."

"Did you..."

"Where..."

Carrie began laughing. "One question at a time. One question at a time." She found herself settled between her mother and father on the couch as eventually the flood of questions slowed then stopped. Kelly, her youngest sister, squeezed in between her and her mother and snuggled against her.

"Oh Mam." Carrie gave her mother one last tight squeeze, which was reciprocated.

Mrs. Classet had tears streaming down her face and made no effort to hide her joy. Carrie looked around. Even her father and brothers looked emotional. How could she have even thought of not returning!

But all too soon the storm of emotion passed. It was then that she noticed the silent presence of four strangers. They wore the uniform of the Presidential Guards.

"What happened, Carrie? Where have you been?"

The question came from Derrick, but Carrie was unable to answer the question. She stared at the Guards in growing terror. "Dad?"

There was an uncomfortable silence as Mr. Classet followed her gaze.

Before he could reply, the leader of the Guards smiled. It was not a pleasant smile. "I take it you are the missing daughter?"

Carrie lifted her chin at his tone. "I am Carrie, yes. Who are you?"

"Carrie," her father cautioned. His voice sounded incredibly weary, further shocking Carrie. She had never heard him sound so defeated "The Presidential Council sent a force of over one hundred men, nine cycles ago. They have been investigating your kidnapping and would have been leaving within one cycle. This is Commander Ryan and his deputies. I am under arrest."

"Arrest!" Carrie asked wide-eyed.

He nodded grimly. "Yes."

"But ...But... What is going to happen?" Carrie looked around as her unease mounted. Both her older brother and Derrick were scowling— Derrick in anger, Dave more in disquiet. Her mother was definitely fearful and so was Kelly. Even Scot, normally the most carefree, was looking worried.

"What will happen is that we will finally be able to carry out our mandate." The commander was unquestionably satisfied. "We were sent to take both you and your father into custody. Now that you have decided to return home this will be possible."

Not liking his tone and the implication that somehow, she had deliberately stayed away, Carrie quickly spoke up. "I was kidnapped." As she sniffed, her father passed her a handkerchief. She wiped her face and blew her nose. She could not believe that, although she was finally home, her problems were just beginning.

Now her family was staring. "What!" The response came from Dave.

"By who?" Her father asked his tone grim.

Carrie began explaining. "I got up that light to go the fluar's watering hole. When I stepped into the barn some men were discussing stealing moonglitter from you Dad."

"Stealing!" Derrick exclaimed.

Carrie quickly explained how she was kidnapped and taken to the cabin in the mountains by Chris. "Fortunately, I escaped," she ended.

"Mine robbers. Blinking stars! Mine robbers! Here!" Dave stared in disbelief.

"Describe the man you think is the leader," her father asked.

Carrie described the man she had not recognized.

"Any ideas," Mr. Classet asked as he looked around.

"Sounds like Mr. Kolling," Derrick commented. "He moved to Arapmo just about six weeks ago. The time fits. And Carrie has never met him."

"Who is he?" Carrie had never heard the name and she knew just about all of Arapmo's citizens.

"He opened another general store in town," Derrick frowned as he answered. "Perhaps two weeks before you were kidnapped. But even before that he was staying in the hotel. Said he was checking out the town."

That was not unusual. It was a common practice for a single-family member or even single men to check out the town before finally moving in or bringing their families.

"We would need to take her to town to prove this," Dave suggested.

Her father had stood during her explanation, a scowl gradually growing on his face. He started pacing. Their lounge room was large, with the furniture arranged about a low center table. But with two large sofas, a huge fireplace, scattered single lounge chairs, plus the addition of the entire family, there really was not much room for pacing. He stopped to rest his elbow on the mantel of the fireplace, before turning to the commander. "Surely you see that this is something that needs to be addressed. A crime was committed. We are going to have to find this cabin—perhaps even catch them in the act."

"Yes," Derrick agreed. "Isn't the Presidential Council interested in stomping out crime? This man will no doubt continue his criminal activity—perhaps even in New World City—if he is not caught. We should take Carrie to town. Have her identify this Kolling."

"Or perhaps find the cabin first," Dave voted.

But the commander was not having it. "Perhaps if I really believed this crazy story that your daughter concocted; I would be more concerned." He looked around with a tight smile. "But I find it hard to believe. It seems to me that this only further proves your guilt on obstruction charges. In fact, I wonder if your entire family is not in collusion." Again, he paused. "But we have our orders. Your father's arrest is for obstruction of a Council's order. No citizen can be allowed to deliberately flaunt the orders of the Presidential Council. Now that Carrie has been found she will naturally be taken to New World City for an immediate marriage. We already have the agreement from her new prospective husband. The first prospect we now consider too good, considering that she is the daughter of a dissident."

"No!" Carrie cried in horror. "I..."

"Carrie!" her mother warned sharply. "Remember Commander Ryan is with the Presidential Guards. They have more men sleeping outside and also have a garrison of close to one hundred men stationed in the town."

Carrie gave her family a panicked look. It was obvious that the Presidential Guards had come prepared for war. The Arapmo Town Council has assumed they would be given a chance to argue their point. But it was now clear that the Presidential Council was not interested in anyone's point of view. Every hint of dissent would be crushed. And there was no way that Arapmo could compete with the force that they had sent. But after knowing Zooric, how could she go to New World City and marry a stranger? Carrie bent her head to stare at her tightly clasped hands, looking up only when she heard a whispered conversation between the commander and one of the deputies.

The commander looked sternly at her. "There are still unanswered questions. Where were you all this time? According to your parents you disappeared a little over five weeks ago. They were unable to find any trace of you."

Carrie licked her lips, her head jerking between her parents and her older brothers.

"Carrie be...," her father began.

"Silence! Allow her to answer," the commander ordered.

"I..." Carrie could feel her face heating. She stopped. Oh no! This was it, she thought.

Could she possibly tell the truth? How would it affect her father's case? There was no hope for her to avoid a marriage but she did not want to make her father's situation worse.

There really was no choice now but to tell all. What other reason would she give for disappearing for over five weeks? Carrie took a deep breath. "We aren't the only people on this planet."

"What!!" They all stared blankly at her.

"Carrie what the lightening are you talking about?" Dave finally asked.

"She is tired," her mother began hesitantly.

"There are other people on this planet. They are called Owoons. One rescued me and accidentally killed Chris." At their disbelieving stares, she turned to her mother. "Mam. This is true. I... I'm not making this up. If you go to the cabin, you will find Chris' body. It was buried outside."

Commander Ryan snorted. "Come. You could do better than that." He turned his furious stare on her family. "I begin to suspect that you were persuaded to take her out of hiding when you realized the seriousness of your infraction against the Council."

"I am telling the truth!" Carrie insisted.

"Enough. You father can explain his case to the Council."

"There is no doubt that she was kidnapped." Mr. Classet objected. "You can easily confirm the evidence of her kidnapping."

"The only thing we have is your word — the word of a dissident. As it stands, shortly after you petitioned the Presidential Council to stop her arranged marriage, your daughter and one of your workers went missing for over five weeks. She reappears, suddenly, the cycle before we are scheduled to leave Arapmo with an obscure story of aliens." Again, he glared at the group. "Do you imagine we are stupid? I think it likely that Chris too will show up soon."

There was silence in the room. Carrie looked down at her tightly clenched hand. A small hand silently reached over to touch her. It was Kelly's.

"I believe you Carrie," the little girl said softly.

"Thank you darling," Carrie blinked. She looked up. Her family was extremely worried and Carrie did not know what to do. How could she convince the commander that she had truly been kidnapped?

"I believe Carrie too," Scott said glaring at the commander.

Derrick, after a slight hesitation, also came to her defense. "I know Carrie is not stupid. She wouldn't have made up a tale like that unless it's true." Carrie smiled at him. She had been half in love with Derrick before her kidnapping.

One by one her other family members also came to her defense.

"It is so outlandish it has to be true," Dave said giving her a rueful look.

As her mother nodded, her father began pleading with the commander. "Derrick is right. My daughter is not an idiot. She would not have invented such a tale. Had she initially been a runaway why would she return just to get us into more trouble. At least let her finish the tale."

"Very well," the commander folded his arms and looked mockingly at Carrie. "So perhaps you will tell us why this alien suddenly decided to release you after fifty cycles?"

Carrie saw no option but to continue her story. "The Owoons live about twenty weeks travel from here. They look somewhat like the Blacks, the darker Colonists in the original landing party."

Matters of race were so complicated, Carrie thought. Originally, the colonists who had first landed had been a mix of races from the planet Earth—in addition to whites there were Blacks, Asians and numerous Latin Americans. Although the colonist population was now more blended, they were not yet homogenous. Many still had darker complexions; some even had distinctive Asians features, and hair color varied from blond to black with all the shades and textures in between. The current population even had a range of eye colors.

But it was the rising objections to the fast spaced approach to creating a single race that was the driving force of the major rebel groups. One group believed in keeping all the distinct races separate—by force if necessary. Carrie's father led another faction. His group objected to any form of forced marriages. In fact, although for the moment Mr. Classet had joined forces with members of the other opposition faction; he totally disagreed with their objectives and goal.

Some radicals were even calling for the death or the forced sterilization of children from all mixed marriages! Under their rule all interracial marriages would be banned. Such a course would immediately render Mr. Classet's marriage illegal. Because, although technically Mrs. Classet should not be considered Black, from their study of ancient history, that is the category she would fall into. And Carrie had inherited her dark complexion. She was the darkest member of the family, even if she had inherited her father's features. Even Derrick— who when compared to the other settlers, seemed to have a permanent tan—came in a distant second if comparing only skin color. Dave had inherited their father's coloring— blond hair and pale complexion— but he looked more like his mother. Scott and Kelly were more mixed—both had brown hair—although they also both had blend of their parents' complexions.

"The Owoon who rescued me was in this area exploring," she continued after her inner reflections. "Their government knows about us but did not want any contact. They are small in number and feared they would be taken over or killed. The Owoon was here on his own and without the permission of his government. Shortly after rescuing me, he fell and broke his leg. We could not travel. So, we ... We found a cave. We stayed there until his leg healed enough so that he could lead me home."

"So where is this alien now?" the commander demanded.

"More than likely on his way back home," she lied. "As I said, his people do not want to contact us. As soon as he was able to travel, he brought me down the mountain."

Commander Ryan stared angrily at her. "Enough! I have had enough of this nonsense. Since you vanished once, you can vanish again. A watch will be placed in front of your room this dark."

One of the deputies suddenly spoke up. "Sir, she has been living with this man for over fifty cycles, perhaps she is no longer a maiden."

There was dead silence.

The commander smiled. He actually rubbed his hands together. "And she did not leave. Were you tied up for fifty cycles Carrie? Is that why you did not leave this alien when he couldn't walk?"

"No! I mean..." Carrie frantically tried to think. If she admitted to sleeping with Zooric she was doomed. The rules were particular rigid for girls. If a girl was not a maiden at the time of marriage and it was determined that her loss of virginity was due to a rape, she would still be forced into an undesirable marriage. If her loss of virginity was due to consensual sex, she could be forced to becoming a comfort woman, bed partners for any of the upper ranking Presidential Guards. The Council would determine her years of 'service' for the crime of losing her virginity. A long term of service could see a woman moving down the ranks until she was servicing ordinary citizens. At the end of her 'service', the girl would then be forced into marriage with generally an older or very poor man.

"My daughter was kidnapped. We have already discussed this," her father now insisted. "You cannot further victimize her for doing what was necessary to survive."

"I didn't know the way down. I was afraid of an attack — afraid of paws." Carrie frantically appealed to the commander. "He would not have been able to survive either. Not on his own. He was hurt. I... I... I couldn't leave him. Not after he had rescued me."

"So, you admit to sleeping with him?"

"This is insane," Mr. Classet interrupted furiously. "You cannot interrogate her in this manner."

"I am the commander here," The commander stated forcefully. "I have full authority to interrogate prisoners as I choose." Again, he turned to Carrie. "Answer the question! Did you sleep with this man voluntary or are you claiming you were forced?"

"Do not answer Carrie," her father ordered.

The commander glared at him. "I will insist that she be examined before her marriage. If what I suspect is true then your daughter is no longer a maiden. She will answer the question or I will personally see that she is convicted of deliberately violating the will of the Council by voluntary running off with a man." Again, the commander turned to her. "So, did you sleep with this man during the fifty cycles that you stayed with him?"

Anguished, Carrie bent her head.

Her silence was damming!

The commander nodded decisively. "For too long the Council allowed this town to flaunt its rules. This family will be set as an example to others. It is true your daughter met someone in the woods. I suspect Chris was her lover and she ran away with him. Perhaps another man discovered her and being the trollop that she is, she was quick to switch from one man to another. Perhaps the new man she picked up killed Chris. The Council will have to examine all the evidence and make a judgment. But in the meanwhile, I am arresting the entire family on charges of obstruction of justice. You will all be kept apart to avoid further collusion."

The speech threw her family into a panic. "Please Carrie," her father turned frantically to her, "Tell him you were forced."

Calamity loomed. Her eyes swimming in tears Carrie looked around at the fear and anger on the faces of her family. "I... I..." She couldn't. How could she deny Zooric and what they had shared? But what was the alternative? Her family! And could she endure being forced to sleep with total strangers—repeatedly? A sob escaped.

The commander smiled. It was not pleasant. "We have it on record that she was not forced. And naturally she will be examined in New World City to determine her status."

"Carrie?" her mother pleaded.

Bending her face into her hands, Carrie began crying. Her mother reached over to comfort her, but there was little she could do for her daughter.

The commander motioned to the deputy who had spoken. "It is late. Take her upstairs now."

"Can I go with her upstairs?" Mrs. Classet asked the commander.

"No," Again the commander motioned to the deputy.

The deputy was smiling as he stood. "Sir, do I have your permission to make sure she is settled for the dark?"

"No!" Her father, Derrick and Dave shouted at once.

Carrie also jerked, but not because of their shouts. Zooric had contacted her!

"*Caree*," he called again. "*I do not like it that you are so upset and afraid. I will be coming to your room. Wait for me there. I should not be long.*"

Carrie was so relieved to hear him she almost smiled. Her lips trembled; she really loved him— arrogance and all. She looked up and realized that in listening to Zooric, she had missed something. Her family was extremely upset. What now?

"It is not your choice to make," the commander was saying smugly.

Carrie looked around in confusion. "I don't mind going upstairs with the deputy," she said hesitantly. In fact, she was now extremely eager to leave. But her father held his clenched fists by his sides, and both Derrick and Dave were looking angry. Carrie was bewildered. Why was her mother looking so fearful now? She gave them all a reassuring smile. "Don't worry I will be okay."

"I will k..." Dave began.

"Dave!" His father cautioned.

Dave gave both the commander and the deputy a glare but remained silent, in impotent fury.

Carrie could not understand the helpless look on her mother's face. Nor could she fathom why her father, Derrick and Dave were silently seething. Later she would think about the whys. She was so focused on getting to Zooric, she did not even protest when the deputy roughly grabbed her arm to lead her upstairs. He was grinning the entire way, but Carrie ignored him. At her door she turned to bid him goodnight.

"Not so fast," he said tightening his grip on her arm as she opened the door.

"What...?" Carrie turned to him; then scowled at the hand still gripping her arm. "Let me go!" she ordered.

Instead, he pulled her even closer. "Don't you want to compare my kiss with your alien," he asked with a smirk.

Carrie lifted a clenched fist to strike his chest, but he quickly grabbed that arm as well then forced her backward into the room.

"Let me go!" she screamed as she tried twisting out of his arm.

Remembering earlier lessons from her brother, Carrie tried to bring her knee up into his groin. She almost made it. At the last minute however, he twisted slightly causing her knee to slam harmlessly into his thighs.

He laughed, roughly pushing her further into the room. Carrie lost her balance and landed hard on her bottom, just in front of the bed. Scrambling to her feet she ran for the window. Again, he laughed. "What are you planning to do? Jump?" After kicking the door closed, the deputy slowly advanced. He stopped to light a small candle beside the bed, grinning as Carrie backed away just as slowly. Then, as he lunged for her, she made a dash for the other side of the room. He caught her by one end of her skirt. Unbalanced, again she fell to the ground and before she could rise, he was on her.

Choked by fear, she began screaming.

****

Chapter 16

At Carrie's scream Derrick jumped up.

"Sit down!" the commander ordered. "Bolt..." Derrick began.

"Arm!" the commander ordered his two remaining deputies. As they pulled guns he again turned to Derrick. "The first bullet will take out your knees—the next will kill you."

Dave dragged Derrick back to the seat.

"I will inform every citizen of this deed," Mr. Classet voice was shaking in anger.

The commander only looked amused. "Who in the Presidential Council will believe, the words of a dissident and a whore?"

Furious, Mr. Classet started to stand.

A loud thud sounded from the room upstairs, startling them all. Carrie's room was not directly above, nevertheless what they heard sounded suspiciously like someone landing heavily on the floor.

In the silence that followed, everyone in the room strained to hear more. Abruptly the sound was repeated. Then Carrie's anguished cry was heard again.

"Bolt!" Mr. Classet was on his feet again, about to take a step forward.

"Dad! Sir! No!" Both his son and Derrick screamed at once.

"Take another step and you will never walk again," the commander promised. "Sit!"

For an instant it did not look as if Mr. Classet intended to obey. But Mrs. Classet reached for him. "Dennis! Please!" she pleaded. Silent tears were already streaming down her face.

She dragged him back to the sofa and, as the Classets hugged each other in grief, Derrick stared hard at the commander. These Guards would pay for this, he vowed. There were no longer any sounds coming from upstairs. But more than likely that was because the deputy had closed Carrie's room door. He gritted his teeth in fury and was unable to stop clenching and unclenching his hands.

Dave noticed his anger. "Take it easy," he muttered. "We have to stay calm... to think."

Derrick did not respond. He couldn't. Although he had never approached Mr. Classet with his plan, he had always intended to marry Carrie. Now he could only strain his ears, trying hard not to imagine Carrie's horror, as his eyes became grainy. However, there were no sounds — only an awful silence. Again, he clenched his fist. Just thinking about what had happened to Carrie brought a lump to his throat. He would gladly kill the deputy who had left with Carrie, even if it meant his own death.

Even before coming to live with the Classet's, he had been Carrie's protector. Neither of her parents was aware of the taunts Carrie used to suffer as a child. As the darkest child in Arapmo, the children of some of Mr. Classet's rivals had tried to pick on her. That was before Derrick got big enough to beat to a pulp anyone who sneered at her. Now his inability to protect her was especially painful. He took another deep breath as the commander spoke again, this time to Mrs. Classet.

"My deputy will accompany you and your youngest daughter to the bedroom."

Mr. Classet reluctantly released his wife. She nodded silently and with a terrified Kelly pressed to her side, stood.

"Sleep well this dark," Mr. Classet said gently. There were no other words he could offer in comfort.

His wife nodded silently. Then moving with an equally silent and scared Kelly, they followed the deputy upstairs. There were eight bedrooms, including two suites and a master bedroom suite. Since the arrival of the Guards, Mrs. Classet had been sleeping in a room with Kelly because the commander had taken over the master suite. Also, for the past nine cycles, Mr. Classet had not been allowed to spend any time alone with his family, and during the dark he would sleep alone in one of the bedroom suites with a guard outside his door at all times. All the boys slept in another room, while the other rooms were occupied by the commander's deputies. In fact, once in bed, no member of the family was allowed to leave the bedrooms during the dark, and the only person allowed to wander relatively free during the light was Thia, their housekeeper. She was also the only person who had been allowed to keep her bedroom.

Now as the deputy moved to take Mrs. Classet upstairs, he turned to the commander. "Should I check on Curtis?" he asked, referring to the deputy who had escorted Carrie up.

The commander smirked. "No. Don't interrupt him. You will get your turn when he is finished. First, we need to get them all safely in their rooms for the dark."

With a grin the deputy left the room.

"Damn you!" Mr. Classet grounded out.

Derrick, the Classet males and Thia watched as the three left the room. They heard the light treads of Mrs. Classet and Kelly as they climbed the steps, followed by the heavier treads of the deputy. Next, there were the sounds of the deputy's voice as he commanded the two women to stay inside their room for the dark. The bedroom door slammed shut. The deputy's treads were heard, presumably as he walked toward Carrie's room. They heard his crude shouts of encouragement to his fellow deputy as he headed back down the stairs.

"Curtis is having too much fun, sir. Perhaps we should interrupt." The deputy was grinning at the commander as he entered the room.

The commander glanced at his watch then motioned to the two deputies. "Curtis will guard Mr. Classet as soon as he gets out. One of you can get a turn with the girl and the other will take Derrick and Dave to their room."

Derrick and the Classet's males said nothing. What could they do? Curtis had been in Carrie's room for over ten minutes. It was painful even thinking about what Carrie was suffering.

A few minutes later the commander again looked at his watch. The other deputies exchanged glances. There was silence upstairs but that was understandable, the walls of the house were relatively thick and low sounds really did not carry well. Yet, somehow, the silence was beginning to feel ominous. As the silence lengthened the mood changed.

Derrick flicked a glance at the commander then discreetly looked down at his watch. Almost fifteen minutes! What the bolt was he doing to her?

The silence lengthened.

Dave fidgeted. "Something is wrong," he muttered.

Derrick nodded after another quick glance at his watch but did not look at Dave.

Another few minutes later the deputy was still not back. There was no sound from upstairs. What was happening?

The commander, who had been absently flicking through a paper, finally motioned to the other deputy.

"Go to the bottom of the stairs and call him."

The deputy did as he was bid, but after a minute of calling, the only response he got was from Mrs. Classet who mistakenly assumed that they were looking for the deputy who had accompanied her to her room. She popped her head out of her room to reply.

"The deputy left some time ago. He is not in here."

"Close your door and stay inside," she was ordered.

Mrs. Classet quickly complied. From Carrie's room there was silence.

"Perhaps I should check on him," the deputy suggested as he returned to the main room.

Without answering, slowly the commander pulled out his gun. He was not the only one uneasy. The eyes of everyone were repeatedly drawn to the direction of the stairs as anger gave way to alarm. Derrick had been straining his ears for the past few minutes. But he had heard nothing.

Using his gun as a pointer, the commander indicated that he wanted them all to move to one side of the room—away from the door. Then, with a savage grin at Mr. Classet, he vowed, "if there is foul play and my men are in any way hurt, I promise that you and your family will be imprisoned for the rest of your lives and your wife and both of your daughters will become comfort women."

"We're just as concerned as you," Mr. Classet retorted angrily. "We've no idea what's going on. You were the one to okay the assault on my daughter."

Ignoring his comment, the commander jerked his head towards the deputy who had just returned from the stairs, "Take Derrick. Use him as a shield. Find out what is happening. Check both rooms." He also motioned to the last deputy. "Get some back-up. Go outside and wake the others. Have the men surround the house. It is possible she came back with her lover."

The last deputy slipped out just as Derrick was ordered to walk up the stairs in front of the other deputy. Their booted treads were heavy on the stairs as they slowly moved out of sight of the group in the main room.

Without knocking first, the deputy opened Mrs. Classet's door.

"Find out if he is in there," the deputy ordered.

Mrs. Classet jerked to a sitting position on the bed as Derrick cautiously looked in.

"What is it?" She asked. "Carrie?"

"Not Carrie," he reassured her. "The deputy here just agreed that I could check on you." He looked around, but apart from Kelly curled up on the huge bed, the room was empty. "He is not here," he tautly told the deputy before turning back to the room. "Did you say the deputy left some time ago?"

"Yes." Her eyes were swimming in tears. "Oh, Derrick. Carrie!"

Before Derrick could comment, he was rudely shoved out of the way. The deputy entered, gun drawn and made a quick sweep of the room before starting to back out.

Derrick's lips tightened. "Try not to worry Aunt Irene. Try getting some sleep." He continued heavily. "We will see what happens in the light."

"In the light?" She seemed to be fighting back fresh tears, but Derrick was unable to comfort her. The deputy was already gesturing for him to leave.

They moved to Carrie's bedroom. Again, he pushed the door open on the deputy's instruction.

The room was dimly lit. Derrick looked around quickly and could just see the forms of two people lying on the bed.

Looking over Derrick's shoulder, the deputy gave a laugh of relief. "Curtis didn't you hear us calling? The commander is worried. What's taking so long?" Thrusting Derrick ahead of him he pushed further into the room.

Derrick's fists were clenched. But the deputy beside him gave another laugh. "Commander, it's alright," he shouted. "They were just taking their time." As he turned back to the room, he lowered his gun. "Hey, Curtis, you had your turn. Did you even give...?"

Like a switch his voice was abruptly cut off. Derrick, who had been straining to make out the activity on the bed, whorled around.

"No!" A strange voice warned. "Do not move. No sound."

A blade was pressed to his neck!

****

Once she realized what the deputy was about to do, Carrie went frantic with fear and anger. She could not fight him off!

"No! No!" Sobbing, gasping for breath, she strained and bucked to move him. It was impossible.

Savagely, he pulled at her shirt, ripping it open, despite her struggles to hold him off.

Saving her breath to fight, she continued to struggle in silence. This time his retaliation was swift. He viciously squeezed her exposed breast.

"Keep still!" he ordered.

Carrie whimpered in pain, her breath coming out in gasps as she stared wide eyed at the deputy. Then, with one hand still clenched on her breast, he reached to release himself. Again, she tried to move but stopped on a moan of pain, as he deliberately twisted his fingers into her breast.

"We can do this the hard way or the easy way," he grinned down at her. "It makes no difference to me. So why not give me a nice, good kiss and we can both enjoy this?"

He was enjoying himself! She glared up at him. No way would she voluntarily allow this —no matter what he did to her. "You dirty paw feeder!" she cried, and then gasped in pain as he gave her nipple a painful squeeze.

Angry color had flooded his face at her insult. Deliberately he squeezed her breast again, and, as she cried out in pain, he began forcing her legs apart.

"No! Please no! No!"

Abruptly, the hand twisting at her breast loosed. He fell heavily on her. Gurgling sounds were coming from his throat, but Carrie only knew she was no longer in pain. For an instant she went limp with relief, then, galvanized by the fear of returning pain, tried frantically to ease out from under him. She did not have to worry. His weight was abruptly removed. She gasped. Zooric! She could actually feel his fury. Fortunately, it was not directed at her.

The deputy was still trying to speak, but Zooric maintained a death grip on the man's throat. His eyes began bulging in terror as he realized he had made a colossal mistake in attacking Carrie.

"Wait, *Sous* Zooric!" Carrie heard an urgent voice. "Deal with him later. We do not want to warn them of our presence. Do not do anything yet."

"They will hear nothing." Zooric promised. He released the deputy with a slight shove that sent the man stumbling backwards. "You will die," he said abruptly.

The man's eyes widened in shock; there was no other reaction. There was not even a groan as he collapsed to the ground.

Carrie whimpered as the acrid smell of death filled the room. Zooric immediately turned to her.

"Zooric!" Sobbing, she ran into his arms. Zooric staggered slightly because of his leg, but he still pulled her close before turning to where the deputy had fallen. "Unfortunately, it was a quick death." His voice still reflected his fury.

"Oh, Zooric," Carrie was shivering in reaction.

"*Hush Caree.*" Zooric turned back to her. "*Link with me.*"

She did, although she realized that there were at least one other Owoons in the room with them. She was too upset to care. It seemed Zooric was equally upset, because he too ignored the presence of the others, as he brought his mouth down on hers to deepen the link.

It was a while before she was calm enough to even relax and enjoy the link, but as her terror died her passion rose. She shifted urgently although she was aware enough to realize that they could not go any further with this link. Others were present!

Reluctantly, Zooric broke the contact. He lifted his head but again crushed her to his chest. Carrie breathed in deeply. She was calmer now, but Zooric still had not regained control. She was still getting his panicky thoughts plus she could feel the frantic thudding of his heart. He was still upset.

Smiling, she wrapped her arms around him. It was just another in the long list of signs that showed Zooric cared deeply for her, although he did not seem to know how to say so out loud. "I'm fine now," she reassured. "He did not..."

"*I know. I know.*" He ran his hands up and down her back ceaselessly. "*You will not leave me again,*" he muttered.

Carrie's smile deepened at his familiar arrogance, but she was tolerant, recognizing that his fear was for her.

He was silent for a few more minutes, just holding her. But when she stirred in mounting embarrassment, he finally shifted her slightly away from his body. "Are you sure you are alright?" he demanded.

She nodded and lifted her head to look around. There was not one but two Owoons in the room! *Gaads* Trateen and Egell. Both smiled at her. Carrie shyly returned the smile. She could not help the self-conscious heat in her face. Not from what the deputy had tried to do but from the link she had just shared with Zooric. She knew they both must have sensed it. Since Zooric had now regained control of his thoughts, she tried to ease further away from him. But he was not having it.

She felt embarrassed as he took a deep breath. "Zooric, I am fine now," she said as she looked up.

His look was enigmatic as he met her eyes. Then, ignoring both her comment and her attempt to move out of his arms, her turned to the two Owoons.

"Did anyone downstairs respond?"

"If they heard anything they are ignoring it," *Gaad* Trateen replied, "No one is coming."

"What are you all doing here?" Carrie asked *Gaad* Trateen. She could only turn slightly since she was totally unable to get Zooric to release her.

"Ask *Sous* Zooric." *Gaad* Egell said wryly. "He insisted, so naturally we had to accompany him."

Zooric ignored that. "Tell me what is wrong," he asked Carrie.

She quickly told him everything ending with, "I don't know what to do. This is so horrible."

"You will not be going with these guards to New World City," Zooric decided firmly.

"But what of my family? I can't just disappear. They would all be arrested and taken away."

He frowned. "How many of these guards are there?"

"Four... Well three now." Carrie darted a quick glance at the dead deputy. Zooric had to have given him a powerful sizzle to kill him so quickly and silently. *Gaad* Trateen immediately moved to cover the body with the sheet from her bed. "But there are many more stationed right here at the outpost. And more in town."

"Perhaps *Loya* Modnar will help," *Gaad* Egell suggested.

"He is already angry that I came here." Zooric sounded doubtful.

Gaads Trateen and Egell exchanged looks. Then *Gaad* Trateen cleared his throat. "*Sous* Zooric, I seriously doubt he will remain angry for long."

Carrie silently agreed. From what she had gathered, *Loya* Modnar was willing to do just about anything to keep Zooric happy. If Zooric insisted, she was sure that *Loya* Modnar would indeed help.

Zooric frowned but nodded. "We will need a plan of action. I will contact *Loya* Modnar."

Zooric's contact with *Loya* Modnar took some time as they planned what to do, while Zooric transmitted *Gaads* Trateen's and Egell's input.

"Someone is coming," *Gaad* Trateen suddenly warned.

Zooric turned his attention to the door. "It is more than one person."

"We cannot let them warn the others," Carrie cried. "The commander will kill my family!"

"Get on the bed," Zooric said.

"On the bed..." Carrie stared blankly at him.

"Now, Caree!" Swiftly he pulled her toward the bed. "*Gaad* Trateen?"

"Do not worry we will take care of them."

****

Chapter 17

With the knife pressed into his neck, Derrick froze. Zig shit, as Dave would say, he thought grimly, then stared as Carrie sat up in the bed. She was clutching the front of her shirt. "C..!" he began.

"No sound!" the voice warned again.

The blade pressed even deeper. Derrick stiffened.

"*Gaad* Trateen, be careful. He is family ... well not quite but don't hurt him." Carrie whispered. She jumped off the bed, still holding her shirt as she came to Derrick's side. "Derrick it's alright. These are the... ah...aliens I told you of." She allowed her voice to trail off at the astonishment on Derrick's face.

The other 'form' on the bed was not Curtis as Derrick had imagined. It was.... he stared. The man swiftly got up revealing himself to be tall and dark skinned. But this man was taller than any human that Derrick had ever met.

More candles were being lit and as the room got brighter, Derrick's eyes almost popped. Not one but three aliens were in the room. And they were all huge.

He swallowed nervously. Bolt! His eyes flickered from Carrie to the aliens then back to Carrie. He swallowed again.

"Get his promise to keep silent Caree." The alien who had just left the bed was now standing in front of him.

"They are willing to help us," Carrie said urgently. "Derrick?" she prodded when he did not immediately respond.

"Shit!" Derrick muttered. Although he had agreed that Carrie was telling the truth about her kidnapping, he had been equally convinced that somehow, she must have been confused. Perhaps she had suffered a blow to the head that had affected her ability to reason or even see. She must have somehow confused a settler with an alien. Now as he was finally able to take in the rest of the room, his astonishment grew. There was a very neatly tied up deputy. He assumed the other covered mound was the body of the first deputy.

"*Gaad* Trateen will remove the knife if you promise not to call out," Carrie again called softly, trying to get his attention.

But Derrick was still in a daze, staring unbelievingly at the scene in the room.

"Derrick?" Carrie whispered urgently.

He finally focused on her.

"Promise you will not call out," she repeated. Carrie seemed to understand his shock; she touched his arm urgently. "They will help us. Just nod your head and *Gaad* Trateen will remove the knife"

Derrick blinked; then nodded slowly. The knife was removed but not sheathed as the alien stepped back. Derrick knew he would have to be cautious. "Bolt! Carrie what the... What's going on?"

"Explanations later," the same alien who had spoken said. "We need to know the positions of your family and the other guards."

Derrick wasn't sure he could handle this. His heart was pounding in a pure adrenaline rush as his body prepared for... He just didn't know what. This was ... This was ... it was unbelievable.

"Derrick!" Carrie again prompted.

Derrick gave the aliens an uneasy glance. "How...?"

"Later we explain," again the same alien interrupted. "Where are the other guards standing?"

Derrick gave Carrie an uneasy look.

"They are willing to help us," she reassured.

"The positions. Quickly!" the alien urged.

Slowly, hesitantly, Derrick began describing the room, the position of the commander and the rest of his family. "The commander is armed," he finished. "And the other deputy has already left to get help." He did not see what they could do and even if they got rid of the commander, what of the force outside? "Carrie this is useless. We..."

But Carrie motioned him to silence as the alien spoke again. "Will the commander see us from the stairs?"

Carrie answered. "No. Not if he is where Derrick says he is. But you have to be absolutely sure. My family..." her voice trailed off as Zooric nodded then moved swiftly with Trateen toward the stairs.

Minutes later an unearthly scream of pain ripped the air. It continued for less than five seconds, but even before the screaming ceased the alien was shouting to Derrick. "Tell your family all is okay. Tell them not to panic."

Derrick rushed out before he finished speaking. He was aware of the alien following. As he passed Mrs. Classet's room the door opened.

"Stay in!" he screamed at her. "Stay put! Do not come out."

Thankfully the door slammed shut because he could not stop to give further explanation.

There were shouts of confusion coming from downstairs. "Sir, tell the others it's okay."

Derrick shouted as he bounded down the stairs. At the foot were the two aliens. Derrick ignored them, reaching the room in record time. He looked around then gasped.

The commander was unconscious. His body was a crumpled heap. Yet there was no visible sign of injury. In fact, the only thing unusual was the evidence of the extreme agony the man had suffered before losing consciousness. He seemed to have literally been trying to remove clumps of his hair. His slackened fingers still held strands of hair.

Derrick looked with shock at his family. Dave was clutching a crying Scott. Mr. Classet was shakily returning to his seat on the sofa. Thia was lying on the floor in a dead faint.

"What happened?" Derrick asked.

Dave shrugged. "He just started screaming and grabbing his head. Then he fell. Is he dead?"

"I..." Derrick began.

"More men are approaching. Do you want them stopped?" The question came from the open door.

Derrick was startled. He had almost forgotten about them. One alien stood just outside the room. Although he was out of sight of the other family members, everyone in the room heard the question.

"Who is that?" Mr. Classet asked rising.

"Carrie's alien." Derrick squeezed his eyes tightly shut. But when he opened it again the scene was the same. In fact, the alien by the door was actually grinning at him.

"Bolt!" he muttered. "I don't believe this."

"Derrick what...?" Mr. Classet had now spied the aliens. "Who... What... What's going on?"

"Zig Shit!" Dave backed up with Scott.

"It's the alien," Scott cried, with the easy acceptance of a child.

As the family stared in shock, Scott wiggled out of Dave's suddenly slack finger. "Did you come to rescue us?" he asked.

"Yes," was said with a smile.

"I see," Derrick swallowed. Could they trust these aliens? Since Mr. Classet and Dave were still confused, he explained. "Curtis is dead and the other Guard is tied up."

"They killed the commander?" His father asked in disbelief.

Derrick nodded.

"Your commander is not dead, just stunned," the alien commented.

The family was still confused. "How?" Dave wanted to know.

They all looked toward the door. There were now two aliens looking in. After a pause one finally responded. "You will have to ask *Sous* Zooric."

"And the Guard killed—was he the one who took Carrie up?" Dave asked.

"Yes," the alien replied.

Dave smiled. "Good!" There was a wealth of satisfaction in his voice.

"What about Carrie?" her father asked. "Is she alright?"

"Yes. She looked fine." Derrick turned to look at the alien again.

"*Zerah* Caree is well taken care off. *Sous* Zooric rescued her before she was seriously attacked." The alien responded before repeating his original question. "More men are approaching the house. Did you want them stopped?"

"Stop them?" Clearly Mr. Classet brain was still fuzzy from shock.

"Those are more Guards," Derrick said urgently. He did not even think to ask how these aliens knew the Guards were approaching. They would deal with the questions later. "The Guards will be attacking us any minute."

"Bolt! The deputy warned the force outside. They will be back to wipe us out within minutes." Dave said grimly.

"No. We are pledged to support you. We will eliminate this force that you speak of, if it is your wish." He raised his voice and turned to the stairs. "*Sous* Zooric!"

As he spoke a warning shout came from outside.

"Commander! Is all okay?"

"Get down!" Mr. Classet shouted. They all dove for the floor then began a scramble for the weapons which were kept in a locked cabinet since the arrival of the Presidential Guards. Dave grabbed a chair and quickly smashed in the glass doors of the cabinet. They were passing out rifles just as the other alien, the one called *Sous* Zooric, appeared. As he came further into the room, they noticed that he walked with a slight limp. From outside came another shout requesting that the commander show himself. Crouched low, the Classets waited. They did not have to wait long.

One of the aliens in the room shouted a warning in his strange language then added in English. "They are coming closer!"

"This is hopeless," Dave cried. "This house wasn't built for defense."

His father nodded grimly. The house had a front porch that gave all the front lower rooms easy access to the outside. This main room faced the porch. Carrie had entered directly from the porch as had the Guards. The Guards could also fire directly in on them because the entire front of the room was made of glass windows and glass doors. They were protected only by the drapes. There was nowhere to hide.

Mr. Classet raised his rifle to fire out into the darkness.

"We cannot waste any bullets." Derrick shouted. "Let's wait until they come in."

Zooric looked at them. He had slowly made his way to the low sofa and was now crouching behind it. "Once they start shooting you will be in the direct path. We have to attack first because there is no place to hide."

As he spoke, he turned back to look at the draped outer walls, then, before any of the Classets could answer, there was another unearthly scream. Derrick almost jumped a foot. Then he remembered. He looked over at the alien called *Sous* Zooric.

"Bolt!" Derrick muttered.

"What?" Dave asked. "What happened?" he eased his head up slightly from his hiding spot behind another sofa.

"Keep down," Zooric warned. "They are confused." As he spoke a staccato of gunfire riddled the glass front of the room.

"Get down! Get down!" Derrick shouted. As the entire glass wall shattered under the hail of bullets, the Classets scrambled for cover.

"What the hell is happening?" Mr. Classet demanded.

There were screams and confused shouting from outside. The room was again bombarded with gunfire.

"It's the alien by the sofa. Look at him." Derrick whispered.

Both Dave and his father turned to watch. Zooric was entirely focused on what was happening outside. His gaze was fixed on the now shattered glass walls, as he turned his head in a slow arc.

"Zig shit." Dave was incredulous. "He's causing it. But what is he doing?"

"I think he is taking care of our problem," Derrick was grim.

"Some are moving to the back of the house," one of the aliens by the door warned.

Ever practical, Mr. Classet gestured to his son. "If he is taking care of the ones in front, we may as well take out the ones coming in from the back. Come."

None of the aliens stopped them as they scrambled out of the room, keeping as close to the ground as possible. They were gone none too soon. As Derrick rushed into a back room, he spotted a Guard attempting to rush the house.

Boom! The man toppled over in slow motion. "One down." Derrick called grimly.

"Scott! Get back!" Dave shouted as his younger brother slipped into the room.

"I want to help."

"Then get Mam. Take her and Kelly to the middle rooms. Quickly!"

Scott turned to run.

"Keep down!" his father shouted. The younger boy dived to the floor then continued snaking across the room toward door. From there they could hear him running up the steps. Satisfied that his youngest son was safe, Mr. Classet called to Derrick and Dave "I'll take the right side; Dave can take the left. Derrick you can stay here," he shouted as he rushed away.

The battle raged on for almost twenty minutes, but slowly the shots from the outside petered out then died. Silence reigned.

"Do you think we are safe?" Dave asked, coming back to Derrick's side.

"For now. They are either all dead or they fled."

Mr. Classet joined them. "Let's check on Scott and the girls." They had all been ignoring the terrified cries from Kelly for the past few minutes.

Scott had a gun and was standing by the door of the lounge looking into the main room. Mrs. Classet, Carrie, Kelly and Thia were with him. Thia was now conscious, sitting and staring blankly at nothing. She seemed to be in shock. Kelly was crying inconsolably in her mother's arms. The little girl was terrified. Carrie looked up from where she was bending over her sister.

"Is it finished?"

"We think so. Where are they?" She did not have to ask whom he was talking about. "*Gaads* Trateen and Egell went outside to check on the wounded. Zooric is still in the main room." She turned back to Kelly. "It's okay now Kelly. See. There is Dad, Dave and Derrick. Everyone is okay."

As she spoke Zooric entered. He quickly scanned the room then immediately went over to Carrie.

Mrs. Classet looked dazed as she took a good look at the alien then rushed over to her husband. Kelly, still holding tight to her mother, actually stopped crying and began staring in fascination.

"I believe it is safe now," Zooric said.

Thia started to rise but stumbled slightly. "You okay Thia?" Derrick asked.

"Just shocked. Still trying to absorb this." She waved her hands in the direction of Zooric.

Dave moved over to Thia who they all regarded as one of the family. "You and me both," he said.

Derrick looked around, "What do we do now?" As he spoke the other two aliens entered the room.

The three aliens came together and exchanged words in their language. Then the alien called *Sous* Zooric moved back behind Carrie, his arm rested easily on her shoulders as he surveyed the room. Carrie in turn smiled at him. She was still clutching the front of her shirt.

Derrick stiffened. Helping them was one thing. Thinking they could have Carrie was quite another. Almost as if aware of his negative feelings, the alien's glance focused on him. Derrick held his breath. But the alien continued to regard him expressionless for perhaps a second before turning to look down at Carrie. Then he moved, startling Derrick. But he was merely removing an outer robe; this he slipped over Carries shoulders. She smiled again, then looked embarrassed as she turned back to her family and realized she was the focus of all eyes.

Mr. Classet cleared his throat. "Perhaps we should introduce ourselves?"

Carrie nodded hesitantly. "This is *Sous* Zooric," she introduced. "He rescued me from Chris." She then pointed to the other two aliens. "*Gaads* Trateen and Egell."

Turning to her family, she introduced each member by name.

Scott broke the silence following the introductions.

"Did you kill Chris the same way you killed the commander?"

"Scott!" Carrie cried looking embarrassed.

If Zooric was upset Derrick didn't see it. The alien's face was totally expressionless as he scanned the family without answering. Into the short silence he abruptly inserted. "It is time we left."

"Leave!" Derrick, Dave and Mr. Classet stared at him, astonished.

"But what of the other Guards?" Dave asked.

"Yes, there is an even bigger force in town." Derrick said grimly.

"Many of the men escaped." Zooric said with a slight frown. "I am not sure how many. Since they have no leader, many began running when they realized the battle was hopeless for them. They took their dead or injured with them. It is likely they are headed for the town to warn the others. It will take them perhaps half a cycle to get to the town, then another half cycle to return. We can do nothing but rest for the next battle."

They gaped at him. His absolute assurance was almost mind boggling.

"Listen, we er..." Derrick began then stopped as a groan came from the other room.

"The commander?" Dave asked.

Following the lead of the aliens, they all reentered the main room. The commander was indeed awake. He was also neatly tied up, gagged and terrified.

"He was making too many distracting sounds," Zooric explained.

Carrie just grinned. "These are the aliens I told you about," she sweetly informed the commander.

But it was doubtful that he heard her. The man was absolutely terrified.

"Did he hurt you? Do you want him dead?" Zooric asked seriously.

"No," Mr. Classet hurriedly injected.

Derrick raked a hand through his hair as he gaped at Zooric's emotionless question. It gave him chills. What exactly was this being? What had Carrie gotten herself into?

As her father paused, Kelly, having overcome her fear, spoke up. "You look like the pictures in my history book," she told Zooric.

At that Carrie smiled. "I told him so."

Hesitantly Mr. Classet asked. "Are you sure, that is not exactly what happened?"

"What do you mean Dad?" Dave asked.

"I remember reading about..." he again hesitated. "I seem to remember from our history that some of the original colonists vanished without a trace. At the time we assumed that the revos dragged their bodies off. It is possible that they defected and formed a separate colony. That could explain... you do have the look of the only male that vanished."

Carrie's answer was slow in coming. "I don't think so, Dad." And as she hesitated her family assumed she was unsure of the Owoons history.

Then before she could elaborate, Dave took up the point. "Why not? Is could be possible."

"No human could have disabled the commander the way he did," Derrick said slanting an angry look at Zooric.

"Maybe," Derrick's analysis short-circuited Dave's reasoning. "I had forgotten about that."

Derrick nodded; it was in fact easy to forget they were aliens because they really looked human. Plus, as Kelly said, they looked like history had come alive. They really could pass for the original Black colonists. He knew that was why his entire family had so easily overcome their fear. Too easily he felt. They had no idea what these aliens were capable of. Seeing Carrie's hesitant look, he gave her a sardonic look. "Don't even try making up some story now to let us believe that they are human."

"I was not thinking of making up a story," Carrie responded with quiet dignity. "I was thinking of telling you the truth."

Derrick gave her a derisive look. Remembering past episodes, Dave quickly interrupted before a full-fledged verbal war broke out between the two.

"What will we do with him," he asked pointing to the commander.

"Perhaps the tack room behind the kitchen," Mr. Classet suggested.

Gaads Trateen and Egell moved toward the commander. The commander arched backward in terror. But he was too securely tied to go anywhere. They easily snagged him, and although he continued to make muffled sounds, he could offer little resistance as they dragged him from the room.

With the commander gone, Derrick stubbornly brought the conversation back to the aliens. He turned to Zooric. "Do you mind telling us how you did it?" This alien had strange powers — powers not known to them.

As the only alien left in the room, Zooric was now the focus of all eyes — not that it fazed him. He was still viewing his surroundings, his interest apparent more by his actions rather than his facial expression, and he made no attempt to answer.

Carrie cleared her throat. "We have to tell them." She muttered almost as if taking to herself.

Zooric shrugged. His hand was still on her shoulder. Now he ran it down her back in an unconscious caress. Unconscious for him that is; Carrie seemed well aware of his actions and her family's surprise. She tried pulling away. Zooric immediately looked down.

"No," he said aloud. Although he did not sound angry, his tone was nevertheless final.

It was that finality the sparked Derrick's anger. "Release her," he scowled. "She wants you to let her go."

Zooric's eyes narrowed. "Caree and I are bonded," he stated firmly.

"Zooric!" Carrie wailed, her tone expressing her deep mortification.

"Does bonding mean what I think it means?" Dave asked the room at large.

Mr. Classet was frowning. "My daughter was forcibly removed from her home. Although I appreciate your rescuing her, I will not allow her..." his voice trailed off at Zooric's scowl. It was not so much the alien's glare, but rather the wave of displeasure emanating from him.

"First, is must be understood that Caree is mine." Zooric's intent gaze flicked the room before resting on Carrie's father. "You were not there for me to ask, but you will now agree that Caree will not go to this New World or marry another."

"Zooric! You are embarrassing me," again Carrie tried to move away from him.

Zooric glanced down at her, and although they did not see or hear him say anything, Carrie was suddenly still, a discomforting expression on her face.

Before Mr. Classet could respond, Derrick spoke up, his voice laced with aggression. "Just because you took her by force does not mean she has to marry you."

"Derrick!" Mr. Classet cautioned softly. But Zooric only looked mildly confused.

"I would not take Caree anywhere by force," he said.

The alien did not quite understand, but Derrick did not care. "Was she given a choice? Could she leave whenever she wanted?" He was unable to stop, furious that this.... This alien had taken Carrie. True nothing had been finalized between them, but he had always assumed that Carrie would be his.

"Careful Derrick," Mr. Classet again warned.

"Unless he is a eunuch, he took her. Bolt! You would have her remain with that thing?" Derrick demanded forcefully.

"The choice was Caree's to stay with me and it has already been made." Zooric said calmly, refusing to get riled by Derrick's comments.

Carrie, fully aware of Derrick's meaning, spoke quickly before things could get more heated. "I was willing Dad. I was always willing." She glanced uncomfortably at Derrick before turning back to her father. "I love Zooric.... I know you don't know him yet but Zooric is...," her voice faltered at Derrick's snort of disgust.

Derrick scowled. Aloof... arrogant.... He could easily think of a number of suitable words to complete her sentence. He was both angry and upset. He and Carrie could easily squabble for hours, but he was also her biggest defender, biggest protector. True he had never pushed for any deeper relationship between them, and he had never given up on his other relationships, but Carrie didn't know about them. He never approached her mainly because of the confusion as to her pending marriage status with the Presidential Council. He had been waiting for this matter to get settled before declaring himself. How could she leave him for a...? Derrick's scowl deepened.

It was Scott who relieved the sudden tension. "You can't be married to her," he told Zooric. "We didn't come to the wedding."

"Wedding?" Zooric gave him a puzzled look.

"Shut up, Scott," Dave advised.

But Kelly was nodding. "Yes. You have to have a wedding, and we all have to come before you can be married."

Zooric turned to look at Carrie. "This wedding will not change our bond. You did not tell me of this."

"You didn't ask," she retorted in clear annoyance.

Again, Scott inserted. "You also must ask Dad first. Then, when you get his permission, you ask Carrie."

"No, you have to ask the Presidential Council," Kelly disagreed. "And Carrie is to marry someone else, so you can't marry her until they say no."

"That's enough you two," Mr. Classet hastily intervened.

But Zooric did not seem particularly worried about the missing steps in his relationship with Carrie. He was unperturbed as his hand, which had been resting on Carrie's shoulder throughout the discussion, again slid down her back.

"We will leave now."

"Leave?" Her family protested as one.

"I can't just leave," Carrie protested as she turned in Zooric's arm. She looked up at him. "I need to spend some time with my family. Perhaps you could come back in the light."

He frowned.

"What about the force in town?" Mr. Classet asked before Zooric could answer. He thought it best to bring the conversation back to the main concern. "There are close to one hundred Guards there. Once these men report to them, they will be planning an attack. In fact, I am not sure if we are not in deeper waters after this..." he waved vaguely encompassing the entire property.

Zooric looked out of the windows. "No attack will come before perhaps the end of next cycle. We will help you then."

"Exactly what weapon did you use?" Dave asked, showing he was just as curious as Derrick.

Carrie took a quick glance at Zooric's face before replying. "The Owoon have an ability that is different from ours."

"Are you the only one with this strange ability?" Dave had noticed that only Zooric killed.

Again, Carrie looked up at Zooric, giving him an anxious look. "Zooric..."

He touched the pad of his thumb to her lips silencing her. "Do not worry about the Guards in town. I told you we will help you take care of them before we leave."

But the Classet males were all frowning. Why the secrecy, they seemed to say?

"Why the secrecy over your weapons?" Derrick demanded. "Perhaps if you explained how you maimed the commander; we wouldn't be so suspicious of your future plans."

****

Chapter 18

Carrie sighed. "We cannot just leave it at that Zooric. My family needs an explanation," She glanced to where both *Gaads* Egell and Trateen stood by the door. With a shake of his head, *Gaad* Trateen indicated that both were comfortable and not inclined to move. "Come Zooric," Carrie turned to Zooric, dragging him over to the sofa. As they both sat, she began. "The Owoons have electro-sensory abilities. The ability to transfer electrical energy to the surrounding." It took a while and there were numerous questions before Carrie completed her explanations about the special 'powers' of the Owoons. With the focus increasingly concentrated on the Owoon's powers, Carrie found it hard to point out how similar Owoons were to the Colonists. She tried twice.

"There really are not much different from us. In fact, you could almost say they are humans like us..."

"Humans can't zap others with thousands of volts of electricity." Derrick abruptly cut her off.

"I'm not saying they are totally human..."

"They are in no way human," Again Derrick did not wait for her explanation. "Just look at them."

"Derrick!" Carrie cried angrily. But Zooric was not offended. In fact, he looked slightly amused as he exchanged glances with *Gaads* Egell and Trateen. Carrie, however, was more than mad enough for them all. She was getting extremely annoyed by Derrick's confrontational attitude. "Everyone can't be the same. On planet Earth there were lots of different races. They were all different, but that didn't make them any less human.

The Owoons are just like the original Black colonists. Even Kelly noticed that."

Her anger did not deter Derrick's sneering attitude. "Is that how you convinced yourself to...?"

"That's enough Derrick," her father interrupted.

Grateful for a voice of reason, Carrie turned to her father. "Dad, all I am saying is that they are as human as we are."

But Derrick was not convinced. "Get real Carrie."

With lips compressed Carrie glared at him.

"Let's just stick to the facts at this point," Mr. Classet urged. "You say they all have this power..."

"No. Only a few are like Zooric—they are called Soosans."

At that they all glanced nervously at Zooric. He had been totally silent throughout Carrie's explanation, although he seemed to be concentrating intently and following the conversation.

"Are you saying that only a few among them have these extra powers?" Mrs. Classet asked.

Carrie nodded. "Only the Soosans. The ordinary Owoon like *Gaads* Trateen and Egell have only limited electro-sensory ability and could not even stun someone. They certainly can't use their ability to kill."

"This is unbelievable." Mr. Classet said.

"I could not believe it when first I heard the story," Carrie agreed. She relaxed back on the cushions. Her original intent was to tell about the Azars and then link the Owoons with both the original colonists and the Azars. But now, with Derrick's vehement objection to seeing the Owoons as humans, she decided against forcing the issue. Later perhaps she would explain more. Her family, and especially Derrick, did not seem ready to believe that the

Owoons were connected to the colonists in any way. Besides, she would have to explain another alien—the Azars. More detailed explanations could wait for another time, she decided. Carrie even decided against mentioning their ability to mental-speak. Clearly it was too much for her family to absorb all at once.

"So how many Owoons are there?" Derrick now asked.

"Zooric said we outnumber them. They were always afraid of us. That is why they stayed away."

"Afraid of us," her father was frowning. "Why were they afraid of us? We have no electro-sensory powers."

As Carrie hesitated, Zooric finally spoke. "From writings in our history, we feared you did have dangerous powers."

"Well, there is no going back to not knowing each other. We need to have some formal meeting between our two governments. We will need to respect each other. We both will have to live on this planet and accept each other as equals."

Carrie was nodding. "There are representatives from the ruling government nearby."

"Are these the Soosans that you spoke of? The ones with greater electro-abilities?" Derrick looked at Zooric as he spoke. His disgruntled expression clearly indicated his unwillingness to accept the Owoons as equals.

"Yes," Carrie nodded.

Mr. Classet stood. "We will have to meet with them."

Zooric nodded agreement. "That can be arranged."

"Good!" Mr. Classet, unlike Derrick, was clearly excited. "This will be an Arapmo's affair, regardless of what New World City wants to do. I will have to meet with the Town Council to decide how to handle the Owoons." He looked around. "If we are attacked within the next cycle or two, we will have to get rid of the Guards without our Council. But later we will head for town and inform the Council. We'll travel together. There may be other Guards in town. I don't want to take the chance of any of us getting separated and captured by any of them."

At the mention of the Council, Derrick's lips tightened. "What of the Presidential Council?"

"We'll tell them. We will eventually have to release the commander—perhaps with a message for the Presidential Council. But I intend to keep our affairs separate from theirs. Our town will decide its own future—whether to have contact with these aliens or not. They can do what they want in New World City, but we will do what is best for Arapmo."

It was a tough speech, yet they all knew that they could not fight the Presidential Council—not without outside help. Mr. Classet seemed to be throwing his ambitions for the town into the hands of the Owoons. Yet the future was still murky.

Zooric stood up. "Now this is settled Caree will..."

"Zooric," she pleaded placing both hands on his chest. "I really do need to spend some time with my family. There is no longer a threat." She smiled at him. "I wish to stay with my family this cycle."

His glance was impenetrable as he looked down. Then, after looking up and noting the interested look of her family, he abruptly turned, putting his back to her family; effectively hiding her from their concerned gaze. Carrie must have given a very persuasive argument because finally Zooric nodded. As he turned around, he again surveyed her family. "Do you know where these Guards are stationed in the town?"

"We will need a rough map," *Gaad* Trateen said. Since he had remained totally silent through the brief discussion, his words now startled them. The family all looked to where both he and *Gaad* Egell were still standing by the door.

Soon the center table was littered with maps and drawings of the outpost and the town. The entire family joined the planning. Mr. Classet's outpost was to the north of town and there was one main path into the outpost. However, no one expected the Guards to travel that route. The path meandered up and down gentle slopes, bordered by low ridges. Along its long length, there was enough cover on either side of the path to hide an army of men. Still, they would have to set up a watch. They would also need a watch at two possible alternative paths. Attack by way of the mountains they discarded. It would take much too long for the Guards to circle those mountains and launch an attack.

Actually, the joint venture calmed everyone, to the extent that Mrs. Classet soon decided to take Kelly up to bed. By mutual consent they all decided to leave the issue of Carrie's relationship with Zooric for now and concentrate on the present threat. As the planning wrapped up, Mrs. Classet pulled her husband aside and spoke privately with him for a few minutes before bidding them all a restful dark.

****

"What about the men in my room?" Carrie asked as her mother started up the stairs.

297

Both *Gaads* Trateen and Egell looked at Zooric. Carrie's family had noted that Zooric seemed to be the person in charge. The other two both deferred to him.

"They are still there," he said. "Where should we put them?" he asked, turning to Carrie's father.

"Perhaps with the commander," Mr. Classet said as the two Owoons moved off. "Incidentally, should we involve our men?" Mr. Classet looked at his older son and Derrick.

Derrick frowned. "We should. We need more help. It's just that we would have to go to the town to get them." During the time that the outpost was occupied by the Presidential Guard, all the workers were sent to the town.

"We'll need at least three men as look out," his father decided as he began folding up the maps. "We cannot let the Guards get close enough to attack the house."

Both young men nodded in agreement. They all feared that defending the house would be a logistics nightmare.

"You are right," Dave said. "Perhaps we should move the women?"

"We will not let anyone attack the house," Zooric reassured them. "Caree and your women will be safe here. My people will stand guard at the paths and take care of any attack."

"What about a two-pronged attack?" Derrick objected. "They have over one hundred Guards"

At Zooric's blank look, he explained the possibility of an attack from two directions at once.

"We should not have a difficulty," Zooric stated as soon as he understood.

The Classets were unconvinced.

"There is nothing else we can do Dad," Dave pointed out after a pause. "It will be next to impossible to get to the town. We are on our own. If the house does come under attack, the women could hide in the cellar."

"That might be the best," Mr. Classet said. "There is nowhere else for them to go on such short notice," he said turning to the Owoons. "Are you sure you will be able to keep the Guards away?"

Zooric was positive. And even Derrick was inclined to believe him. Although he did not like the alien, he suspected that Zooric would never endanger Carrie's life. If there were even a remote chance of an attack on the house, he was sure Zooric would suggest another safe hiding place.

"What will we eventually tell the town Council about the Owoons?" Dave asked, now that they had settled the details of the counterattack.

"That they are descendants of deserters from the original colonists who choose to go off on their own." Mr. Classet decided. "Superficially they look the same."

"I doubt that will work." Derrick was shaking his head, one eye on Zooric, as he conferred with Carrie. "They will have heard from the Guards how they were zapped. The town will know that these are not your typical human beings. Besides, what happens when these Owoons accidentally show their electro- powers? And it will happen."

The other two Owoon reappeared. They had removed the Guards from Carrie's room and checked on the conditions of any Guards outside.

"We left all three in the room behind the kitchen." *Gaad* Trateen said. "There is none left outside. If any were shot by members of your family, their bodies were removed and all those *Sous* Zooric stunned have since recovered and fled."

"I though he killed them," Dave asked his face mirroring the surprise on everyone's face.

"No, they were stunned as the commander was," *Gaad* Trateen responded.

"They wouldn't have been missed," Dave said. He was positively not ready to forgive the Guards anytime soon.

"Should we leave the living with the dead?" Derrick asked frowning.

Gaad Trateen shrugged "*Eeng.*"

Derrick opened his mouth to question that. Mr. Classet stopped him. "Let them stay. After what they put us through these past few cycles they deserve to suffer. Are they still tied up?"

"*Eeng.*"

"Good. They can remain tied." Like Dave, Mr. Classet was not interested in forgetting what the guards had tried to do with Carrie. "We will release them next light. They can dig a grave to bury their deputy, then we'll retie them until this is sorted out."

Zooric suddenly stood. "*Loya* Modnar approached. I will go and confer with him." He turned to Carrie but she shooed him away.

"Go. I will be safe now. Please Zooric. Let me stay the dark. I'll be with my family. Return at first-light."

Zooric stared silently at her for a few seconds. She smiled reassuringly. Finally, he nodded. "I will not let anyone approach the house. And I will send word on the situation with the guarding of the paths," he informed them. With a brief inclination of his head, he slowly left the room, favoring his recently healed leg.

"Zig shit!" Dave muttered.

Derrick looked over at Scott who was fighting a losing battle with sleep. "Thia, could you take him up to his room?"

Thia nodded with a smile. Although she seemed fully recovered, she had remained silent throughout the discussion and still seemed nervous around the aliens.

As soon as Thia and Scott left the room, Carrie turned to Derrick. "Why do you hate him so?" she demanded.

Derrick's mouth twisted. "Perhaps because I can't imagine how you could let that thing..."

"Derrick!" her father warned.

Lips compressed; Derrick turned away. "What about you Dave. You see nothing wrong with what Carrie has become."

"Not if they get married..." Dave began hesitantly

"Married! You would legitimize it!" Derrick said incredulously.

"Carrie is fine, so let's just forget that for now," her father advised. "Dave, take Carrie to her room. Make sure it is cleaned up and there is nothing there to give her nightmares. It won't be many hours until the next cycle. We need to rest."

"I'll take her." Derrick jumped up and pulled Carrie to her feet. "Come Carrie."

Mr. Classet hesitated, and then nodded in agreement.

****

Chapter 19

Silently, Carrie and Derrick moved toward the stairs. Half way up Carrie again turned to Derrick. "What did Zooric ever do to you?"

"When you come to your senses, you'll see what he's doing to you!" He said tightly.

Carrie's lips compressed as they walked along the corridor to her room.

"He cares about me Derrick. I know he does. And I know he would never hurt me in any way."

"A pet wouldn't hurt you either," Derrick said brutally, "but I wouldn't make love to one."

"Derrick!"

Without responding to her shock, Derrick shouldered her door open. It was clean —not a spot of blood. He bent over and lit a few more candles. Then he walked over to the window and looked down. The rope the aliens had used to climb in was still attached to the window by a strange looking hook. Grimly he pulled up.

"Was he planning on sneaking back during the dark?"

Carrie did not answer; she was still upset at what he had said. As she made her way to the bed, she was aware of Derrick's building anger. But she too was getting angry. "Zooric is good for me. If you care for me at all, isn't that what you should want? A man who will treat me well?"

"Yes, a man. But you went and picked up a thing."

"Zooric is just like any man here," Carried retorted angrily. "They're all practically like us except they are tall. You know they look exactly like some of the original colonists that we read about in our history books."

"You've absolutely no idea what you're talking about. This thing isn't even human! Have you seen any other man's body— examined them? How do you know he has the same parts? Bolt Carrie!"

"He is human! You just don't want to listen. He's as human as we are and I love him. That's all that should matter."

"All!" Derrick turned about the room in frustration. "What about us?"

"There was never really 'us' and you know it," Carrie retorted. "We were always fighting over everything. And don't pretend you weren't seeing other women."

Derrick's cheeks reddened. He looked away, unable to meet her eyes. "It didn't mean anything. You don't understand...."

"It meant something to me," Carrie interrupted fiercely. "All the feelings were on my side. I was never sure if I meant anything to you."

"So is this to get even."

"No!" She glared at him. "Zooric has nothing to do with you—with us. After I met Zooric I realized that what I felt for you was nothing but friendship."

But Derrick was still furious. "Do you realize that you could be breeding a monster now," he sneered. "Did you even think about that?"

For a few seconds Carrie was startled— she had never even thought about pregnancy— then, as his implications sank in, her anger rose. Her fist clenched in fury. "Any child I have would be perfect—just perfect. Do you hear! How dare you! I always read about the original colonists and wished that the Presidential Council didn't choose to eliminate the other races of people that were here...."

"They didn't eliminate them," he interrupted.

"How do you know what they did? They say they encouraged marriages across the races to create just one race. But that's what they said. We'll never know what they actually did."

"They did it for a reason."

"Yes! They did it because they know there can be bigots like you!" she shot back. "You're worse than the Separatists living in town."

"That's unfair and you know it. I wouldn't have anything against another race of humans but you picked up an alien. Zig shit! He could've been infected with anything, and you slept with him. For all you know, you may be carrying some weird disease now."

"The Owoons knew about us. We are the aliens on this planet, so if anything, we would infect them and not the other way around. Besides, Zooric has never slept with another woman so he couldn't give me any disease."

"How the bolt do you know?"

"He told me."

Derrick gave her an incredulous look. "Carrie," he said with a condescending smile, "Men have been telling women that for ages."

Carrie decided to ignore his tone. She knew that Zooric had never had a woman before. But she could not explain how she knew, to Derrick. That would involve letting him know just how different Zooric was from other Owoons!

"I believe Zooric," she stated positively. "He was just as..." Remembering their first time together she felt her cheeks heating and turned away. "I believe him."

"You're an idiot! You haven't heard anything I said."

"You've nothing against Zooric except fear and prejudice."

Derrick stared at her in baffled fury. "Do you realize your child will be even darker than Mam? After what you suffered as a child, you would put your child through the same torture."

"I'll live with Zooric. His people are all dark skinned. Just because you are hung up over skin color doesn't mean that I am too."

Derrick refused to go there. And Carrie knew why. She knew it had never been easy for Derrick. It was their shared frustrations more than anything else that had brought them together. In New World City, there were others with dark complexions but not so in Arapmo. Her mother was the darkest citizen here, then her, next Derrick. And although a majority of Arapmo's citizens did not support the views of the Separatist, there were many Separatist sympathizers.

Mr. Classet's wealth insulated him from many of the town's racial undertones. But all of his children and Derrick were well aware of the simmering tensions. There were even some Separatists who were pleased when Carrie was given a marriage contract. The thinking being that she would leave Arapmo. She should, according to the Separatist, marry only someone of her own race to avoid further dilution of the races. And since the races were already mixed because of the policy of the Presidential Council, this would mean marrying someone her complexion or darker. The dream of the Separatist was to recreate four or five distinct races by banning all intermarriages.

Now Derrick's only response was. "If you leave with him, you'll be disappointing your Mam and Dad."

"I know Mam will understand, and Zooric promised that we'll be able to visit. I hope Dad will understand too because I have to go with Zooric. He needs me."

Derrick gave her a scowl of frustrated dissatisfaction. "He wants you and he's using you. They have probably never seen a woman like you before. But it will never last. When he dumps you, you'll be back. Just don't come crawling back to me with an alien monster in your belly." With those brutal words he slammed out of the room.

****

Derrick returned downstairs to find Mr. Classet and Dave still working on a strategy for dealing with the town Council.

"What's wrong," Dave asked on seeing his face.

"I'm wondering if that alien has somehow infected her mind. She doesn't what to listen to a single bit of reasoning."

Mr. Classet sighed, his look subdued. "She's young and in love. She's not going to listen. It's much better not to put much opposition in her path right now."

"There are more than enough human men for her to fall in love with. Sir, you can't let her leave with that thing. It would even be better if she went to New World City to marry."

"I know how you feel. I too hoped that you and her..." Mr. Classet gave an understanding smile. "Don't worry. I am not yet resigned to him having her. But we will have to be careful."

"Careful! It isn't even human." Derrick was determined to dehumanize Zooric.

"He looks human enough to me," Dave said mildly. "He looks like some of the original colonists."

"It looks human but it isn't!" Derrick snapped before turning to Mr. Classet. "We don't really know what this alien is capable of. Even if she wants to, we shouldn't let her leave with it."

"So how are we going to stop her," Dave asked. "You saw the man. He is almost seven feet tall. I would not like to get into a fight with him. Plus, he has the ability to zap us with thousands of volts of electricity. Can you just imagine us telling him not to take Carrie? He would kill us on the spot."

"Perhaps, perhaps not," his father looked thoughtful "But did you ever consider that he may not really want Carrie. He could just be fascinated by a woman who is different from his own people."

Derrick brightened. "Could we offer him another woman then?"

"Who?" Dave snorted. "And what woman will even consider going with him."

"Perhaps we could get one of the women from the town to consider him," Derrick suggested. "Mrs. Editon, for instance. She will sleep with anything in pants. If we pay her, she..."

"She would be scared shitless." Dave disagreed. Mrs. Editon was a widow whose favorite hobby seemed to be 'men.' "Carrie has had weeks to get accustomed to these aliens. No woman is going to just jump into bed with one."

"I want to retch whenever I think of that thing touching her," Derrick grounded in frustration. "She was totally innocent. He could have four male parts and she wouldn't know the difference."

"Take it easy Derrick." Mr. Classet did not share Derrick's racial fears, and as Carrie's father, did not carry the baggage of ambivalent feelings of rejection. "She hadn't been hurt. So, whatever he has done, he's been gentle with her. She wouldn't want to stay with him otherwise."

Derrick stared, clearly blind-sided by Mr. Classet's words.

"I have my reservations," the older man continued with a rueful look. "But perhaps the best way to go about this is to introduce him to other women and also get them both to stay here for a while. I don't believe trying to break up the relationship at this point would be successful."

"You mean get them to stay and bring Mrs. Editon here as well?" Dave asked.

"Not here. Your mother would never allow that. But perhaps once we have sorted out this situation with the Guards, we could take him into town, introduce him to others, especially women. He could well take the bait."

Derrick began smiling. "It could work. Bolt! I just hope she is not pregnant."

"Zig Shit!" Dave muttered.

"Whether she is or not, once they are living here, we will keep them apart as much as possible." Mr. Classet rubbed his jaw. "If there is to be a baby, we can deal with that later.

Meanwhile, we can just tell him she needs time to prepare for a proper wedding." He looked around for agreement. The others nodded.

Satisfied that he had done all he could, Derrick moved back to their immediate danger. "Do we need to keep watch this dark?"

After a moment of thought Mr. Classet nodded. "I somehow don't believe that they will harm us or let anyone approach. He really seems committed to keeping Carrie from harm. But just to be sure, who will take first watch?"

Derrick offered. Since that was settled, the others headed for bed.

****

Carrie was much too angry to fall asleep after Derrick left. Fighting back tears, she quickly stripped off her clothes, took a quick wash and put on her nightshirt. Now she was in bed but unable to sleep, as she twisted and turned trying to get comfortable. She also missed Zooric. She finally sat up, hugging her knees. "Oh Zooric, why did I tell you to leave?" she said aloud. Much as Carrie loved her family; she knew she would have to choose Zooric over them. She could not, would not, give him up. What was she going to do? Would she ever be able to convince her parents to accept Zooric? Derrick, she had already given up on. Carrie squeezed her eyes shut and hugged her pillow.

"*Caree.*"

Carrie's eyes flew open. Zooric! She looked around half expecting him to be there, but he wasn't. Yet his mental words continued.

"*Caree why are you again upset? You said you wished for time with your family. I left only because I believed you would be safe with them. What have they done?*"

"Oh Zooric." Carrie sniffed. "Nothing. They haven't done anything." She didn't care that he couldn't hear her.

"Should I return for you Caree? If you remain upset I will."

"I want to stay, but I am so afraid." She sniffed again, but already she was relaxing slightly. "I wish I hadn't told you to leave."

Zooric must have sensed her changing mood. *"I am missing you, Caree. I ... How am I going to get through the dark without you? I am not sure how I survived without you before. What are you thinking about Caree? Are you missing me?"*

"Yes," Carrie whispered. "Yes. I miss you Zooric." Why couldn't she have the ability to mental-speak too? It just wasn't fair. "I love you Zooric," she whispered.

"Think of me as you go to sleep. Sleep Caree. I need you to fall asleep. Lie down. Are you in your bedroom?"

Carrie bent forward and snuffed out the candles then snuggled down under the covers. Listening to Zooric was incredibly erotic and soothing. She felt comforted. It was almost as if he were with her.

"Are you in bed Caree? Hug your pillow. Think of me. Imagine what we would be doing if I were there with you."

Carrie followed Zooric's instructions by burying her face in her pillow. "It's not the same," she wailed. "This is nothing like having you here. Why did I tell you to go?"

"I'm going crazy here Caree. Why did I tell you that? Forget what I just said. Just go to sleep."

Carrie giggled.

Zooric's mental sigh came over loud and clear. *"At least you are no longer so sad. Sleep now, Caree. I will see you in the light."*

Smiling, Carrie closed her eyes. Yes, she was much happier now. And yes, she was sleepy!

****

In his mountain camp, less than a fifteen minutes pageen ride away, Zooric ruefully looked down at himself. There was no emotion coming from Carrie now, hopefully that meant that she was asleep. But he did not have much hope of that happening to him. Sleep was the furthest thing from his mind now. Yet he was curiously at peace.

He was not usually into self-analysis and he had no wish to revisit the mind-numbing fear that had gripped him when he recognized that Carrie was being attacked. He had always wanted Carrie, he now recognized that he also cared deeply—and needed her to be safe. His initial plan had been to leave her with her family while he went with *Loya* Modnar to Caleel, this because he did not want to risk taking her into the uncertain dangers of the Soosan, and he also wanted to get her away from Raekon. Now, he was not sure. He did not wanted to contemplate living without her. Before Carrie came into his life, he had often worked himself to the point of exhaustion just to get a few hours sleep. He knew his insomnia was related to his past—and fears of nightmares. Much as he had tried to confine his childhood abuse to a mental graveyard, it was during sleep that the events would come back to haunt him.

It was not completely an exaggeration to say that he had been sleeping much more peacefully throughout the past few cycles, since meeting Carrie, than during the entire time from his escape from his abusers. He was in fact far less exhausted, both mentally and physically, since meeting her—more satisfied too. Unbelievably satisfied, he grinned, then stretched, and reached to rub his leg. It was still a little stiff but only slightly painful, even after the unexpected stress he had placed on it by walking without the crutch. Soor, who was sleeping by his side twitched in reaction; but did not awaken.

"Lucky you," Zooric said with an affectionate look at his pet. He folded his hands behind his head and stared up at the endless Segaan skies. What would it be like to travel to a distant planet? Caree said that it would take many many cycles to travel to Earth, the original planet of her people. What would the Owoons do if more of her people came? They had to have superior technology to travel into the skies. And if they could send one ship into the skies, they could send others. Besides, surely, they would worry about the disappearance of their first ship. But if more were coming, why had they waited so long? The Tifoosas landed here over 300 alifees ago.

The skies offered no answer. Zooric decided that since there was nothing he could do; it was pointless worrying about the possible arrival of a new group of aliens to their planet. Actually, they had enough worries with this group. His thoughts switched to Derrick. What was he going to do about this Tifoosa? He would not be able to avoid him indefinitely. As a close friend of the family, Derrick would always be around. Zooric's only hope was to quickly solve the problem of the Presidential Guards so that he could leave with Caree.

As he squinted, the moon blinked behind a cloud. There was only a half moon out this dark. Caree said that Earth had only one moon. Here on Segaan they had four. Zooric knew from his readings that it was the result of the rotational actions of the four moons that Segaan had cycles rather than the definite days of the planet Earth. The second-light would actually be a dark were it not for the light of usually two and sometimes three moons. Still, there were many similarities between Segaan and Earth, which perhaps accounted for the development of similar type life forms.

The Azars, in the distant past, did not have electro-sensory powers. Electro powers were an artificial creation. In tinkering with their genetics to create an indestructible race, the Azars had destroyed themselves. The tinkering had also led to the creation of the Owoons. Would any Owoon exist in the future? There was the chronic fertility problems suffered by many Owoon women that resulted in families with only one or two children. His family of three was a rarity.

It was impossible to predict the future. Certainly, now that *Loya* Modnar had met Caree, he and the others were less worried that the Owoons, and their way of life, was threatened. Still, *Loya* Modnar wanted to proceed with caution and had only reluctantly agreed to provide further help. The Soosans were intelligent enough to realize that they would have to meet with representatives of the Tifoosa's government—if only to convince the Tifoosa's that they in turn would not be harmed by the presence of the Owoons. With careful planning, the Tifoosas and the Owoons could learn to live together even if they never came to like each other.

With a sigh Zooric rolled over to his side. Caree was asleep and she was fine. He did another quick mental check of his surroundings and knew there was no danger—not with Soor peacefully sleeping. Nothing. He was getting no emotions. The entire camp was asleep. It was past time he slept too. Next cycle, they would be busy. He needed to rest. Zooric closed his eyes and was pleasantly surprised by the pull of sleep. ****

Chapter 20

The next light there was no sign of the aliens.

"Do you think they left?" Scott asked.

"No. Zooric will not leave me," Carrie stated positively.

Her family was not so sure. They had been up early, and her father and Derrick had already checked on the men in the tack room. They had even allowed the captured Guards to dig a grave for the dead deputy. Everyone was now gathered in the kitchen.

"How are they?" Mrs. Classet asked.

Derrick gave a satisfied grin. "Scared— terrified more like. I think the deputy is losing his mind."

"Good. I can't say I feel sorry for them. Not after what they did to us and to Carrie," Dave said.

"What did the aliens do with the rest of the Guard?" Thia wanted to know.

"They must have all escaped because there are no bodies outside." Mr. Classet was frowning. "The attack will come. There is no way the rest of the Guards can ignore the tales these will tell."

The others nodded but as the light dragged by, without an attack or any sign of the aliens, they became increasingly nervous. No one strayed far from the kitchen.

"If they don't come back, we are doomed." Derrick said grimly.

Mr. Classet did not respond. Like everyone, he was bitterly aware of their precarious position. They could not hope to fight the Guards on their own. If the aliens did not return, they would have to surrender immediately, and he did not want to think of the consequences afterward. He ran a weary hand through his thinning hair.

"Should we try to hide?" Dave asked.

His father shook his head. "We cannot survive in the mountain for any long period. Immediate surrender is our best option," he replied quietly.

"Oh, Dennis." As Mrs. Classet openly wiped her eyes, he reached for her, folding her into his arms.

"Zooric will return, Mam." Carrie insisted. "I know he will."

The others did not share her confidence. "So you've been saying for the last few hours." Derrick retorted. "It is now almost first-dark. Perhaps since you gave him what he wanted he is no longer interested."

"Derrick!" her mother chided.

Carrie jumped up in fury. "You...you...bigot! I hate you!" Her family could not fail to notice that she and Derrick were no longer best buddies. She had been deliberately snubbing him all of first-light. So far Derrick had ignored the numerous insults. However, with the tension of the wait, his nonchalance was fast deteriorating.

"Derrick, that was going too far," Mr. Classet weighed in.

But Derrick's temper was spiraling. "Too far... don't you realize what that ...that alien did? He set us up then left us in the lurch. We are sitting ducks because of him and his promises."

Hugging herself in an effort to control her anger, Carrie glared at him. "He hates Zooric just because Zooric is different Mam. He is like the Separatist. They too claim to like all races yet would ban interracial marriages." Her voice was breaking up. Carrie stopped and sniffed.

"Zooric cares for me. But Derrick just can't see beyond the fact of Zooric's skin color. He told me... he told me..."

Mrs. Classet left her husband's side to comfort her daughter. "Hush dear." She too was now glaring at Derrick.

"Oh, Mam." Turning her face onto her mother's shoulder, Carrie began to cry. She relished the comfort her mother offered. She couldn't remember the last time she had broken down crying on her mother like this, but she missed Zooric. He had made no effort to contact her since last dark, and that omission surprised her. What if he had somehow gotten hurt? It was now almost first dark. She knew Zooric would never voluntarily leave her. But there was Raekon and the simmering hatred between the two. Carrie wished she could just stay in the comfort of her mother's arms and cry her eyes out, but Kelly was getting scared. The little girl was even now beginning to cry.

"Mam.... Mam," Kelly was holding to her mother's dress, crying and trying to get her attention. The stress and violence of the last cycle was beginning to have a serious effect on Kelly. Ever since the Presidential Guards arrival, Kelly had become sad, and since last light she was terrified at the slightest sound. She was becoming clingy and more and more anxious— totally unlike her usual outgoing, cheerful self.

Carrie pulled back, sniffing and wiping her eyes. "I'm fine Kelly. I was just upset," she said giving her little sister a watery smile before lifting her head. Her parents, Dave and Thia were all looking worried. Even Derrick seemed upset at her loss of control.

"Carrie, I'm sorry if I upset you," he now said stiffly.

He might be sorry she was upset, but Carrie was convinced he did not regret what he had said. He still did not believe Zooric was right for her. She turned away.

"Carrie..."

"It's okay Mam I am fine now. I really am. I'll take Kelly upstairs; we can play in the playroom for a while. Come Kelly," she urged.

The change of scenery would be good for Kelly, and getting away from Derrick might be for the best. They had always been so close. Like a pendulum, Dave would swing from being a merciless tease to the invaluable peacemaker. Derrick, however, was constant. Carrie knew that her mother, unlike her father, was well aware that her mixed race set her apart from many of the town's people. Oh, they were not outright in their disapproval, the Separatist were too slick for that. But they were still upset that her father had chosen to bring his entire family to Arapmo. Carrie even knew of two Separatists living in town who refused to bring their wives and children from New World City. Not because the marriages were forced, but because the wives were of a mixed race. One was a Council member, and so far, he was smart enough not to get a house or settle anywhere permanently—the excuse he offered to the Presidential Council on why he had left his wife behind. She knew her skin color, and possibly Derrick's, would always set them apart in this town.

However, since coming to live with them, Derrick had become a part of the internal dynamics of their family. Although Derrick and Dave had often been paired together because they were boys and close in age, somehow Carrie had always been able to insert herself into the mix. And it was to Derrick she had often turned to for companionship. Kelly was too young, and if anything was often paired with Scott. But she was beginning to suspect that it was this closeness she had shared with Derrick that was causing the problem. He did not want to let go of her, and now his protective instincts were out in full force. She hoped that was all. As much as she cared for her family and Derrick being an integral part of it, she had no intension of giving up Zooric just to keep them all happy.

****

Kelly was now giving her mother a frightening look.

"Go on dear," Mrs. Classet prodded.

As the two left, Mr. Classet turned to Derrick. "Leave Carrie alone."

"But Sir..."

"Your tactics will drive her more into Zooric arms. Leave her alone. Unfortunately, she will have to come to her own realization that he is using her."

"Who says he is using her," his wife objected.

The males exchanged looks.

Mrs. Classet in turn glared at her husband. "He did not have to save her from Chris. From what she says, he could easily have captured her and forced her to go with him to his people or abused her then left her to die in the mountains. I believe he cares for her. By allowing her to come back to us, he took a big gamble. She could have decided to stay. Bringing her back to us shows he wants to please her. He wants her to be happy. Good god, he even left her here with us against his better judgment this past light. I could tell he didn't really want to leave her." With a final glare at Derrick, she added. "And I believe Carrie. He'll be back. I find it impossible to believe he took all those risks just to abandon her."

318

Mr. Classet was stunned at the unexpected attack. "Well..."

But Mrs. Classet was on a roll and did not stop. "Don't you dare do anything to break them up," she warned concentrating her ire on Derrick. "Carrie is happy. My only fear is that he will not let her return once she leaves with him. But I intend to speak to him about that."

Mr. Classet cleared his throat. "Perhaps they should stay here for a while then," he began tentatively. "After all, he is a stranger. We need to get to know him better."

"Yes," his wife nodded. "That's a good idea. He could stay here. We'll bring that up as well."

"You mean have him live here?" Derrick said incredulously. "In this house!"

"Why not," she challenged. "Since you are so concerned, it will give you a chance to get to know him. To find out if he really cares for Carrie."

Derrick was astute enough to know when to back down. "Yes Ma'am," he muttered.

"This could get interesting," Dave commented with a grin. "I can just see the headlines—Vicious man to man fight between settler and alien."

"Dave!" his father warned.

Scott, who had been quiet throughout the unexpected outburst of anger, giggled.

Annoyed by the giggles, Derrick scowled. He was about to retort when there was a shout from upstairs.

"They are coming!" Carrie shouted.

"What?" her family stared as she came running down the stairs. Kelly was right behind her.

"They are coming! Zooric is coming!"

"How the bolt do you know?" Derrick demanded.

"I ...I..."

They were all staring at her.

"I heard them."

Derrick was skeptical, but before he could respond, the others heard it too. It was the steady pounding of racing animals.

Frowning, Dave moved to the window. "That doesn't sound like a zig."

Carrie smiled. "It isn't."

"Fluars!" Dave shouted. "They are riding fluars!"

The others rushed to see. Sure enough, two aliens were fast approaching the house both riding the tall graceful fluars.

"You knew?" Dave turned to his sister.

She nodded. "I rode one on the way back. It is an unbelievably smooth ride compared to the zig."

"But how..." Dave did not hide his astonishment, which was also reflected on the faces of the others.

"There is a simple secret to it. We just need to get two fluars. They have a primitive form of electro sensory ability. They have to send impulses back and forth between each other to survive. One cannot live without another."

"That simple," Mr. Classet said still amazed.

"Yes." Carrie said.

"And Zooric told you this?" Derrick asked, wanting to know.

"Yes," but she answered absently, her attention already focused on Zooric as he dismounted. Zooric's face was impassive, but Carrie sensed his tension. He must have registered her previous anger. Why had he not contacted her? Was something wrong?

Zooric carefully scanned the room as he approached her. He still had a slight limp.

"How is your leg?" Carrie asked.

"It is healing. Are you fine?" he asked her.

"My family was getting worried that you would not return," Carrie told him with a tremulous smile. When he did not smile in return, she stared but it was impossible to read his face. "Zooric?"

"Why were you so sad?" he asked privately. *"Why do you wish to stay if they make you sad?"* He pulled her to him as he spoke, bringing Carrie to less than a foot away. She placed both arms up on his chest to prevent him from pulling her in closer.

"Zooric!" This time it was an embarrassed protest.

Zooric frowned. He did not release her.

"We will speak later," Carrie soothed. She pressed again at Zooric's chest to gain her release. "Please..." Her father was approaching.

Zooric looked up, finally releasing her, as Mr. Classet stepped forward.

"I am not sure if Carrie told you of our efforts to tame these animals." He said giving Zooric's fluar an admiring look.

Zooric gave a brief nod. "Caree did mention your frustrations, yes."

Scott slipped up beside his father. "Can I touch it?"

Zooric flashed a smile. "Yes. They love petting."

Of course, Kelly immediately stepped forward. "Can I pet your fluar too?" she asked. At Zooric's nod of permission, she too began stroking the belly of the fluar. She and Scott were both too short to reach the animals' neck. Dave, and even Derrick, joined them, and the next few minutes were spent discussing fluar training techniques and capture.

Mr. Classet could not wait to try out some of the tips on fluar rising. "We need to get rid of these Guards as quickly as possible," he said. "What of the plans?"

"If you get the maps, I will show you how we have arranged the lookout."

Within a few minutes they were all gathered in the kitchen, and the table was strewn with maps. Zooric pointed out where the Soosans would stand guard. "These are the points you told me that are most easy to guard. Two people will stay at each look-out point, a Soosan and either another Owoon or one of you," he told Mr. Classet. "I will remain here. If there is any sign of an attack at any of the look-out points, the Soosans will let me know."

"We have not met any of these Soosans," Mr. Classet frowned. "Are they the ones with the special powers like you?"

"Yes," Zooric gave a brief nod. "You will meet them when this is all over. They are already on their way to the lookout points. With a Soosan at each lookout point and I here, we will easily get messages across."

Now all the Classet males looked blank.

"How?" Derrick voiced the question in all their minds.

"We didn't tell them," Carrie touched Zooric's arm to interrupt, then turned to her family. "A part of the special electro-sensory skills the Soosans have is the ability to communicate mentally with each other."

Everyone stared.

"You mean they can read minds?" Dave asked in horror.

"No!" Zooric said emphatically. "We cannot read your minds but we can communicate mentally with each other."

"Zig shit!" Dave backed away.

"I told you not to trust them," Derrick cried, staring at Zooric in both fear and anger. "I told you..."

"Just a second," Mr. Classet interrupted. "Are you saying you can just zoom information back and forth to each other?"

"Only from a Soosan to others." Zooric did not elaborate.

"I don't like this, Sir." Derrick gave Zooric a hard stare. "It looks to me as if we are totally dependent on him and his alien friends."

"You are welcome to join the Soosans at any of the look-out points." Zooric pointed out.

"Easy, Derrick," Mr. Classet cautioned, resting his hand on Derrick's shoulder. He turned to Zooric. "We will let your people handle the look-out."

"But Sir what if..."

"We either trust them or we don't," Carrie's father decided. "We cannot fight the Guards on our own Derrick. So, we will have to decide to trust them." He was staring straight at Zooric as he spoke. But Zooric almost seemed to have tuned them out. The tall alien was standing staring absently out the windows. Tuning back to his family Mr. Classet added, "I'm betting that if Zooric is here the house will be safe."

But Derrick was still frowning. "I still don't like this."

Zooric turned to give him a cool look. "As I said, you are welcome to go to one of the look-out points with a Soosan."

Derrick started to respond, but again Mr. Classet interrupted him. "If they are going to mess up, we will pay with our lives. But I can't imagine why they would help us during the light only to get us killed now."

This time Zooric responded to Mr. Classet's words with a faint amused smile. He then gave a brief nod but did not attempt further reassurances. "That is settled. Everyone should be at his post before first-dark. Since you do not wish to stay at the lookout points, I will so inform *Loya* Modnar. Three other Owoons will head out to stay with the Soosans."

Again, Zooric turned slightly away from them to stare blankly out the windows. Mr. Classet watched him for a few seconds as the realization dawned. "Is he conferring with these Soosans?" he asked Carrie.

She nodded. "You can trust Zooric, Dad. I know he will not let anything happen to us."

Mr. Classet was indeed convinced that Zooric would not let any harm come to his daughter. He was not sure however how far the alien would go to protect her family. "Are you 100 percent sure that they cannot read minds?" he now asked.

"I am positive." Carrie reassured him.

Her father nodded, then turned to *Gaad* Trateen who was still standing by the door. "And you cannot send these mental signals."

"I cannot," *Gaad* Trateen confirmed. "Only a Soosan can."

He nodded, satisfied. "Now our biggest problem will be during the dark. What if the Guards creep up on them?"

"We can all sense movements even at night. It will be impossible for them to pass the lookout points."

"Let's hope so because this house was not built for defense, and we are stretched way too thin. If the Guards attacked from three directions, we would have to retreat to the house to fight off the attack."

"We will not allow any Guards to approach the house." *Gaad* Trateen reassured. "They will all be stopped."

Reluctantly satisfied with the Owoon's plans, the Classets decided to resume their normal chores. There were no incidents. In fact, first-dark was fast approaching when the Soosan reported their first sighting on the main trail.

"A group of men are approaching." Zooric relayed. "They are carrying a white flag. They do not look to be professional guards and are not dressed in uniforms."

"We cannot attack them if they are flying a white flag." Mr. Classet decided. "It means that they come in peace. Dave, perhaps you had best ride out. Just be careful."

"No problem, Dad," Dave was already rushing out.

Less than twenty minutes later, Zooric gave them a report. "Dave has ridden down to these men. They seem friendly and are greeting him. They are all continuing and should be here soon."

Indeed, half an hour later, an ecstatic Dave rode up with a group of men the family recognized. It included Ron, their foreman, some of their workmen and even some of Arapmo's citizen. The entire family rushed out to greet them.

"What is this I hear about a secret weapon?" Ron demanded, as he dismounted from his zig.

"Dave refused to explain. Wait until we get to the outpost, was all he would say."

Mr. Classet laughed. "It is good to see you. How did you get out of town?"

Ron chuckled. "When we heard that there was a fight here last light, we decided you needed help. We crept out one by one and regrouped just outside the town."

"The Guards came back with a weird story about a strange killing weapon," another man called out.

"You don't know the half of it," Derrick muttered. Fortunately, the men did not hear that.

"Come in. Come in. I'll explain everything." Mr. Classet was already urging them inside. Soon all fifteen men were packed in the kitchen. A quick glance showed him that both *Sous* Zooric and *Gaad* Trateen had disappeared at the men's approach. Good. He had every intention of telling his men about the aliens but thought it better not to surprise them with the aliens' presence immediately.

"Listen up. I have what will be a shocker. We don't have any strange weapons. However, what we do have is strange help."

"Did someone from the town help you?" Ron asked, as the spokesman for the group.

"Don't wet your pants, but there's another race of people living on the planet with us. Carrie met them and brought some back, or they brought her back. They helped us this past light to defeat the Guards. They will be helping us again. We knew you were coming because they are watching the trails for us."

The men were all looking blank. Most were disbelieving.

"What do you mean by another race?" one man questioned cautiously.

"If you promise not to faint or do anything silly, I'll have them come out."

"They're here?" Immediately some of the men began looking nervously around the room.

"They're in the other room," He was actually just assuming—he had no idea where they had disappeared to.

"Aliens!" someone else repeated. "Bolt!"

Mr. Classet couldn't help smiling. "Are you all ready?"

No one answered. But one of the town's men lifted his rifle. "I don't like this. We should get out of here!"

As he started backing up toward the door, three other men followed him. "Maybe these aliens have taken over their minds," one said.

Mr. Classet did not stop them. "Go if you're going. We aren't going to stop you." There really was no easy way to do this. They would eventually believe since he had the aliens as final proof, but there would always be the odd man who would refuse to accept reality.

At his calm the men hesitated.

"What do they look like?" someone asked.

"Like the original Black colonists." Mr. Classet explained. "Very normal looking."

That bit of information halted the beginnings of panic.

"What do you mean?"

"Just that they are the image of pictures from our history books."

"Are you sure they aren't just colonists who deserted the original party?" Ron asked.

At that Mr. Classet shrugged. It they wanted to believe that so be it. Perhaps it would even help ease their fear. "Could be." He surveyed the fearful group. "I'm going to call them in. You will be able to judge for yourself. Whatever you do, just don't shoot. We are depending on them to help us defeat the Presidential Guards."

One man gave a nervous laugh. "If they are deserters, that wouldn't make them aliens."

"I'll let you decide." He said as he raised his voice, "*Sous* Zooric! *Gaad* Trateen!"

Gaad Trateen appeared, but Zooric did not follow.

There were startled gasps, and some of the men quickly backed up.

"Bolt!" someone called out. "He's a giant!"

There was nervous laughter, as Mr. Classet began the introductions. *Gaad* Trateen, meet some of our citizens. They are here to help us in any way they can." Turning to the men he said. "Meet *Gaad* Trateen. His people call themselves Owoons and the live about twenty weeks travel south of here."

The men were undoubtedly curious. Yet, just as Mr. Classet suspected, meeting one of the aliens actually allowed their fear to recede. One obvious reason was the normality factor. These Owoons looked like people they were all familiar with. Every settler studied history as a child, even if it was just elementary school history. All knew the story of the first landing. *Gaad* Trateen, at over seven feet tall, differed from the original Black colonists only in height.

The men were now jostling and shifting positions, each trying to get a clear view of the Owoon. *Gaad* Trateen seemed just as curious, and a little more cautious. He carefully scanned the men before volunteering to speak.

"I am pleased to meet you all."

There were gasps of surprise.

"Hey! He speaks our language!"

Gaad Trateen actually smiled. "All Soosan guards learn the language of your people. Yet, I do not have much skills."

"Bolt!" The comment came from Ron. "Is there a written history of your people?" Ron was still pursuing his theory that these were not true aliens but deserters from the original colonists.

Gaad Trateen gave him a puzzled look. Either he did not understand enough English to get Ron's meaning or he understood and was puzzled by the question. Either way Derrick did not wait for a response.

"We have already gone through that. They aren't human," he stated bluntly.

"It's impossible for them not to be," Ron insisted.

Others were nodding.

"Yes Dennis, just think for a minute," Ron turned to Mr. Classet. "How could humans leave planet Earth, travel over fifty light-years, and then find a planet that has a race of people looking exactly like us. That just strikes me as next to impossible."

"They're not exactly like us," Derrick muttered.

"Close enough to be the same. The Blacks were considered another race on Earth not another species. These people," here he waved in the general direction of where *Gaad* Trateen still stood, "they are as human as we are. There is no doubt in my mind. They must be! They are likely deserters from the original colonists. Weren't some of the lost colonists Black?"

The Classets exchanged uneasy glances. Put like that, it did seem inconceivable that the Owoons were not human—but how to explain their extra powers? Could their electro-sensory powers be caused by other factors on the planet itself? Mr. Classet turned to *Gaad* Trateen, wondering how much of this the Owoons understood. But although *Gaad* Trateen was still watchful, his expression was carefully neutral. He had in fact almost perfected Zooric's impossible to read look.

"You know," Dave mused. "I really think I agree." He looked around at his family. His mother was already nodding.

"I think so too. It just seems too much of a coincidence."

But Derrick was skeptical. "So how do you explain their extra abilities?"

"What extra ability?" Ron wanted to know.

"The so-called secret weapon that the Guards reported is actually the Owoons. They can generate a powerful burst of electricity, enough to kill." Mr. Classet's tone was grim.

His words caused shock ripples through the townsmen. This time the exclamations were fear related, forcing Mr. Classet to spend a few minutes reassuring the men. "They are on our side," he pointed out. "They are willing to fight the Presidential Guards for us."

"I still think their being here is too much of a coincidence. This ability could be genetics. You know. A slight mutant gene." Ron looked around at the nodding men. They were all agreeing with him. He turned back to the Classets. "We really should check out their history further. I'll bet anything we'll find that they are as human as we are."

"If they didn't keep a record, there's probably no way to know for certain," Dave said.

"They told Carrie they weren't human," Derrick pointed out.

As everyone looked at Carrie, she bit her lips. "I didn't say that. Remember when I tried to explain to you and no one would listen."

"This is ridiculous." Derrick jumped up. "Are you now saying that they are human? Do you really expect us to believe that now?"

"I never said they weren't human, all I said was..."

"This is zig shit!" Derrick burst in. "I can't believe..."

Mr. Classet broke the bickering. "Listen let's shelve the theories for now and get back to winning this war."

"But..." Ron began.

"No Ron." Mr. Classet held up his hand for silence. "Let's wait to finish this discussion. We will agree that there is a strong chance that they are as human as we are. But there are differences."

"Major difference!" Derrick could not help inserting.

"But what happens after we get rid of the Guards?" Ron wanted to know.

Mr. Classet looked puzzled. "They will likely live in their town and we will live in ours."

"But what's to stop them from taking over?" someone shouted.

There was a short pregnant silence. What was to stop them?

Into the silence Zooric spoke. "We cannot take over your town. Our numbers are too small."

Everyone swiveled in the direction of his voice. They had been too busy arguing to notice his entrance. The town's men now stared in fascination at this new alien.

Still, Ron's tone was belligerent as he asked, "What happens when your numbers increase?"

At that Zooric shrugged. "By then is it hoped we would have developed a mutual respect and there would not be a power struggle for dominancy. Besides, only the Soosan among us have this special ability that you fear. And Soosans are few in numbers and likely to remain so for the foreseeable future"

They all stared at him. Not all were reassured. But what could they do? They were in the middle of a battle. And right now, they needed the Owoons help to survive.

"I just hope we're not jumping from one fire into another." Derrick muttered.

Frowning Mr. Classet started slowly. "What do you mean? Why will there always be few Soosans?"

But Zooric refused to clarify. "It requires much explanation. After this battle is over, we can have a long discussion."

"You can't just state something like that then expect us to forget it," Derrick said angrily.

"I do not see why not," Zooric tone was calm. It was unlikely that any insult was intended; nevertheless, the result was the same.

Derrick exploded in fury. He hated the dismissive tone that Zooric had used. Fists doubled, he had already taken two steps towards Zooric when both Mr. Classet and Dave grabbed him. Each held one of his arms.

"Calm down Derrick!" Mr. Classet warned.

"Calm down! He needs someone to...." Derrick struggled against their hold.

Dave stubbornly held on, shouting. "Have you forgotten what he did to the commander? Do you want to get your brain fried?"

As Derrick finally calmed, Mr. Classet turned to apologize to Zooric, only to pause in surprised shock. The alien had backed away. Zooric was actually leaning against the wall, his eyes closed. He definitely did not look well. What was going on?

"Wha...?" he was so surprised he released Derrick. But before he could comment, Carrie moved rapidly toward Zooric. She placed both hands on Zooric's chest and ignored the growing hum of voices as everyone expressed concern, surprise or both. What was this? *Gaad* Trateen had also moved protectively closer, and his face mirrored the concern on Carrie's face.

"What happened?" Dave demanded.

Someone called out the same question. "I think Derrick did something to him." Mr. Classet held up his hand. "Quiet everyone."

"I didn't..." Derrick began.

Mr. Classet gave a grim smile. "Well, something is not quite right." Zooric's eyes were now open. "Well *Sous* Zooric. I think you owe us an explanation."

"Your explanations will have to wait," Zooric said calmly, "Your Guards are coming."

"How do they know?" Ron asked. "We will explain later," Mr. Classet said urgently. "Where *Sous* Zooric?"

****

Chapter 21

It was now almost full dark, so the ten men who set out had to travel carefully to the point indicated by Zooric. The others remained at the house as backup just in case an attack came from another direction. The backups did not have to wait long. The Guards had planned a two-prong attack! Within minutes the men were racing out.

Derrick went with the first group of men. When they arrived at the scene, the confusion was unlike any battle he had ever seen. The Guards were dropping or falling off their zigs—literally dying were they stood and creating a confused mass of uncertainly. Derrick could just imagine their terror. They could not see or even hear the enemy. As he and the other men took up positions and began shooting at the milling Guards, he almost began to feel guilty. This was so easy, it was criminal. Even as the thought entered his head, some of the Guards broke ranks and started riding desperately back to town. Good! They were retreating!

"Don't shoot if they are giving up!" Mr. Classet shouted. His words—crystal clear— seemed to galvanize others to follow the lead of the few retreating Guards. Soon, there was a mass exodus as the retreat gathered steam. The battle was over! As silence slowly returned, the Classets and their men edged down the slope. The destruction was appalling. Between them, the Owoons and Settlers had killed over twenty Guards.

Even though many had fled, the totals did not add up. That meant there had to be another attack somewhere else. Derrick surmised. "Let's hope our people were warned."

Ron rode up beside Mr. Classet and Derrick. "Mind explaining some more of this?"

Mr. Classet spoke as they rode back to the outpost. There they learned the results of the other wave of the attack. The other Guards had suffered an equally humiliating defeat at the other lookout point. There were even more dead Guards — over thirty.

****

Second-light found everyone gathered on the porch comparing notes on the battle.

"I think we wiped out at least half of the total," someone gleefully exclaimed.

"I think so too." Dave grinned. "This means the rest are back in town — perhaps some on their way to New World City to tell of our powerful invisible weapon."

"What do we do next?" one of the townsmen asked.

"I say we head back to town. Confront them there," Derrick said.

"Will the Owoons support us?" Mr. Classet turned to the two Owoons.

Gaad Trateen was sitting in the kitchen. He was propped up on a stool, slightly swinging one foot. Zooric was nowhere to be seen.

"Where is *Sous* Zooric?" Derrick demanded.

"He is in the house," *Gaad* Trateen gave a slight shrug.

"Where is Carrie?" Mrs. Classet suddenly asked.

"Shit!" Derrick shouted. He turned forcefully to *Gaad* Trateen. "Where are they?"

"In the room you call the library," *Gaad* Trateen explained mildly.

Derrick rushed out with the Classets close behind. Bolt! Trust Zooric to use the opportunity to get Carrie alone. The library was at the back of the house and had been specially constructed to provide privacy. Few if any sounds from the other rooms penetrated the silence of the library. Although expecting to interrupt a private scene, Derrick pushed the door open. Peals of laughter greeted him— laughter from Kelly. He stopped abruptly—so suddenly that Dave crashed right into him propelling him further into the room. Their shocked gaze took in the scene. Zooric was giving Kelly a ride on his back. Carrie was curled up on the sofa watching. She now lifted startled eyes.

"Dad!" Kelly cried in delight. "*Sous* Zooric gives the best rides ever." The little girl gave another gleeful laugh. "Giddy-up," she squealed tugging at Zooric's thick mat of hair.

He grinned. "Sorry little one. Ride is over for this cycle."

Derrick stared. The grin had transformed Zooric from a frighteningly intense warrior to a mischievous teenager.

Derrick looked around and realized he was not the only one startled by the change. Dave was only now closing his mouth. His father wore a bemused expression. And Carrie—well Carrie was definitely amused. Her expression clearly said, I told you.

Derrick noisily cleared his throat and as Zooric looked up, his features settled in its accustomed expressionless immobility.

Zooric slowly lowered Kelly to the ground. "Was there something that you wanted?" he asked Derrick.

"No," Derrick hesitated. "We were just wondering where you were."

Zooric stared. "And now that you have found me?"

It was a mildly worded question delivered without inflection, yet again Derrick was annoyed. He was convinced that Zooric was deliberately taunting him. He exchanged a 'see what I mean' look with Mr. Classet.

Mr. Classet smoothly filled in before Derrick could explode. He did not want to pursue a Derrick/Zooric confrontation at this point. "The fighting here is over. We plan to go into the town to deal with the rest of the Guards."

Kelly turned to look up at him. "Did you kill all of the bad Guards Dad?"

"Most of them honey. But some escaped to the town. So, we will have to go get them. Well *Sous* Zooric?"

Zooric first glanced down at Kelly. A smile briefly shifted across his features — so fleetingly — it was gone in seconds.

Derrick frowned as he remembered how sick Zooric had looked earlier. He was sure it was somehow related to his actions. But he had done nothing — nothing obvious. Yet something could bring them down. He just had to figure out what. Was it simply his anger? That just didn't make any sense. But these aliens were so focused on mental communication it could just be....

"Can I introduce *Sous* Zooric to everyone Mam?" Kelly turned eagerly to her mother. Her fear was gone, but best of all she was smiling again. Whatever Zooric had done, he had definitely been good for her.

"Go ahead darling," her mother now encouraged, despite the fact that the settlers had already met Zooric.

"This is *Sous* Zooric," she stated importantly. "He is very nice so you don't have to be afraid of him.

"*Sous* Zooric, this is Ron that I told you about and this is..." Kelly went through introducing all of the men one by one as they squeezed into the library.

Her family gave her just enough time to finish before they were off again. They had a town to retake!

****

Retaking their town proved to be ridiculously easy. Dave and seven men remained at the outpost with Mrs. Classet, Thia, Scott and Kelly. The others transported the dead back to town, while the rest accompanied by Zooric and *Gaad* Trateen, set out for the town.

But the Presidential Guards were in full retreat by the time the Owoons and the settlers reached town. In fact, as they approached the town, settlers were rushing out to let them know the Guards had left.

"You got rid of them. They are crawling back to New World City."

That fact called for a celebration. Both Zooric and *Gaad* Trateen decided that if there was not going to be a war, it was best that they not enter the town. The Classets agreed. And no one objected as they quietly slipped away before the town's people noticed their presence.

As Zooric pointed out, "It would not be wise to surprise the people of the town with our presence at this point. The introductions need a more controlled environment."

He had a point. Yet Derrick was still uneasy as he rode off. "I still don't like him," he muttered to Ron.

"I'll admit, he is a bit stiff and arrogant and needs to learn how to smile more. But..." Here Ron shrugged. "He really doesn't seem that bad."

Derrick scowled. "You wouldn't think that if he were after the woman you were supposed to marry."

"Carrie?" Ron was startled.

"Yes." Derrick was grim. "He claims he is bonded with her — I guess that is some form of marriage among his people."

Ron looked thoughtful. "Does anyone know?" Before Derrick could answer, he answered his own question. "No. The Council can't know yet."

"What does that have to do with anything?" Derrick demanded.

"Just wondering what the separatist on the Council are going to think."

"Carrie's marriage plan is none of their business..." Derrick began furiously.

Ron's hands were raised in mute surrender. "Don't take my head off. It was just a comment. Besides, you know you wouldn't have been able to marry her anyway. She was headed for New World City. You don't know who she would be paired with."

"It would not have been an alien. And have you forgotten we were challenging the Council?"

"True but remember what we are fighting for."

"What the bolt has that got to do with her marrying an alien."

"It's her choice. This is what this is all about. Freedom to choose."

But the truth did nothing to sooth Derrick's anger, and Ron soon left him to his scowls.

****

It was well into the second-light before the Classet males returned to the outpost. Members of the Town Council accompanied them. Rumors and speculations about the aliens were rampant. Every Council member wanted to see an actual alien. The Council had also decided that it was in Arapmo's interest to release the commander and his deputies. The commander would be allowed to return to New World City with an official message from the Arapmo Town Council declaring Arapmo's independence from New World City. As radical as the move was, a quick vote at the last dark had shown that a majority of Arapmo's citizens supported the move. Those who didn't were given the option of leaving town.

Back at the outpost, the one meeting that the Town Council craved did not happen. There were no aliens waiting at the outpost.

"Their leader wanted to speak to them and insisted that they all return," Carrie explained.

Derrick was immediately suspicious.

"When are they coming back?" he wanted to know.

"Zooric said next cycle," Carrie ignored Derricks scowl and turned to her father to change the subject. "How are the plans going Dad?"

"Fine." Her father smiled at his daughter's anxious look. "Don't worry. Arapmo will survive. We have rid the town of all of the Guards. I think we should invite one or two of these aliens to the town — introduce them to the people. Let them speak to the Town Council. And get everything in the open."

"Why not have them come here instead Dad," Carrie suggested. "It might be better to introduce them all at once. Perhaps bring the town's people here then have them come into the house in groups to meet the Owoons."

Dave was nodding at Carrie's plan. "She's got a point Dad. If we tell them about the aliens, then give them too much time to think about it, they might just start running scared. We have to show them that there is nothing to fear."

Some Town Council members wanted to wait, but after a bit of conferring they finally decided to leave and return within the next cycle. The Classets would give out invitations to the entire town. This way, they would all get a chance to meet the aliens, and there would be no surprises later.

The next task was to oversee the release of the commander and his deputy. The Classets and all Council members went to the tack room. The commander was totally subdued, and the deputy seemed to have collapsed mentally under the stress. The man was almost foaming at the mouth, and to prevent him from harming himself and others, he had to be restrained again as soon as he was released. It was a slow procession that took the two Presidential representatives back to the town. The departing Guards had left their dead, so once again the commander was forced to dig graves. Some settlers helped just to speed the process along.

Later the commander would travel to New World City with those citizens choosing not to remain in Arapmo.

After they left, as the Classets began their big preparations, Carrie suddenly turned to her father. "Dad, what about Tim and the other man who attacked me?"

"Zig shit!" Dave shot up.

"They must have left town." Mr. Classet frowned. "I really don't remember seeing them." He turned to Derrick and his son. "Did any of you?"

"No." Derrick scowled. "You're right. They must have left. In all the excitement none of us checked. We will ask the men but I am sure that as soon as they heard you were back and that we had won, they packed up and left town."

"Pity," Mr. Classet murmured. "I would have liked to have a little chat with the leader."

Both Derrick and Dave nodded.

Carrie sighed. "So now we will never know."

"Don't worry," her father reassured her. "Now that he is gone, he is unlikely to return, and once this is over, we will visit the cabin where he took you. Perhaps we will even set up a watch just in case there are others involved. Now that I know what some folks are capable of, they will not catch me unaware again."

Although disappointed, Carrie nodded. There were too many preparation chores to complete, leaving very little time for moping. None of the adults got much sleep that dark. The front glass wall, which was destroyed in the fighting, had to get a temporary fix—so it was boarded up. And although the women from town were bringing food, the Classets were still expected to ensure that there was enough variety for everyone. The cooking and general repairs kept the entire family busy well into the dark.

****

Chapter 22

The next cycle the sun was only just clearing the horizon when the Classets were awoken by the arrival of the Owoons. The Classets were in for another shock. They finally got to meet another Soosan, since *Loya* Modnar had accompanied Zooric, *Gaads* Trateen and Egell. Carrie quickly explained who *Loya* Modnar was, and she was pleased that both her parents showed sufficient respect to the Soosan elder. Unfortunately, *Loya* Modnar could not speak aloud, so after the introductions he stood silent as Zooric and Carrie took turns explaining the Soosan's method of communication.

"And you dare to call them human," Derrick muttered under his breath.

Carrie heard him. She gave him a furious glare before turning back to her father. "Dad, *Loya* Modnar wants to discuss how our two governments will coexist."

"Explain to him that the Council members will be here within a few hours," Mr. Classet began.

Carrie interrupted with a smile. "Remember, *Loya* Modnar can hear you, Dad. He is just unable to speak aloud."

"My apologies *Loya* Modnar," her father tried again. But he was hesitant, and Carrie could see he was uncomfortable.

So could *Loya* Modnar apparently, because the Soosan turned to Zooric who translated, "*Loya* Modnar wants to know if there is anything he can do to help you adjust."

"No. No," Mr. Classet gave an apologetic smile. "We'll adjust with time. My main concern now is having you speak.... er... well presented at one of our Council meetings. The members of the Council will be here within hours. Perhaps you can attend."

"He has agreed," Zooric confirmed.

Having decided to leave weighty discussions until the entire Council was present, Mr. Classet spent the next few hours showing *Loya* Modnar around his outpost. He did not get to complete his tour. Within hours, settlers from the town started showing up. Parties in Arapmo were usually a town affair and with the excitement of meeting aliens as an incentive—well no one wanted to miss out. So, with the Owoons inside the house, the party was in full swing when Mr. Classet invited the six other Council members to meet Zooric. He choose Zooric because, as intimidating as Zooric could be, Zooric spoke almost perfect English, plus he also spoke aloud—something that *Loya* Modnar could not do.

"I hear they look like some of the original colonists," one man said.

But apart from a smile, Mr. Classet refused to answer any more questions until he got them in the main room. "Have a seat," he indicated. This was not an official Council meeting so both Dave and Derrick were present, along with the six other Council members.

"So, where's the alien?" Jade Feld asked as he looked around. Jade was a close friend of the Classets and like all the Council members; he was one of the original twenty settlers to found Arapmo.

Mr. Classet stood. "I invited all of you here to prove that there is nothing to fear. The Soosans want to meet representatives of our government. I want Arapmo to represent Arapmo. I don't care what New World City plans to do. We now run our own government. I want us to consider the Soosans a foreign government and negotiate with them as a nation. We have to meet them someday, so it's better now than later. They have advanced technology that we will find useful. They also saved Carrie." he paused. "Some of you saw her this past light."

There were nods of agreement. Then one of the members called out. "Come on Dennis. You're killing us with tension here. Save the lecture and just bring them out."

Smiling, Mr. Classet asked, "But are you all ready?"

"Ready as we'll ever be," another man said.

"*Sous* Zooric!"

Zooric walked in. There was a gasp. Jade Feld half rose then sank down again "Bolt!"

Carl, another Council member, had his mouth hanging open. He closed it with a snap.

Zooric looked amused. "I am pleased to meet you," he said.

"You said he wasn't the only one. Where are the others?"

"There are eight of us in the valley," Zooric answered.

"Bolt!"

After a few minutes of chatting, *Loya* Modnar, *Gaads* Egell and Trateen were introduced. Although the Councilmen were uncomfortable, the meeting actually went well. *Loya* Modnar's lack of speech forced Zooric and the two Owoons to become interpreters. But that was not their biggest problem. Just about every Council Members was fearful of the powers of the Soosans. They wanted reassurance. But most of all, they wanted explanations. Again, and again the Soosan had to reassure the Council that Soosans were not interested in controlling Arapmo. Both peoples could maintain a separate existence without interference in each other's affairs. It was actually *Loya* Modnar's suggestion that they work on establishing a border between their two nations. This seemed to finally calm most of the settler's fears.

"So," Mr. Classet asked as the meeting began to wind down. "How should they be introduced to the others — one at a time or in groups?"

"I am finding this hard to swallow," Jade said.

"Do you know your history?" another asked.

"Here we go again," Derrick muttered.

Surprised, more than one Council member looked at him. Jade frowned. "Did they tell you before?"

"Actually No," Mr. Classet looked inquiringly at *Loya* Modnar. "We should solve this problem now."

Loya Modnar was looking politely puzzled until Mr. Classet turned to him and explained what the problem was. "We, many of our people, suspect that your people are descendants from early colonists. Do you know if this is true?"

"But of course," *Loya* Modnar was smiling as *Gaad* Egell spoke his reply.

Pandemonium broke out.

What!!!

"Did Zerah Caree not tell you our story?"

Loya Modnar wanted to know. He was looking at Zooric as he said this. Zooric shook his head even as he interpreted *Loya* Modnar's words.

"No!" Mr. Classet confirmed. "Carrie told us nothing of how you came to be here."

The colonists listened in silence as the *Loya* Modnar related the story of the final experiment of the Azar race. It took a while since *Gaad* Egell had to repeat all of *Loya* Modnar's mental words aloud.

"I can't understand why Carrie did not tell us this." Mr. Classet was perplexed.

Zooric answered. "Caree tried but you were not willing to listen."

Derrick, who was still spoiling for a fight, did not appreciate Zooric's blunt approach. "She didn't try very hard," he said, giving Zooric a hard look. Zooric, however, was unwilling to oblige him with a rebuttal. The Soosan shrugged.

"So, in reality they're practically as human as we are," Jade muttered.

"I knew it!" Dave said. "I just knew that it was not possible for them to be true aliens. Not looking so much like us."

It was some time before the settlers had exhausted all possible theories on how the original people of Alloca lived and died. *Loya* Modnar promised to organize a trip to the nearby Azar sector to explore the Owoons' roots. It was a trip that excited even Derrick.

"We definitely will hold you to that promise," Mr. Classet warned. He then moved to another topic. "*Sous* Zooric mentioned that your numbers are small and will always remain so. Can you explain this?"

With *Gaads* Egell and Trateen translating, *Loya* Modnar carefully explained the concept of the Soosan. Although there were startled looks from the settlers, no one commented directly on the Soosan's lifestyle, although Derrick directed a pointed and angry look at Zooric.

However, Mr. Classet's quick frown shushed any comment Derrick might have thought to make. At the moment none of the settlers were aware of Carrie's relationship with Zooric, and he did not want it revealed, at least not for the next few cycles. Mr. Classet did not want any controversy in this initial stage of contact with the Owoons. Apart from himself, Jade was the only other Council member who was a fully committed Freechoicer. Two other members tended to vote with them but could not always be trusted. The Separatist also had two committed members and one waffler. The Freechoicers, therefore, had a tentative majority. He wanted nothing to stop the Council from voting unanimous on full mutual recognition between them and the Owoons.

He finally interrupted some of the Council members.

"We need to move on. The others are waiting outside."

The meeting broke up with a final vote to take place among the Council Members in the next cycle, after more private discussions. It was now time to introduce them to rest of the town. Taking up to four people at time—they were brought in—until all had met the Owoons. Six women fainted. One man reached for his gun but was disarmed by a pulse from Zooric, which threw the man half way across the room.

Stunned, the settler landed in a crumbled pile, alive but momentarily unable to move. There were murmurings of bemused disbelief as what most assumed to be a demonstration of the Owoon's special 'skills.'

Derrick glared at Zooric. "Did you have to do that?" Derrick, while less aggressive, was still the furthest from accepting Zooric.

"With Caree here I did not want to take the chance of him firing a weapon," Zooric stated calmly. "He is not hurt."

"And to hell with us all if Carrie was not here," was Dave's imprudent responses.

"Would you have your sister hurt?" Zooric demanded.

"No! No!" Dave raised his hands in surrender. The Classets were beginning to realize the extent of Zooric's focus on Carrie. That fact was demonstrated even more acutely later in that cycle.

****

As soon as all the townspeople had their individual introductions, it was decided that *Sous* Zooric and *Gaad* Egell should mingle with the settlers. As an excuse, they would take out more supplies plus another table. Dave and *Gaad* Egell lifted the table and together with *Sous* Zooric and Derrick, the four started walking outside. But they just managed to clear the porch when the shooting started. All four men dived to the ground ducking behind the fallen table. It was Roger, the same man who Zooric had disarmed earlier. He was standing far off to the side shouting insanely.

"They'll take over our minds. They're going to kill us." Boom! "We'll all be killed." Boom! Boom! "They're going to kill us."

"Bolts!" Dave screamed as the settlers scattered.

Boom! Boom!

"Bolt! We have no cover." Derrick shouted. They didn't. Apart from the table, they were in the open just beyond the front door. There was no other cover. In fact, if Roger hadn't been crazed with fear, he would have been able to pick them off with ease. As it was, some shots were coming uncomfortably close.

Boom! Boom!

"*Sous* Zooric can't you stop him at the distance?" Dave shouted, as he pressed even closer to their only cover.

Zooric looked over at him. "This is not my problem. Caree is safe inside."

Gaad Egell gave what sounded suspiciously like a hastily converted laugh.

For a second, both Dave and Derrick stared at him then Derrick burst out.

"Firebolt! He's shooting at us, you..." words failed him.

Dodging another shot, Dave turned to glare at Zooric. "If he kills you, Carrie will likely die of heartbreak," he pointed out.

Without responding, Zooric turned back to look at the settler. Abruptly, the man went flying through the air.

"What's happening?" Mr. Classet called from the porch.

"Roger when berserk and started shooting at us, but unfortunately since Carrie wasn't in harm's way, *Sous* Zooric didn't see that as a problem." Dave reported blandly as he stood and dusted off his clothes.

His father looked from the angry faces of Dave and Derrick to the amusement on *Gaad* Egell's, before resting on Zooric who was unhurriedly brushing off his robes and ignoring them all.

"I had a similar problem," he said dryly.

"What do you mean?" Dave asked.

"*Loya* Modnar's only concern was whether *Sous* Zooric was safe or not."

"Zig shit!" Dave muttered. "Talk about one track minds."

"He is one of yours. It was not my problem to solve," Zooric said mildly, proving that he undoubtedly followed what they were implying.

"He was shooting at us," Derrick grounded out. "It couldn't get any closer to your problem than that."

Clearly deciding that he had had enough of the conversation, Zooric turned to Mr. Classet. "I will go to Caree."

"Carrie is fine."

"I know she is fine." He inclined his head in a formal farewell gesture before walking off—a grinning *Gaad* Egell accompanied him.

"Isn't he the one who rescued your daughter?"

Two of the Council Members had followed Mr. Classet onto the porch.

Mr. Classet hesitated. Carl Robert, one of the Council's most radical Separatists, was asking the question. Before he could formulate a reply, the man smirked.

"I guess it's fine that he wants her. She certainly wouldn't find a husband among any man in town."

"What are you implying?" Mr. Classet demanded, glaring at the Council Member.

"Come Dennis. It is best if she is removed from Arapmo. She would only further dilute the whites here if she were to marry one of us."

"Why you..." In blind fury Mr. Classet took a swing at the man, his fist landing an uppercut that sent Carl reeling.

Swearing, Carl scrambled to his feet. Jade managed to grab him in time, pulling him away even as both Derrick and Dave stood beside Mr. Classet with clenched fists.

"Now that we are free of the Presidential rule, there are no laws barring my daughter from marriage to any man in Arapmo." Mr. Classet grounded out. "And as long as I am on the Council there will never be."

"We will see," Carl threatened, still furious at the attack. "It is past time for us to ensure that our race and others stay pure. Now that we no longer have the Presidential Council forcing their policies of mixing up the races, I intend to get Separatist control of the Council. You can't control all the votes. We'll see what the majority wants." With a satisfied swagger he walked off.

"We may have another war on our hands Dad," Dave commented.

Derrick stared after the man. "He's right, you know."

"What?" Mr. Classet swung around.

"You're ... you are accepted here," Derrick muttered. "But because of our skin color, Carrie and I were never fully accepted. In New World City there is so much mixture it doesn't matter. But here, where the population is all white, they see us as different. And they like the idea of preserving a pure breed. Although the majority here hate the Presidential polices of forced marriages, they are loath to the idea of integration of the races and they think nothing of showing their disdain for innocents like Carrie and myself.

"You never mentioned this before," Mr. Classet said giving Derrick a look of wounded amazement. "Did someone say something or do something?"

"Apart for the subtle and not so subtle actions many upright citizens took just to make sure I knew I didn't belong here." Derrick gave a mocking laugh even as he shook his head. "No Sir."

"I didn't know..." Mr. Classet seemed almost dazed.

"No one would dare do anything too overt. Mostly, there were just snide remarks and petty acts."

Mr. Classet ran his hand through his hair. "Your father was like a brother to me...."

But Derrick interrupted with an abrupt dismissive movement of his arm. "I know that Sir. It isn't anything to do with you. What they did... do is often so subtle it really isn't worth mentioning. I know it is just the attitude of some of the people of this town. It's true that many here in Arapmo came to escape the policies of the Presidential Council, but the Separatist definitely came because they wanted to stick with their race."

"I still believe that most people want to be allowed the freedom to choose their own husband or wife," Mr. Classet insisted. "The battle that we just fought has given us a chance to escape Council policies. I think the majority will vote for freedom. They will dislike the Separatist policies of banning all mixed marriages even more than the previous Council policies."

Jade hesitantly spoke up. "I agree, but Derrick is also right. Many Separatist sympathizers don't see it that way. They just see their race disappearing under the Council's policies. It isn't just the whites. Until I saw these aliens, I hadn't ever seen anyone so dark skinned. Not even in New World City. And when was the last time you saw a true Asian." He stopped abruptly at the incredulous look he was receiving from the Classets.

"Do they have another convert in you too Jade?" Mr. Classet asked ironically.

"No. I don't agree with the Separatists, but unlike you I understand their position."

"I can't understand how anyone would vote to have the Council control their lives again." Mr. Classet shook his head. "Besides, if people are allowed choices, what makes you think they will choose to integrate?"

"You may have a better chance of getting them to see things your way if you stressed that."

"I can see another battle coming," Dave repeated grimly.

"I am not afraid of wars," His father said implacably "If we fight to win, we'll succeed, no matter how long it takes."

"This time we had help Dad," Dave pointed out. "And have you noticed that their Soosan leader is none too pleased that *Sous* Zooric is attracted to Carrie. All humans—and they are human—like familiarity. We like the safety and security of interactions with people just like us. Everyone has a personal comfort zone—and that applies especially when dealing with others of a different race. If we force them to stray too far from their comfort zone, the people of Arapmo will rebel."

Mr. Classet sighed. "You have convinced me. I am willing to stress that we are for freedom. Pure freedom! This means freedom to associate with whomever you please, wherever you please. We must protect the rights of those who would exercise their freedom of choice by marrying someone of another race. We must ensure that all our people are equal and free no matter their color, class or condition.

"I agree," Jade was nodding. "You don't have to convince me."

"Then let's take this one thing at the time." Mr. Classet looked over to where the crowd around Roger was gathered. "At least he is not injured." Roger was already sitting up.

"I believe I will go and calm Carl's nerves before he gets all the other members riled up." Jade said.

"Good idea." Mr. Classet grinned at his friend. "I lost it for a moment there. Thanks. Let me know if you hear anything worth knowing."

"Sure thing. But I doubt you have anything to worry about just yet. They are all still afraid of the Presidential Council. Right now, there is safety in numbers. No one will dare try to break away."

There was a brief silence as Jade walked off.

Again Mr. Classet gave a sigh. "I hope he's right. If not..." he shrugged.

"Why not just concentrate on sticking to plan A for now." Derrick suggested. "We need to get *Sous* Zooric to mingle."

"Would you believe *Sous* Zooric watched Roger shooting at us for a good minute and did nothing because Carrie was not in any danger?" Dave said in disgust.

"I believe you," Mr. Classet began thoughtfully. "He needs to focus on someone other than Carrie. You're right Derrick. We should get him back out here where he can meet other women. Perhaps we can redirect his attention."

"Isn't that the Separatist idea?" Dave murmured cheekily.

"We are not banning their marriage." his father disagreed. "To have true freedom of choice one must be given choices."

"And I doubt *Sous* Zooric has had an opportunity to check out other women," Derrick added not giving up.

"I don't think it will work," Dave said as they reached where the townspeople had gathered around Roger.

"Why not?" Derrick demanded.

"You met the man. He seems totally focused on Carrie—only Carrie. And you heard Carrie. I think she loves him."

Derrick looked thoughtful. He was also worried about the bond Carrie seemed to have formed with Zooric. But he was not convinced that there was nothing he could do about it. Carrie was a sensible girl. How could she commit her life to an alien?

"Can it really be true love when they are so different?" Mr. Classet asked. "They have interacted with each other only under stressful conditions. They haven't had the opportunity to see each in a natural environment."

Dave shrugged. "They seem totally committed to each other. I just don't think it's a fleeting emotion that will disappear just because we want it to."

"She met him only fifty cycles ago." Derrick scoffed. "She can't possibly be in love with him. I think she is grateful because he saved her life and she is transferring that gratitude into something else. And he is just using her."

Mr. Classet shrugged, "If it is love, if they are that committed, then I'll not stand in their way. But I do agree with Derrick. Fifty cycles is not a long time to learn about someone. Carrie is young. Her emotions can swing like a pendulum. We need to see how strong their commitment is to each other is." He turned back to the problems at hand. "I'll stay here and calm the jittery crowd. You two go get *Sous* Zooric. Get him back outside."

****

Chapter 23

By and large, the settlers disregarded the incident with Roger and stayed the entire light. First dark was approaching before parties large and small began heading back to the town.

As the party winded down, the male members of the Classets household headed inside to join Mrs. Classet. Ron and the other men were busy shuttling people back to the town. In fact, all of the men would be sleeping in town to return later in the cycle. Mr. Classet realized that starting the next cycle, much that had been neglected since the arrival of the Presidential Guards would have to be corrected. They would all have to get back to work!

Kelly bounded down the stairs. "Is Carrie still here?"

"Why shouldn't she be?" Derrick asked.

"The alien could have taken her away since it's now dark," Scott reasoned as he followed his older brother.

Derrick scowled at him.

"How is she?" Mr. Classet asked as he took off his hat and raked his hands through his hair.

Mrs. Classet smiled, "She is fine, just a little tired as we all are."

Surprising to the Classets, it was *Loya* Modnar who had convinced Zooric to leave the outpost this dark. But as Dave later pointed out, this was further proof that *Loya* Modnar was even more against the match between Zooric and Carrie than they were. *Loya* Modnar pressed Zooric to give Carrie time with her family before trying to take her away and had insisted that Zooric leave with him. Although Zooric had complied, he had been noticeably reluctant, and Carrie had been clearly upset.

"Will the alien come back and take her Mam?" Kelly asked as she helped her mother clear away the remains of their big picnic.

"I'm sure that even if she leaves for a while Carrie will come back."

"We've perhaps a full cycle to convince her to stay," Dave said, flopping down at the table.

Derrick pulled away his seat and prepared to sit. "We have to stop her from going with him Ma'am. He is so...so..."

Dave grinned, "Arrogant... offensive."

Derrick snorted rudely. "Yes, to both of those." He turned to Mrs. Classet, "And he was acting stranger than usual this cycle."

"What did he do?" she asked.

"He treated the town's people as if they were contaminated or infectious. He absolutely refused to shake hands with anyone. Even the *Loyas* shook hands, but Zooric insisted on bowing."

"That's the Owoons method of greeting," Mrs. Classet defended.

"So *Loya* Modnar explained. But after we explained the handshake, *Loya* Modnar shook hands without a problem. *Gaad* Egell shook hands with everyone. *Sous* Zooric refused. Twice I took him aside and explained to him that hand shaking was our preferred method of greeting. He just gave me an expressionless stare and continued bowing. No explanations."

"Perhaps Carrie can speak to him. I'm sure he means no harm." Mrs. Classet hesitated. "He seems to be very reserved, and I somehow doubt that he takes hints very well."

"There was no 'hinting' involved Mam," Dave said humorously. "We did everything short of applying force. I lost count of the number of times people tried to greet him with a handshake. He just ignored them."

"I'm sure he understood exactly what we wanted him to do." Derrick scowled. "He just refused for whatever reason. The fact the *Loya* Modnar tried to explain away his refusal shows that even they were aware that he was being objectionable."

"And he definitely hid any embarrassment well," Mr. Classet grumbled. His effort to get Zooric focused on other women had been a total failure.

Contrary to what the Derrick and Classets thought would happen, the women from the town were clearly fascinated by the aliens. Mrs. Editon had actually begged to be introduced to Zooric, yet after the introduction, Zooric refused to get closer even as she had tried to devour him with her eyes. Not that her apparent enthrallment appeared to have any effect on Zooric. He had literally circled her, treating her as if he would a strange wild animal. And many of the other men and women from the town got similar wary treatment. As Mr. Classet finished describing the incident, Dave began laughing.

"You should have seen her face. Zig Shit!" Dave said.

Even Derrick was mildly amused.

"Tact does not seem to be *Sous* Zooric's strong point," Dave said still grinning. "He made it clear he wanted nothing to do with her or any other woman. In fact, I don't think this is a good idea. Zooric will not take kindly to interference in his affairs."

"What is a good idea?" Mrs. Classet asked looking confused.

"I wanted *Sous* Zooric to meet other women." Her husband insisted. "We can only know if they are truly right for each other if Zooric meets others."

Although she looked troubled, Mrs. Classed finally nodded. "I just hate the idea of her going so far. Perhaps we could let them stay here for a while."

"You mean Carrie is not leaving with the alien?" Kelly asked excitedly.

The adults all looked at her. They had forgotten her presence.

It was her father who first responded. "Maybe not little one," he said patting her head. "We're trying to see if *Sous* Zooric will stay here for a while."

"You mean the alien will live here with us?" Scott asked, his voice hushed in wonder.

"We will have to ask him first."

"This is great. We will be living with an alien. Just wait until I tell my friends."

Smiling in amusement, his mother turned to her husband, "Is everyone gone now?"

"Yes. We decided to give the men the dark off. They will all be returning at second- light."

Carrie stepped into the room. "What is this I heard about Zooric staying here," she asked as she made her way across the room.

"Carrie!" Kelly cried. "Mam said...." she stopped as they all turned to look toward the door. There were steps on the pouch. Someone was coming!

"*Sous* Zooric?" Derrick looked questioningly at Carrie.

She was shaking her head slowly. "Nooo."

Derrick did not ask how she knew. He scraped back his chair and jumped to his feet. But he had only gone two paces in his attempt to reach his rifle on the wall, when the door pushed open.

****

"Raekon!" Carrie paled.

Raekon smiled in delight. "Hello Carrie."

"Who is this, Carrie?" her father asked urgently.

"Zooric's enemy." Carrie was staring at Raekon, her eyes huge "Where is Zooric?"

"Not here." Raekon grinned at her then continued in his language. "And if he should come. Look what I have." He took out a small flat band of metal. It was just long enough to fit in the palm of an adult's hand.

Carrie recognized it instantly. It was the kooknor, the ancient weapon Zooric had found. Zooric had finally fixed one to demonstrate it to *Loya* Modnar. More than likely *Loya* Modnar had told *Loya* Meestric about the weapon. After that it was easy to see how Raekon had acquired it. Carrie, however, did not see how it could possibly help Raekon.

In an abrupt movement, Derrick, the farthest from Raekon and the weapon, suddenly lunged for his rifle. He didn't make it. Screaming in agony, he suddenly fell to the ground.

Carrie jumped to her feet, her hands flying to her mouth in horror. She scarcely heard her mother's, Thia's or even her sister's cries of terror above her own.

"Do not move!" Raekon shouted above the din. "Tell them not to move or I will kill them," he continued in Gavaa as he turned to face Carrie.

Tearfully, Carrie translated Raekon's words. Her family was now motionless in shock. Derrick remained abnormally still. Now the only noise was Kelly's cries of fear.

Raekon eyed Kelly in agitation. "Tell her to stop the noise. Tell her now or I will sizzle her."

Since Carrie was the only one to understand his words in Gavaa, she turned anxiously to her sister. "Kelly, please stop." She gave her mother a pleading look. "Mam, we have to get her to stop before he sizzles her. Kelly, please darling, you must stop crying."

"What's a sizzle?" her father asked urgently as Mrs. Classet began pleading desperately with Kelly, even covering the little girl's mouth to silence her cries.

"What he did to Derrick." Carrie was crying silently now, tears streaming down her face. "Oh Dad, I am so sorry." She wiped her eyes as Kelly hiccupped in fright, still unable to stop crying despite the desperate pleas of her mother. In the middle of another hiccup, she suddenly screamed in terror — then crumbled.

"No!" Mrs. Classet reached for her daughter but was unable to stop Kelly from falling to the floor.

"Do not move!" Raekon shouted again as the older lady made to rise. Like her older daughter, Mrs. Classet began silently crying. With tears running down her face, she stared at her now quiet daughter. Kelly's body lay crumbled on the floor. It was impossible to tell whether she was dead or alive.

With silence at last, Raekon's grin re-emerged. "Come here Carrie." He motioned to his side. "Now, I will find out about this linking you have with *Sous* Zooric."

With a renewed feeling of control, Raekon was now calm enough to speak in English. But Carrie could not move. She continued staring at Kelly's body in mute shock.

"Come!" Raekon was beginning to get angry. "Come or I will sizzle another of your family. No. I know what I will do." He motioned for Scott to come to him. "Come!" he ordered.

"No!" Carrie screamed, as she pushed her chair back. "I'll come. Please. I'll come. Don't hurt him."

But Raekon was bent on his own particular form of amusement. "No! Stay!" he now gestured at Carrie. "You come." Again, he spoke in English while motioning to Scott.

Scott was wide-eyed with terror. He looked at his father who reluctantly nodded. There really was nothing they could do.

As soon as Scott was within Raekon's reach Raekon grabbed him around the chest. Grinning widely, he gestured to Carrie. "Now you come. He will ensure that you behave after we leave."

Slowly, like a zombie, Carrie moved away from her chair. She stopped short. Zooric was close by.

****

"Do not go, Caree," he told her mentally.

Raekon's eyes flashed. "*Sous* Zooric!" He crowed. He swung the weapon in a wide arc as he continued. "Come join us."

The entire Classet family turned to watch as Zooric stepped into the dining room from the interior of the house. He approached calmly, his movement sure and alert. It was something they had noticed about him; it would be next to impossible to take him unawares. He was constantly scanning his surrounding–always aware of the movements of those around him–always on guard.

Raekon continued grinning as Zooric approached. His grin slowly faded, however, when Zooric did not stop.

"*Tveex*! Stop!" He yelled. "*Stop or I will sizzle you.*"

Zooric lifted an eyebrow. Compared to Raekon's expressive face, his was like a statue. "Sizzle me then you die. *Loya* Modnar is approaching." He continued his steady approach.

Raekon's eyes flickered nervously. Scott whimpered as Raekon unconsciously squeezed him. "*Stop right there or I'll sizzle you,*" Raekon repeated. He lifted the weapon, pointing the tip directly at Zooric.

Zooric gave him a cold smile. "The kooknor does not give you extra powers. Sizzle me if you dare. It will be your last act." He was now glad he had not revealed the true power of the kooknor.

Raekon backed up, pulling Scott with him. Then abruptly he shifted, the weapon now pointing it at Carrie "*I'll kill her. I swear I will. Stop or I'll kill her.*"

Zooric stopped. "I will kill you slowly," he announced without expression. "Before you die you will wish for death."

Raekon licked his lips, clearly intimidated. His hand holding the weapon was visibly shaking.

As casually as possible, Zooric slipped his hands inside the folds of his robe. His fingers closed over the smooth surface of his kooknor as he coolly assessed the positions of everyone present. The Classet family was terrified yet heartened by the distraction. They were all staring at him with varying degrees of hope, well aware that Raekon felt threatened.

"I would suggest that you kill me first." Zooric's expression was icy. He was literally exuding menace. "Killing Caree will guarantee your death. With my death your chances are slim, but at least there is a chance."

Without looking at Carrie, he continued privately. *"When I say 'now', drop to the ground – like a dead faint. Can you do that Caree? A dead faint. Nod your head if you can."*

At Carrie's nod, the weapon in Raekon's hand wavered; then quickly shifted back to Zooric. *"What are you saying to her? If you try anything, I will kill you. I will kill you instantly. Then I will leave with Zerah Caree and the boy Tifoosa and you will not stop me..."* his mental words trailed off at Zooric's amused stare. Swallowing, he began sending a plea to both *Loyas* who were close by. *"I didn't mean any harm. It was not right that he should have the Tifoosa. I will not hurt her. You know I would not hurt her."*

"Scott!" Zooric was looking directly at the boy.

Scott jerked. Unbelievably his eyes, already widened by fear, became wider.

"When I say, 'now,' bite his hand as hard as you can. Then, as soon as he releases you, run away from him. Drop to the ground if you can but get away from him. Can you understand? Nod if you do."

Raekon did not even see Scot's wide- eyed nod. He was still pleading with *Loya* Meestric.

Zooric interrupted his pleadings. "Raekon! You are dead!" As Raekon's eyes widened in fear, Zooric pulsed his kooknor while instantaneously shouting, "Now!" to both Carrie and Scott

Startled by Scott's bite and Zooric's shout, Raekon's arm jerked. But his kooknor was still pointing directly at Zooric! The electro pulse leaving the kooknor was lightning fast and should not be seen yet midway between Raekon and Zooric, there was an amazing firework like explosion. The brilliant flash of light was accompanied by a sound that rocked their eardrums.

Zooric, meanwhile, had dived to the ground as Carrie gave a very realistic faint. Even before the rest of the family could absorb the rapid sequence of events, Raekon's body was lifted and thrown a good two feet. Then, as Scott scrambled away, Raekon began screaming. The Owoon had grabbed his head with both hands and was tearing at his hair. His blood curdling yells sent chills up and down Carrie's spine. Scott ran to his mother as Raekon's screams abruptly stopped.

Carrie, who had remained motionless on the ground, looked up when she smelled charred flesh.

"Zooric!" she cried since it seemed that Zooric was intent on burning Raekon's body to a crisp.

He immediately became concerned and shifted his intense focus from Raekon. "Are you okay?"

At her nod, he got up. With four swift strides, he picked up the weapon that Raekon had dropped and slipped it in his robes. Then, without looking at Raekon's body, he continued to Carrie's side.

Crying, Carrie hugged him. "Oh Zooric." He was bending to kiss her when he suddenly jerked his head up. "The *Loyas* are coming." Zooric said looking around at the shattered Classet family.

Both Mr. and Mrs. Classet were bending over Kelly.

"Is Kelly...?" Carrie asked fearfully.

"Kelly should recover soon. She was stunned only," Zooric said.

"Thank God," Mrs. Classet said still sobbing.

"She will be fine. She is a high receiver like Caree." Zooric murmured to her. "Derrick is also a high receiver, so it is unlikely that the pulse Raekon used would kill or maim him."

Thia and Dave had been examining Derrick's still form. "He's barely breathing," Dave announced fearfully. "It that normal?"

Taking Carrie with him, Zooric went over to examine Derrick. He tentatively touched two fingers to the man's temple.

"What are you doing?" Dave demanded.

"I will not hurt him," Zooric muttered. "He should wake up soon. And our medic is coming."

They all looked around. Sure enough, at least three more Owoons were running toward the open door.

"They will not harm you." Zooric called out. "One is a medic and will help Derrick."

Despite his reassurance, the males all reached for their rifles. Dave lifted Kelly's still unconscious body as the entire family backed away from the door and watched the arrival of the Owoons.

Two came swiftly to Derrick side, one opened a bag and they were soon injecting a clear fluid into a vein in the unconscious man's arms.

"How do you know this medicine will not harm him," Mr. Classet asked with a worried frown.

Zooric looked up. "It should not. The ancient writings showed proof that much of our biology is the same."

It was not much reassurance, but what else could they do? Still uncertain, the family continued to watch. Kelly groaned.

"She is awake," Mrs. Classet announced tearfully.

"Mam!" Kelly immediately began crying again. "My head aches," her voice was fretful from both the pain and recent fear.

"One of the Owoons working on Derrick looked up. "We can give her medicine for the pain," he said reaching inside his bag. He handed the medicine to Zooric who took the vial of liquid over to the family.

"This will help the pain in your head," Zooric said, smiling at Kelly who returned a tearful smile. The little girl looked first at her mother, then satisfied with her mother's reassurance, took the medicine.

"What do I do with it?" she asked. "Drink," Zooric indicated.

"Does it taste bad?"

"No. It is very sweet."

She lifted it tentatively to her head and took a tiny sip, then pleased with the taste, drank the lot.

"How long before it works?" Dave wanted to know.

"Within a few minutes her head should be fine. It may make her sleepy."

"I will take her to bed as soon as I know Derrick will be okay," Mrs. Classet announced. She moved to position herself to hide Raekon's body from her daughter. Seeing her action, one of the Owoons removed his robe and covered the dead Soosan.

Mrs. Classet smiled her thanks; then looked quickly toward Derrick as she heard him groan. Minutes later his eyes snapped open. He moaned again, bringing both hands to his head.

"More of them are coming," Dave suddenly announced.

"They will not hurt you," Zooric reassured.

It was the *Loyas* and *Gaad* Keefav. After grimly surveying the room, the Owoons worked quickly, following instruction from *Loya* Modnar that Zooric did not feel like translating.

"He could have buzzed him," Loya Meestric kept saying. *"There was no need to kill Sous Raekon. Modnar you cannot agree to this."*

Whatever *Loya* Modnar's response, it was heard only by *Loya* Meestric. Although *Loya* Meestric calmed somewhat, he still seemed in a state of shock, saddened by Raekon's death.

When things returned to a semblance of normality, Mrs. Classet decided to take Kelly upstairs to bed. As she was about to leave, Scott suddenly tugged at his mother.

"He spoke in my head." With the natural resilience of youth, his eyes were bright with excitement.

"What?" Mrs. Classet asked distracted by her concern over Kelly.

"The alien spoke in my head," Scott repeated.

They all stared at him but did not get a chance to comment as Scott began an avid recollection of the events. "He told me to bite the bad alien and I did." Scott grinned at Zooric.

Now everyone was staring at Zooric. "Is that true?" Carrie's father asked.

Scott nodded eagerly, pleased to be the focus of attention. Again, he turned to Zooric. "Can you speak in my head again?"

"Yes." Zooric responded to Scott alone.

"He did it again," Scott shouted in glee. "I heard you. I heard you."

Zooric looked amused at Scott's excitement but not so the others. They were clearly astonished.

"I thought..." Mr. Classet began. "I did not realize that you could speak mentally to us too."

"Speak to me in my head too," Kelly pleaded with Zooric.

Zooric complied, bringing a squeal of delight from the little girl.

Loya Modnar turned to stare at Zooric. He was clearly astonished. *"How could you speak to him?"*

Loya Meestric was also staring. *"He is a child!"*

Zooric shrugged. "It is possible to speak to children."

"How is this possible?" came the response from *Loya* Meestric.

"He does not have a frequency." *Loya* Modnar was clearly puzzled. *"Sous Zooric we have discussed your strengths in detail. You did not mention your ability to speak to children. Can you also speak to Owoon children?"* It showed the extent of their shock that both *Loyas* were discussing Soosan business publicly, and in the presence of other Owoons.

"I have never tried," Zooric said cautiously.

"But could you?" *Loya* Modnar asked demanding an answer.

"I suppose it is possible. I can 'sense' them."

Loya Meestric turned to say something privately to *Loya* Modnar at which *Loya* Modnar shook his head. *"Sous Zooric, you will learn that the Soosans do not like surprises. Why did you not mention this ability?"*

"I spoke in an emergency to Scott, until then I had never tried to communicate with a child mentally."

"You must have suspected that it was possible, yet you did not speak of it." Loya Meestric was now angry.

"I..." again Zooric shrugged. "I... I did not think of it before."

"Zig shit," Dave muttered turning to Carrie. "They are arguing, aren't they? What are they saying?"

Carrie quickly explained and began interpreting.

"An alien within the aliens." Derrick said softly. His tone was not complementary.

Zooric heard him. He gave Derrick a hooded look but remained silent.

Loya Modnar finally realized the inappropriateness of discussing Zooric's abilities so publicly. *"We will discuss this later,"* he started turning away only to swiftly turn back with another thought. *"Are there other high receivers like Zerah Caree here?"*

"Eeng," Zooric admitted. "Caree's mother, Derrick, and Kelly are high recievers—also some of the Tifoosas from the town both male and female. I was able to pick up some signals but I did not pursue the source."

"What do they mean by a receiver?" Derrick demanded. Although still weak from the effects of the sizzle, he shakily got to his feet.

Loya Modnar turned to him and with *Gaad* Trateen interpreting said. *"Zerah Caree is a high receiver."* He explained the concept.

Now it was Mr. Classet's turn to demand more explanations. In fact, he was very annoyed that the Owoons had hidden such important information from them. *Loya* Modnar apologized, but explained that only Zooric had this special ability, and it was something that even he did not fully understand.

Derrick suddenly remembered something. "Why is *Sous* Zooric having anything to do with Carrie? You mentioned that Soosans live in an all-male society."

The *Loyas* exchanged looks. Finally, *Loya* Modnar said. *"This is perhaps not an appropriate time for this discussion. We must see to Sous Raekon's burial. Then we will return to answer your questions."*

Loya Modnar turned to Zooric. *"Sous Zooric."* It was a clear command for the younger Soosan to follow them.

But Zooric objected. "If we leave now, Carrie will be forced to answer all questions," he pointed out.

Reluctantly, after a private exchange of words between the *Loyas, Loya* Modnar nodded. *"Very well. Sous Zooric you will explain."*

Zooric was none too happy but reluctantly faced the Classets as he began. "Among my people there are those who are strong transmitters and receivers of electro skill —these are the Soosans and weak transmitters and receivers — other Owoons. In Caleel all strong transmitters and receivers known by the Soosan are males. A strong receiver who is female is unknown in Caleel and a strong transmitter can only mate with a similarly strong receiver. Carrie is a strong receiver."

"Are you saying," Mr. Classet began delicately. "You cannot er... mate with anyone else in your village."

"I have not tried." Zooric shrugged his disinterest. He was in fact sure that he could. He was now convinced that his mother was a strong receiver. That meant there were other females like her. The Soosans had never thought to test women! "It is..."

But Derrick interrupted with a look at Carrie. "So now we finally have the truth," he burst out. "Do you realize he is using you? They are all using us." He turned to Mr. Classet in fury. "What's going to happen to us when the next Soosan goes berserk?"

"Zooric is not using me." Carrie stormed. "He already told me there could be other females in his town that are high receivers. No! He is not using me."

But Derrick was beyond listening to reason. "We need to get them all out of here before they destroy us," he insisted. He was glaring at all the Owoons when Zooric moved to touch Carrie's arm. Derrick exploded in fury.

"Take your hands off her," he stormed reaching to push Zooric away.

No one could quite explain what happened next. Zooric stepped back to avoid contact with Derrick but somehow tripped, possibly because of his recently healed leg. Yet, Derrick still reached for him, in a reflex action to prevent him from falling, Zooric gave a startled gasp of pain. He pulled away from Derrick, but the movement overbalanced them both. Derrick screamed—his voice laced in agony.

In panic, Derrick tried to jerk away, but in their fight for balance, they both fell to the ground—on each other. Zooric gasped again, then he groaned aloud.

****

Zooric was totally blind-sided by Derrick's mental attack. He had never particularly cared whether Derrick liked him or not. Mostly he ignored Derrick and generally tried to block him out, totally. But if Derrick projected fury, or any strong emotion, he could only achieve a total block if there was no contact between them, which was why he had stepped back sharply when Derrick reached for him. He did not want the contact. Yet the very thing he feared most was happening. One minute he was mentally reaching for Caree; the next second Derrick's fury hit him. Instinctively Zooric reacted, sending a low intensity buzz to disable Derrick. The Tifoosa screamed in pain! It was then Zooric realized that although Derrick was still projecting fury, he could not buzz the Tifoosa again. Derrick was just recovering from Raekon's attack; even a low intensity buzz by Zooric was likely to permanently maim him. Zooric knew he could not do that to Caree's friend.

He was now being blasted by both Derrick's terror and his fury, yet he was unable to retaliate — unable to stop the intensity of emotions. Blocking such strong signals was usually only partially effective; with contact it became impossible. He doubled over in agony. He was losing control! Caree! He needed Caree! But as with Carrie, once weakened, his brain automatically sought a low-link. This time the link created was with Derrick. Fear swamped him as the linking brought all his old anguish and nightmares to the surface. For a fraction of a second, Zooric lost it. It was a spiraling effect. He did not even realize that he was screaming mentally — literally sending out a panic signal to everyone within reach.

****

"Zooric! Stop! You are paralyzing everyone in sight!" Carrie dropped to the ground, cradling Zooric's head, crying as she tried to calm him.

The others were either screaming or shouting. Then, as abruptly as the mental screams started, they stopped. Zooric had lost consciousness. He was now slumped in Carrie's arms.

"No!" Derrick was struggling to his feet. "No!" he tried to stand.

Mr. Classet came over to assist him. "My God! What happened?"

Carrie began crying as she tried to rouse Zooric. "He's not waking up!" she wailed.

The *Loyas* joined the crowd around the two.

"Oh, Zooric," she sobbed. Carrie refused to let him go despite *Loya* Modnar's attempt to intervene.

"Gaads Egell and Sorgan will see him,"Loya Modnar urged her.

Carrie forced herself to release Zooric and allow his examination by the medics. She glanced tearfully around. The others were hovering around, some still clutching their heads in near panic. Mr. Classet and Dave were supporting Derrick, helping him to his feet.

"Is he ok?" Derrick asked.

"He is being checked," Loya Modnar said without turning his attention from Zooric,

Derrick's head jerked up. "I can hear you now." He stared at *Loya* Modnar. "I can hear you." This time, his glance flickered between *Loya* Modnar and Zooric.

Loya Modnar swung around. Both he and *Loya* Meestric turned to give Derrick penetrating stares.

"You can hear my mental words," Loya Modnar requested confirmation.

"Yes," Derrick was still staring.

"What is going on?" Mr. Classet demanded.

"I can hear when the *Loyas* speak mentally."

"Zig shit!" Dave muttered.

Now the Classets were gaping at Derrick, their initial terror, only partly subsided, was clearly rising again. The interruption by Egell was a welcome relief.

"He is totally unresponsive *Loya*, but his vitals seem to be stabilizing."

Loya Modnar turned his worried gaze to Derrick. *"Can you explain what happened?"*

"He... I guess... I am not sure. First, he tried to buzz me then he abruptly stopped. I started getting his thoughts.... I don't know..." Derrick rubbed his face. "He seemed... I know he was in a lot of pain."

"Your emotions can hurt him," Carrie said wiping away tears. "You are a high receiver so your emotions can hurt him."

Everyone was staring at her.

"Explain. Sous Zooric did not mention this." *Loya* Modnar was now frowning.

Still fighting tears, Carrie told them about the earlier incident when her fury had caused Zooric pain. "He can only partially block the pain of someone's emotion if there is no contact. But since they fell on each other, most likely he was totally unable to block. At the time he told me that the pain was like missiles in his brain."

"He did not tell us this. Why? Precautions could have been taken."Loya Modnar was visibly upset.

"I don't know," Carrie shook her head. "And I don't know why he didn't stop Derrick's fury from reaching him."

"He tried; then stopped because he was afraid he would hurt me." Derrick's voice was subdued. "He didn't want to hurt me. Bolt. I can't believe it... He didn't want to hurt me because I am your friend." Derrick raked his hair with his fingers. "I... I was getting his thoughts. He didn't... I was too panicked to realize what was happening. He felt that after the buzz by Raekon, my mind would not be able to absorb another so soon." He looked helpless at Carrie. "I'm sorry Carrie. Bolt! I had no idea what was going on until it was too late."

"Oh Zooric!" Carrie sank back to the ground, sobbing uncontrollably, her head buried in his chest.

After a short silence her mother came over to urge her up. "Come darling. He is still alive. Perhaps he is just stunned." She turned to her husband. "Can we move him? Maybe to the sofa... or somewhere more comfortable."

After another examination by *Gaad* Egell, it was decided that Zooric would be moved to one of the upstairs bedroom suites. Zooric did not stir during the move but as everyone kept reassuring Carrie, his vital signs were stable.

With Zooric ill, none of the Owoons seemed inclined to leave; besides they had to arrange Raekon's burial. After consultation it was decided that they would bury him in an area that the Classet's had originally reserved for future family burial. Not everyone agreed with Mr. Classet's decision. After all, Raekon had tried to kill some of the family members. But since another enemy, the deputy, was also buried there, Mr. Classet decided that the area was already contaminated anyway. He would now have to dedicate another plot as the family burial site.

Gaad Egell stayed with Zooric while the other Owoons attended the burial. The Classets assumed correctly that they would be having guests for the last light meal. The family was just settling down to eat when they were startled by the howling bark of what they thought was a wild animal. Derrick and Dave grabbed their weapons and were ready to rush outside when *Gaad* Trateen shouted out.

"It's Soor!" He was yelling. "Don't shoot. It's Soor!"

"What is a soor?" Dave asked.

"*Sous* Zooric's pet." Trateen was already dismounting as the Classets gathered on the porch.

"Trust him to have a bizarre pet," Dave said shaking his head wryly.

Although Soor was standing docile, proving he was well trained, no one came closer.

"What is it?" Scott finally asked.

"A rocleer." Trateen explained.

For a few minutes the rocleer was the focus of attention, then the *Loyas* dismounted to perform formal introductions. All seven Owoons would be staying and after they were assigned rooms, Soor was taken up to be with Zooric. As the other family members and guests sat down for a very subdued meal, they could hear the mournful howling of Soor.

****

The Owoons were all settled in the spare bedrooms and Carrie, who had not eaten, had at last been convinced to leave Zooric and go to bed. She was still teary as she prepared for bed and knew she would get no sleep. Then she felt it. A bolt of pain lanced in her mind. Zooric!

Carrie ran. She was not the only one to feel Zooric's pain. He must have had absolutely no control if he was transmitting to everyone. The others were all running in the direction of Zooric's room even though the intensity of pain increased the closer they got to Zooric. As she entered the room, Carrie was actually beginning to feel nauseous. Even the *Loyas* were gasping. *Gaad* Egell was frantically trying to inject something into Zooric's arm. Carrie held her head, as she leaned weakly on the door. Zooric was retching. He was violently sick, and now with each heave he was projecting his pain.

"Take it easy." Derrick said supporting her.

"He has no control," Carrie cried.

"I know I can feel it too."

Slowly, as the medicine took effect, the intensity of pain decreased; then it finally stopped. Carrie moved further into the room. She ignored the others as she approached the bed and tenderly ran her fingers along Zooric's cheek. He had to recover!

"It is only a sleep aid," *Gaad* Egell explained as Carrie's fingers combed through Zooric's hair.

"This is not good." *Loya* Meestric said. *"What if he does not regain control?"*

No one answered.

"How long will the sleep aid last?" *Loya* Modnar asked.

"Perhaps half a cycle. It depends." *Gaad* Egell was re-packing his medicine bags. In his hurry to inject Zooric with the sleep aid, he had spilled most of the contents on the floor.

"I want to stay with him," Carrie said

"There is nothing you can do." *Loya* Modnar pointed out.

"I don't care. I just want to stay."

"Carrie... "Her father began.

"Please Dad."

The *Loyas* exchanged glances then *Loya* Modnar looked at *Gaad* Egell who shrugged.

"It will not hurt," Egell said cleaning up beside the bed where Zooric had been sick.

"We give our permission," *Loya* Modnar nodded.

Gaad Egell translated *Loya* Modnar's agreement for Mr. Classet.

Classet signed. "Very well Carrie. But ..." He hesitated then, without completing the thought, turned to Dave. "Let's go. We both have to get some sleep. We are heading to town next light. Remember, I'm meeting with the Council."

Dave nodded. He and Mr. Classet moved away.

"Are you coming to town with us, Derrick?" Dave asked.

Derrick hesitated. "If you don't mind sir, I'd like to stay," he said addressing Mr. Classet.

The Classets gave him worried frowns. Neither had failed to notice that Derrick had been downright subdued since Zooric's injury.

"Derrick, you couldn't have known what effect your emotions would have on him." Mr. Classet reassured.

"I felt his pain," Derrick said softly. "I knew I was causing it."

Carrie looked up at Derrick. "You didn't do it deliberately."

"No," he agreed softly. "But... I hated him. Yet he tried to save me."

"It was still an accident," Carrie said firmly.

He gave her a lopsided grin. "Call me if you need me, okay."

She nodded.

****

Chapter 24

"We don't want these aliens living here," Carl insisted.

Dennis Classet signed. He had expected dissent at this Council meeting but even the other Freechoicers where having trouble siding with him after he suggested that the Owoons could help in their war with the Presidential Council.

"Listen. We don't have a choice here. We must convince them to stay because we need their help. There is no way that we'll be able to defeat any attack by the Presidential Guards. And the Guards will attack again. I don't see them just giving up."

"You promised we would negotiate with the Presidential Council," Sam pointed out. "We never planned to fight."

Sam Donald often sided with the Freechoicers but he was not dependable. Dennis knew that if he couldn't convince Sam the vote would be lost. "They gave us no choice. I admit that I underestimated them. I didn't expect the Guards to come with such overwhelming force, without even giving us the option to negotiate. But we cannot back down now."

"I don't trust these aliens," Carl was adamant. "I say we kill all the Soosans and drive out or kill the others — the Owoons. We already know that we outnumber them."

Some of the Council members were actually nodding.

Classet was appalled. Such extreme thoughts he expected from Carl Robert or Evans Bradley. They were both radical Separatist. But for the others to agree... "So, our first act as an independent nation is to sanction the mass murder of an entire people."

"It will be them or us," Carl shouted. "Get real Dennis! What do you think their leaders will do next? We'll either become their slaves or we'll be killed."

"You've met two of their leaders. I'm comfortable with their sincerity." Classet hesitated; then decided to tell them about Zooric. It would relieve everyone's mind to know that the Soosans were not invincible.

"Are you telling me they can send thousands of volts of electricity into someone but a shout can kill them?" Evans was skeptical.

"Believe me. I was as shocked as you are. *Sous* Zooric was unconscious for hours and when he woke, he was in such intense pain their medics had to put him to sleep again. He was still sedated when I left this light."

"We need to know exactly how this works," Jade Feld said.

"It seems some of us are what they call high receivers. We can receive their electro signals but it looks like we also have a direct link to their brain." Classet continued his explanation.

"Did they tell you who else had this ability," Jade asked thoughtfully.

"In my family it is Irene, Kelly, and Carrie. Derrick also."

"I'll admit this information relieves me somewhat," David muttered.

David Hill was another moderate who could go either way so Dennis was glad that he had shared the information on Zooric's weakness. "Then I say we need to build alliances now. We need to secure our border. It looks like we share this planet. It is us, New World City and the Owoons—Three nations. We can live in peace if we respect each other. The first thing on our first agenda should be to plan and consolidate our win. We need to get our constitution in writing and determine how this town should be governed. The Soosans have already agreed to recognize us. They have maps of the entire planet. There are vast stretches of unexplored area. We need to decide now rather than fight wars over territory later. They would like us to have borders that both nations can respect. They are willing to help us, yet instead of moving ahead we are bickering. Kicking them out now would be suicidal."

"I don't believe the Guards will come back," Carl stubbornly insisted. "They know what they are up against. We just need to get rid of these aliens and get our lives back."

"I'll not leave my family defenseless. The Guards mean business. They will be back."

"You lead us to this point," Al muttered. "We challenged the Presidential Council and look what it got us."

"It got us our freedom," Dennis Classet pointed out. Al Gerin was another hopeless Separatist, although not as radical as Carl and Evans. But Gerin and Sam were close neighbors and Sam could be influenced by his vote. "We suffered no losses and we emerged victorious— with the help of these Soosans. We would be stupid not to at least try convincing them to help us further."

Carl grunted scornfully. "We are selling our soul to these alien devils. What if they kill us all?"

"If that was the plan, I believe that they would have done so already," Jade pointed out mildly. "Beside you just heard. They are not invincible."

"I think Dennis is right," David was hesitant. "There is no way we can ignore these people. Their settlement is what, less than twenty weeks travel distance." He looked at Classet for confirmation. At Classet's nod he continued. "We are better off learning as much about them as possible."

"This calls for a vote," Al stated.

Dennis Classet looked around the room. He could not afford to lose this vote. He was almost positive he could count on David's vote. Sam still had him worried, but the argument had been going on for some time now and it seemed pointless to continue.

"I propose that we allow the Owoons to stay as needed and request their help dealing with the Presidential Guards." He announced. "We will negotiate with them as one government to another. Is there a second?"

"Second," Jade immediately called out.

"Those in favor so indicate by a show of hands."

Three hands went up.

Shit! Classet looked at Sam. Slowly, reluctantly, the man raised his hand. They had won!

"You'll regret this." Carl was furious. "We should be passing laws and minding our business instead we are mixing with a bunch of aliens."

"We're going to be a nation in our own right, separate from New World City," Sam pointed out. "We'll be passing our own laws. But Dennis is right. We need to build alliances with these aliens."

The argument was starting all over again!

"Enough!" Dennis pounded on the table for silence. "The motion was passed. The Owoons will stay if they want to. I'll return with them next light. The sooner we get started on getting our borders settled, the better."

"Let just one of them touch any of our women..." Carl was still spoiling for a fight.

"Our women are free individuals." Classet stated flatly. "It they choose to associate with any of the Owoons..."

"There will be no mixing!" Carl stormed.

"This town will be a free society," Classet insisted. "We did not leave the yoke of the Presidential Council to take on ..."

David Hill interrupted. "I did not vote to have my daughters mixing with these aliens."

Again, Classet pounded the table. He did not want to tackle the Separatist now. As mad as he was over the comments, he would have to take one thing at a time. "I'll inform the Owoons to respect our women."

"They can damn will continue sleeping with each other and leave our women alone." The angry comment was typical of Carl.

"Enough!" Classet glared at him. "I'll make arrangements for us to meet with the Soosans."

He was still angry as he left the meeting. Jade Feld hurried after him. "Calm down. You got the vote."

"The bolt I did," Classet grunted. "These Owoons will be coming to the next meeting. What happens after that will be anyone's guess."

"At least give them credit for agreeing with your plan. Think about this. These aliens have a life style that is totally different from ours yet our people are willing to accept them."

"You call what happened in there acceptance?" Classet's look was ironic.

Feld sighed. "Let's drop the subject. Are you traveling back before dark?"

They both paused at the entrance of the building. Although officially the town's library, it was often used as the Council's meeting room because of its central location. They descended the steps directly into the street, which was actually Arapmo's main road. There was no sidewalk, just a shallow depression that separated the road from the building. The main purpose of the depressions was drainage to avoid water flooding into the building. Theirs was really a one street town but the settlers had spent a lot of time and effort building their main street. To build the surface they had used an old-world technique of layered stones, packed tightly, to withstand zigs plus people travel. The main street was winding and held the library, all the shops and business plus a few residential homes. It led directly into and out of the town. In addition, to the main street, there were only five minor cross streets for residences only. The quality of the paved surface of the side streets depended on the wealth of the residents. Some streets had the same high-quality stone pavement but others were just hard packed soil.

One thing the town did not lack was trees. New World City was almost devoid of large plants – possible because of its extreme temperature. When the settlers first arrived in Arapmo their fascination with the larger trees had led them to practically build their town around the vegetation. The winding main road and numerous trees gave the town a picturesque quality of peace and tranquility. If only the town could live up to its image!

Classet now looked up at the sky. It was a one light travel by zig to his outpost. As he had travel to town during first-light, and the meeting had dragged on, second-dark was now fast approaching.

"You are welcome to stay at my place." Feld offered. He owned, Feld Hotel, the town's only hotel and had built his house on the side street beside it.

"Thanks, but I promised Irene I would return this dark," Classet said, referring to his wife. "Besides Dave and a few of my men are waiting over there." He waved in the direction of the general grocery store. "We also needed to pick up supplies. You wouldn't believe the damage the fight caused to the outpost." He grimaced. "I definitely don't want another war at my doorsteps." He jerked his head in the direction of the library. "They will never understand the fear, the total helplessness." He shook his head. "Never again! We must convince the Owoons to stay!"

Feld nodded. "I can understand. I would feel the same if my wife and children were threatened"

As they continued down the street Classet continued. "Perhaps I'll take you up on your offer for the next meeting. If the meeting drags, I don't need to be worrying about getting back."

Feld nodded. "You can stay as long as needed. We're got the space."

"Remember the Owoons and Soosans will be with us."

"Not a problem," Feld grinned. "I'm not afraid of knowing them and my sons and even my wife and daughter have been unbelievable curious."

"Thanks," Classet said. "I owe you."

"You owe me nothing. We got the vote, which was the important thing."

"Some of it," Classet agreed grimly. "Could you find out—just a rough estimate— how many people actually support the Freechoice movement?"

"Dennis," Feld warned, "we can't afford to stir up the people at this point."

"We may have to." Classet frowned. "We certainly can't afford not to be prepared. You heard Evans' threat and just how he and Carl sounded almost as if they were planning something. I don't think they'll back down on this. Once we sort out the Presidential Guard issue or even during this mess, they're going to push for laws legalizing racial separation. "

"Nobody will vote to split the town."

"Maybe, maybe not. But I think we should strike first."

"How?"

"First, we need to know just how many sympathizers they have. If most people haven't made up their minds it's not too late. We can sway them."

"I'll do what I can. Although I still think you're getting unnecessarily agitated."

"I would agree with you if I hadn't just gone through this experience with the Presidential Guards." Dennis said soberly. "I would never have dreamed that they would come on so strong. Commander Ryan would have allowed his men to rape Carrie! No. I'm not going to be caught unprepared again."

They had been walking toward the general store and some of Classet's men had emerged.

"Meet you at the zig stables," he called out.

As the men nodded in response, he turned back to Jade. "Will you be able to make a start this light?"

"I will. I'll get my boys to help," he said referring to his two older sons. "Lots of town folks linger in the hotel bar during the first-dark. But I also get another crowd just before second-dark. I'll ask then also."

"Careful."

Jade nodded. "We'll just ask around, very causally."

Dennis nodded. They had reached the zig stables. "I'll see you at the meeting next light."

****

Irene met her husband at the door.

"How did it go?" she asked.

He grimly described the meeting.

"What happens next?"

"I wanted to take the Soosans to the next meeting—at first-light. Jade has offered his place so we can stay in town for a while. How is *Sous* Zooric?"

"Not much change. He woke but he was in pain again. Carrie linked with him." She smiled as she said it.

"Linked?"

"The Owoons explained that it was the transmission of a low electrical signal from one person to another."

"Something else? I really don't like this slow trickle of information."

"Which is why living with them is a good idea. We can't learn everything all at once. But all their little quirks will come out over time."

He grunted. "So, what is this linking supposed to do?"

"Carrie insisted that it would help his pain and help him heal. She says that was the method she used after he broke his leg. He fell asleep naturally afterwards so I just hope she is right."

"Where are the Owoons?" Dave had joined them.

"The Soosans are in the library working on maps," his mother explained. "The others spent most of the cycle with Derrick. They were teaching him about fluars. One of their medics is still with Zooric."

"And Carrie?" her husband asked.

"Sleeping. After Zooric fell asleep, I convinced her to go to bed. She was exhausted."

****

Later that light Mr. Classet was in the library with the *Loyas, Gaads* Trateen and Egell, when *Gaad* Sorgan brought the news.

"*Loyas*! He is awake and in control." *Gaad* Sorgan declared, not hiding his joy. He was grinning from ear to ear.

Loya Modnar's grin was equally relieved. "*We must see him.*" He stood quickly and the entire group headed upstairs.

Zooric was indeed awake but although he had control, it was clear he was not pain free. He was sitting up on the bed, abnormally still. His eyes remained closed even as they entered.

Loya Modnar approached the bed, "*Sous Zooric?*"

"*I can hear you,*" he transmitted. His eyes remained closed.

Since Zooric rarely used mental-speak to them, *Loya* Modnar knew his control was shaky. "*Gaad Sorgan?*"

"He did not want anything for the pain," *Gaad* Sorgan explained.

391

"I am most happy you are recovering," Loya Modnar said touching Zooric's hand in comfort — briefly — to avoid any emotional exchange. *"And I am trying hard not to berate you while you are ill,"* he added.

Zooric gave a faint smile as his hand moved restlessly on the bed. *"Carrie?"*

Carrie had left his side as the others entered the room. She now came forward, knelt by the bed, and held his hand.

"I'm here."

"Leave us!" Zooric commanded everyone.

Carrie flushed at the abrupt order but did not attempt to pull away as Zooric's fingers locked with hers.

"We will leave you to rest," Loya Modnar did not look insulted. In fact, he was smiling in relief as he left the room.

Although neither Zooric nor Carrie came down for the last-light meal, the atmosphere during this meal was totally different from the previous. The relief that Zooric was recovering was almost palpable. In fact, only Derrick still seemed somewhat subdued.

After the meal, Dave and Derrick were at the rear of the group heading toward the family room.

"What's wrong?"

Derrick shook his head. "Nothing."

"Who are you kidding?" When Derrick didn't answer, Dave continued. "Are you still feeling guilty over what happened?"

"Somewhat," Derrick shrugged. "He saved my life," he said quietly.

Dave gave him a considering look. "Don't beat yourself up over it. You know he did it for Carrie's benefit not yours. Besides, he's recovering."

Derrick nodded. "I... I hated him, mostly because of Carrie. But..."

Dave's lips twitched. "But mostly because of Carrie?"

Derrick gave a reluctant grim, "Okay. Okay... only because of Carrie."

"Let her go," Dave advised. "I think she really loves him and he seems to love her."

Again, Derrick nodded. "He does. I've been going over... trying to piece together stuff. When he panicked, I started getting some of his thoughts. He was terrified that any hurt to me would hurt Carrie."

"That sounds like Zooric."

They both grinned.

Dave clapped him on the back. "By tomorrow he will be back to his impossible arrogant self and you will have no trouble wishing to wring his neck."

****

The next cycle Zooric was substantially better, so Mr. Classet brought his entire family to town. He was not about to leave his wife and children at the outpost without protection, especially since he wasn't sure how long he would remain in town. They arrived close to first-dark accompanied by all the Owoons and were soon settled at Jade's home. Jade Feld's house was a mansion. They would not have to worry about tripping over each other.

Both *Loyas*, with *Gaads* Trateen and Egell as translators, would be present at the Council meeting. It was decided that Zooric needed more rest. He had not traveled well and was still having severe headaches. *Gaads* Sorgan and Keefav would remain with him. Mr. Classet expected the meeting to drag on and he was not disappointed. Sitting in one of the larger rooms of the library, they arranged four tables to form a square, which gave everyone an equal view of everyone else and allowed them to easily shuffle papers around as needed.

They bickered for most of the light over the borders. The settlers had not realized that the planet was so huge. The two peoples were actually clustered on a large continent, which was in reality only a fraction of the planet! Finally, they decided to carve the continent into three sections. Since they were unable to agree on the rest of the lands, they decided that the rest of the planet would remain unclaimed land. On their continent New World City got the Northern half, while the Southern half was split between the Owoons to the far south and the Arapmo settlers in the middle. This left New World City with the largest area, but since the north had extremely high temperatures; the Arapmo settlers and the Owoons decided it was a fair deal. If New World City didn't like it, they could go exploring!

They also wanted to decide on a single name for the planet. The Owoons called it Alloca while the settlers had named it Segaan. However, after a vote it was decided to leave the two names.

They also managed to finalize plans for an expedition to explore the Azar sector. The expedition would take place within the week because the Soosan wanted to return to their town as soon as possible. Mr. Classet was disappointed when he could not convince them to stay. He was also unable to convince them to sign a mutual protection treaty. What he really wanted was the Owoons help in defending Arapmo against any further attack from New World City. However, both *Loyas* felt they would need to consult with their elders before committing their nation to such a plan. At least they agreed that the Azar sector of Yotse was in Arapmo's territory. This meant that any finds would be Arapmo's to keep, sell or trade with the Soosans.

They were about to adjourn the meeting when Evans asked. "Are any of us high receivers?"

Loya Modnar looked at Mr. Classet. *"Have you explained all to them?"*

Gaad Egell interpreted.

"Yes. And they know about *Sous* Zooric's injury."

"Ah." *Loya* Modnar nodded his understanding. *"Unfortunately, it would take a considerable amount of time for us to test everyone here. Sous Zooric is the only one capable of telling instantly if any of you are high receivers. We do not have his detection skills."*

"I see." There were still some puzzled looks, and Jade Feld asked the question on everyone lips. "Why is *Sous* Zooric so different from all Soosans?"

Loya Meestric took over and with *Gaad* Trateen translating explained. *"Sous Zooric is one of only a few Soosans born of Soosan fathers. His father, who was a powerful Soosan medic and ruler, arranged his birth. All Owoons are tested at puberty to determine their electro skill, however, Sous Zooric avoided testing by living in the wilderness outside Caleel. In fact, the Soosan only recently learned of his existence and his powers. We still do not understand fully all of his powers, but we do recognize that the Soosan needs him."*

Loya Meestric turned to Mr. Classet. *"The Soosan needs him without the distraction of your daughter."*

His comment had the room in an uproar.

"Are you saying you do not wish a marriage between *Sous* Zooric and my daughter?" Mr. Classet demanded.

Loya Modnar touched *Loya* Meestric in a restraining gesture, but *Loya* Meestric clearly disagreed.

"We need to discuss this at another time ..." *Gaad* Egell began translating for *Loya* Modnar.

But *Loya* Meestric would not be restrained. He indicated that *Gaad* Trateen should continue his translations then turned to *Loya* Modnar. *"We need to speak truthfully with these people. They will be our neighbors."* Turning back to the Council members he continued, *"The truth is that Sous Zooric must live within the Soosan sector. His special skills need the protection of the Sector. He would not be able to survive in the general population. Our people are much higher receivers than anyone here in Arapmo and witness the harm an Arapmo citizen was able to do to him. He also has no means of support outside the Soosan. The next question is will the Soosan accept your daughter. I would not wish to send my child to a distant land where her welcome will be uncertain."*

"I will admit that I had my reservations..." Mr. Classet began.

"Hah!" Carl Robert immediately pounced. "So, you admit that your policy of mixing races is flawed."

"I admit no such thing. Allowing freedom of choice has always been my goal. You would impose even more restriction on the citizens of Arapmo with your bigotry."

"My bigotry would preserve our race and our future!" Robert shouted.

"What you believe is your belief. It should not be forced on the entire population. I am not forcing the population to intermarry. All I am saying is — give them a chance to make their own choices."

"If given the choice, the different races may well choose to go their separate ways," Jade Feld pointed out.

"Is this a new policy?" David Hill asked frowning.

Recognizing an opening, Mr. Classet quickly pressed the point. "This has always been the policy of the Freechoice movement. The Separatist would tie us to rules as rigid as the Presidential Council. Now that we are free of the tyranny of the Presidential Council, I intent to publicly present the true policy of the Freechoice movement. I dare any Separatist to be equally honest with our citizens."

"Sometimes policies are set for the good of the majority even if it is a policy of the minority." Evans Bradley added just as forcefully as Carl. "Our future will be shaped by policies acted on now. Besides, a majority decision can be just as bad as a minority decision. We are the leaders. We should set the policies. It should be our decision what is best for Arapmo. I have never heard anything good coming out of a stew where everything is thrown in. If you want to talk about honesty, why not honestly admit that you do not want your daughter marrying an alien?"

Before Mr. Classet could respond, *Loya* Meestric, who like *Loya* Modnar, had been silent as the settlers argued their point, interjected—with *Gaad* Trateen interpreting. *"We can well understand Council Classet's fears. Caleel, our community, is many cycles of travel from here. If his daughter leaves, how will he know she is well?"*

Mindful of the public nature of this discussion, Mr. Classet was careful. "I will not object to their marriage if I can be assured that my daughter will be well looked after and well protected."

Loya Modnar enlisted *Gaad* Egell's aid to respond. *"We can understand your concerns, but the decision on marriage must remain Sous Zooric's. I will also admit that Loya*

Meestric and I do not fully agree with Sous Zooric choice. But the Soosan is more than willing to accommodate his needs." He gave *Loya* Meestric a warning look before continuing. *"In the short time that I have known Sous Zooric, I have come to respect his decision and would not do anything to alter the course that he is plotting. It is inappropriate to even try to reach a conclusion without his presence."*

It was clear that *Loya* Meestric disagreed but could not publicly argue further with *Loya* Modnar. Robert and Bradley were still raring for a fight, but Dennis Classet had had enough. He quickly adjourned the meeting. They would meet again to decide who should travel to Yotse.

****

Chapter 25

The Classet's party arrived back at Jade's home just as the two youngest members of his family were finishing their last-light meal.

"How did it go?" Dave asked as his father entered their suite.

"I wasn't able to convince them to stay." Mr. Classet raked his hands through his hair, his disappointment keen. "We will be on our own if the Presidential Guards attack again." He went over to greet his wife, Kelly and Scott. "Ready for bed?" he asked the children.

"No." Scot scuffed his toe on the carpeted flooring. "Why did I have to eat early? I wanted to eat with you. I am ten."

"Me too." Kelly said.

"You're only eight," Scott retorted.

"When it is just family at home, you can both can eat with us," his father promised. "But we are not at home, we are guests, so off to bed with you."

They were still grumbling as Thia shepherded them from the room.

As they left his wife asked, "If they leave now, what of Carrie?"

Mr. Classet signed. "I want to believe I can trust *Sous* Zooric, but I am not sure I have total confidence in his people. *Loya* Meestric brought up some serious issues. The Soosan is an all-male society. The more I think about it, the less I like the idea of her going to live there—as the only female. From what I understand these Soosans thought they couldn't have any form of relationship with women but *Sous* Zooric has proved that wrong. So do they prefer males by choice or because it was their only option? Somehow, I don't think putting a single female in the mix is a wise idea. It's guaranteed to cause fighting. And there is no way Zooric – one man – can protect her. I don't think I want Carrie to travel with them. If *Sous* Zooric is that committed to marrying her, he can stay here with her. "

"Zig Shit!" Dave muttered. "When are you going to break the news to Zooric?" His father grimaced, "Definitely not this cycle."

"Is that the only option? Where would Zooric live if he remained here?"

"I don't know," he shrugged, "According to the *Loyas*, the strange powers that he has makes it difficult, if not impossible, for him to live outside the Soosan. I'll ask for more details. I'll admit I don't really understand it. I'll eventually have to sit with him and sort out the facts." He scrubbed at his face. "I'm really most worried about another Presidential Guard attack. I was counting on the Owoons help. But now..." His voice trailed off.

"We'll just have to mobilize everyone," Dave said grimly. "We can't be caught unprepared."

"I have to first convince the Council that an attack is very real. They didn't have our experience. But if the Council remains unconvinced, I will take steps to protect my family — even if it means leaving Arapmo and perhaps travelling with the Owoons to their city."

"Shit!" Dave said softly.

"That's a last resort option. I just hope we don't have to use it. I don't know what will happen, but we definitely will not leave ourselves open to attack if our town refuses to prepare for war."

His wife gave him a quick hug. "You are tired. A meal and some relaxation will help clear your thoughts. Maybe you'll think of something else."

He gave a brief nod but was clearly still worried. "How is Derrick?"

Dave answered. "He and Zooric have been circling each other for hours. Zooric say he accepts Derrick's apology but it seems to me that Zooric wants to have nothing to do with Derrick." Dave shrugged. "You know Derrick. He just keeps pushing."

"So Zooric is better?" his father asked

"Well enough that he, Carrie and *Gaad* Sorgan took Zooric's pet out for a walk."

Mr. Classet raised an eyebrow. "How did the town react?"

Dave grinned. "Carrie said they attracted a following, but everyone kept their distance. Zooric didn't want any company and had his pet growl if anyone came close."

****

Within a half hour the Classet and Feld families were gathered in the great dining room. They had not had time for proper introductions earlier, so a few minutes were spent exchanging names. Jade's wife Jenny was unflappable and his two older sons Josh and Jim were just plain curious. Like Mr. Classet, Jade had sent his younger son and daughter to bed. After the introductions were made, they sat in the formal room for the meal. It was decided that *Gaad* Egell would translate for *Loya* Modnar while *Gaad* Trateen would do the same for *Loya* Meestric.

401

"I am curious," Jade Feld asked. "Do you all have only one name?"

The Soosans and Owoons exchanged puzzled looks.

"I am Jade Feld," Mr. Feld explained, "but I got your name only as *Loya* Modnar for example."

Ah, *Loya* Modnar nodded in understanding. *"Owoons have one name only."*

"But doesn't it get confusing?" Dave asked.

"We are a small society," Loya Meestric smiled. *"Only in the Soosan is it sometimes a problem. There, young boys may be required to change their names to avoid confusion. In the general society, our titles often act as separators. An adult male is referred to as Zha, a married adult female is Zhara and an unmarried female is Zerah. Perhaps as we grow, there will be confusion but at present we do not have a problem. Someone could be Zha Egell from outside Caleel or Zha Egell from Caleel or Zha Egell son of Zha Trateen."*

Mr. Classet turned to Zooric. *"Sous* Zooric, I am not sure how you should be addressed. Are you a Soosan or Owoon? "

"We are all Owoons," Zooric stated. Without directly addressing the question, he continued. "Owoons who are sensitives are called Soosans."

"Sous Zooric is a Soosan," *Gaad* Trateen said interpreting *Loya* Modnar's emphatic response. "The title *Sous* denotes that he is a young Soosan and not a part of the Soosan hierarchy. *Sous* Zooric is in an unusual situation because most Soosan become aware of their nature at puberty. *Sous* Zooric chose not to be tested."

"Why?" Dave was curious. He had not heard the explanation at the Council meeting.

Loya Modnar turned to Zooric, *"Sous Zooric, you will explain."*

Zooric looked up. After a pause he gave a brief and totally unrevealing explanation. "I did not wish to live in the Soosan."

There was silence. As the silence lengthened it became clear that Zooric had no intention of explaining further.

****

Derrick gave Zooric an irritated look. "You are among your prospective in-laws and friends. The least you could do is offer a complete explanation."

"Do not interfere in what is not your concern." Zooric did not even look at him.

"They... We deserve a reasonable explanation!"

"Derrick!" Mr. Classet was clearly worried at Derrick's persistence.

Zooric, however, unexpectedly flashed Derrick a look of muted anger then abruptly pushed back his chair. "I wish to be left alone. I will return to my room."

Carrie, who was seated next to him, started to rise. Zooric indicated that she should stay. She threw him a worried glance but remained seated.

Loya Modnar looked over at *Gaad* Sorgan who immediately rose to follow Zooric.

"I do not need a guide, a guard or a sitter. *Gaad* Sorgan must remain and eat."

Gaad Sorgan remained standing, seeking guidance from *Loya* Modnar.

Derrick also stood, "I would like to speak with you privately," he said to Zooric. When Zooric did not immediately respond, Derrick stepped forward.

"Do not come any closer!" Zooric actually took a step backward.

"Zooric!" Carrie was appalled at his rudeness.

Derrick flushed. "Bolt! I would not hurt you." But to everyone's surprise, Zooric winced.

"Sorry," Zooric muttered. He had closed his eyes briefly, now he opened them. "When you are close, I cannot easily block your emotions," he finally and reluctantly explained.

"What!"

"Your emotions. Since our link they... I can sense them stronger."

"Can you pick up all of our emotions?" Mr. Classet demanded.

"No, only the emotions of high receivers, and usually I can block. But I find that after a link, contact with the person, blocking becomes difficult."

"That is why you didn't shake hands with anyone," Dave exclaimed. 'You did not want to create a link with anyone."

"This is yet another reason you must live in the Soosan. You cannot live among the Owoons. You would be mentally exhausted and uncomfortable if you attempted to block all the time. Also, you have no resources to support a mate." Loya Meestric seemed determined to press his point.

"A hand shake does not create a link," Zooric stated flatly. Without offering additional explanation he continued, "I had planned to live in the Soosan."

Since *Gaads* Egell and Trateen had been translating the *Loyas* response, everyone was following the conversation. Mr. Classet frowned as he now remembered their discussion at the Council meeting. "*Loya* Meestric brought up an important point at our meeting. He stated that the Soosan, being an all-male society would not necessarily accept my daughter. Could you guarantee that Carrie would be protected and safe under such conditions?"

"Are you saying that Caree would not be safe in the Soosan?" Zooric demanded of *Loya* Meestric.

"*No!*" *Loya* Modnar insisted. "*Loya Meestric is overstating...*"

"I will not risk Caree by taking her where I cannot be sure I can protect her," Zooric was frowning.

This was the perfect time to.... "Perhaps," Mr. Classet began slowly, "You should return to your people alone. Carrie can wait here for you."

"No!" Zooric was emphatic.

"*It is a reasonable suggestion,*" *Loya* Meestric was frowning heavily.

Zooric did not respond. He looked at Carrie. "*I need to link with you.*"

Carrie was alarmed. She looked around in embarrassment, although no one could have heard Zooric's private request. "I cannot."

"Cannot what?" Dave asked as he regarded them curiously.

Carrie flushed. They were all staring at her expectantly.

Neither of them answered, and Zooric again turned to Carrie. "*Why can we not go to your room and link?*"

Carrie shook her head and turned slightly away without answering, unwilling to have her family know that Zooric was communicating with her mentally. But Zooric seemed to take her lack of words for consent, and he began gently rubbing her upper arm with his thumb.

Carrie, perhaps realizing that being subtle was not going to work with Zooric, finally decided to be blunt. She looked steadily up at him. "I cannot go upstairs with you because it just is not done. My family doesn't recognize us as married. And we can only do what you are suggesting if we are married.

"Are you saying you will not..." he began.

"Zooric!" Carrie interrupted. "Please! You are embarrassing me," she looked around at the interested gaze of her family then covered her hot cheeks with both hands.

However, Zooric scowled. He clearly was not in a good mood. We are already bonded. We can therefore link."

Seizing the opportunity, Mr. Classet rushed in. "Surely you can accept that my daughter should have a marriage that is recognized by her people. Perhaps in a few months' time..." he allowed his voice to trail off at Zooric's furious stare.

"I will not wait for a few months," Zooric stated flatly.

"Why not?" Carrie implored. She was still angry, furious in fact that he had voiced his wish aloud and embarrassed her, "It will give us a chance to get to know each other better without the cloud of... of..." She suddenly stopped talking. Her reason was the sudden lack of expression on Zooric face.

Abruptly, he released her and turned away from them all, taking a step toward the door.

"Zooric!" Carrie's voice turned to panic.

He flicked her a glance. Of course, he knew she was upset...but over what? There was no way he could leave her like this. Stopping again, he turned to Carrie.

"You need to tell me what is upsetting you. I cannot read your mind."

Carrie nodded. "Are you going to leave me?"

His eyes flickered to her watching family. Suddenly, he stepped forward and took her arm again. "Come, we will speak privately."

****

They all watched in silence as she rose and left the room with Zooric.

"I cannot allow my daughter to go into an uncertain situation. I really do not feel comfortable sending her to live where there could be danger. How serious is this issue?" Mr. Classet asked.

"Very serious," Loya Meestric insisted.

"But it can be easily resolved. The Soosan is more than willing to accommodate any special needs of Sous Zooric," Loya Modnar was firm. *"I can assure you, Council Dennis, your daughter will not be harmed."*

Mr. Classet was not convinced, in fact, he was more certain than ever that Carrie should not go with the Owoons when they took their leave of the town.

****

Another dinner conversation was taking place in the hotel room of Carl Robert. Ever since moving to Arapmo Robert had rented a suite of rooms at Feld Hotel. He did not want or like his wife and children who were of mixed race, and without a permanent home in Arapmo he had a reason — that satisfied the Presidential Council — for not bringing them to Arapmo.

"We should just kill them. Or kill the one they call Zooric." Carl was scowling.

"That would be tricky." Evans did not even look surprised by Carl's statement. "And what about the other two Soosans?"

"They are not as powerful." Carl was dismissive. "If we get rid of Zooric, I suspect they will just go back to wherever they came from."

"I don't like it." Al looked nervously at Evans. "The other two are likely to get mad and try to kill us all."

"Then we could kill the girl." Carl was still fixated on his killing theme. "The only reason these aliens are hanging around is because of her. If we get rid of her, we will automatically get rid of them."

"That would be killing one of our own." Al again looked at Evans but Evans was not sharing his thoughts. "And if we kill the girl, her father is likely to get riled up."

"So what do we do?" Carl was annoyed.

"*Loya* Meestric could be our ally," Evans Bradley finally said.

It was a casual dining arrangement and they were seated comfortably on sofas in the sitting area. A low table was available for their plates and glasses.

"How so?" Carl asked.

"He doesn't want the girl going with them. Like us, he is for separation of the races."

"But we want her to leave," Al protested. "Good riddance, I say. We should convince them to take Derrick with them also."

"You are right in one sense but the main issue is our policy. We need to pass new laws now," Evans munched thoughtfully. "If we plan this right, we will have only whites entering the town. Now is the time to push our agenda."

"Getting the town to support us might still be complicated," Al said. "Dennis is pushing his Freechoice policy. There was a lot of talk in the bar last dark."

"What kind of talk?" Evans was frowning.

"Against us. They were saying that we want to tie the citizens up with rules just as restrictive as the Presidential Council."

Carl nodded. "I heard it too. And some people were listening. They claim they don't want any Council telling them who to marry."

"That sounds like the spouting of the Freechoice movement." Evans frowned.

"We need to get rid of him," Carl was blunt.

"I don't know if I want to murder anyone," Al murmured a weak protest.

"Listen." Carl stabbed the air with his finger as he spoke. "This is the best chance we'll ever get to shape the policy of this town. Our policy is to create a white only town, and drastic situations calls for drastic action. If we plan this right, we could even blame his death on the aliens."

"I don't like it," Al was still hesitant but he was again looking to Evans for guidance.

"Look at the facts." Carl was intent. "We really just want to pass Separatist laws. The person stopping us is Dennis Classet. You know that Sam and David will support us if we push them. Jade can do nothing on his own. We need to act now!"

"So, we kill Classet?" Evans was thoughtful.

"This might be our best chance. With these aliens here... As you said *Loya* Meestric could be on our side."

"Maybe," Evan, although equally intense, was not as impulsive as Carl. He usually avoided hasty decisions. "Let me think about this some more.

Remember, if *Loya* Meestric helps, he's not likely to have his people take the blame for Classet's death."

Their meeting broke up shortly afterwards. Al headed for his home in town while Evans turned and began walking toward the zig stables. He lived outside the town, but not far — just a short zig ride away.

****

Zooric and Carrie had decided to take a short walk outside. Only Soor accompanied them. It had been Zooric's idea. He did not really like the closeness of Jade's house.

"After your experience this cycle, I didn't think you would want to leave the building again," she teased.

"I want privacy." He gently pulled her to his side. "I need a deep link with you. We cannot be private inside.

Carrie tried pulling away. "Zooric please. The streets are public!"

Zooric refused to release her. "Where can we go?"

Carrie's mind was blank. She couldn't think of anywhere private. "I don't know..." She was shaking her head helpless. "Besides we cannot be private until we are married. I promised Dad. Besides I could get pregnant!"

"Pregnant!"

"Have a baby." Carrie explained because he was staring at her in shock.

"I did not think... The Azar did not..."

From his total confusion, Carrie realized that Zooric, steeped in the history of the Azar, had forgotten that unlike the ancients, humans reproduced in a traditional manor.

"When will this marriage take place?" he now demanded.

"I don't know." Carrie again tried moving away from him because with his confusion fast fading, it was being replaced by a clear sexual intent. "Everything has been happening so quickly. We haven't really got a chance to discuss anything."

Zooric abruptly released her and started walking away from the Feld's house.

Soor, after a moment of hesitation and a questioning look at her, followed him.

Carrie bit her lips. "Zooric!"

"Come!"

"But we cannot..." she began.

"We will not." Zooric pulled Carrie gently into the deepening shadows of one of the native trees. With his back to the street, he wrapped his arms around her and before she could react, kissed her. They immediately linked.

Carrie felt her knees buckling as Zooric deepened the link and poured into her. Were it not for his lips covering hers, she would have moaned aloud. As it was, he absorbed her cries greedily. It was a few minutes before he finally lifted his head, releasing her lips. Then he bent once again, resting his forehead on hers.

"Now tell me why you are so upset?"

"You... My family."

"What of me and your family?" Carrie slid both hands up his chest, but her eyes were downcast as Zooric gently began tracing the contours of her face with his fingers.

"Well?"

"You do not ask. You always make demands," she muttered. It was only a partial reason, but she was running scared. What if the *Loyas* insisted that Zooric leave — without her?

"What is it that you wish to be asked?"

Gathering her courage, she looked up. "Will you leave me?"

Zooric gave her a look of astonishment. "Leave you? Caree, you know I do not wish to leave you even for a single cycle."

"I thought... what *Loya* Meestric said..."

"I am afraid," he said seriously. "You know this Caree."

She did know. From the link they had just shared, she knew that he was afraid her family would influence her away from him. Yet he was also both excited at the thought of her pregnant with his child and fearful of the future. Although *Loya* Modnar had convinced him to return to the Soosan, he would not take Carrie with him if her life were in danger. However, apart from those facts, his thoughts were so chaotic that Carrie had no clue what his plans were. Did he intend to leave her here alone? Would he stay? Could he stay?

"I will not let my family tear us apart Zooric. But I am still worried. How can we live here? And what will you do if the *Loyas* insist that you leave with them?"

"The *Loyas* know better than to insist that I leave without you or force me to go with them against my will." Zooric murmured. "Do not worry so, I will find a way for us to be together."

Soor gave a low growl.

Carrie became startled and immediately tried to pull away, but Zooric held her tightly.

"It is Evans Bradley — the Council member."

"How can you tell?"

"I met him before. He is a high receiver. Soor!" Softly, he added a command in Gavaa.

The animal immediately slid flat on his belly. With his black coat, he was now invisible in the shadows. Evans was on the other side of the street walking briskly toward the zig stables. He did not see them, and they both remained still as he disappeared down the street.

"Is it true when *Loya* Meestric says you cannot block the emotional signals from high receivers?"

"I cannot block if I am in contact with the receiver, but I could buzz the person to prevent injury to myself."

"But... wouldn't you get buzzed too?"

He shrugged. "Yes. It would create a circuit but at least the emotional signals would stop — I think. Besides, a buzz is much less painful than the emotional signals. I did not buzz Derrick because he had just been attacked by Raekon."

Carrie nodded her head in understanding then moved to her other question. "Will you link with someone when you shake hands? I remember when we first met, you did not want to touch me."

"That was before I realized that I have control. A handshake will not create a link, but if the person is a high receiver, I cannot block their emotions during the contact. I prefer not to have the constant bombardment of unwanted emotions.

Loya Modnar is actually wrong." Zooric continued. "It cannot be that difficult to learn how to stop sending emotional signals. You did not send me any emotional signals when you were angry with me."

Carrie looked at him in surprise. "I didn't? When?"

He reminded her of the time after she threw dirt at Raekon.

Carrie remembered.

"See," Zooric grinned. "You just stopped sending your emotions."

"Oh!" Understanding dawned. "I can do it. I do have control." She frowned at him. "Why didn't you tell me?"

"When you stop sending your emotions, I feel that a part of me is missing," He was absently rubbing her arm and did not even look guilty.

"Zooric!" Carrie was not really annoyed. How could she be seriously annoyed with someone who clearly cherished her?

"I will feed you my emotions if you wish," he offered.

"No thank you," Carrie firmly shook her head. "I cannot imagine how you can concentrate."

"When I concentrate on your signals, I can block everything else much easier."

"Except Derrick's."

He shook his head. "The low-linking I shared caused a road map to be drawn. His emotions are now just as sharp as yours, and just as hard to block." He paused in remembrance. "I think my mother too is a high sensitive. I had just as much difficulty blocking her."

"Your mother?"

He briefly explained.

"But Zooric," Carrie said excitedly, "That means there definitely are other women among your people who are high receivers. Do the *Loyas* know?"

"No. I will tell them if or when I go to Caleel. I would like to check another theory first."

"What other theory. And wouldn't it be better to tell them now," Carrie asked hesitantly. She worried that Zooric was too insistent on doing things his way.

"No, it would not." Zooric was decisive. "When I trust them totally, I will confide more." At her continued frown, he brought his mouth down to kiss her briefly. "It is better this way. I get very conflicting emotions from Meestric. Also, I wish to learn more on how the Soosans conduct first-link. It is a one-way link and totally unlike anything that I have tried."

Carrie gave up on a sigh.

"When my headache finally clears, perhaps I will meet with Derrick and teach him how to stop sending. His guilt and concern is driving me crazy. His hate was much easier to deal with."

He only grinned at Carrie's reproachful look and touched her nose with the pad of his thumb. "You will also stay away from Derrick."

"Zooric...," Carrie began, annoyed with his returning arrogance.

His thumb moved to her mouth gently silencing her. "Derrick liked you before. Now he has some of my mental images of you. I do not want that liking to go further. I will not share."

Carrie felt her face heating. "You don't know...."

"Yes, I do," Zooric interrupted firmly. "It was a few seconds, but he got much of my thoughts.

Carrie decided it was in her best interest to change the subject. "Zooric you need to explain yourself more," she told him seriously. "Everyone would have been less upset if you had explained some of this earlier."

"Perhaps," Zooric shrugged. Clearly, he was not convinced.

Although Carrie was exasperated, she was smart enough to recognize that her effort to change him was pointless. It was not worth it to press him further. "Can you totally block my emotions?"

"Only for a short time. When I was angry with you, I tried to block you. It takes a lot of concentration even when we were apart. I think blocking would work much easier if we were at a great distance from each other. The only time I did not get your emotions was when you wandered away in the woods near Yotse and when I went exploring Yotse sector with the others. But I also think that the more links we share the harder blocking will get. I am sure that a time will come when I cannot block you."

"So, the number of links and also distance are important." Carrie said.

He nodded.

"If I don't send any emotion, will you still know if I am close?"

"Of course. I would still be able to send signals to you. As the signals go back and forth between us I would 'sense' you."

"Did Evans pick up your signals just now?"

"No. I did not try to contact him mentally. You sense my presence only because when we are apart, I am always actively 'seeking' you. I did it unconsciously even at the very beginning, and now it has become a habit. A very comforting habit," He grinned down at her.

"I see," Carrie gave him a reluctant grin in return. The man was impossible! Again, she ran her hand up his chest. "We should get back. They will be wondering where we are."

As they turned and began walking toward the Feld's home, Zooric mused. "I am thinking I will stay here with you. I will not leave you."

"But where would we live? And what of *Loya* Modnar's wishes."

"I did not particularly wish to go to the Soosan. *Loya* Modnar convinced me to go, but if there is a danger to you it would not be wise to take you there. Look at the problem we had with Raekon. If I cannot convince some of your people to travel to Caleel, I do not think that it is wise to take you there alone."

He had not answered the question of where they would live, and Carrie did not press him. There was no answer to that question.

"*Loya* Modnar calls. He is worried that I am not in the house. I just told him I am coming."

Loya Modnar was more than worried. He was very angry that Zooric had left the house without a Protector. In fact, the entire household was waiting at the door from them.

Sous Zooric, it was most irresponsible of you to leave the house." Loya Meestric said.

"I cannot believe you went outside ... alone!" Derrick was staring. At Zooric's frown he backed up a bit in consideration of Zooric's headache.

"We did not go far," Zooric tried to explain. His brief explanations of his need for privacy satisfied no one, and as they continued to berate him, he finally got annoyed.

"I am not a child," he informed them coldly. "I will go out as I please."

"*You will follow the dictates of the Soosan.*" *Loya* Meestric told him furiously.

Zooric's eyes flashed his anger. Once again, he was unconsciously projecting his fury.

Involuntarily, everyone took discreet steps backwards.

"Zooric," Carrie took his arm soothingly. There was an immediate link. She flushed as the Owoons all stared. They had all realized what had happened!

However, even the settlers noted Zooric's now calm stance. "What did you do?" Mr. Classet demanded of his daughter.

Carrie gave Zooric a quick glance but remained silent, no doubt in embarrassment.

Derrick wondered if he should tell. He gave Zooric an ironic glance. Zooric coolly dared him to say anything.

Never one to refuse a challenge, with a wicked grin, Derrick turned to Mr. Classet. "They just shared the equivalent of an intimate kiss—Owoon's style."

"What do you mean?" Dave looked puzzled.

"They just linked."

"I have yet to get a reasonable definition of linking," Mr. Classet grumbled.

"And I am totally lost," Jade laughed. Zooric was not in the mood to offer explanations. He took Carrie's arm. "I will accompany you to your room." With that he led her from the room totally ignoring the other occupants.

****

The silence was broken only as his and Carrie's steps were heard on the stairs.

"I could feel his fury," Jade sounded more amazed than fearful.

"*He unconsciously projects his emotions when he is angry*" *Loya* Modnar explained.

As *Gaad* Egell translated, *Loya* Meestric inserted.

"He has little control when he is angry. This is what I fear..."

"Loya Meestric!" The rebuke in *Loya* Modnar's voice was clear.

Since the last two statements made by the *Loyas* were not translated, Derrick was the only non-Owoon to 'hear.' He glanced sharply at the *Loyas*.

"I think *Sous* Zooric has excellent control." He stated coldly, then turned to the Classets and Felds. "*Loya* Meestric thinks *Sous* Zooric lacks control. I disagree. Anyone who could deliberately choose to injure themselves rather that accidentally inflict hurt on another has excellent control."

"Sous Zooric was thinking solely of Zerah Caree." *Loya* Meestric pointed out.

Derrick waited as *Gaad* Trateen translated the *Loyas* statement before continuing. "The fact remains that he was thinking — rationally. He was not acting uncontrollably."

Loya Modnar nodded. *"I agree with you. Sous Zooric has excellent control over his skills. I do not believe he would ever harm someone unnecessarily or without cause. However, he is young, impulsive and believes himself invincible. That is why I fear he will rashly harm himself or unintentionally harm others."*

On that note the *Loyas* retired for the cycle. The older members of the party also decided to retire, but after a short debate, *Gaads* Egell and Trateen accompanied Derrick, Dave, Josh and Jim. They planned on spending some time at the Feld's bar.

****

At the next Council meeting, the members finalized plans for the expedition. Four Council members and four of the town's citizen would accompany the Owoons up the mountain. With Zooric present at the meeting, Jade repeated his original question.

"Are any of us high receivers?"

Typically, Zooric response was ambiguous. "There are many high receivers among your people."

Jade persisted. "Are there any high receivers among the Council?"

"Only Evans," Zooric replied.

Evans looked immensely pleased. "Well. Well."

Mr. Classet looked over at Zooric—now he understood the seating arrangements. In the original arrangement, Zooric was placed to sit between the *Loyas* with *Gaads* Egell and Trateen at the ends. However, Zooric had switched seats with *Gaad* Egell, which placed him next to *Loya* Modnar. Mr. Classet had assumed that because of the last confrontation, Zooric did not wish to sit next to *Loya* Meestric. He now realized that Zooric had placed himself at the furthest point from Evans.

"Perhaps with a first-link we will be able to communicate with Evans," *Loya* Meestric now suggested.

As *Gaad* Trateen translated Zooric spoke. "There is no need. I can project his frequency. I can also project the frequency of the others."

At that both *Loyas* stared.

"Are you saying that we could speak mentally to everyone if we had their frequency?" *Loya* Modnar demanded.

"I do not see why not."

"I cannot believe you did not state this before," *Loya* Meestric glared at Zooric and would have continued berating the younger Soosan if *Loya* Modnar had not firmly calmed him with a private word.

Loya Modnar then turned to Zooric, "How?"

"The same principle happened with Derrick. I discovered it then. I gave you his frequency by projecting through him."

He turned to the Council and explained what he was about to do. As he spoke, he suited words with action.

"Hey! I can hear him in my head," Evans was blinking rapidly.

"*Can you 'hear' me now?*" *Loya* Meestric asked.

"We all can!" Mr. Classet exclaimed as he glanced around the room.

"Yes. By God!" Evans was still wearing a remarkable pleased expression, one that Mr. Classet did not trust.

As the meeting broke up, Evans issued an invitation to the *Loyas*. "I would like to invite the Owoons to my house for the last light meal." He turned to Dennis Classet. "I think you have monopolized them enough. It is time they heard from the other side."

The Owoons had traveled separately to the Council meeting, so during the ride back to Feld's Hotel there was no opportunity for Mr. Classet to caution them about Bradley's friendly overtures. As he and Jade Feld got into their carriage, he wondered whether he should. The two were still debating the issue when the carriage carrying the *Loyas* pulled up behind theirs. They had arrived home.

"I think you should leave it." Jade advised as Mr. Classet climbed down. "Our campaign is underway. The town will decide one way or another."

Their campaign plans, to start by the next light, included blanketing the town with posters publishing the view of both sides of the issue. Mr. Classet hoped his preemptive attack would foil any plans of the Separatist to influence the people of Arapmo.

Following Jade's advice, Mr. Classet merely wished the Owoons an enjoyable meal and did not follow up with any warnings. Still, it was with considerable misgiving that he later watched them leave.

****

"I wouldn't worry too much. *Sous* Zooric assured me that he would not be swayed." Derrick reassured him.

"When?" Mr. Classet asked with a frown.

"We met just before they left."

"Just the two of you?" Dave asked.

"Yes. We finally cleared the air," he grinned. "Actually, he was remarkable open. I was unconsciously sending him my emotions, which was disturbing—disturbing for him that is. He taught me how to control, so that I no longer send him my emotions."

"I thought that was impossible."

Derrick looked thoughtful. "It's not impossible. However, knowing *Sous* Zooric as I do now, I don't think he plans on repeating the process anytime soon. So unless he discovers another way, he is going to keep blocking the emotions of others. There is no way that he would want to do this with everyone."

Since the others were puzzled, slowly, reflectively, Derrick began explaining. "He has to link with me mentally to allow me to identify how my emotions are being sent to him. He calls it a low-level of linking. It's very personal. I can get his thoughts and emotions whereas he only gets my emotions. I can, in effect, read his mind. The longer the link lasts the more information I get. He was so tense that he aborted the link the first four times we tried it."

422

"I can't imagine *Sous* Zooric tense," Dave commented, his voice mirroring his amazement.

"He hated the very idea of revealing anything about himself to me."

"What convinced him to go ahead," Jade was curious.

"Just to even the score and to help him relax, I told him some personal stuff. I understand him a lot better now," Derrick was still reflective. "He is reserved yes. He ran away from a child abuser and lived in the forests outside his village during his teenage years. During that time, he had no interaction with others — with his people. Also, just about all he knows about us is based on what he's read from the Azar's. That gave him the bare clinical and statistical details but not the practical everyday knowledge. Nevertheless, he has a strong moral code, and he is neither impulsive nor uncontrolled."

"Child abusers?" Dave queried.

Derrick nodded. "It is rare in their society but it happens. He was an unfortunate victim and still has painful memories."

"But are you certain he can be trusted to remain on our side?" Mr. Classet was still frowning. "I am worried that Evans will be able to sway him or the *Loyas*. The last thing we need is to have the Owoons on the side of the Separatist."

"He can be trusted," Derrick was adamant. "He needs to work on his social skills, but I would still trust him with my life. And *Loya* Modnar will always side with *Sous* Zooric. *Loya* Meestric could be a problem. He doesn't really like *Sous* Zooric because he was bonded with Raekon, and Zooric killed Raekon."

****

Chapter 26

It was the middle of mid-cycle when Zooric topped the rise. He was just outside the boundary of Mr. Classet's outpost. Halting his pageen, he stood silently as he watched *Loya* Meestric enter the abandoned cabin. His senses told him that Evans Bradley was already inside. Soor used the stop to conduct his own investigation of the surrounding shrubbery.

Loya Meestric had traveled with *Gaad* Trateen, but he had left the Soosan Protector some distance away. Although Zooric knew he could get closer without detection by Meestric, to hear the conversation he would have to definitely come within Meestric's range. With a mental whistle to Soor, he turned and headed back to where Trateen waited.

Before he came within sight of the Guard, he called out mentally. *"Gaad Trateen. I am approaching."*

Trateen was expecting him and watched as he rode up.

"Where is *Gaad* Keefav?" Trateen asked with only mild curiosity.

Zooric shrugged as he dismounted. "Possibly at the outpost." Soor flopped down to lie in the shade.

"I take it you did not follow orders and left without him," Trateen did not seem surprised.

He moved back into the shade of an Aceed tree and leaned against the trunk.

Zooric did not bother to answer. He nodded in the direction of the cabin. "Do you know that he is meeting someone there?"

Trateen frowned. "No. I was told to wait here. I did not know his plans."

"He is meeting with Evans."

Trateen's eyes widened. "Council Evans Bradley?"

"Yes. I am interested in finding out what their plans are."

"*Sous* Zooric, we should allow *Loya* Modnar to settle this."

"*Loya* Modnar will suggest that Meestric has every right to pursue a relationship with a Tifoosa just as I have. However, Evans is using him. Evans is anti-race mixing and unless planning something unsavory, would not have any contact with Meestric."

Trateen looked uncomfortable. "You cannot know."

"You were present at their end cycle meal. It was a deliberate brain washing session."

"We should still follow *Loya* Modnar's lead," Trateen said.

"How long have you been a Soosan Protector?"

Trateen blinked at the change of topic. "Since twenty alifees of age—for almost seven alifees."

"Do you always agree with the Soosan?"

Trateen's eyes widened. "*Sous* Zooric!" He protested. "You are well aware that disagreement with the Soosan is never allowed."

But Zooric only looked amused. "It is always possible to disagree. The key is learning how to safety or legally voice your disagreement."

Trateen hesitated for a second before accepting Zooric's challenge. He nodded. "It is as you say, *Sous* Zooric. I have disagreed with the Soosan."

Zooric grinned, "My name is Zooric." Having established to his own satisfaction that Trateen could be flexible, he turned back to the problem at hand. "Meestric is perhaps driven by anger. His anger at me is seeking an outlet, but he cannot be allowed to pursue this path." Again, he seemed to change the topic. "Did *Loya* Modnar have a mate?"

"He did, but it is almost four alifees since the death of his mate. Theirs was a committed relationship. He has never sought another." Embolden he added. "I would not suggest dropping *Loya* Meestric's title when in *Loya* Modnar's presence."

Zooric nodded absently. "*Eeng*. I am well aware of the significance of titles. And I do recognize that *Loya* Modnar firmly adheres to the tenets of the Soosan." Then with telling casualness he continued. "Did Meestric have another mate before Raekon?"

"*Eeng*," Trateen wisely decided to ignore Zooric's clear insult to *Loya* Meestric. "*Loya* Meestric tends not to take the bond seriously. It has been sometime since his first mate died. He bonded with *Sous* Raekon shortly before we left Caleel. Many of the guards felt that *Sous* Raekon deliberately pursued *Loya* Meestric. We suspected that *Sous* Raekon was more interested in increasing his own standing in the Soosan by associating with a Soosan in the hierarchy.

Zooric suspected that Raekon was more interested in being included in the planned search for him. "So Meestric can move on. Which is the more common behavior among the Soosans, his or *Loya* Modnar's?"

"It varies." Trateen shrugged. "It does not reflect badly for anyone if they choose not to have a committed relationship as long as their pairing does not result in conflict or tension. I believe the Soosan actually hold court to solve major problems of conflict."

Zooric nodded. "Then the contact with Evans may also be driven by need. He is vulnerable at this time. Perhaps Evans recognized this."

"If Council Evans is not planning a relationship with *Loya* Meestric, why else would they meet?"

"Information. Evans wants control of the town Council. The only person stopping him is Caree's father. This expedition might be dangerous."

"What could Council Evans possibly do?"

"Plan an ambush... kill us... kill Mr. Classet. Anything is possible. The mountain path is treacherous in places. Evans is likely seeking information of our plans — our strengths and weaknesses. We will have to be careful."

"But a death on the outgoing journey would immediately cancel the expedition."

"I do not believe they would want that. The attack is likely to take place after we have finished exploring the sector — perhaps on the return journey." He looked up. "They have concluded their meeting. I will follow Evans."

"*Sous* Zooric! Zooric! You cannot follow him into the town," Trateen cautioned.

"I will not go into the town. It is likely he will return to his outpost. It is not far. I wish to find out who he meets with next."

Trateen was not happy with Zooric's decision. "Be careful. *Loya* Modnar will have my head if you are hurt."

"There is no need to tell him of these events."

"But should they not be warned?"

"Mr. Classet, *eeng. Loya* Modnar, *zte.* Remember, he will always follow the tenets of the Soosan, and this is not yet the time to confront Meestric." Zooric mounted.

"Come Soor." Then he said to Trateen as he rode off, "I will speak with you later."

****

Trateen stood by the window. Where the dees was Zooric! He was out of sensing range and he had not returned. It was now close to second-dark. The worst possible scenario is that he was dead. But he could be hurt and out of range. However, this total absence of any signal from him was not good.

With Mr. Classet's help, *Loya* Modnar was organizing a search party.

"Thank you, Council Classet. The Protectors will cover areas to the north of your outpost if your men take the southern areas."

Mr. Classet nodded, "The town is to the south. He is actually less likely to have headed in that direction."

"Was *Gaad* Keefav the last person to see him?" Derrick looked at Carrie.

She nodded. "He spoke to me at the beginning of second-dark. He said he wanted to check out something and would be out of contact for a short time. That is the last time I heard from him." She bit her lips worriedly. "Usually, he contacts me constantly so I can sense him, but I haven't sensed anything."

Keefav looked apologetic. "After we packed, he wanted to check on his pageen. He told me not to follow him."

"You should have," Loya Meestric stated.

"There is no way *Gaad* Keefav could have followed *Sous* Zooric without being detected," Derrick pointed out.

"He is most irresponsible. He did not want to go on this trip. I hope he did not plan a disappearance in the hope that we would leave him."

"Zooric would never do that," Carrie defended angrily "When I spoke to him, he was unhappy yes, but he was fully resigned to the travel. He would never hide from his responsibilities."

Loya Meestric turned to *Loya* Modnar, and it was obvious from his gestures that he was conversing with *Loya* Modnar privately.

Trateen turned back to the window. Should he let them know that Zooric had followed Council Bradley? He would never forgive himself if Zooric got hurt. And the Soosan would never forgive him. He knew that if it was ever discovered that he had lied about Zooric's whereabouts, his career as a Protector was over. At the same time, he was beginning to develop a healthy respect for Zooric. If he spoke up now, Zooric's wish for secrecy and caution would be ruined. And Zooric would be furious.

He was eager to start the search. At least he would be doing something. Standing around doing nothing was getting to him and despite *Loya* Modnar's orders, he planned on circling around to the south— the direction Zooric headed after leaving him.

Loya Modnar suddenly looked up. *"Someone is coming!"*

"Is it *Sous* Zooric?" Trateen asked.

"I believe so ..." *Loya* Modnar frowned slightly; he did not have Zooric's ability to identify others from a distance. "The person is heading for the zig stables."

They did not have to wait long.

"It's him." Carrie said nervously. "He's finished taking care of his pageen. He's headed straight for the house.

"Did he tell you where he disappeared to?" Loya Meestric asked.

"No. He is coming."

Zooric looked dusty and tired. As he entered the room, his eyes immediately focused on Carrie. She was standing with her arm hugging her body. "What is wrong?"

"No one knew where you were," she said tremulously. "We were worried."

"Sous Zooric!" *Loya* Meestric said sharply since Zooric seemed intent on ignoring everyone else as he started walking toward Carrie.

Loya Modnar stopped any further comment. *"We will speak privately with Sous Zooric."* The *Loya* turned to Mr. Classet. *"Thank you for your offer of help – if you will now excuse us."* He directed his next command at Zooric. *"Sous Zooric we will speak with you now."*

It was obvious that Zooric was speaking privately with Carrie. She was nodding but still looked upset. He began absently playing with her fingers while still ignoring the *Loyas*.

When he did not move, she pushed him in the chest. "Go! We can speak later."

Zooric reluctantly turned to face them. "My apologies for any worry by absence caused. I was exploring."

"Exploring! At this hour!" Loya Meestric scoffed.

"I am tired and hungry. I..."

"Sous Zooric we will speak privately," Loya Modnar interrupted. He was already at the door.

Reluctantly, after giving Carrie's hand a final squeeze, Zooric followed the *Loyas* from the room.

****

The planned start of the expedition was early first-light. There were the six Owoons including the two *Loyas*. From Arapmo there were Al Gerin, Evans Bradley, Jade Feld, Dennis Classet and four other men from the town. It would take them little more than full cycle to reach Yotse, then they planned on spending at least a week — ten cycles — exploring. The men were already gathering even thought it was not yet first-light! But with a contagious excitement running throughout the crowd, not many could remain sleeping. And there was a crowd. Almost the entire town was at the outpost eager to see them off.

Mr. Classet looked out of the windows of the library. "More people are heading in. Where is Derrick? We have to go outside soon."

"I don't know," Dave said. "He told me to grab you and Mr. Feld. He was getting *Sous* Zooric."

"This had better be important."

"He said it was..." Dave began.

"It is!" Derrick announced as he walked in. He firmly closed the door. "Sorry I can't get Zooric. He insisted he needs to speak with Carrie first, and we definitely don't have enough time." He gave Mr. Classet a rueful grin. "I think we will have to scrap that plan to fix Zooric's interest in someone else. Right now, he is literally acting as if he is leaving for a year instead of a few cycles."

"The Soosans are planning on leaving immediately after the expedition," Mr. Classet said.

"Would they leave without first returning here?"

Mr. Classet ran a hand through his hair. "I wasn't able to convince the *Loyas* to stay. Last night after their talk with *Sous* Zooric, I met with them in the library." He shook his head. "God knows what *Sous* Zooric did or said, but

Loya Meestric was not in a good mood. According to the *Loya*, there is absolutely no chance of them staying."

Jade Feld patted his friend's back. "I know you were depending on them."

Mr. Classet only gave a grim nod. "What about Carrie?" Dave asked.

"I asked," Mr. Classet gave a reluctant laugh. "I should have kept my mouth shut. I simply told *Sous* Zooric that I couldn't allow Carrie to go with them because I needed more time to get to know him and his people."

"Oh..." Dave eyes widened. "How did he take that?"

"I was very coolly informed that there is no way I would be able to prevent him from taking Carrie away."

Derrick sighed. "Yes. That sounds like Zooric!"

"As you can imagine, I was thoroughly annoyed." Mr. Classet turned to look out the window. "I spoke to Carrie. She promised she wouldn't leave without our permission. I just hope he isn't now trying to convince her to change her mind."

After a moment of hesitation, Derrick spoke. "I think Zooric hopes to convince the *Loyas* to stay."

"That was definitely not the impression he left me with," Mr. Classet grumbled.

Again, Derrick hesitated. "Sir, you can't push or threaten Zooric. He will refuse to cooperate. He also tends to retaliate in a totally arrogant and obstructionist manner."

Since that was exactly what had happened, Mr. Classet had to credit Derrick with his understanding of Zooric's personality.

"Sometime during the next few cycles, I'm going to have to sit down and have a very serious talk with him."

Mr. Classet turned to Derrick. "You seem be getting along with him. What do you think he will do?"

Derrick grinned. "He is prickly as hell, but yes, we get along now. Somehow, I don't think he would take Carrie against your wishes. For one thing, he wants Carrie happy and I am sure she wouldn't be happy if there was any estrangement between her and us."

"Could you impress on him that I am not against his marriage to Carrie. But I am concerned. I can't let Carrie go into a situation where she could be unsafe."

"He knows," Derrick assured Mr. Classet seriously. "The problem is: what work would he do here in Arapmo? It's impossible for him to work at the outpost. He just doesn't understand the concept of authority—he follows orders when it suits him and just ignores those he disagrees with. I personally don't see how he will fit in the rigid structure of the Soosan either."

"Difficulty following instructions is not his only fault!"

Although he no longer hated Zooric, Derrick well recognized Zooric's faults. "I know. Remember his history. He's a loner, but I'm working on improving his socialization skills."

"His history explains his lack of social skills but not his arrogance," Mr. Classet muttered. "He is important to these Soosans. Would the *Loyas* even allow him to stay here by himself?"

"Do they have a choice?" Derrick countered seriously. "As I said, Zooric follows his own counsel. If he decides to stay, he will stay with or without their consent. I think you should ask him his plans when you sit for that discussion."

A shout sounded from outside. It had them all looking up.

"We need to get going," Jade said. "What is this meeting about?"

"Zooric thinks that Evans might be plotting something. And *Loya* Meestric is involved." Derrick quickly explained how Zooric had followed Evans last light. "Evans headed back to his outpost. He met with Carl Robert, Al Gerin and Ryan Swenson. They were there for a while before their meeting broke up."

"This doesn't necessarily mean anything," Jade Feld pointed out. "And why didn't he tell us before?"

"Remember, *Loya* Meestric seems to be involved. He doesn't want the men to know he's onto their plans."

"I still don't see why we need to conclude that they are plotting something," Feld was frowning.

"Evans is a radical Separatist who is anti any mixing of the races! Why else would he meet with *Loya* Meestric except to plot something that is bound to affect us adversely?"

"I'm inclined to agree with you," Mr. Classet was nodding. "This doesn't sound good."

"Zooric feels that Evans might be using *Loya* Meestric. Personally, I agree. Zooric likes neither of them and doesn't trust Evans. I can see no other reason for them to get together. Zooric says that *Loya* Meestric is vulnerable right now because he lost Raekon and may be looking for a relationship."

"With Evans?" Mr. Classet looked doubtful. "You know the Presidential Council has always frowned on any such relationships between men, besides Evans is anti-race mixing."

"You are right, but *Loya* Meestric doesn't know that," Derrick pointed out.

"Even if Evans is trying to lure *Loya* Meestric into some sort of fake relationship, how could that possibly affect us?" Jade Feld was still skeptical.

"The town is swaying toward the Freechoicers," Dave said. "Maybe they're feeling threatened and hope to use *Loya* Meestric's powers somehow."

Mr. Classet's campaign was working especially since the Separatist had yet to come up with a coherent message.

"True, but still, I don't see how the *Loya* could help them." Jade was not convinced.

"I don't either, but sir, I don't think you should ignore Zooric's warning. He thinks there might be a real threat—possibly to your life or to Mr. Feld's."

"I'm not going to take any chances," Mr. Classet was more inclined than his friend to believe that something was up.

"And I'll watch your back," Jade Feld promised. "Although, I still think you're all overreacting. I don't see Evans as a killer."

"What does *Loya* Modnar think of this?" Dave asked.

"He doesn't know, and Zooric feels that to tell him would be to warn *Loya* Meestric and possibly Evans," Derrick hesitated. "Sir, this threat is very real. Zooric would not have warned me otherwise. Remember, he can pick up the emotions of all high receivers. Evans Bradley and Ryan Swenson are both high receivers. Both of the *Loyas* are also high receivers."

"Zig Shit!" Dave said.

****

Chapter 27

Zooric restlessly prowled the camp. Even Soor had given up on him. The rocleer was relaxing near the open fire keeping an eye on Zooric but showing no inclination to follow him. They were only at the halfway point, but some of the men were finding the uphill travel a bit of a challenge. Since it was first-dark, they had decided to stop and take a break. The clearing was not the same one Zooric had used when he was traveling with Caree so many cycles ago. But this clearing also had a small cave which was now crowded with the resting settlers.

Like him, Evans was prowling, annoyingly close at times, which only compounded Zooric's unease. Zooric knew it would be dangerous to wander far, yet he was seriously thinking of giving himself a mental break by moving out further. The emotional onslaught from Evans was getting very irritating—and this was just the first cycle. Also, he had lost contact with Caree.

"*Sous Zooric*" *Loya* Modnar called. The *Loyas* were sitting near the large fire. The fire would keep away all but a very determined attack. Most animals very sensibly would seek easier prey and unless threatened, they would most likely steer clear of their camp.

Zooric slowly approached the *Loyas*. Since Evans had joined them, he stopped a good distance away. Soor ambled over. "Is there a problem?"

"*Council Bradley wanted to know if you had explored any other area on these hills.*"

"I did not." He immediately turned to go.

"*Sous Zooric.*" *Loya* Meestric called out angrily. "*You will...*"

But Zooric was tired, irritated and worried. He had even less patience for social niceties. "Council Bradley projects his emotions. I find it very irritating. I prefer not to linger near him."

Loya Meestric looked satisfied. "*I knew you would not be able to tolerate the emotional sending for long. This is proof that you cannot live here. Nor can you live in Caleel. Just imagine the emotional onslaught. It would drive you crazy.*"

"The emotional impact from Council Bradley is greater because his hate is being forcefully directed at me," Zooric said coldly.

"How dare you! I have no feelings for you," Evans shouted.

Zooric stood his ground, but his expression became taut. Soor gave a low growl.

A quick frown from *Loya* Modnar showed his concern. The *Loya* turned to calm Evans. "*Sous Zooric perhaps used too strong a word.*"

"*It may well be true that Council Bradley doesn't like you, but it is ridiculous to suggest that he is deliberately directing hate at you,*" *Loya* Meestric inserted. "*You are an extremely sensitive detector, and to blame others for your problem is irresponsible. It will ruin the comradeship of this expedition.*"

"I am not mistaken in believing that Council Bradley's hate is purposefully directed at me."

Their loud voices had woken up members of the expedition who were trying to sleep. Everyone began crowding around.

"Is there a problem?" Mr. Classet asked.

"Zooric is being particularly insolent," Evans stated coldly.

"Sous Zooric is merely an extreme sensitive." Loya Modnar was now frowning at Evans' use of Zooric's name without a formal title. His emphasis on *Sous* was telling. *"We will appreciate if you and your people employ the correct title of respect when addressing our citizens."*

"We in Arapmo believe respect can only be earned," Evans was smug.

"I am glad, Evans, that for once we are in total agreement," Zooric's tone was silky.

"Enough!" Mr. Classet directed a warning look, first at Zooric and then Evans. "We are grown men here. Let's act accordingly!"

As Mr. Classet spoke, Zooric glanced at *Loya* Meestric. The older Soosan was getting so upset that a flare of his emotional signals was breaking through Zooric's block. It denoted an unusual lack of control. Zooric abruptly took another step back. He did not want to have to give the Soosan a buzz, but buzz him he would if he dared project his anger. He gave them all a brief bow.

"I will, of course, respect your appeal for restraint, Council Classet." Turning, he walked off. Soor easily kept up with his swift pace.

****

Loya Meestric watched him with a deep frown. *"Council Classet, I deeply apologize for Sous Zooric's behavior."*

"From the little I heard, *Sous* Zooric was not alone in throwing insults." Mr. Classet was in fact secretly pleased that Zooric had stood his ground against Evans.

"Are you accusing me?" Evans glared at him.

"I'm commenting on what I heard." He was not about to get in an argument with Evans. "Now gentlemen, if you will excuse me. I'd like to get at least a few minutes of rest before we have to resume our journey again." He too turned and walked off.

Since the excitement seemed to be over, the other men soon dispersed. In fact, when Mr. Classet looked over, he was surprised to see Evans and *Loya* Meestric still in discussion. *Loya* Modnar was nowhere nearby.

Was Zooric right?

He got no more proof of a conspiracy that cycle, although Zooric remained moody and fractious for the entire trip. Second-dark was fast approaching as they entered what the Owoons indicated was the Travelers Reviewing Center of the ancient Azar sector. As soon as they arrived in the sector, Zooric disappeared. Mr. Classet had been hoping to sit him down for a chat. After a quick check he inquired about Zooric's whereabout.

"The walls of the sector block electrical signals." Trateen explained. "I suspect *Sous* Zooric needed privacy."

"But where did he go?"

"Deeper inside the sector proper or perhaps in one of the front rooms."

"I see." None of the Owoons seemed worried so Mr. Classet gave up the search.

It was in fact five cycles into their trip before he got to sit down with Zooric. The cycle after they arrived, they had decided to organize collecting trips to various parts of the sector. Each group generally consisted of two settlers and one or two Owoons. One group would stay at their base camp—which remained at the Receiving Center— while the other three groups fanned out. Although he participated in the scout trips, opened doors and helped catalog the items found, Zooric still tended to spend most of his time alone. He was always a part of Mr. Classet's group and made sure he was never paired with *Loya* Meestric or Evans Bradley. He even avoided *Loya* Modnar and because he refused to eat with any of the groups and would disappear unexpectedly, it was hard to arrange a meeting with him, besides Mr. Classet did not want a planned meeting. He was hoping a more spontaneous talk would work in his favor.

None of the Owoons seemed surprised by his behavior and after *Loya* Modnar explained Zooric's problem, the settlers were surprisingly understanding. In fact, Mr. Classet was delighted to discover that among the settlers, Zooric was extremely well respected. He pulled his weight and treated everyone equally.

As one settler commented, "He doesn't say much but does his work and more. I can't complain."

Occasionally, during second-light—after their meal—Zooric would sit by himself experimenting on a host of Azar instruments. He was trying to figure out want worked and what did not and was often abrupt with anyone who dared to interrupt him—including *Loya* Modnar or Meestric.

With that in mind, Mr. Classet approached cautiously. "Can we talk?" he asked.

Zooric did not look up. "What will this talk be about?"

Since he wasn't bluntly told to leave— the response Zooric had given more than one of the settlers—Mr. Classet sat. He decided on the direct approach.

"Do you have any specific plans for the future?"

Zooric looked up. "I will remain in Arapmo. I have decided."

"I see," Mr. Classet was cautious. "Have you thought some more on what you would do?"

"Your people will need someone here— perhaps not permanently—but until you decide what to do with this site, you will need someone to manage it for you."

Mr. Classet thought for a bit. "You do have a point. And you are fully qualified for the job. Does *Loya* Modnar know of your plans? "

"Not yet," he admitted. Then he shrugged off *Loya* Modnar's possible reaction to concentrate on what was clearly more important to him. "Caree says that we must get married before we live together. I am willing to ..." he paused then continued in a careful neutral tone of voice. "To follow the rules of your people."

"Are you?" Mr. Classet smiled.

"I am willing to try," Zooric responded seriously. "When will this marriage be?"

"How about in forty more cycles. That should give me time to get to know you a little better. I also need to get the Council's permission for you to manage the sector." He decided to trust Zooric's judgment. Zooric obviously was not worried about *Loya* Modnar's opinion.

Zooric nodded. "During the wait I will stay and work at your outpost. I cannot stay here without Caree. I cannot sense her. I do not like this," he admitted.

Zooric was clearly not asking permission. Mr. Classet looked at him in astonishment, both at his arrogance and his candor. "Well... that does explain your ah... crankiness," he said hiding a smile.

Zooric took his comment entirely at face value. He had already moved on. "Forty cycles —it is not an unreasonable wait. I will tell Caree when we get back." Having satisfied his only interest, he now waved Mr.

Classet away. "You can now leave. I wish to be alone while I finish these," he indicated the Azar tools at his feet.

Mr. Classet was barely able to stop his jaw from dropping open. Seriously! Derrick was right; the Owoon needed socialization skills.

"One more thing before I go." He ignored Zooric's impatient look as he continued. "I would like, actually, I will need your help in fighting the Presidential Guards. Should they return, Arapmo cannot win an outright battle alone. Can I count on you?"

"Of course! Living here I will be one cycle away. It is best if you post one or two permanent rotating guards along the travel routes. We can work out the details later, but with posted guards they will not be able to catch us unprepared."

Mr. Classet gave him a brilliant smile. Zooric's unconditional and immediate consent had just removed a gnawing burden. "Thank you. With your promise to provide help, the job as manager of the Azar sector is your... even if I have to twist the arm of every Council man."

Zooric grinned. "Good!"

****

They had collected a vast quantity of artifacts from Yoste. As before, as they travelled down the mountain, they decided to give both adults and animals a break at first-dark. The approach to this clearing was heavily forested with dense, thick trees and shrubs. The immediate path was long and narrow. On the upward journey the settlers had tried widening the path, but, even so, it allowed only a single file of riders. They were entering the clearing one by one. It was a slow process, dismounting, leading the mounts in, making way for the next person, and then unpacking the mounts.

Zooric was traveling behind Mr. Classet. The others had already dismounted. As they waited their turn, he became uneasy. The return trip was the most dangerous part of the journey and with Evans' constant signal bombardment, he couldn't lower his guard but... He did a quick scan. Dees! Meestric was sending a private signal. But to whom was he sending them? Evans? They had been traveling together, and both had already entered the clearing. Frowning he tried again, this time focusing on the surroundings.

"Someone is near. Get down!" As he shouted, he grabbed Mr. Classet, pushing the older man to the ground just as a shot rang out.

The bullet bored into the earth, inches from where Mr. Classet had been standing! Zooric rolled into the forest taking the older man with him. Pandemonium broke out as everyone began scrambling for cover, and the mounts began rearing in panic.

Boom! The shooter was definitely aiming for Mr. Classet. The shot was altogether too close for comfort.

"*Saac ga!*" Zooric turned swiftly, trying to locate the shooter. He had him!

A high piercing scream ripped the air.

"Zooric!" Trateen had jumped to his feet. "Are you hurt?" he asked.

"I am fine," Zooric called out. "The shooter was aiming for Mr. Classet."

"And I am fine," Mr. Classet got to his feet, stumbling a little, "Thanks, *Sous* Zooric!" Zooric gave a slight grin as he too got to his feet.

"Who was it?" Someone else wanted to know.

"Ryan Swenson." Zooric said calmly. "You will find him on the rise?" he pointed.

Trateen was about to dash off when *Loya* Modnar halted him.

"*Gaad* Egell is a medic. He will go."

Egell and two settlers quickly rushed out.

Since Mr. Classet still looked shaky, Zooric turned to help the older man, but Mr. Classet brushed him off.

"Thanks, I am okay, just a bit unsteady. See to the animals."

Zooric automatically began sending soothing signals to each animal. It calmed them instantly. It abruptly dawned on him that he had been doing this all his life in the wild— using a low-link to calm, to heal. Within minutes they were leading the animals into the clearing. It was then that Zooric noticed Evans. He was talking with Meestric. And Meestric appeared... Again, Zooric lowered his block. Meestric was worried almost to the point of panic.

He walked over, "Was this the plan Evans?" he asked.

"I have no idea what you are talking about."

"Meestric sent a signal as we approached." He gave Meestric an inquiring look, "You were conferring with Ryan. Did Evans tell you...?"

In an explosion of fury, Evans rushed at Zooric.

Zooric gasped as Evans' emotions reached him in a flash of pain. Swinging around he sent a buzz to disable the man. However, even as Evans screamed in pain, he was still bent on lunging himself at Zooric. He knew Zooric would not be able to block if they were in contact!

Meestric abruptly launched himself at the settler. All three went tumbling down. Zooric did not hesitate. He didn't want to go through the torture of another bout of emotion-induced pain. He buzzed Evans again. However, because of the contact, the current surged through all three men. This was not a low level linking!

Zooric was gasping in pain. Evans screamed again. Meestric choked off a cry, rolling away and doubling over. The entire camp rushed to their aid. Momentarily stunned, Zooric was trying to catch his breath as Sorgan bent over him.

"I... I..."

"How is your head?" The medic asked as he checked Zooric's pulse.

Zooric took a deep breath. "Just a mild ache. Nothing like before."

As he struggled to sit with Sorgan's aid, he looked over at Evans and Meestric. *Loya* Modnar was helping Meestric to his feet while Evans was being helped by Ben Helms. Further away, Egell and the other settlers were carrying Ryan Swenson in. The man was still unconscious.

"What happened?" Someone called.

"Evans has been sending me his emotions throughout this entire trip. While at Yotse, I finally figured out one possible reason. With Evans' constant blast I had to maintain a high block. I could sense nothing around me."

"So how did you know Ryan Swenson was there?" Mr. Classet asked.

"I started giving myself random breaks. Every few minutes I would lower my block and do a quick scan. I became even more cautious after sensing *Loya* Meestric's signal, just as we entered the clearing. I suspected that something was about to happen. When I scanned again, I found the settler."

Zooric turned to Evans. "The plan was to kill Mr. Classet, was it not?"

Evans glared at him. "You can prove nothing."

A very subdued *Loya* Meestric spoke up. *"I believe you are right. He told me he was planning a surprise and asked me to send a message to Zha Helms. I was told to tell exactly when we approached and where Council Classet was. Just now he was trying to buy my silence."*

"Evans befriended you only to pump you for information," Zooric commented. He related how he had followed them the cycle before the expedition.

"Why did you not tell us this?" Loya Modnar asked in bewilderment? *"Sous Zooric, I cannot understand you."*

Zooric hesitated. Meestric had actually tried to help him just now. He shrugged as he looked over at the *Loya*. "I am sorry *Loya* Meestric, but I recognized that in your grief over Raekon's death, you were angry with me and not likely to believe any theory I would present."

Meestric nodded in agreement. *"It is true. I was grief stricken. I too am sorry."*

****

Chapter 28

They arrived at Mr. Classet's outpost just before second-dark. A jubilant crowd was there to greet them. Not even the presence of two prisoners could dampen the crowd's sprits. They were all too excited about the finds, which the town planned on storing in the library until a museum could be built. It was only later, as the crowd settled down, that the questions began.

Evans had finally stopped pleading innocent. No one had believed him anyway. However, he still refused to talk. Fortunately, that did not matter. Ryan had recovered and he was not about to take full responsibility for a planned killing. Under questioning by the settlers, Ryan not only pointed the finger at Evans, but he also implicated Carl Robert and Al Gerin in a complicated and sordid plot to gain control of the town Council by killing Mr. Classet. They had befriended *Loya* Meestric with the promise of a relationship with Evans.

Arapmo had no justice system—no courts, judges, jail or even a police force. The town would need all four to deal with conspirators. In the meantime, four settlers were deputized to round up Robert and Gerin. They would all be kept under guard in a secure room in Sam Donald's house until the town organized a proper legal system.

After spending most of the dark coordinating the capture and detaining of the plotters, Mr. Classet was exhausted yet excited about the new possibilities for governing his town. True Arapmo still had Separatist sympathizers, but with their leader jailed, the organization was in such disarray, it was no longer an immediate threat. He could breathe easier. It was almost the middle of the first-dark, but he was determined to head back to his outpost. Still on a euphoric high over their success, the other Council members decided to accompany him. They wanted to finalize plans for a justice system. In fact, they were riding on such a high that it was almost first-dark before they realized that the Owoons were missing.

"They must have left last-light as soon as we arrived," Jade Feld commented. The Council had gathered in the library of Mr. Classet's outpost for their impromptu meeting. It was now a Council of five.

"Impossible!" Mr. Classet said. He could not believe Zooric would have simply left. "I'll check with Carrie."

"Dennis," Jade cautioned.

Dennis knew he was being cautioned against building up his hopes but he could not, would not believe that Zooric would let him down, not after saving his life. As he stepped outside the lounge and headed for the kitchen, the first person he met was Derrick.

"Derrick! Do you know where Zooric is?"

"No." Derrick looked puzzled. "Was he supposed to be here?"

"Where is Carrie?" Mr. Classet was suddenly urgent. This was just what he had feared!

A quick search of the house failed to find Carrie.

"She promised me she wouldn't go."

"What if he took her by force?" Sam Donald asked.

"I know Zooric," Derrick defended. "There is no way he would take Carrie by force!"

"Then where is he? Where are they? "Jade Feld asked.

They were all gathered in the main room. Mrs. Classet came over to hug her husband. There were tears in her eyes.

"He can't have left," her husband insisted. But he could provide no proof, which was not very reassuring for the others.

"Should I alert the men to start a search?" David Hill asked.

"Let me try something first," Derrick suddenly jumped up.

"There is no point searching for them if they have left," Jade Feld pointed out. "And I can't imagine all of them suddenly getting lost."

"I'm not suggesting a search," Derrick explained. "I'm going to try projecting my emotions. If Zooric is near, he will sense them. He will also know something is wrong because he showed me how to stop projecting emotions."

"That isn't going to work if he is blocking," Dave pointed out.

"He doesn't block all the time. He can't. He finds it too uncomfortable. It's like losing the ability to hear... or the see."

****

Derrick stood by the window. He stared out at the still chaotic scene in the front of the outpost. There were makeshift tents, carriages and wagons everywhere. Many of the settlers had spent the dark and much of first-light at the outpost. First, he tried projecting fear but couldn't quite get fearful. Next, he just tried calling Zooric's name — saying it over and over in his mind, projecting as much worry into it as possible. He was not sure how long he stood there, but suddenly he got a response.

"Derrick?" Zooric sounded puzzled.

Derrick wished he could mental-speak. He turned with a jubilant smile. "Zooric just responded."

"Where is he?" Mr. Classet asked tensely.

"I have no idea. I can't mental-speak. I tired projecting worry. He is close enough that he got my emotion. He called my name and he sounded very puzzled. He'll be here soon." Derrick was so confident; he was grinning even as he spoke.

Dave was also grinning. "That means they can't be far. They didn't leave."

"I just got another mental signal. He is meeting with *Loya* Modnar and will be returning shortly."

The tension in the room eased. "I think I just aged about ten years," Mrs. Classet sighed as she dabbed at her eyes.

Mr. Classet squeezed her tightly. "It will be alright." He gave a shaky grin. "I was almost positive Zooric would never leave, but Carrie's disappearance had me worried."

Derrick's confidence did not dim although it was another twenty minutes before they heard the approaching fluars. The Owoons were returning, and Carrie was with them.

"Where are the others?" Mr. Classet asked as he greeted the approaching group.

With Carrie were *Loya* Modnar, Zooric, Trateen and Egell.

Carrie was looking guilty as she entered the room, Zooric's arm firmly about her waist. He did not release her even as his eyes sought Derricks.

"Is something wrong?" Derrick got the same message from both *Loya* Modnar and Zooric.

"You were missing. Carrie was missing. We were getting worried," Derrick explained.

Zooric immediately turned to Mr. Classet. "Did you think that I would not honor my promise to you?" he demanded.

There was stillness to his face, and Derrick realized that he was hurt by Mr. Classet's lack of trust.

Mr. Classet realized that also. "No!" he said immediately, giving Zooric a rueful smile. "I will admit however that Carrie's absence had me worried. For that I apologize. This past cycle has totally twisted my world."

Zooric stared at him in silence. Everyone was waiting for him to respond; yet it was impossible to read his face.

It was Carrie who broke the uncomfortable silence. Turning slightly, she touched Zooric's arm "Zooric, I promised Dad I would not go with you without telling him. Since he couldn't find me, he was naturally worried." She continued to her father, "I am sorry Dad. Zooric woke me early. He did not want to leave me here while he met with *Loya* Modnar. We were just outside the outpost."

Zooric finally gave a nod signaling his acceptance of Mr. Classet's explanation. He then glanced over at Derrick. "Your method of contacting me was brilliant."

"It wouldn't have been necessary if you'd taken the time to contact one of us before running off with Carrie," Derrick pointed out.

Zooric suddenly grinned. "You do not stop, do you? It is a good thing I will not be living here. Your irritating nudges and advice would drive me insane."

"Don't stop Derrick," Carrie urged, "Maybe with both of us nagging him, he will be forced to change."

Derrick only grinned. "I wouldn't bet my life on that if I were you." He suspected that Zooric's go it alone approach was a product of his solitary childhood and was deeply ingrained.

The others could only stare in surprise, not only at the relaxed expression on Zooric's face but also at the obvious friendship between the two men.

"Council Classet, I wish to apologize for any worry we caused. We were indeed planning to leave," Loya Modnar was speaking, *"However Sous Zooric has convinced me that we need to stay here to get to know each other better. Misunderstandings between our two nations must be avoided and if we recognize our differences yet appreciate each other, we will develop trust and commitments that are not easily destroyed."*

Mr. Classet was pleasantly surprised. "Will you all be staying?"

"No. Loya Meestric with Gaads Sorgan and Keefav are preparing to leave. Gaads Trateen and Egell both volunteered to stay. The others will take back an account of our time here to the Soosan. Incidentally, Sous Zooric has told me about a valuable weapon that is important to the Soosan but useless for you. I would like to send four of these weapons with the returning party." He produced a Kooknor.

"That's the weapon that Raekon had," Carrie explained.

"What does it do?" her father asked.

"It stops the sizzle. This was how Sous Zooric was able to disable Raekon. He had one hidden in his robes."

"The loud burst of light." Dave stated in a flash of understanding.

"What light?" Derrick asked.

"You were unconscious," Mr. Classet briefly explained what had happened for the benefit of the others. "In the confusion afterwards, I totally forgot about that."

Loya Modnar nodded. *"In this case, it was wise of Sous Zooric not to share this information with us because Raekon was unaware of the true use of the Kooknor. He assumed it would boost his powers, which was of course false. However, to have a weapon capable of stopping a sizzle,"* he shook his head, almost in disbelief. *"I cannot tell you how important this is to us. I wish the Soosan to have it immediately. Also, Sous Zooric tells me that you need our help. Since we will be staying, of course you have our pledge of support should the Presidential Guards return. We will assist you in any way that we can."*

After a glance at the other members of the Council, to check for objections, Mr. Classet nodded. "Thank you *Loya*! I cannot tell you what your support means to us." He could not hide a pleased smile. "We have no objections to your taking some of the weapons, although we would like to keep one in our museum if it is safe to do so."

Derrick stared thoughtfully at the weapon in *Loya* Modnar's hands before slowly looking over at Zooric. Typically, Zooric was totally ignoring the conversation. The Owoon had cornered Carrie, completely blocking her from them all and was now engaged in what was obviously a totally private conversation. Derrick wondered if the *Loya* realized the subtle control that Zooric wielded. Zooric gave out information according to his rules not the *Loya's*. He also clearly expected his edicts to be carried out—hence his current unconcern. Before, Derrick had questioned how Zooric would survive under the rigid rules of the Soosan. Now he realized that it was the Soosan's very existence that should be of concern. If

Zooric did not like the rules, he would undoubtedly ignore or change them!

Loya Modnar did not hesitate, *"According to Zooric there are many more. That should not be a problem. I would also like to give you the opportunity to send a letter from your council government to the leader of our government, our Jirga."*

"Good idea!" Mr. Classet agreed, and the other Council members nodded.

"Zooric has stated that we will be allowed to live in the sector during our stay here. He further states that we will stay here at the outpost until his marriage to your daughter." Although the *Loya* paused, he was obviously waiting for confirmation, not a rebuttal.

Mr. Classet was momentarily speechless. Derrick frowned. Was this Zooric's monumental confidence at work or another carefully calculated plan of action? Somehow Derrick thought it was the latter. The response of the Council and Mr. Classet did not surprise him.

"Of course, we will be happy to have you. Again, thank you for your willingness to help." There was no way Mr. Classet could turn down the offer. There were no protests. For the town, this was just too good to be true. Arapmo now had a fighting chance of survival.

****

About the Author

Liv Joanka writes science fiction and contemporary romance. Her books often highlight the diverse nature of our society with all its flaws and contradictions.

****

Thank you for reading **In Love with an Alien**. If you liked this book, or any other of our releases, please consider rating this book at the online retailer of your choice. Your ratings and reviews are appreciated by the author and will help other readers find new favorites.

Visit https://peltrovijan.com/ for more interesting titles by this author.

Liv Joanka

In Love with an Alien

Liv Joanka

www.ingramcontent.com/pod-product-compliance
Lightning Source LLC
Chambersburg PA
CBHW060725190726
48285CB00001B/68